Embers of Destiny

Hannah's Heirloom ~ Book Three

Rosie Chapel

First printing 2016
ISBN 978-0-9945053-5-4

Ulfire Pty. Ltd.
P.O. Box 1481
South Perth
WA 6951
Australia

www.rosiechapel.com

Cover artwork by H.E. Rodgers

To my wonderful friends both near and far,
thank you for coming with me on this journey.
Your support, encouragement and ability to make me laugh
when I'm out of sorts,
makes you worth your weight in gold.

Acknowledgements

My profound gratitude to Helen for her amazing artwork.

My heartfelt appreciation to Janet and Moira for being so
generous with your time throughout the editing process. Your
patience and attention to detail has been invaluable.

Special thanks to Bill Thayer for his kind assistance with some
Latin abbreviations.

Embers of Destiny

Hannah's Heirloom ~ Book Three

Chapter One

It was one of those glorious spring days, full of promise, from the hint of warmth in the sun, to the heady scents of the blossoms. The air was like champagne and the dazzling blue of the sky was softened here and there by an odd white cloud floating like a huge marshmallow on an azure sea. I was sitting on the bench near the back door, my fingers wrapped around a mug of hot tea. It was not quite seven thirty and I didn't need to be at work for another two hours.

There was something very special about these early mornings, just the sunrise and me. I loved to watch the colours change from the palest rose flush of the dawn through an almost opalescent hue before morphing into the bright cerulean blue, typical of most days since I'd been here — since we'd been here.

I leaned back and let my thoughts roam free, watching the shadows retreat as the sun began its slow climb across the heavens. The bench was in the garden of a comfortably large cottage, nestling near the bottom of a hill in Northumberland, not far from Hadrian's Wall. The cottage was not particularly close to either of our regular jobs, but we didn't care, it was perfect.

Within the traditional whitewashed walls and slate roof dwelt an old three-bedroom cottage, which had been renovated to suit a more modern lifestyle. The main rooms downstairs had been knocked through to create one large integrated living room-kitchen area; but by preserving the original wooden framework near one end, the illusion of two rooms had been retained, while benefiting from the extra light the open space provided. Across a narrow hallway, there was a study, utility room and cloakroom. Upstairs, the rooms had been reconfigured to create a master bedroom with small ensuite, two guest rooms and the main bathroom. There was a huge fireplace at one end of the main room and the cottage was also centrally heated.

Outside, at the back, a flagged courtyard large enough to accommodate an outdoor setting and a barbecue led up to a grassed area across which the washing line was strung. The front garden was a riot of colourful flowering plants and bushes, organised along a stone path to the front gate. A low stone wall up which firethorn and buddleia grew surrounded the whole plot. I didn't know much about horticulture, but it was a very pleasing garden and seemed to have been arranged so that there was colour all year round.

My name is Hannah and over the last two years I have experienced more than most people will in a lifetime. First, I accompanied my best friend Max Vallier to Masada in an attempt to trace the origins of a ruby clasp, a gift from my long-dead grandmother. Once there, somehow I connected with an ancient ancestor, also called Hannah and began to experience events, starting with a rebel ambush and culminating in a massacre, as they unfolded through her eyes. A healer, she was caring for three Roman soldiers injured in the ambush, one of whom she fell in love with at about the same time that I realised that I had fallen for Max. As my two worlds collided, I realised that the only way to save those I loved and survive the horror that would be wrought on Masada by both Zealots and an avenging Roman army was to rely on instinct and my knowledge of what would happen on the citadel, without changing history.

Then six months ago, we visited Pompeii, where once again I was drawn into my ancient world. Rather than a rebel massacre, this time the destruction would be in the form of a natural disaster, namely the cataclysmic eruption of Vesuvius. Hannah, now married to Maxentius — her Roman — had accompanied him to Pompeii where he had been given command of a peacekeeping force sent to quell ongoing riots. While there, Hannah had joined a team of physicians or medici at the Gladiators' School, where she helped care for prisoners of war now forced to fight in the arena. I must admit that trying to warn those whose lives had touched mine — well her's — about the danger, without seeming as though I was completely mad, was rather difficult. I had to leave everything to the last minute and it was touch and go for a while, but thankfully I, we, managed to escape, although I fear that many whom I had known did not.

The clasp — the clasp is gorgeous, a deep red stone nestled in an intricate setting of burnished metal. I had received it twice, once from Maxentius, who gifted the clasp to me — okay, not really me, the other Hannah on the birth of their daughter, which is how, nearly two thousand years later, it came back into my possession. It is my talisman and I believe it is what connects me to my other life.

Max and I went through our own transition. As though what happened at Masada wasn't difficult enough for anyone, let alone someone who loved me, to comprehend and accept; I feared that the pressures of our everyday lives would tear us apart. On top of this, even though it was the other Hannah who loved, married and had a child with Maxentius, in my mind I had spent longer with my ancient family than I had with Max. I needn't have worried; it seems that it would take a whole lot more than this to scare Max away and before we left Pompeii he proposed.

We were married about four months ago, during Christmas week. By our choice, it was a very quiet affair, just immediate family and a few close friends. Our honeymoon was spent in this same cottage, which was owned by Max's family and had been presented to us as a wedding present. Despite its isolation, we loved it and had decided to live here permanently, selling my apartment and renting out Max's. The privilege of watching the sunrise over this wild yet breathtaking landscape was worth any commute.

I hadn't been aware of my ancestor since we returned from Rome; no dreams or visions of what she was doing. I wasn't naive enough, however, to presume that our connection was broken. I had accepted long ago that our lives were somehow entwined, that she would always be with me and funnily enough, I was comfortable with this.

I heard movement behind me and turned to see Max coming out through the door, hair still damp from his shower and my heart did its usual flip-flop. Tall, dark-haired and green-eyed, my husband — oh how I loved using that word — was incredibly handsome, yet wholly unaware of it. An engineer by profession, he was happiest working on an interesting project or immersed in anything to do with archaeology.

"Morning, Sunshine. Sleep well?" I smiled back, nodding as he sat next to me, draping one arm over my shoulders and pulling me against him. "How long have you been up?"

"Just long enough to watch the sunrise."

"So, a good hour then?" He grinned down at me, amusement glinting in his eyes.

"I couldn't get back to sleep, so it seemed kinder to get up than to disturb you."

"Another headache?" A seemingly innocuous question, but I had been suffering from them for several weeks now and both of us were concerned that they might be related to my accident on Masada. A severe head injury had put me in a coma for over a month and until recently any after-effects hadn't plagued me, so the sudden onset of these headaches was somewhat disquieting.

I had been inclined to ignore them at first, but when they increased in frequency, Max had insisted that I consult my doctor who had referred me to a specialist. A scan had proved inconclusive; they couldn't see any damage, but neither could they rule out the possibility of an underlying problem. They would monitor me and repeat the scan in six months, suggesting that I refrain from spending too much time in front of a computer. Not helpful when a large part of your job involves research.

"Not a bad one." I assented. "I haven't needed to take anything for it. The fresh air and this tea seem to have done the trick. A cup of coffee before I go to work will probably knock it on the head, so to speak." Max chuckled, but his eyes were a little shadowed. I reached up and stroked his cheek. "I'm okay, Max, they're just headaches."

"I know, but..."

"No buts. We have to trust the doctors; they didn't seem too worried. I refuse to let a few headaches interfere with my life." Then, distracting him, "What time do you leave?" Max was travelling north today to inspect some equipment being constructed for his current project and would be away for a few days.

"I think the taxi's coming about ten. The flight is at lunchtime."

"Everything packed?" He nodded and, having diverted his attention away from my headaches, I started chatting about our plans for the weekend.

Eventually, we had to get ready, Max for his pick-up and me for work. The museum I usually work for had decided to give their antiquities department a complete overhaul and although it had been in the pipeline for some time, it meant that I was effectively without a job for the duration. They offered to transfer me to their sister museum, but the travel was just too far. Fortuitously, Nate — yes, he of Masada and Pompeii fame and who was guest lecturing for a year at Newcastle University — had contacted me, asking whether I'd be interested in doing some cataloguing at one of the museums along Hadrian's Wall.

The timing was too good to be true and I jumped at it. The museum was recording artefacts from some of the older forts recently discovered following aerial surveys of the land alongside the Wall. It appeared that there had been garrisons stationed here long before the construction of the stone forts and the Wall itself, living in what would have started out as temporary marching camps, evolving into more permanent structures the longer they stayed.

The problem was that there was scarcely any historical record between around AD84 and the reign of Hadrian. Thus, we had no idea whether these forts were part of the initial conquering force sent in to subdue the local tribes forcibly or otherwise, or simply constructed to police the borders to ensure trade and so on was not disrupted. The archaeologists were hoping that these new finds would shed light on that dark period.

The museum itself was quite close to our cottage, within cycling distance and the hours were very relaxed. As long as I did my allocated time each week, I could fit them in whenever the museum's archive office was open. Making sure I had my lunch and a bottle of water, I went out to the garage to check my bike tyres. Strolling back into the house, I waited for Max to come back downstairs; this would be our first night apart for many months and he knew I struggled when he wasn't near.

I was sitting on the arm of the sofa, staring at the view through the window, when he came up behind me, stroking his hand down my hair. As I made to stand up, he drew me close, wrapping me in his arms and I leant into his chest, breathing him in, fixing him into my mind. With one hand cupping the back of my head, he tilted my chin and very gently kissed me, his lips barely brushing mine. I gazed up at him and our eyes locked.

"I'll miss you," I whispered. "Please take care."

"Always," he murmured, resuming his kiss, which slowly deepened, sparking the slow burn so familiar to me. We lost ourselves in each other for long moments until, reluctantly, I drew away.

"I have to go," I sighed wistfully. "I'll see you Thursday evening." Pausing for one last kiss, "I love you, Max."

"I love you too, Sunshine. Be careful on that bike." I grinned and, grabbing my backpack, went out of the front door quickly, turning to wave once, unaware that he watched me until I was out of sight.

By the time I reached work, I felt less upset. I was a grown-up; I could manage a few nights without my husband. I had a job I loved and the cottage was a haven, safe and peaceful. Concentrating on the task at hand, I was soon absorbed in the world of Roman Britain circa AD80. Many of the artefacts, although exciting in that they had survived so long, were actually quite mundane. No treasure hoards or large items, just things people would discard without thinking: mainly broken tools or shards of pottery, the odd piece of armour or leather. Nothing like the writing tablets that had been uncovered at Vindolanda, which was a shame really; a very clear 'Caecilius was here in AD83 to calm the masses' would have been perfect.

The finds did, however, offer an insight into everyday life on a frontier of Empire and I was fascinated by what they might reveal. Little did I realise how much that would be.

Chapter Two

Caught up in some cataloguing, I lost track of time and it was quite late by the time I got home, so I quickly reheated something from the fridge and settled down in front of the television for half an hour of mindless escapism while I ate. Once I'd eaten and tidied everything away, I took a glass of wine outside and watched the sun going down, the colours deepening in the waning light. The evening was clear, if cool but snuggled into one of Max's old baggy jumpers, I was comfortable enough.

I'd been sitting there for some time when Max called. We chatted for a while and then said our goodnights, distance and a bad signal making our conversation a trifle unsatisfying. Unable to do anything about that and, comfortable where I was with nothing else demanding my attention, I remained in the garden until it was completely dark, waiting for the stars to appear. This was as close as I could get to the breathtaking night sky I'd experienced at Masada and I never tired of it. Here the stars were undimmed either by light from urban conglomerations or other pollutants. I watched as they began to twinkle into existence as though some invisible hand was drawing back a veil, the earth below illuminated in their ethereal glow.

Eventually, I turned in, securing the doors and making sure everything was switched off. Our bedroom was in the centre of the upper floor, large bay windows jutting out from under the eaves. I opened them wide, letting the air circulate and ignoring the fact that I felt lonely without Max, curled up under the covers and tried to get some sleep.

.......oooooOOOooooo.......

The smell of woodsmoke woke me and I sat up, disorientated; where was I? Glancing around, I saw an opening to my left and peered through, suddenly remembering that I was in a tent. It was still very early, dawn was only just breaking, but people were milling around, the aroma of hot food making my stomach growl. Forcing myself to get up, I wrapped a large blanket around me and stepped outside, shivering a little as my bare feet came into contact with damp grass.

Movement to my right caught my eye and I turned to see my husband striding towards me, attired in full armour. Spotting me at the door of the tent, he smiled, his face lighting up.

"Good morning, my Hannah, I'm sorry this clatter has woken you, I had hoped after yesterday you could sleep a little longer," dropping a kiss on my head as he reached me. I grinned back at him.

"Nothing more than I'm used to at the moment. How much longer do you think we will be travelling?"

"Not sure; less than a week." I grimaced and may have harrumphed. Much as it was very nice discovering a new place, the journey was becoming rather tedious. I am as good a rider as any man, but I was fed up being in the saddle day after day after day. "Soon we will be there and we can settle into one place again for a time." Maxentius cupped my cheek in his large hand, tilting my head so that he could look onto my face, which I knew must look tired.

"I'm sorry, I don't mean to be such a grump."

"Do not think of it, my love, it cannot be easy with the little one. Maybe we should have..." I forestalled the rest of his sentence by placing my finger on his lips.

"I could not have left him; he is too young. It was hard enough saying goodbye to the others, to leave Luc would have broken my heart." As though he heard his name, a small wail came from inside the tent. I ducked under the flap and lifted our small son out of his wraps, cuddling him to me. He was still breastfeeding, so there was no way I could have left him in Rome, despite the fact that a wet nurse would have seen to his needs.

Maxentius followed me in, taking the baby from me as I worked out the most comfortable way to feed him while sitting on the floor. I leaned against the central wooden post and held out my arms. Maxentius handed me our son and sat with me while I staunched the child's voracious appetite. As when Claudia was born, Maxentius was in awe of this child and spent hours just watching him. Our youngest daughter was now nearly nine years old and I had long ago given up on having any more children, assuming that as it hadn't happened it probably wasn't likely to. You can imagine our surprise when I discovered that I was pregnant again.

We already had three children, our Claudia and the two older ones, Efraim and Liora, whom we had adopted after the deaths of their parents — my brother and his wife. Occasionally it had troubled me that Maxentius didn't have a son of his blood, but he'd said he already had one, assuring me that Efraim and for that matter Liora, were as much ours as though I'd given birth to them, so I'd stopped worrying.

Luc, full name Lucius Marcus Valerius, was born eight months after the eruption of Vesuvius, while we were in Rome and his birth had been uneventful, by which I mean that I'd survived it. As with Claudia, we disregarded convention, naming him for Marcus, Maxentius' comrade and best friend as well as the brother of my heart. However, since we already had a Marcus, we decided on Luc as his everyday name, less confusing.

Maxentius' mother and sister were incredibly supportive, looking after the other children, allowing me to rest while I recuperated. For their part, my three had loved staying with their grandmother and when this latest commission had been assigned, Claudia, Maxentius' mother, asked whether we would consider allowing them to remain with her, rather than accompany us on what could be a dangerous posting. Efraim would be able to continue his education uninterrupted, and my two girls could begin their training in the social graces expected from the women of the elite. Good luck with that, I thought. Both our daughters were like me — tomboys — and although they loved dressing up, were happier climbing trees and riding horses than worrying about etiquette, deportment and decorum.

As I had been when they had first accompanied Claudia and Antonia to Rome, I was torn. I knew that staying would give them opportunities undreamt of, but the thought of such a long period without them with no chance of visiting made the decision very difficult. After much discussion and yes, I admit it, many tears, I was persuaded eventually that it would be best for the children to stay with their grandmother. The children themselves, much to my well-concealed dismay, were ecstatic for they had begun to settle in the capital of Empire and loved the vitality of that most exuberant of cities.

That was a little over two months ago and once that decision had been made everything else fell into place very quickly. The posting was to one of the forts on the northern frontier of Britannia, and it sounded like a cold and bleak place after Masada, Pompeii and Rome, but one did not argue with military orders. Thankfully, a few familiar faces would be accompanying us, Marcus, who would again act as Maxentius' second-in-command, Petronius my fellow escapee from Pompeii and most surprisingly, Julius.

I was certain that Julius had been killed in the devastation that had engulfed Pompeii, as we had neither heard nor seen anything of him for quite some time. Then one day out of the blue, he appeared at one of the barracks outside the city, asking for Maxentius. He had taken my warning to heart, helping others flee the town, before eventually making his way to Rome and trying to locate what remained of his garrison.

I knew many of the other soldiers too; they who had been part of the peacekeeping force at Pompeii and had left prior to the eruption, accompanying Maxentius and Marcus when they had escorted the agitators to Rome. Sadly, several others had been killed in the catastrophe.

Leaving Rome was harder than I could have foreseen; not so much the city, for it still confounded me, but the children and Maxentius' family. We had become very close in the few months we had been living nearby and knowing it was unlikely we would see them for at least four years, left me utterly bereft. There was also Aliza, the children's grandmother, now ensconced in Ostia with her new husband. We had visited them several times and she was very happy in her new life. Living together for so many years, however, we had become much more than just friends and I missed her company, not to mention her cooking.

At least we had Luc with us; he was enough to keep my mind from dwelling on the separation and my very patient husband was there to mop up any tears and calm my fraught nerves; added to which, the anticipation of a new adventure was a fairly effective distraction.

Our main route was by sea, the voyage taking about four weeks and we disembarked somewhere along the east coast of Britannia, at a bustling port called Petuaria. From there the journey had taken us by horseback — or for most of the soldiers on foot — across country to the great road that would take us north. The distance was reckoned to be around fifteen to twenty days, depending on weather and road conditions and we had been moving for eight.

The fort Maxentius was to take over as commander was called Magnis; the current legatus, or general in charge, having just completed his term of office. As such, our contingent of soldiers was not very large — two centuries, which amounted to one hundred and sixty men, plus auxiliaries and horsemen — to augment two detachments of soldiers taken from garrisons based elsewhere in the province and already established at the fort, some of whom would be leaving with the outgoing legatus.

Such a relatively small number of soldiers would normally move much more quickly, but we had an inordinately large number of wagons carrying supplies, equipment and weapons, so 'fast' was not a term we could use to describe our progress.

We had passed the fortress town of Eburaci, a huge military base with a burgeoning vicus, or civilian settlement, adjacent to it. Obviously undergoing some redevelopment and expansion, its plethora of amenities and businesses reminded me of Pompeii. It was everything you expected of a Roman town and the diversity of goods was an eye-opener, so far from what many would call civilisation.

There was all manner of food shops, dry goods and materials, along with leather, metal, stone and glass workers. I had spotted stalls with herbs and oils and itched to investigate whether they could be used for medicinal purposes. Sadly we did not have time to explore, but I hoped that we might be able to come back and visit this surprising town someday soon.

Now, more than half way to our destination, the scenery was changing; the gentle slopes and vales had become windswept hills and steep valleys. It was a wild, untamed landscape, but I found it pleasing; it had an unspoilt beauty. Flowers and bushes, strange to my eyes, were strewn across the expanse of dull green and brown, their myriad of colours like gemstones sparkling in the sunlight. Maybe it would not be so bad this new land. It was summer here, yet the temperatures were not as uncomfortably hot as those of Roman Italy and the nights remained cool. The days were long, the sun not setting until very late, making the nights short. The skies, however, were usually crystal clear and the delicate hues of evening wrapped themselves around you, soothing the weary traveller. Such beauty — I could have admired it forever.

Back to the journey. It never ceased to amaze me how quickly Roman soldiers could strike camp. By the time I had fed my son and inhaled some food, the tents had been packed away and the wagons were ready to roll. Unwilling to hold up the train, I hurried to secure Luc, who was fussing a little, in his carrying pouch and using the step of one of the wagons, mounted my horse, whose name is Gemmula — yes, she of the wild ride from Pompeii. Happily, we had managed to get her back to Rome where she had been stabled at the garrison. Maxentius swung his horse around, coming alongside me, resting his hand on my leg.

"You sure you are ready, my love? Is Luc settled?" peering at his grumpy son. I smiled.

"He'll go back to sleep as soon as we start moving and yes, I'm ready. I always forget how quickly you soldiers pack up." My husband grinned at me and nodded to the soldier at the front of the column. An order was shouted and we were moving again. "Soon," I whispered to my baby, "soon we will be there and hopefully we can rest."

My name is Hannah, by the way. I am a physician and a Roman citizen of Hebrew heritage. My life has been changed in ways I never anticipated and I carry a secret known only to my husband and Marcus — oh and one other, but she's nearly two millennia away.

.......oooooOOOooooo.......

Chapter Three

An incessant ringing permeated my brain, I couldn't wake up, the bed was so comfortable and warm and I had been lost in dreams. Reaching out, I hit the alarm, but the ringing continued. Oh, for goodness sake, how did this thing turn off? I opened my eyes and realised that it was my mobile phone ringing, not the alarm. Grabbing it from the bedside table, I answered rather groggily.

"Yes, hello, who's this?"

"It's me, Hannah, are you okay? Did I wake you?" Max's cheerful voice bounced out of the speaker.

"Hey there. Yes you did, but that's okay, what time is it?" I asked, peering at the clock. My eyes wouldn't focus, so I gave up, resting my head back on the pillows. It was light outside, but I didn't think I'd overslept.

"Not long after seven, sure you're all right?" I assured him I was fine, just still half asleep.

Max's early morning calls were the next best thing to waking up next to my husband; somehow he made me feel as though he was right there. We chatted for a little longer and he told me he'd text me through his flight details for the next day. I couldn't wait for him to get home. I had planned a lovely meal — an impressive feat for someone who can't cook — and had found a rather nice bottle of bubbly to go with it. Once we'd hung up, I showered and dressed; then before I ate, took my cup of tea into the garden and watched the day begin.

It was another gorgeous morning: clear blue sky as far as the eye could see and although cool this early, would probably get quite warm as the day wore on. After enjoying a leisurely breakfast with a cup of coffee, I made sure I had everything I'd need for the day and set off for work. While I was cycling, I remembered my dream — well, tried to — it hovered just out of reach. There was something teasing at my consciousness, but it refused to be pinned down. I mulled it over all the way to work, still nothing. I ran my mind back over everything I'd done yesterday, there hadn't been anything unusual; all the artefacts had been much the same as every day, nothing stood out.

Mentally shrugging, I pushed it aside and settled down to my pile of boxes. It would take quite a long time to work through all of them, there were plenty in the office they had allocated to me and apparently there were many more in the storage room. I think everyone was hoping for one of those eureka moments when some innocuous looking artefact knocks the socks off everyone and changes history. I loved their optimism.

By the middle of the afternoon I was starting to feel weary. Concentrating on small items was interesting, but my head was beginning to ache so I decided to finish the boxes I was working through and call it a day. Carefully, I lifted out the last three. One held some pottery, it looked like Samian Ware, which must have been imported from France, or Gaul as it was known in antiquity. It appeared to be part of a large platter or serving dish and was a beautiful piece, the glossy red hardly dulled by its long years in the earth.

The second box was a little heavier; the item was wrapped in layers of soft cloth and I couldn't work out what it was. It felt like a cricket ball, which made me smile, envisioning a group of bored Romans inventing the game one Sunday afternoon on the edge of Empire. As I placed the artefact onto the thick cushioned mat used for preventing anything rolling off, my world trembled and there was a loud whooshing sound in my ears. Blinking, I tried to concentrate and examined the piece closely. It was made from wood, a rich almost dark bronze colour owing to its age and pigment leaching into it from the soil. I turned it over, noticing that one side was smooth, but the other had been whittled into some kind of shape.

As I ran my gloved fingers over the ripples, tracing the design, pictures formed in my head. A sun drenched plateau, a soldier, a young woman, sparkling water and pomegranate trees; a shelf above a fireplace, a wild ride and a town engulfed in ash. How could it be here, so far from where I'd last been aware of her? Even without the images, in my heart I knew what I was holding; it was just taking my head a little longer to catch up.

It was the pomegranate. The one Maxentius had carved for his Hannah in the aftermath of the massacre and during the rebuilding of Masada. She had carried it across the sea, first to Rome, then to Pompeii and back to Rome after she had escaped the eruption of Vesuvius. How had it come to be here? My mind kept circling back to this question, even though the answer was obvious. They must have been posted to Britain. How long were they here? I knew that generals were assigned to forts or the much larger fortresses as commanders for a given period, three or four years usually. Maybe I would be able to trace Maxentius through military records. Had he been granted retirement? Did they stay on afterwards? Or had the beautiful carving been mislaid somehow? That didn't sit well with me, for I knew how much Hannah had loved it, nearly as much as her — our — clasp.

I sat back, my mind spinning, the headache becoming intolerable. I took a couple of painkillers and waited until they started to take effect, then wrapped everything back up. I would deal with this tomorrow. I needed to talk to Max. This was not something I was prepared for, so far away from where I expected my ancient family would be living.

I locked the door and waved my goodbyes to the other staff, making my way around the building to where I had locked my bike. I leaned on the wall for a moment, breathing in the fresh air, gazing out across the countryside. It was quite late in the afternoon now and the light was enchanting. There was the merest hint of pink on the horizon and the bright blue of the day had mellowed to a paler shade, suggestive of a cold night. The restorative powers of scenes like this can never be underestimated. This view along with the painkillers went a long way to banishing my headache.

Once home, I secured my bike in the garage and sorted out some food. I couldn't face a large meal, so I plumped for toasted teacakes, slathering the butter on so thickly that it dribbled down my chin when I bit into the hot bread. Very decadent, I thought. Then, after making a cup of tea and shrugging into the same jumper I'd been wearing all week, I sat outside to watch the moonrise. The jumper smelt of Max's aftershave, helping me feel closer to him and tonight I needed it more than ever. I rang him, but it went straight to voicemail; frustrated I left a brief message. Typical, the one night I really wanted to talk to him was the one night I couldn't get through.

I rested my head against the wall of the house, the headache still pulsing behind my eyes and I knew I would need more painkillers before I went to bed or I wouldn't sleep. Suddenly I thought about my dream and wondered whether it and the wooden pomegranate were connected. Try as I might, I couldn't recall it, but it was still there, lurking on the fringes of my mind. It was too hard to fathom and made my headache worse, so I gave up and just watched the sky.

The phone interrupted my reverie and grateful for the distraction I answered quickly.

"Hey, Sunshine. Sorry I missed your call; was still in a meeting and my phone was on silent."

"It's ok, Hon, just didn't expect you'd be working so late."

"We had a sticky problem that needed more than a five-minute fix. I was worried it might mean an extension to this visit, but it's all good now and I'll still make it home tomorrow." He paused. "How was your day?"

"Great, I got loads done, but..." I trailed off, unsure how to phrase the next bit.

"What happened, Hannah?" Max knows me too well; I am incapable of hiding anything from him, even at great distances and over the phone.

"Errrmmm...well...it was like this..." Stopping abruptly, I shook my head; my mouth didn't seem capable of forming words. Taking a deep breath I started again, telling him more or less coherently about the artefact. It took a little time, as I kept second-guessing myself, but eventually I think he got the gist of it.

"So what does this mean, Hannah? Do you think they were here? Have you had any dreams?" I was about to say no, when I remembered the one from the night before.

"No...ooo..." hesitantly "...not that I'm aware of, but I can't be sure." Going on to say that I'd had one the previous night and couldn't recall it, but that it was still nagging at me.

"Well, I'll be home tomorrow, we can talk about it properly then. Where is this pomegranate thing now?"

"Wrapped up in a box in my office, its safe, but obviously I can't tell anyone. I can't say that I know who carved it and when, how it was taken from Masada to Pompeii and that it somehow ended up in the ground near Hadrian's Wall. I'm not sure what to do. It was hard enough leaving it there, I wanted to bring it home with me." Max chuckled and I could picture his expression.

"Don't let it worry you, sweetheart, maybe leave it 'til I'm back and we can examine it more closely together." I realised that this would be a good idea and felt better about the whole thing. We chatted for a few more minutes, but too soon it was time to hang up. "I'll call you in the morning, Sunshine, sleep well. I love you."

"Love you too, Max." The disconnect tone rang in my ear and I put my phone down, running my finger across the screen as if I could reach through and touch my husband. Pulling a face at my whimsy, I picked up my teacup and went inside, locking the door and going up to bed.

After giving in and taking a rather strong painkiller, I sat in bed for a while with the lights out and the windows open, watching the sky. The cool breeze wafted through the room, and all was quiet. I started to feel drowsy as the tablet started working and pulling the comforter up to my shoulder, let slumber take me.

.......oooooOOOooooo.......

Finally, after what had seemed like a never-ending journey, we were here. The last few days had been quite arduous as the terrain was not easy along this frontier region compared with the great north road. There was a road of sorts under construction, the army engineers widening and strengthening it, but long stretches were still more like a well-beaten track and it was rather narrow in places. A few broken wheels had resulted as the wagons got stuck in the ruts, causing some delay. I knew it was part of an important trade network, though, so the improvements would be essential.

Never mind, we'd made it and it was another lovely day. The landscape had changed yet again; here it was harsher, miles and miles of stark moorland, but I could see rolling hills in the distance. The grass was quite sparse, the area around the fort covered with scrubby bushes and low trees, all laden with white and yellow blossoms. A little way off, there were dark forests, pine, if the scent in the air was anything to go by and I speculated as to what — or who — hid in their dark depths.

We trundled up to the huge wooden gate, open to allow the long train to enter. Although not on the scale of the fortress at Eburaci, the fort was enormous, or so it appeared to my uneducated eyes. I had visited the garrison at Pompeii once or twice, but this was huge in comparison and, on our approach, I had noticed the defensive ditch that surrounded the palisade and the turf ramparts, giving me an immediate sense of security. As we rode through, I spied row upon row of long wooden buildings at either side of the main gateway, a large square building right in front of us and more buildings beyond. Their layout seemed deliberate and Maxentius told me that this was typical, so that any Roman soldier or civilian, arriving at the fort would know exactly where everything was. I was looking forward to exploring.

As we dismounted, soldiers materialised to take our horses to the stables and our contingent organised themselves into rows for inspection, while the auxiliaries started the long task of unpacking the wagons. The outgoing commander strode towards us in full battledress and the formalities began. Unsure of what I was supposed to do, my status being somewhat unusual, I moved to the edge of the company and waited. Luc had slept much of the day, but he was stirring and I knew he would demand sustenance soon. Rocking him in a vain attempt settle him, I watched the two men greet each other, immediately falling into an animated discussion and I deliberated, idly, as to whether they had met before.

They walked through the lines of soldiers, one scrutinising, the other observing and there seemed to be a lot of nodding and talking. I hoped this wouldn't take too long; I wanted to see where we'd be living and was desperate to feel properly clean. I'd even suffer the bathhouse, were such a thing part of the set up here, if it meant I could have hot water. We had been travelling for days and had been able to manage only cursory washes, except at Eburaci, but even that had been rushed. Luc fidgeted again, trying to get out of his wrap, his tiny hands fussing at my clothes and I knew I would have to feed him.

Glancing round, I tried to see if there was anywhere I could go, a quiet corner where no-one would see me, but I was wholly unfamiliar with the layout. Catching my husband's eye was pointless; he was totally occupied in the business of the army. Looking down the lines of soldiers, I spotted Marcus standing facing the troops, waiting for his commander's orders. As I moved, he looked across and I motioned for him to meet me. He made his way over and I explained my quandary. He smiled down at his namesake and said that I should be able to feed in one of the rooms in the commandant's house. I glared at him in frustration. Men — they have no idea.

"I can't just go into someone else's home, Marcus. For a start they don't know me, for another I have no clue where it is and Luc will scream the place down if I don't feed him soon." Knowing my son's lung capacity, Marcus chuckled and told me not to worry, we were expected and there would be guest rooms set aside for our use, forgetting that I would have no clue where the residence even was in relation to where we were standing.

"Yes, that's all well and good, but where?" I muttered, exasperation clear in my tones. "Please, Marcus, you need to help me. I know that there are protocols, but I don't imagine anyone wants me to feed my son in the middle of the quadrangle. I can't ask Maxentius, he's being all important and official," I said trying not to sound aggrieved. "We've been riding all day; I'm tired, your boss's son is about to deafen the whole camp and I have no idea how this fort is laid out or where I'm supposed to go."

Marcus glanced at me and I knew I looked weary and fed up. I was the only woman accompanying the soldiers and, even though I wasn't trained for long marches with heavy packs, I had never once held them up or asked for special treatment and I'd carried my son since we'd disembarked at Petuaria. Grinning at my expression, he walked calmly over to Maxentius and the other legatus and had a quiet word. They both looked over and I blushed, uncomfortable being the recipient of such attention. There was a moment of discussion and Marcus walked back to me, taking my arm and leading me out of the quadrangle, to a large building at the edge of the fort.

He shouted something as we entered the atrium and a tall man, wearing civilian attire came to meet us. Marcus asked him where I could feed my son and we were ushered into a small chamber to one side of the entryway; simply furnished with a couple of chairs, a table and a rather ornate cupboard. Thanking them both, I sank into the chair, unwrapping Luc from his travel pouch and letting him feed. It was a relief for both of us as he suckled with gusto. I stroked his cheek as he fed, marvelling that I had created this tiny human. He had a mop of dark hair, just like his father and, although blue at the moment, I hoped that his eyes would be green. As I watched him, I thought about what our other children might be doing, feeling the familiar tug at my heart strings and considered how I might be able to get messages to them while we were so far away.

Marcus was still chatting with the man who had shown us the room and whom I assumed was in charge of running the household. I could hear snippets of their conversation; they were discussing the change over and who would sleep where until the current commander and his staff left. I could feel my eyes getting heavy and, try as I might, I could not fight the wave of exhaustion that came over me. Comfortable in the chair, in this quiet space, I nodded off.

.......oooooOOOooooo.......

Chapter Four

I didn't sleep well, waking at dawn and padding down the stairs to take yet more painkillers and make a cup of very strong coffee. My dreams had been convoluted and I was fairly certain Hannah and Maxentius had been in them. I felt their presence at the edge of my consciousness, but could not interpret it. I didn't know whether it was because of the pomegranate, or that they were indeed close. I hoped that I would be able to find something today that would tell me whether they had ever been near here.

There was a new database, which although still in the development phase, already held a mind-numbing amount of information about the movement of legions, their commanders and how long they spent in particular places. As an archaeological museum with military archives, we should be able to access it; the problem was that there was a dearth of information concerning the period I was interested in. If these artefacts were dated to any time after AD84, I doubted I would find anything useful. I just had to hope that there was something recorded prior to this date, which might help me work out where Maxentius was.

Making myself comfortable on the sofa, I sipped my drink, breathing in the heady aroma and willing the caffeine to kick-start my morning. It was quite dull outside; the clouds seemed heavy and a bit oppressive. I hoped it was just localised and wouldn't prevent Max from coming home this evening. His flight was due in about four, meaning he should be home a little before six. I decided that since I was up early, I might as well prepare the meal now rather than leave it until I got home; then all I would have to do would be to turn the oven on, shower and change. Good thinking, Hannah. The bubbly was chilling in the fridge and the dessert was ready; I was surprisingly organised, for someone who can't cook.

I mooched about the kitchen, happily peeling and chopping vegetables and browning the meat, thinking about the coming evening and having Max home. As if in tune with me, the phone rang, I glanced at my watch; it was only half past six.

"Morning, beautiful." I grinned down the phone, as I replied.

"Morning Max, how did you know I'd be awake?"

"Just born lucky. You okay? I've been worried about you since our chat last night."

"I didn't have the best night and..." I hesitated; did I want to share this over the phone?

"...and what, Hannah?" I could hear it in his voice; he already knew what I was going to say. I was quiet for a long moment. "Hannah?"

"I dreamed about them, but before you say anything, I don't know whether it was because of seeing the carved pomegranate. Might be nothing at all."

"But you don't think so, do you?" I pondered his question.

"I really don't know what to think, Max. I am going to try accessing that new military database this morning to see whether there's any record of Maxentius being posted here. It's worth a try."

Our conversation circled this for a while and then maybe as a distraction, we moved onto other, more mundane matters. We had a few family birthdays coming up, so we talked about whether we'd be able to get to any of the celebrations. Neither of us was particularly comfortable in large groups of people, me especially, but family get togethers were usually fun and pretty relaxed affairs. Eventually though we had to hang up, both of us had busy days ahead and time was moving on.

"The weather okay with you?" I asked. He told me it was a perfect day, still and cool, so I didn't bother to elaborate. It must be localised. "Safe flight, take care and I'll see you this evening."

"I will, can't wait. Love you, Sunshine."

"Love you too, Max." We disconnected and I stood for a while, staring into space my hand still on the phone. "Come home to me, Max." I whispered as, inexplicably, I felt a chill ripple down my spine.

Gathering myself, I finished preparing our dinner, ate a fairly decent breakfast and made a sandwich for lunch. Another strong coffee — I'd be bouncing off the walls if I wasn't careful — and I was ready. The sky was still threatening but it was lighter at the horizon, so I thought it might clear before long.

Once at the museum and before I did anything else, I turned on my computer opening up my usual tabs relating to antiquity in general and Roman Britain in particular, including my favourite website, LacusCurtius. This site had translations of pretty much any historical text I would likely ever need in my line of work — so much easier than wading through dusty tomes — run by a gentleman who was very helpful if I came across a knotty issue with an ancient source or some Latin that I was unsure of. Then I logged into the new database and set up a search. I let it run through the parameters while I carried on cataloguing the artefacts, carefully avoiding the one box on my desk that enticed me. Every time the search came up with no results, I'd change the parameters and try again, all the while cataloguing and recording the finds.

Lunch came and went and I was about to give up for the day, when the computer pinged, a rather happy little sound, which I trusted meant that it had found something. Hardly daring to breathe, I moved the screen, so I that could see it properly. There it was, two fragments from an inscription. It wasn't all there, but the transcriber had made a best guess from what had survived and the suggested text read, 'Under the command of Legatus L. Maxentius Valerius, soldiers from COH II PR LEG XX VV and LEG II A at Magnis made this.'

Double-checking through my plethora of websites, for my own piece of mind more than anything, I confirmed that COH II PR was the second praetorian cohort; this was the contingent from Pompeii. Although unusual for a Praetorian unit to be so far from Rome, these were Maxentius' soldiers and, I assumed, a small detachment — probably to replace those departing with the outgoing commander — a maximum of two centuria, not the full cohort. I already knew that LEG XX VV was the Twentieth Legion Valeria Victrix and LEG II A was the Second Legion Augusta. Both of the latter were legions based elsewhere in Britannia but vexillations were often sent to police the frontiers, or to augment other garrisons.

Magnis was under where I was sitting, well pretty much. It was presumed to be the earlier name given to Carvoran Roman Fort, whose ruins were adjacent to the museum I was working in. Not much left now, but it was believed to be one of the forts set up by Agricola as he worked his way into Scotland. Plenty of tombstones, altar stones and fragmented inscriptions had been found in the immediate vicinity of the fort, providing a wealth of information for later occupation, but so far very little dated to the time period we were investigating.

Initially a temporary camp eventually evolving into a large fort, it was rebuilt many times and was still in use in AD160 when it was reconstructed entirely in stone; indicating that it was one of the long-term settlements along what had become Hadrian's Wall. I speculated about what might have been made. Was it some part of the fort, or a road, or a bridge? We would never know — never say never a small voice whispered at the back of my mind. I studiously ignored the voice and printed off the page.

Unable to stop myself now, I pulled on a new pair of cloth gloves and opened the box in which the wooden pomegranate rested. So, my ancient family had definitely been here, but how did Hannah lose this? With infinite care, I held the artefact, turning it over and over, struck again by the intricate detail, the clever hand that had carved this. Maxentius' face flashed into my mind, his unruly black hair and deep green eyes, so familiar. Nothing else came though, no images or information about them.

I held the pomegranate to my heart for a long time, unwilling to let it go yet knowing I had no choice. Eventually, I rolled it back up into the soft cloth and placed it gently on its cushion of cotton wool, making sure the lid was clipped on. I wrote the description on the label, adding that it was not yet catalogued, in case someone decided to file it away. I had put in a day's holiday so that Max and I could have a long weekend and, although as a general rule no one else interfered with my work, you could never be sure. Glancing at my watch, I noticed that it was after half past three and my day was over. Before leaving the office, I picked up the sheet with the inscription from the printer; it was something Max and I could talk about if we had time over the next few days.

Wishing everyone else a good weekend, I left and cycled home. The day had brightened up, still not as blue and sunny as they had been, but no longer dull. The breeze was lovely, just enough to keep me cool as I rode along. Suddenly, very happy and excited about seeing Max, I could not stop myself from singing. I'm sure it sounded awful, but I didn't care, my husband was coming home.

Arriving home, I locked my bike away and going into the house took the lunch box and water bottle out of my backpack, placing them in the sink to wash later, then turned the oven on. The casserole would take a couple of hours and I wanted to be sure it was done for when Max came in. The house was clean and tidy. I opened all the windows, letting the fresh air in and went upstairs to shower and change. Half an hour or so later, I was back downstairs, checking the dinner and laying the table. I turned on the television, its volume low and just enough to provide a little background noise and had been pottering around for about ten minutes, when an item caught my attention.

The reporter was saying that they had some breaking news: a small plane, carrying seventeen people had crashed on take off and had burst into flames. Police, fire and ambulance were on scene, but at that stage it seemed unlikely that any on board had survived. I stared at the television as a terrible fear made my stomach clench. Picking up my phone, I scrolled through to the text Max had sent with his flight details. I looked back at the screen; the flight number was rolling along the bottom along with a phone number for relatives. The flight numbers matched.

I couldn't take it in; that pile of fiery wreckage strewn across the grass held my Max? My Max was dead? No — it wasn't possible. My head started to hurt and my breathing went all wonky. I leant against the table, gripping it with one hand, while my other still held the phone. What should I do? Should I call the number on the screen, or would they call me? I was next of kin, but how would they know? I tried the number, but it was busy; of course it was busy, seventeen people were dead, seventeen families needed to know whether any one of them was their loved one.

I looked at my phone again; were the numbers the same? Maybe I'd made a mistake. The pain in my head increased. No, there was no mistake, the numbers still matched. I felt the world around me darken, shudders began running down my spine and I still struggled to breathe. The headache became excruciating and I couldn't see properly. I glanced back at the television. The last thing I saw was the wreckage burning fiercely and knew no-one had a chance. My love, my life, my destiny, everything I held dear had been destroyed in those charred embers, which were dancing lazily in the breeze before vanishing, lost forever. Then blessed oblivion, as my head exploded in pain and I slid to the floor unaware that I had shattered the quiet with a cry wrenched from my soul.

****

A tall man had just got out of a taxi and was walking up the driveway to his cottage. He had managed to get an earlier flight and was home long before his wife expected him. His wife — he loved rolling those words around in his head — he had missed her these last four days and couldn't wait to see her. The thoughts of their reunion, quite likely very passionate, made him smile, but just as he reached the gate, he heard an agonised wail, a sound he'd heard once before and never wanted to hear again.

Running into the cottage, he saw his wife sprawled on the floor, her phone in one hand. Dropping his bag, he bent over her. She was breathing but it seemed to be erratic and her face was sheet white. The television was on and, as he glanced up at it, he saw a report about a fiery plane crash. Registering the flight number, he realised what had happened: his wife thought he'd been killed. Horrified, he tried to wake her.

"Hannah, it's okay, I'm here and I'm not dead. Hannah!" She moaned a pitiful sound, but didn't come round. Remembering her headaches, Max dug out a telephone number and called the specialist, a Dr Stephenson, who had been treating her. He was with a patient, so Max left an urgent message. Gathering his wife in his arms, he carried her upstairs and gently laid her on the bed.

Hannah's head felt very hot, but the rest of her was ice-cold. Tremors were running along her slender frame and occasionally she moaned again. With no clue about what to do, Max just sat with her, holding her hand and talking to her, trying to call her back from whatever dark hole to which she had retreated. After what seemed like forever, the phone rang and Max told Dr. Stephenson what had happened, asking whether he should take her into the local hospital. Seemingly, though, the cottage wasn't far from where the specialist lived, so he said it would be easier if he called round on his way home; he could bring the equipment necessary to establish what had happened. Before hanging up, he told Max to keep Hannah in a quiet room, preferably darkened.

Feeling more than a little helpless, Max looked down at his wife, the tremors continued to ripple through her body, showing no signs of abating. He sat next to her, holding her hand and stroking her hair, talking to her all the while, desperately trying to make her wake up. He'd been here before, only this time she didn't think he was alive; what did she have to come back for?

.......oooooOOOooooo.......

Someone was shaking me. My dreams held me, I didn't want to break them; they seemed very important, but the hand kept shaking.

"Hannah, we have rooms we can remove to, it'll be more comfortable to rest there if you need to." I opened my eyes into a pair of twinkling green ones and a face smiling down on me. I struggled to sit up. I had slumped down in the chair, weariness overtaking me.

"Oh, I am so sorry, I didn't mean to fall asleep." Embarrassed at doing so in front of people I didn't know and staff to boot, how impolite could I get? Maxentius smiled back at me unconcerned and, as I glanced round, I realised there was only the two of us.

"Where did everyone go?" I asked. "Marcus and another man were here; they were talking; it feels like only a minute or so."

"You've been asleep for about an hour, my love. They decided to leave you as you seemed very tired."

"Luc, where's Luc?"

"Once he was full, he fell asleep too, so Marcus took him to the rooms we've been allocated. Someone is with him." I realised that someone else must have sorted me out as well and looked up at my husband. He grinned, knowing exactly what I was thinking and nodded.

"It's fine, Hannah, I took care of it." I blushed and he leant over kissing me gently. "It's the most natural thing in the world; do not fret." I grasped his hand gratefully. He pulled me out of the chair. I stretched, trying to make my body work.

"What happens now? Are there more ceremonials or do you just shake hands and sign in?" I asked, yawning. Maxentius looked at me curiously.

"What do you mean shake hands and sign in?" A remnant of my other self had risen, using phrases not yet popular; maybe wouldn't be for a long time. I bit my lip and explained, making Maxentius chuckle as he told me how things would be. The current legatus, Servius Fabricius Habitus, would hand over officially the next day and then would leave the fort for Luguualium, about twelve miles away on the first leg of his journey back to Caerleon, headquarters of the Legio II Augusta. Then we would be able to settle in properly. For tonight, we would use the guest quarters.

As I stood, my dream came back.

"Maxentius." Something in my voice made him stop as he was turning to show me through the building.

"What is it, my Hannah?"

"I just had the strangest dream, I think it was about the other Hannah. Her head hurt, she couldn't see for the pain and then she sort of collapsed. I'm sure her Max found her, but he can't wake her. It's as though she is drifting aimlessly." I hesitated and my husband looked at me — waiting. "I have a feeling that she will come back to me very soon." My words were absurd and, other than my husband, there was only one other person who would understand what I was talking about and even then it would seem peculiar. Maxentius took my hand and pulled me close.

"We will deal with it, if or when it happens, my love. We cannot change these things and we both know she is always with you and you with her." I looked up at my tall Roman who, after all these years, could still surprise me with his complete acceptance of my convoluted life. Standing up on tiptoe, I kissed him gently.

"Thank you." He raised an eyebrow. "For loving me unconditionally, you are the rarest of men." He grinned agreeing that he was indeed rare and then showed me through to our rooms.

We had a whole wing of the legatus' house; it was enormous and this was just for guests. We didn't need all this, but I was assured it was quite normal and that we would be able to inspect the rest of the building the next day. A lot of people were moving things about, furniture was being packed onto wagons and large wooden boxes were stacked at one of the entrances. I assumed these were the personal items of Fabricius Habitus being readied for the transfer. Unless he had hated his posting, I knew how hard it would be for this man to leave. Four years is a long time; he would know all the men under his command and presumably much about the local tribes.

Maxentius was this way also; he made sure that he treated all the soldiers in his garrison with dignity and patience and tried to understand as much as he could about wherever he was posted to. Soldiers can be a belligerent lot and, as many came from conquered nations, rebellion was not unheard of. It pleased me that my husband was, in essence, a compassionate man and realised that even though discipline was essential, so was respect. As far as I could tell, within his ranks this respect was mutual. The issues confronting the soldiers on this frontier were not very different from those faced at Masada; it was just a whole lot colder.

.......oooooOOOooooo.......

Chapter Five

Dr. Stephenson arrived finally, about two hours later. Hannah still hadn't come round, although there had been times when Max thought she might rouse. After a thorough examination the specialist said that as far as he could tell there was no underlying concern. He had brought his wife along, who happened to be a nurse, as well as portable x-ray and ultrasound machines; the two of them doing as much as they would have done had Hannah been in hospital. Listening to Max's explanation of what he thought had happened the doctor surmised that she was in shock.

"I know this does not seem serious, Max, but shock can kill, even though Hannah has no physical injuries, nothing that we can treat. The only thing you can do is talk to her; try to make her believe you are not dead. Get her family to come over and do the same thing. Only one at a time, but let them all speak to her, convince her that you are alive and well. It may take some time, or she may come out of it overnight. Grief is a strange master; it often refuses to let go. The scenes from the television would have been too hard to process, so her mind has shut down. You need to persuade her that it is okay to wake up." Max grimaced, knowing how hard it would be to call her back; sadly, it was not something he could share with this doctor.

Max thanked the specialist, who said he'd be back the next day on his way into work; then called Hannah's family and his own parents, explaining what had happened and hoping that they might be able to visit even if only for a few minutes, and that it could make all the difference. Arrangements were made, after which Max just stood in the middle of their bedroom, at a loss. He realised he could smell food and went down to the kitchen, noticing Hannah had set the table with candles and champagne glasses. His heart ached.

He opened the oven door, the casserole smelt delicious, but his stomach roiled at the thought of food. Lifting it out, he left the food to cool on the stovetop, turning the oven off as he did so; the casserole could be reheated in the microwave. Boiling the kettle, he made himself a hot drink and as an afterthought, poured a glass of cold water for Hannah; he might be able to get her to drink something. Taking both upstairs, he pulled the large wing-backed chair over to the bedside and settled himself in for a long night.

****

I could hear noises, people moving around, but I couldn't work out what was happening. Max was dead, my heart was shattered and the pain in my head was unbearable. A voice spoke to me telling me that it was okay and that I could wake up, that Max wasn't dead. Of course he was dead, I'd seen the wreckage, I'd seen the fire. What was the point — if he wasn't in my life, what was the point? I knew this was cowardly, I knew I should throw off this black desolation, but I found I couldn't. The scenes from the television kept flickering through my mind and, try as I might, I couldn't blank them out.

Again the voice spoke, so gently, whispering my name. I fancied it was Max, but that was impossible. Was it his ghost? Was he saying goodbye? I wanted to cry, knowing that if I did, I might find some kind of release, but the tears wouldn't come. I felt hollow and bereft. There was nothing more here for me now. I thought of the pomegranate and the dream. If I let myself fall, at least I would be part of a life; I would still be loved, even though it was through someone else.

I could feel my consciousness receding. My head swirled, the pain came again and I think I cried out. As the spasm passed, the darkness lifted, images began to sharpen. Wooden buildings, soldiers, a soft blue sky on a summer's day. I felt cushioned by a warmth I couldn't explain. The scene was still hazy, but I knew what was happening and this time I didn't fight it, more I welcomed it with open arms — here I was safe.

.......oooooOOOooooo.......

It was about a month since we had arrived at Magnis and I felt we had settled in rather well. The soldiers were an interesting bunch of men from at least two, if not three different countries. They were vexillations, sent to supplement the cohort left behind by the Roman Governor, Agricola, to police the borders as he secured the frontier and continued to push north into Caledonia.

Although it had taken some time, I was now familiar with the layout of the fort and had been very excited to discover that there was a hospital; in fact this fort was extremely well set up all round. Besides the commander's residence and the hospital, there were barracks, the principia, or administrative headquarters, two granaries, several workshops, stores, a bathhouse — although this was outside the fort to avoid the possibility of a fire within — and stables. I was astonished, but once again Maxentius informed me that this was normal, that there was nothing superfluous to requirements, no real luxuries, just everything an army needed to keep it fed, clothed and supplied with weapons.

The principal role of the fort here at Magnis was to guard the junction of two major routes; however, it was also involved in the planning and construction of new roads along our section of the frontier, making communication and travel less onerous. Road building was a rather complicated process; extensive surveys were undertaken to determine the shortest route between certain points, then they had to decide what engineering methods would be required, taking into account lie of the land, watercourses, forests and so on. The roads needed to be wide enough for two wagons to pass and once the surface was completed, were reinforced with support walls and then constantly maintained. It was time-consuming work, but the result was well worth it.

Thus, every day the military engineers marched out, laden with supplies and equipment; their expertise evidenced in the beautifully smooth paved roads that were replacing the old, worn out and, often muddy, tracks. For their protection as well as for those of us within the fort, soldiers constantly patrolled the area, making sure that there was no chance of attack, sudden or otherwise.

Maxentius decided to reap the benefits of his peacekeeping experience and had set up negotiations with the local tribal leaders; understanding that if they had some way of expressing any grievance, it reduced the likelihood of reprisals. He accepted that many of these tribes resented their conquerors — who wouldn't? He met twice a week with all of them at a place of their choice. His time on Masada and in Pompeii stood him in good stead. Patience was something he had in spades.

I had ventured beyond the protection of the palisade. The countryside was beautiful and, despite the vague threat of attack from disgruntled locals, I found I could not be confined. In the company of a guard, more often than not Petronius or Julius, I spent many hours searching for herbs, roots and plants that might prove beneficial for healing.

Maxentius had set aside two rooms within the legatus' — our — house for my use. One room was full of shelves and the other had a large sink and a stone bench, which was perfect for chopping, grinding and blending. Not very large, but enough for me to work in. The tablets on which I had so painstakingly written my symbols, had survived several journeys, as had most of my medicines, and everything was now stacked neatly alongside my supply of bandages, sponges and cloths, some of which had come in handy as we travelled.

The long summer was reaching its finale, yet the days were still pleasantly mild and each afternoon, a gentle breeze would come rustling through the pine forest refreshing the air. This particular day, I was walking over to the hospital, or valetudinarian as the Romans called it, my bag full of medicines. I had been treating a few soldiers for stomach upsets and one for a wounded leg. There was a medicus already stationed here but even though he had auxiliaries, there were several hundred soldiers in the fort many of whom always seemed to be injuring themselves, so I had persuaded him to let me help. Although, my small son took up much of my time, he was still just a baby and slept a lot; being able to assist at the hospital was a lifeline, preventing me from being bored witless and allowed me to use my knowledge. The medicus was quite young and had been trained in Rome, before joining the military. As with so many medical men I had met, he was humble and rather shy, but very much a gentleman and we spent hours discussing treatments of every kind.

To my unending delight, he had a copy of a medical text that until now I had only heard of, written by a physician called Pedanius Dioscorides and called De Materia Medica, or On Medical Matters. It was a vast anthology of information in five volumes, including the details of about six hundred plants as well as minerals and mineral extracts, along with around a thousand medicines that could be made from them. I could not believe this young man had a copy, beautifully scripted on papyrus, bound and rolled carefully into cloth bags. It was marvellous to be able to study the texts and work out whether here, so many miles from Rome, we would be able to concoct any of the medicines detailed within.

Just as I was about to enter the hospital, I felt the ground shudder ever so slightly. Glancing around, I wondered whether there'd been an earthquake, unsure whether they were prevalent here. There was no sound of shouting or concern; no-one else seemed aware of it. A little dizzy, I leaned against the doorframe to steady myself, when suddenly I felt as though I had been punched in the stomach. The breath went out of me and as I tried to suck air back into my lungs, spots appeared before my eyes. My legs gave out and I sank to the ground. What on earth? Unable to move, I remained where I was, hoping that no one would see me. No such luck. Marcus appeared from one of the storerooms and, noticing that something seemed awry, was swiftly at my side.

"What happened, Hannah, are you all right?" I stared at him, unable to speak, still trying to breathe. He went to pull me to my feet, but I shook my head.

"Not yet..." I gasped, "...legs won't work." I tried to smile, but even that was too hard. Marcus squatted in front of me, anxious now.

"Hannah, what's going on? Are you ill?" I shook my head again and sort of waved my hand about trying to gesture that I'd be okay. I wasn't very convincing and, refusing to leave me there, Marcus scooped me up and shouldered his way through the door of the hospital, shouting for the medicus. I was very embarrassed, but quite frankly there didn't seem to be much I could do about it.

Atius or to give the medicus his proper name, Tiberius Atius Camillus came through a door at the side of the entryway, his expression reflecting his shock. Oh, good grief this was ridiculous. I struggled, trying to get down, but Marcus would not let me go, carrying me to where Atius indicated there was a quiet room. My brother laid me on the bed then moved aside to let Atius examine me. By now I was mortified, it was just a funny turn. Atius said something to Marcus who patted my arm and went out quickly.

"Atius," I tried to say, but my words were distorted. I tried again. "Atius, I'm fine." It sounded like gobbledygook. Shaking my head, attempting to rid myself of the buzzing in my ears, I grabbed Atius' arm. "Please, I'm fine." He smiled at me and disappeared into a tiny anteroom. I thought about getting up and leaving but my body had other ideas. I couldn't figure out what was going on, it was so weird. I lay back on the plump pillows, the room was cool and dim and suddenly I felt very weary. Maybe I should just shut my eyes; that might stop the dizziness.

I had barely closed them when they flew open, I knew what had happened. I needed my husband. I fought to get up, determined to go home, but a wave of nausea swamped me and I sank back onto the bed. Atius reappeared, frowning at me, realising what I'd tried to do and I smiled rather diffidently as he handed me a draft of something which smelt a bit peculiar.

"This will stop the nausea and dizziness." I stared at him in astonishment. How did he know I felt sick? I'd only just worked that one out.

"How?" I muttered thickly.

"Lucky guess." He winked and watched until I had drained the goblet. As I handed it back to him, a strange sensation rippled through me. What had he given me? I tried to speak, panic curling through me, but my voice wouldn't work and everything went black.

.......oooooOOOooooo.......

The tall man lingered at the foot of the bed, his face grave. An older lady, so like Hannah that she had to be her mother, sat next to her daughter, talking to her. A serene voice, telling her about what they had planned for the summer — birthday parties and family gatherings — that it was time to wake up because Max was here and he missed her. She talked for a long time; occasionally Hannah moved restlessly, but nothing more. Eventually, she stroked the cool hand lying on the comforter and said she'd be back tomorrow. Standing, she hugged Max.

"She'll come good, Max. Hang in there, Hannah loves you too much."

"Yes, but she still believes me to be dead, Cate. How do we convince her that I'm alive?"

"By repeating everything we've been telling her until she believes it too."

It had been the same with everyone who had visited — his family, Hannah's family — nothing; even her niece's high-spirited chatter didn't register. He was stumped. Going downstairs with Cate, he thanked her for coming, saying he'd update her later in the evening. Cate said she'd be back the next day with David, Hannah's father. Max nodded and watched as she walked down to her car. It was a beautiful day. Hannah would have loved to be sitting on the bench with a cuppa or a glass of wine — nothing to do, nowhere to go, just the two of them. With a pensive glance over his shoulder, Max trudged back inside, locking the door behind him.

The casserole was still on the stove and he reheated a portion, weighing up whether he could get his wife to eat a morsel or two. After finishing his meal, he spooned a small amount into another bowl and went up to their bedroom, very carefully lifting Hannah up on the pillows. She muttered something, but he didn't catch it.

"Hannah, I have some casserole here, please try a bit. You made it for me; it's so delicious. We should be sharing this downstairs with the champagne you bought." He held the spoon to her mouth; unbelievably she took it, swallowing the meat and potato without protest. He tried again; same thing and he managed to get her to eat the bowlful. Her eyes flickered and he held his breath, but she settled again.

"Max?" Barely a whisper.

"I'm here, Sunshine, come back to me." A sob caught her throat and a single tear ran down her cheek. Max leaned in and wiped it with his finger, caressing her face as he did so. She shuddered and the tremors began again, although maybe not quite as frequent as they had been.

"Oh Max, why you?" Her voice, so quiet and full of sorrow and he watched helplessly, as she slipped away again.

.......oooooOOOooooo.......

I fought whoever was holding me down, frantically trying to get them off me. I needed Maxentius; where was he? Someone grabbed my flailing hands and held them tightly. I struggled against them, but they held me fast. In a last ditch effort, I kicked out and heard a muffled grunt; the bed shifted as someone sat on it.

"Hey, that's enough, it's me." I recognised the voice, but couldn't quite place it and attempted to open my eyes but they felt like they had lead weights on them.

"Where am I?" I mumbled, confused.

"You're in the hospital; Marcus found you." Oh, that I vaguely remembered.

"Please let go of my hands." Plaintively.

"Well, don't hit me then." I could hear amusement in the voice and my hands were released. I lifted them to my face trying to prise my eyes open.

"I can't seem to open my eyes, they're so heavy." A cool damp cloth covered my face and someone wiped it over my eyes very gently. That felt better; maybe I could open them now. By sheer force of will, I managed to part my lids. The room was dim, but I could make out a shadowy figure near my head.

"Why am I here?"

"You had a funny turn. Marcus carried you in and Atius gave you a sleeping draft." Now why on earth would he do that?

"Why? I didn't need to sleep; I needed Maxentius."

"Well, now I'm here, my Hannah." His gentle voice wrapped itself around me. How had I not known it was him?

"Oh...you sure? It's really you?"

"Of course, who else?" He sounded somewhat perplexed as he ran his hand over mine and I felt his callouses, rough on my skin. He rubbed his thumb over my palm and I relaxed.

"Sorry, everything's a bit fuzzy. I need to tell you, I know what happened." I whispered, so quietly, that he had to lean right in to hear me. "But not here, somewhere private, I don't want anyone else to hear."

"There is no one near, my love, just tell me." I tried to collect my thoughts.

"It's her, she's here, but she kind of slammed into me like a whirlwind, that's what made me go all funny. She's in my head, but she's distraught. Previously as we've connected, it's been slow, some dreams, some awareness; this time she came so fast. I don't know why and it's weird; normally we just meld and our minds entwine, but she's hovering just on the edge of my consciousness. I don't know how to calm her and her distress is what's making me feel ill."

In the gloom, I could sense rather than see, Maxentius' gaze while he processed this. It was not very long since she and I had last been a part of each other. I had just discovered that I was pregnant with Luc and we had sort of met in Rome, an out-of-time experience for the three of us, as Maxentius saw her as well. She had been so happy. What had caused this anguish and why was she here now? Was there something we needed to be warned about? I knew these same thoughts would be running through my husband's head also.

Maxentius moved up on the bed, settling himself next to me and cradling me against his large frame, one hand stroking along my arm.

"I think maybe you just have to let her be. She'll come when she's ready and hopefully you'll work out why." Our conversation — as ever — was nonsensical. We were talking about another person from another time, just popping into my mind as if it was a normal everyday occurrence. Which, I suppose for us, it was.

"I want to go home, Max, please tell them you will take me home. I need to see Luc, who will no doubt be yelling for me and I need to be in my own surroundings, not in this hospital."

"Are you sure? You were rather unwell earlier and you still look a bit washed out. I could bring Luc here, maybe you should rest some more."

"I'll be fine, I can rest at home, please." I grasped my husband's hand as I was talking; my fingers curling round his in entreaty. He gave up and nodded.

"Ok, but only if you promise to take things easy 'til we know where this is going." I nodded back.

"Promise, thank you, my love." He kissed the top of my head and I leaned into him for a few minutes, drawing strength from him. Then I remembered he shouldn't even be here.

"Aren't you supposed to be out with one of the local tribes?"

"I was on my way when Marcus caught me. He's gone in my place; they know him as well as they do me. He reckoned I was needed here more."

"I'm so sorry, Maxentius, I had no intention of taking you from your duties." I smiled at him ruefully. He grinned back telling me not to worry and helped me up. My legs decided to behave and I was nowhere near as dizzy as I had been, but I might have struggled to make it home without Maxentius' arm supporting me. I was surprised to see that it was still daylight outside; the room I had been in must have been deliberately darkened to let me sleep.

As we approached our door, I could hear a familiar wail and glanced up at my husband, who chuckled.

"Always hungry, just like his father," I said. 'Who's been looking after him?"

"Senna is with him. You know she loves him like he was her own." Relieved, I knew Luc was in good hands, but that wail meant one thing — food. As I turned towards the sound, Maxentius stopped me, guiding me into the large room we had made into our triclinium, or living area.

"Sit down, Hannah, I'll fetch him." Gratefully, I sank into the closest chair, resting my head against its back. Dizziness was still lurking, but only faintly. I knew I'd be back to normal, or as normal as my life ever is, very quickly now.

Maxentius returned with our son, a wriggling squalling bundle, whom he handed to me while smiling proudly.

"He has strength, this child of mine. Maybe he will become a soldier like his papa." I looked at him curiously, while Luc took his nourishment with relish.

"Do you really want that life for your son? A life of danger, of postings to unknown lands?"

"It is a good life, my Hannah. You are well fed, well clothed and danger lies everywhere, sometimes in the most benign of places. It will be his choice, but in some ways I hope he will follow in my footsteps and you never know who you might meet in some far-off land." Smiling at me, his green eyes twinkling, I smiled back, remembering how and where we met in one of those far-off lands, a meeting that neither of us could have guessed would lead us to this corner of Empire.

After I fed Luc, I carried him back to his bedroom, settling him into his cradle and rocking him back to sleep. He had grown in the last few weeks and soon I would be able to try him on more solid foods. We had risked some mashed up fruit and vegetables, which he had eaten under protest, spraying most of it out, disgruntled with the unfamiliar textures. Hopefully he would be better with these different foods soon, as I knew my milk wouldn't last very much longer.

Wanting to be sure he settled properly, I made myself comfortable in one of the chairs, watching him until he was over. I still felt a little off-colour after my shenanigans of the morning, so it was nice to rest for a few moments while I waited for Senna.

Senna was from one of the neighbouring tribes. She seemed quite young, barely twenty years I surmised and I had been surprised that she was not yet married. Happily for me she wasn't; a tranquil soul, she loved Luc and he always behaved when in her care, no small feat for a boisterous baby. Along with Senna, there were quite a few locals working within the fort; mostly domestic staff, but some worked in the stables and others, clever with their hands, in the workshops.

They were just like us — ordinary folk trying to get through life with as little fuss as possible, bearing in mind they were a conquered people. The previous legatus had done much to create a cordial relationship, which Maxentius was determined to uphold. Senna was funny, smart and quick and we were fast becoming good friends. I trusted her with my son and my instincts didn't usually let me down.

I was trying to learn something of their language too, which sounded quite beautiful, rather like they were singing. Senna was helping me and I'm sure anyone listening to us would have found my efforts to be hilarious. Maxentius had told me it was called Brythonic and I usually pick up languages quite easily, but this one was proving a challenge and I knew my pronunciation was atrocious. I persevered, however, and could manage quite a few words. I hoped that I might be able to visit the local tribes and maybe meet their healer with a view to an eventual sharing of knowledge, recognising that having mastered even a little of their language might go a long way to them trusting me.

Senna came into the room, asking whether I felt better. Goodness, who else knew I'd chucked a wobbly? I blushed and told her I was fine, thanking her for her concern. Leaving her to take over the care of my son, I said I'd be back shortly and went looking for my husband. The large house we lived in still flummoxed me and I frequently took a wrong turn, ending up outside rather than in the room I was aiming for. Besides the bedrooms and the triclinium, there were the domestic quarters, the guest wing, my medicine rooms and several smaller rooms, which could be used as offices or extra bedrooms. There was a peristyle courtyard in the centre of the complex, the walkway surrounding it always lovely and cool.

Marcus had been allocated three of the rooms in the main wing and as he had done since I'd known him, joined us for all his meals. Although most of the administrative work was conducted in the headquarters, or principia, both he and Maxentius had offices within the residence and I found my husband in his poring over documents. He looked up as I entered, a smile lighting up his face.

"Feeling better, my Hannah?" I nodded telling him that Luc was now also satisfied and asleep, with Senna on watch.

"Do you have time to talk now, or would you prefer to leave this until later?"

"If you can wait, my love, it might be easier. I have a few things I must attend to this afternoon, which I cannot put off. We can talk this evening it will be more relaxed. I realise that Marcus will be with us, but since he is already aware of your other life, it may be helpful to have his input."

Knowing I should not take him from his work, I agreed. It was not long until the end of the day and I doubted anything would change before then. I could feel her and even though she was just out of reach, I believed we would merge very soon. Her distress frightened me however, I could not determine its cause and it seemed as though she had given up on something. Unable to grasp it, I tucked it away. When she was ready, I would understand, it was always so.

Chapter Six

It was pointless returning to the hospital; Atius would only send me back home. So I unpacked my leather bag, which someone must have brought over to the residence. Tidying everything away, I spent a little time making sure everything was as it should be. I had several bunches of herbs drying out and checked to see whether they were ready to be ground down.

Satisfied that I was on top of things, I went back to Luc. Although he had only been down about an hour, I preferred that he didn't sleep too long in the afternoons for it meant I would be woken several times during the night. I studied his tiny face as he slept, his cheeks rosy from being snuggled up under the blanket, his little hands scrunched up tightly. I folded the blanket back a little to keep him from getting over heated and even though I knew I should wake him, he looked so peaceful that I ignored my better judgement and let him sleep on.

Senna was sitting quietly in the adjoining room, working on something that appeared rather complicated. She was weaving together fine strands of what looked like wool to form one long piece of material, but it was so dainty that I could barely see where the threads touched. I had seen artisans working with large weaving machines in Pompeii, but this was quite different. A memory tickled at the back of my mind — a picture of delicate patterns like snowflakes created by white threads attached to long wooden pins — but I was unable to trace it. Giving up, I watched for a little while fascinated, then asked her to show me how she did it. Happy to demonstrate, Senna spent the next hour explaining the intricacies of her work and I was quickly hooked.

Soon enough, Luc awoke, distracting me from our task and I decided it would be nice to take him outside for some fresh air. It was pleasant strolling through the fort, stopping to watch the military activities, which went on every day; changing of the watch up on the towers, or sword practice, or whatever else might be happening. I spotted Petronius in the stables and we paused for a few moments to have a chat. He took Luc from me, sitting him on the horse that he was in the process of brushing down. Luc gurgled in delight, grabbing the horse's mane in his fingers and trying to stuff it in his mouth. He had started teething, so anything he could chew on was fair game.

Petronius chuckled at my son's efforts and I left them to it, while I went over to Gemmula, who had nickered a greeting to me as I entered the stables. I stroked her, talking quietly and she pushed her nose into my neck, nibbling at my hair. I had never owned an animal and, although I knew of people who kept dogs, I had never really wanted one but I loved this creature and felt we understood each other.

"Maybe tomorrow," I whispered. "Maybe we could go out tomorrow and have a proper run." She blew down my ear as if she knew exactly what I was talking about and after a few more minutes I collected Luc, said goodbye to Petronius and continued with our constitutional.

As we reached the rear gate, I could hear the sound of heavy footfalls and the patrol swung in, headed by a soldier I did not recognise. They marched in, formed their lines and waited to be dismissed. The soldier stalked along the ranks of men, spitting out instructions or complaints or something. I watched in astonishment, I had not seen any of the men being treated with such disrespect. I knew that discipline was essential, but this seemed somewhat over the top. I walked back over to the stables and motioned for Petronius to come to the doorway.

"Who is that soldier?" I pointed. "The one doing all the yelling?" Petronius studied the man for a moment.

"His name is Quintus Gratius Albus. He is part of the Augusta vexillation. He is not a happy man, is he?"

"It's very unusual. I have not met him before and none of the other centurions are so angry. These men do not look sloppy or ill-behaved. What has caused his ire?"

"I shouldn't be asking him if I were you, Hannah." Petronius smiled, knowing my penchant for sticking my nose in where I ought not.

"I wouldn't dream of it, Petronius," I replied haughtily. "That's what my husband is for." Chuckling, my friend went back to his duties and I dawdled my way home, mulling over this soldier's attitude. We didn't need discontent in the ranks. So far the different legions had rubbed shoulders quite well, but having seen this little display of temper, I guessed it might not take much for something to spark them into mutiny.

I fed Luc again, then left him with Senna, and went to change for the evening meal, deciding to treat myself to a proper bath. We had a private room for bathing and I luxuriated in the warmth of the water, taking the time to wash my hair after scrubbing the dust of the day from my skin. I dressed hurriedly. My undershift was of a deep turquoise with a lightweight tunic in a paler shade over the top, cinching the outfit at the waist with a white belt. Completing my outfit with leather sandals, I felt presentable again.

I was about to make my way to the triclinium when the bedroom door opened to admit my husband. He looked tired and it was all I could do not to smooth the lines from his face. He winked at me as he came into the room and stripped off, saying he needed a wash and wouldn't be long. I sat down on one of the rather fine chairs left by the previous legatus and waited for him.

"You tired, my love?" I asked, when he came back in.

"Somewhat. It's been a long day, but it's over now and I can relax for a little while."

"Not helped by your wife chucking a wobbly," I muttered. He heard me and grinned, coming over to where I was sitting

"You couldn't help that, my Hannah and your wobbly saved me from going out to the village. So it wasn't all bad. Anything else happen yet?" I knew what he was asking, and shook my head.

"Not yet, but I do not think it will be long."

He pulled on a fresh tunic and, after pushing his feet into house slippers, held out his hand. Placing my tiny hand in his large one, I let him lift me up out of the chair, but rather than turn to leave the room, he drew me into his arms. Dipping his head, he kissed me soundly and rather passionately.

"Hmmm...what a lovely way to start the evening." I smiled, rather breathlessly.

"I thought so." He smiled back, repeating the gesture until I wasn't sure whether we'd make the evening meal. I pushed him back, raising my eyebrows at his antics. Ignoring my efforts, he kissed me again.

"Come on, Max." I said, when he finally let me catch my breath, "we have a meal and probably a Marcus waiting. It isn't fair on the cook, if we don't partake." He sighed dramatically.

"I know, but I found I couldn't resist." I chuckled and, standing on tiptoe, whispered in his ear, at which he smiled even more widely, wrapping me closer in his embrace.

"I'll hold you to that," he murmured.

"I certainly hope so," I replied. "Now come on, food awaits."

We made our way to the triclinium, where our meals were served — yes served. Here in this outpost of Empire, where such extravagances were only dreamed of, we had staff. In some ways this wasn't a bad thing, for if left alone to feed my family it is quite likely we would starve. Medicines I can blend, herbs I can grind, I'm a dab hand at cleaning and laundry, but cooking is a closed door. I have absolutely no clue and anything I try to make is a disaster — score one for having staff — a much more pleasant term than servants or slaves!

Maxentius' position as legatus came with a whole household of them and an overseer. I still felt uncomfortable about it, but it was out of my hands, not that this stopped me from helping where I could. Plus, these people were given coin for their work, were provided with sleeping quarters and as much food as they desired, so I could not in all conscience deprive them of their positions. It did mean, however, that we had to be careful what we said within their hearing. Much as they were trusted, we were still living on a frontier and there were some who were unhappy with our presence.

The room was lovely; long and narrow with a low wooden table in the centre and comfortable couches arranged around it, in the dining style traditionally used by Romans. I would have preferred something similar to the furniture we had used on Masada: a table you could tuck a chair under and rest a platter on, enabling you to eat without being hunched, or have to recline, in what I can only describe as an awkward position. We hadn't been here long enough to persuade anyone to make one, but it was on my list, along with a few other items I considered to be necessities. Still, it was better than no furniture at all and, for that, I was most grateful.

The legatus' residence, like all the buildings in the fort, was wooden, but the interior had been painted with some kind of pale wash, making the room appear much lighter and there were oil lamps all around, sending a warm glow across the room. The windows had shutters that could be opened, over which I had hung some bright material rather like drapes. It wasn't much, but made the austere space feel more welcoming. Here and there I'd placed personal items, a bowl, or a carving, something that reminded us of home.

In our bedroom, there were pictures of the family displayed on a low storage cupboard. We had commissioned an artist to etch an image of our children onto small flat stones. It was a crude medium, but they were beautifully done and the likeness was incredible. Small things like this made us feel less far from them all.

As I gazed around the room our meal arrived; the many different dishes placed on the table along with wine and water. I knew I needed to have a chat with the cook, whose name was Mabina, to let her know that we didn't require such lavish meals. A simple one-course, properly filling meal would suffice. Maxentius and Marcus worked hard all day; they needed sustenance not frippery, but it would take a lot of tact, something I don't possess much of. We tucked in and despite the fact that it was lots of small portions it was quite filling. The food itself was delicious, some local ingredients, some we had brought halfway across the Empire.

While our staff moved in and out of the room, our conversation remained on mundane matters, but as the last dishes were removed, we could relax and talk more freely. A few administrative matters were niggling the two of them, so they tossed ideas back and forth for a little while, eventually settling on a method of dealing with them. Then Marcus asked how I felt after this morning's strange turn, inadvertently opening the gate for me to talk about the other Hannah. I gazed at my two Romans for a long moment and Maxentius nodded at me imperceptibly. Taking a deep breath, I started to explain what I thought was going on.

"I think that my other self is here, but she's not quite in my head." I knew I wasn't being clear enough. "I fear that something terrible has happened to her and she wants to be here with me, with us, but something's holding her back. When I was unwell this morning, it was because it felt as though she was running into my head at full speed. Normally, there is a growing perception that we're reconnecting more tangibly, a slow and relatively gentle melding of minds. It always makes me feel strange and there are moments when she or I lose memory of who or where we are. Like when I collapsed at Masada after Sergius died." Maxentius nodded, stroking my hand.

I paused, looking at them both.

"Oh I know, I know, that sounds bizarre, but it's the only way I can explain it."

"So, she's here and you think she'll be staying?" Marcus questioned.

"I suppose so, but until she lets go, she is just a flicker at the edge of my senses, a bit like a sneeze that won't come." They chuckled at my simile. "I just wanted you to know it may be that if she is in such distress, I might become unwell again for no apparent reason."

There was the other reason as well, the one that none of us was prepared to voice. Why was she reconnecting? What terrible event was looming that would require her to be with me? We'd survived a massacre and an eruption; couldn't we just enjoy a bit of peace for a while — conveniently forgetting that we were living on the edge of Empire, policing an unsettled and potentially volatile land.

In an attempt to distract the two men, I asked them about the angry soldier, telling them what I'd seen. Marcus said that, as far as he could work out, Gratius Albus had expected the position of legatus to be conferred upon him when Fabricius Habitus left. To be fair, he'd been in Britannia for several years, the last four here on the borders; but he was a centurion, not a general and Fabricius had considered him too unstable to be promoted. That then explained his belligerence.

"Could this end up being a problem Maxentius?" I asked quietly. "I hope he's not going to cause insubordination in the ranks. We don't need to be worried about the loyalty of the soldiers within the fort, we've enough problems beyond."

"I doubt the soldiers want to be persuaded into revolt. They are generally a good bunch of men, hardworking and loyal to the Emperor and Agricola. Fabricius treated his soldiers well, and they would rather be answerable to a fair-minded general than one who only cares for positions and titles; added to which

53

I have my own soldiers, many of whom have been with us for years. Hopefully their confidence in me will be an example to the others."

"I do not think we have anything to fear, but we will keep a watch on him." Marcus said, patting my arm in a brotherly fashion. I grinned at him and relaxed, resting my head against the back of the chair.

As I did so, I felt her circling, was that because I'd just been talking about her? She must know I would be aware of her. Although I tried to call her, she refused to be drawn yet I could feel her grief. It was difficult to ignore the sensations she was creating and to concentrate on what my two Romans were talking about, their words becoming indistinct. For a split second our minds collided and a flurry of images flooded my head — a box with fire in it, a room with strange furniture and the man carrying a woman, the one in my head. I couldn't hold onto it; almost as soon as I saw them the pictures faded and my head cleared.

As my world came back into focus, I registered that both men were staring at me rather anxiously.

"What was that, my Hannah?" queried Maxentius

"What was what?"

"You were muttering about boxes of fire." I gazed at him, trying to find the words to describe what I'd seen. Collecting my wits, I gave it a go, and even though it sounded very muddled and completely implausible, they listened to and accepted my explanation. These men constantly surprised me with their unconditional love and support, bearing in mind I'm talking about things that we would never see and, couldn't even dream of. Without them and their belief in me, I think I might have gone mad long ago.

.......oooooOOOooooo.......

Chapter Seven

The day was waning into the cool of the evening. The visitors had gone; their presence had made no difference. Max leaned against the window of their bedroom, staring out over the undulating landscape, mulling over what to do now. Hannah lay quietly, not asleep, but certainly not awake. Her eyes were open, but she wasn't seeing anything around her; her vision had turned inward. While he stood, Max ruminated on everything the doctor had said to him about this type of shock. He had also spent a fair portion of the day, when someone else was sitting with his wife, researching it on the computer.

It seemed that he needed to find something to talk about that only he would know; something that Hannah would recognise as being between the two of them, something no-one else could possibly be aware of. Max knew exactly what that was, but feared that if he started talking about it, it would only push her further into that other world, her other life, the one with the Roman soldier and a child. A memory teased at him, something she'd said to him not very long ago. He tried to capture it before it skittered away, but it wouldn't come.

Going back to the bedside, he sat down and took Hannah's hand, rubbing his thumb over hers, a gentle gesture and one she had found soothed her when her headaches got too bad. He began to talk about Masada, about how mad she had been with him for not meeting her at Ein Bokek; about the first time they had kissed under the stars. She stirred, her hand gripping his, but Max didn't react, just continued talking, weaving a picture around them. A picture of the isolated rock, of sunny days working on the dig, of long nights in each other's arms away from the world, no one knowing, just the two of them.

He recalled what she'd told him about the pomegranate trees, but was loath to bring them up, as they seemed too closely related to her other life. Then he remembered the artefact, the wooden pomegranate that she said Maxentius had carved. Was it worth asking the museum whether he could borrow it? If she held it, she would recognise that only he would know its significance.

I could hear his voice, he was talking to me about Masada; how could that be? I could see us there. I could almost smell the desert air, feel the chill of those crystal-clear nights and see the millions of stars twinkling in the black sky. Who else would know about Masada, at least those things he was talking about? They were private moments, special to us. A tiny glimmer of hope flickered in my heart, a hint of warmth to melt the ice that encased it. Had he made it out of the wreckage? Was there any chance he was alive? Then the scenes from the television reared up in my head and I shuddered. No, I didn't want to face the world yet; if I was wrong it would break my heart all over again.

.......oooooOOOooooo.......

The days flew by and as I hadn't felt her again, I stopped worrying. It was as though she had retreated to a safe place, one where nothing could reach her, or maybe she had gone back to her own world, but I didn't think so for I was still aware of her distress. Unable to help her, I had continued with my normal daily life — my husband, Luc, Senna and the hospital. All these things kept me busy and I was also supposed to keep a check on the management of our home. Annant, however, the man in charge of the staff, did a far better job than I did; we generally discussed matters once or twice a week and I left him to it. He seemed to be a gentle, kind sort of man and he was always respectful to me, but he ruled the house with a rod of iron. Since everything ran like clockwork, who was I to interfere anyway?

Today, I was back at the hospital. Several of the soldiers had come into contact with some kind of stinging plant and we were trying everything to reduce the swelling and itching that it had caused. I'd never seen anything like it and, although Atius mentioned one previous case, it had been a mild one, nothing like the symptoms we were seeing. I ruminated over whether it was worth going to see where they had blundered into this plant; maybe the locals knew of a remedy. I had asked Senna but she seemed unsure. Checking the patients, I massaged in a soothing balm consisting of camomile and marigold that I had made, which seemed to help, but did nothing to reduce the inflamed bumps all over their legs where the plant had come into contact with their skin.

As I was chatting with Atius, I mentioned that I'd like to see where this plant was. One of the soldiers, whose name I recalled was Livius Atellus, said it was not very far from the camp, close to the edge of the forest, but in a meadow. I looked at him quizzically and asked him how on earth it had happened, for surely it could not have been on the roads or well-worn tracks that they used to patrol the area. He grinned, somewhat abashed, telling us that they'd seen a hare and one of them had suggested it might be good eating. So they'd chased it, straight through the large bed of stinging plants. I bit my lip so as not to laugh, picturing the incident in my mind. Atius was less polite and guffawed, commenting that maybe now they would think twice before hunting small defenceless creatures.

I finished applying the balm to all those who had come to be treated and took my leave, telling Atius that I was going to try to find this plant and possibly speak to some of the locals. While the soldiers were still able to go about their regular duties, the itching had not abated and we were concerned that if we couldn't prevent them from scratching, infection might set in; served them right in this case, but I'd rather not risk being unprepared should unwary soldiers stumble into a similar patch of plants.

On my way back to the house, I saw Julius walking in my direction and asked whether he might be free to accompany me into the countryside. He nodded, saying he'd come over forthwith. I detoured passed the principia to advise Maxentius of my plan; he would be less than impressed if I disappeared out of the fort without telling him. He was busy with Marcus and several other soldiers, discussing duties and rosters, but he spotted me hovering at the doorway and motioned me into the room.

The other soldiers acknowledged my presence, waiting patiently while I explained to my husband where I was going and that Julius had agreed to escort me, if this was acceptable to him. His lips twitched as I said the last part, knowing I was only requesting his approval because his men were there. As he nodded his agreement, I bestowed my brightest smile on him and left quickly, saying goodbye to them all. Marcus chuckled at my complete disregard for military etiquette, but I knew that as soon as I had left the room they would have forgotten I'd been there, totally absorbed by their work.

I had enough time to check on Luc and Senna before Julius appeared. Senna was watching my son shuffle around on his tummy. He was trying to crawl, but had worked out that if he rolled, he could get along much more easily and often ended up under furniture, to the amusement of his guardian. I told her where I was going, that Maxentius knew and that if she was worried about anything, to find him in the principia. Senna said she was sure they would be fine and not to worry; she was going to try feeding my son with solid food again — very brave. I smiled gratefully and left them to it.

Julius was waiting at the main door, and we went out through the rear gate of the fort towards the forest. I explained what I was looking for and he chuckled at the idea of grown men being felled by a mere plant. We searched for maybe an hour, sweeping along the fields and pathways near the fort, without finding anything that resembled the plant they had described. I was just beginning to think they'd made a mistake with where it had happened, when Julius called me over to a huge bed of plants right at the edge of the field we were walking through.

It was the strangest looking plant, dark green with jagged leaves. When I crouched down and studied it more closely, I observed that the leaves themselves appeared to be covered in extremely fine hairs. This must be where the sting is, I thought, it's the plant's way of protecting itself. Knowing I had to touch the plant to see whether this was indeed the one the soldiers had come into contact with, I braced myself for the pain. I brushed the back of my hand gently over the leaves — nothing. Interesting. I pressed a little harder and suddenly I felt as though someone was stabbing hot needles into me, the sudden pain snatching my breath away.

"Wow," I stammered. "That packs a punch; no wonder they were complaining." Scrubbing at my hand, I tried to deaden the pain but it got worse. Pulling up a handful of grass, I wiped it over my hand, but that had no effect either. I had a small jar of vinegar in my bag, something I always carried and unstoppering it, poured a liberal amount over my skin. That stung too, but seemed to reduce the pain a little. I looked at my hand; it was covered in bumps and my skin was bright red, beginning to itch as the pain lessened. I knew that if I scratched at them, I would make it worse but it was very hard to resist. I warned Julius to be careful and showed him my hand.

Wanting to know more about this prickly little sucker, I wrapped my other hand in a thick piece of cloth and plucked several stems, laying them at the bottom of the basket I had brought for this purpose. As we were doing this a small group of locals approached us, no doubt puzzled as to why on earth we would be stupid enough to be close to such a plant. I showed them my hand and asked, with both words and actions, whether they knew of a remedy. I tried a few words in their language, simple words that Senna had taught me and this seemed to please them.

There was a lot of smiling and laughing — yeah, yeah, I thought, daft foreign woman getting stung — but they showed me two other plants and demonstrated how they worked. One had long leaves, which had a fleshy, leathery feel to them the other had bright yellow flowers. The leathery leaves were rubbed over my skin. The effect was immediate; the sting definitely subsided and the redness appeared to diminish. With the yellow flowering plant, they squeezed the sap from the stalk and let it drip onto my hand, then rubbed it over the skin. The same result. I was astonished. Such a simple thing and these plants looked as though they grew in abundance nearby the stinging one.

Thanking them by dint of smiling, bowing and shaking hands, I collected a huge number of both plants and added them to my basket. Before we went our separate ways, one of them, an older woman, came up to me and I gathered by watching her gesticulations that the yellow plant had many uses. I was fascinated and wanted to learn more. I asked the women her name and mentioned Senna. She nodded enthusiastically and said something, which sounded like Breeda. I pointed to her and said, "Breeda," then back at myself and said, "Hannah." She grinned a toothless grin and nodded again. I grasped her hand and squeezed it gently and, hoping I had the words correct, said that I would see her soon.

Julius had been watching this interaction with an amused smirk on his face.

"What's that face for?" I asked suspiciously, as we turned for home.

"I know what you're up to, Hannah Valerius. Next thing, you'll be down at the village, learning everything these tribeswomen can teach you; all the old ways and remedies and treatments. You cannot help yourself, can you?" I grinned at him.

"It's so interesting; there are plants and herbs here that I do not know of and to learn their properties and uses is something I must do if I can. There could be poisonous plants, or roots, or berries or fruits here and we would not know until it was too late. Don't you think it's important to understand these things?"

"Of course, Hannah, this is why we bring you with us." He chuckled at my expression. "Come on, we should make all haste back to the fort; we have been outside for a long time and I have no desire to cause your husband worry." He winked and we set off, wading through the long grass to the main track and turning towards the fort.

I was tired by the time we got back, but wanted to tell Atius about what we'd discovered; so after thanking Julius for his time, made my way over to the hospital. I showed Atius the different plants and explained how the remedy should work. Several of the affected soldiers happened to be there and Livius, who had told us where to find the plant, said he would very much like to have us try it on him. His skin was quite raw, as he'd been unable to stop himself from scratching and I knew infection was now a real possibility if we didn't do something soon.

Taking two of the long leathery leaves, I rubbed them over the sensitive area, the green juices seeping out as the leaves were crushed against his skin. I made sure I covered all of the affected flesh, then sat back and waited. The relief on his face was almost comical.

"I think you must have actual magical powers," he whispered. "The pain, the itching, it's gone, just like that." Encouraged, I went along doing the same to the remaining soldiers who had been stung and got the same response. Their expressions mirrored that of Livius and it was all I could do not to giggle. Pleased with the result, Atius and I discussed how we could preserve such leaves and I pondered out loud whether Marcus could grow some in the garden beds he had begun to nurture. Atius helped himself to one of the leaves to compare with examples in his medicine books, hoping we could trace a genus for it.

Telling them to come back later so that I could re-apply the remedy, I returned home and going into the larger of my two medicine rooms, laid out the plants studying them again. They were rather limp now, having been out of the ground for a couple of hours, so I found a shallow bowl and lay the stems in water, hoping they would last until I could work out whether they would be as useful dried as fresh. While I mulled this over, I thought again about Breeda and how much she might know about what grew locally and how it could be used.

Leaving the plants in the water, I made my way to Luc's room where he was sleeping and Senna was weaving. Speaking quietly so as not to disturb my son, I told Senna about the morning and how the locals had shown us what to do. When I mentioned the woman Breeda, Senna's face lit up; this woman was her aunt and they considered her to be a wise woman. Familiar with traditional remedies and treatments, she was also the one who helped other women through childbirth and was very important within the district.

Explaining my interest in understanding the healing properties, or otherwise, of local plants, I asked Senna whether she would be willing to take me to her village and introduce me to her aunt, formally. She agreed readily and we decided to go the next day. We could take Luc with us and it would be a welcome change from our usual routine.

Letting Senna get back to her weaving, I returned to my medicine room, noting that the plants I had left to soak had revitalised. Digging out a short beaker and filling it halfway up with water, I lifted the plants from the bowl into it, trusting that the cool, dim room would be enough to keep them alive a little longer.

Jobs done, I collected a small handful of the leaves and crossed to the hospital to check on the soldiers. The redness had definitely lessened and they said that the irritation was nothing like as acute as it had been. I wiped away any remnants then reapplied the remedy, adding a binding of cloth soaked in a mixture of cold water and sap from the yellow flowering plant, hoping that this would give them more sustained relief for some of the night. Happy that I had done all I could, I came back home to wash and change. It was late afternoon now and I realised I was very hungry. Somehow, in my enthusiasm for searching out the stinging plant, I had missed the midday meal and had eaten nothing substantial since first light.

Pulling on an undershift of pale green, with an over tunic in a darker shade, I sauntered through to the domestic quarters to see whether there was a light snack I could beg from Mabina. Tutting at me for forgetting to eat, she handed me some kind of savoury slice, which was absolutely delicious and I thanked her profusely as I devoured it. As I got up to leave, she smiled and wagged her head maternally at me; I smiled back and left her to her culinary adventures. It seemed as though our relationship was becoming more cordial.

I heard a familiar wail as I walked along the corridor past the courtyard and I rushed to stem the source before it became too loud. Luc was struggling in Senna's arms, his fists bunched up and he had screwed his face up ready to emit one of his ear-piercing howls. He saw me and stopped abruptly, making himself hiccup. Grinning, I lifted him into my embrace and sitting on the chair by his cradle, let him staunch his hunger.

While I was feeding him, Senna told me that she had managed to get him to eat some of the mashed-up vegetables without him throwing it all over her. This was progress. Seemed that he also enjoyed gnawing on a hunk of bread, although I imagined this might have more to do with him teething, than actually liking it. His little fingers, which had been kneading quite uncomfortably at my breast, started to relax as he suckled quietly. He was getting heavier, this child of mine and I would be glad when he no longer needed me to feed him quite as often.

Making myself comfortable, I lifted my feet up onto the stool in front of my chair and felt myself drifting off. Noticing, Senna said she'd be back shortly and left us alone. I often snoozed when Luc was feeding; it gave me chance to catch up on any sleep I had lost when I needed to get up to him during the night. The house was still, the room was cool and it was just the two of us.

Chapter Eight

I dreamt of the woman; she was lying on a bed, not awake and not asleep. The tall man, her Max, was watching her. Others came into the room and sat with her, trying to get a reaction, but she didn't respond. I wanted to tell her to wake up, that whatever was haunting her wasn't real, but I couldn't make myself heard, or she didn't want to hear. She was in shadow hiding from her life and I still couldn't work out why.

Max held her hand. He was talking to her about Masada, then about Pompeii. He knew what she — what we — had gone through; she had told him. We were the same, she and I: we both had men who accepted that our destinies were entwined and loved us the more for it. As I watched them together, my own world called me back and suddenly I was awake.

I opened my eyes straight into my husband's, as dark as the forest I had been near today. Maxentius was crouching in front of me, rubbing my hand trying to wake me without disturbing Luc. I smiled sleepily and with great care moved to place my son back in his cradle. I managed to do so without waking him; he would sleep until late evening now. Sorting my tunic out, I straightened up, stretching out my tired arms. Maxentius came over and we stood together gazing down at our son.

"He is so perfect, my Hannah," he murmured. "I still cannot believe something so perfect is part of me." I looked up at him quizzically, cupping his face with one hand.

"Why ever not? You are strong, brave and kind, qualities I find perfect every day. Not to mention tall, dark and incredibly handsome." His chest rumbled with suppressed laughter.

"Ahhh, but you are biased, my love."

"Of course I am! What of it? You're my husband and I love you, so I'm allowed." He put his arm around me, drawing me close and we left quietly, going along to our room so that Maxentius could change.

"How was your day?" I asked, half lying on the bed, while he stripped out of his dusty tunic, washing in the large bowl on the cupboard. My heart tripped as I watched the muscles flexing under his skin when he moved, his body still taut and trim, despite him being a little over forty years. There may have been a hint of grey in his hair but, if so, it was barely discernible; he didn't really seem to have aged much at all since the day we first met. I wanted to run my fingers through his hair and kiss the pulse point along his jawline. Really, Hannah! Get a grip woman!

I dragged my attention back to what he was saying, something about having had a good meeting with the locals who wanted to set up another trading network across the frontier. It would do everybody a favour, as we would be able to trade our supplies also. There were many merchants who plied their wares along the roads and tracks, some on horseback, others with wagons; and Magnis was strategically placed nearby two of the major routes. It would negate the need for regular supply runs to Eburaci, which always required far more soldiers to accompany the wagons than we could afford to be without.

Once Maxentius was ready, we walked along to the triclinium; Marcus was already there, chatting to Annant who was supervising the meal. Smiling, he came over and gave me a hug.

"How are you, Hannah? I hear you were out looking for stinging plants today." I nodded, telling the two men about what Julius and I had found and how the locals had shown us what to use to counteract the sting. Waving under each nose the back of my hand, which was still a bit red and bumpy but no longer painful, I told them that we now anticipated a speedy recovery for the affected soldiers.

"I'm going to their village tomorrow with Senna. The older woman, Breeda, is her aunt. I'm hoping they can tell me more about the native plants." I was so excited at the prospect that I was gesticulating with my hands and had begun pacing up and down the room as I talked. Used to my enthusiasm about all things medicinal, my two Romans let me talk until I ran out of anything to say, by which time we were sitting down and eating our meal. "Oh, and Luc managed some solid food today too, without throwing it all over Senna." I grinned at them and finally drew a proper breath.

"I was wondering when you were going to remember to breathe, my love." Maxentius laughed. I glared at him, which only elicited more amusement. Our conversation carried us through the meal and into the evening. Annant brought us some hot calda, for although it was summer, the nights tended to be cool and the spicy drink warmed the body very nicely. Marcus went along to his rooms quite early as he said he had some work he wanted to finish. Maxentius and I sat for a while longer enjoying the peace, before following suit and heading off to bed.

Luc was still fast asleep and Senna had gone to her own room. I left both his and our doors slightly ajar in case my son woke in the night, although I usually heard him before even he realised he was awake. The house was quiet and the world felt safe. I pushed the shutters open and looked out of the window at the stars, realising that there were nearly as many visible here as had been at Masada. Maxentius came up behind me, wrapping his arms around me. I could feel his heart; its steady beat calming my unsettled mind and leaning against him I ran my fingers lightly over his hands, as I covered them with mine.

After long moments, he turned me to face him and my heart thudded as I looked up at this man, my husband, my Roman; the man who still made me go weak at the knees fourteen years after we had first met. Cupping one hand round the back of my head and tilting my chin with the other, he bent down and kissed me very gently. His lips were soft and I felt the inevitable heat flicker in my stomach. My arms went around his neck and I pulled out the leather strip holding his hair back, letting the unruly mop fall over his face. Running my hands through the silky blackness, I did what I had wanted to do earlier and kissed him along his jawline, feeling his pulse quicken under my lips.

He gathered me close, his kiss deepening and his hands beginning to bewitch my body, seducing my senses. Passion flared and I felt my legs begin to buckle as fire licked along my veins. He held me against him, never breaking that mind-blowing kiss. I felt his heart quicken, its rapid beat matching mine. His hands caressed me, teasing and stroking, causing ripples of pleasure to run down my back and unable to stop myself I moaned. His breathing hitched and he lifted me, carrying me over to the bed and after using his heel to close the door, proceeded to make me forget everything except how much I loved him.

Later, as our hearts settled and our breathing calmed, we lay together talking. Maxentius asked whether I had any further awareness of the other Hannah, but although I knew she was near, I had nothing else. I still worried that there was something else, some catastrophe that she was supposed to be warning me of, but that her own troubles were preventing her from sharing her knowledge. I was too tired to keep going over it. I had no control over if and when she came anyway, so we pushed it aside. Maxentius held me close, kissing me tenderly before tucking me against his chest, moulding me to him. Secure in his arms, I cast aside my cares and slept.

The next day, I checked on my soldiers and, using the last of the leaves, managed to treat them all. I added some sap from the yellow flowering plant, which allowed me to spread the little I had left around all of them. Their legs looked much better and they could continue treatment if necessary, but I did not think any of them would require it. Once they were sorted out, I collected my bag of medicines, some of which I hoped to be able to use as trade, and a basket for any plants I found. I needed more of those fleshy leaves anyway. Even though Senna was from the local village and known in the district, Petronius had offered to escort us and he arrived promptly at the fourth hour.

Luc was tucked comfortably in his carrying pouch and was asleep before we had gone through the gate. It was a cooler day; the season was changing and here, so far north, you could almost hear it click over. The light seemed less vivid somehow and the trees were taking on autumnal hues, golds, bronzes and reds; even the air smelt different. I contemplated, briefly, what it was like in winter. I assumed it would be much colder than Pompeii, but how much colder?

We chatted as we walked and in a little under an hour we reached the village, which was not far from where we'd found the stinging plant the day before. Senna went to find her aunt while Petronius and I waited at the edge of the hamlet, unwilling to venture in without invitation. Before long, Breeda came over with her niece as well as a tall burly man, who looked quite imposing. Senna explained that he was Bearach, the headman and he wanted to welcome us to their village.

We followed Bearach and Breeda between beautifully crafted houses, all of which were round with low-profile conical roofs. The walls appeared to be woven from what looked like saplings, the gaps filled in with mud, but I couldn't be certain. The roofs were thatched and, although I couldn't see any windows, smoke curled out through the top of the structure, so I assumed some light entered that way. I was astonished at the size of the dwellings and the one we were led into was huge. It was quite warm inside and a bit smoky but well organised.

In the centre was a fire pit surrounded by large flat stones on which lay pots and bowls. There were baskets stacked up to the left of the entrance and a sleeping area to the right. A large pile of what I could only describe as animal skin rugs and sort of primitive cushions were arranged against the wall opposite the doorway. The internal wall, which was quite low, had been covered with a greyish-white coating and there were rush torches dotted here and there.

A narrow gap between the wall and the roof allowed air to circulate without causing a draft and you could only stand upright in the middle of the house. As everything appeared to be done while seated however, this didn't seem to be a problem. We were invited to sit and I could not help but run my fingers through the furs, which were velvety soft and very comfortable. Senna explained to Bearach the reason why we were here and that I was a healer, interested in learning about their treatments and remedies. There was a lot of nodding and gesticulating. Someone brought us refreshments, which were delicious and still the discussions went on.

After a time and maybe because I wasn't moving anymore, Luc began to fidget in his pouch. I rocked him, hoping he wouldn't decide to yell the place down, but knowing my hope was likely a vain one. Petronius had remained outside, not wanting the headman to think that the army was in any way pressing them to talk to me, so I couldn't ask him to take my son for a few moments while these discussions were continuing. I caught one or two words that I recognised, but for the most part I just tried to look as though I knew what they were talking about.

As I feared, Luc was not prepared to be settled. He started fussing, his little grumbles indicating how aggrieved he was and I knew I would need to feed or otherwise distract him — naptime was over. Senna heard him and said something to Breeda, who came over to inspect my child. She motioned that she wished to hold him and I handed him over gratefully, thankful to be relieved of his weight for a time.

Breeda crooned to him, stroking his cheek, at which he grabbed her finger and held on tight, gabbling in baby talk, trying to reach her hair with his other hand. She laughed delightedly and Bearach got up to join her, amusement lighting up his rather sombre face at my son's antics. Senna told me that they thought my son was strong, with the heart of a warrior but the soul of a poet. Oh great, I thought, my son was a cross between Julius Caesar and Ovid. Maxentius would be well chuffed. I smiled and thanked them, after which Bearach said something and rubbed his hands together, before clapping them.

I had no idea about what had just happened, but Senna was smiling encouragingly at me, so I did the only thing I knew that might convey my appreciation and dropped a deep curtsy in front of Bearach, thanking him in both our languages. It seemed to do the trick, for he nodded and ushered us out of his home. Senna whispered that he was happy for Breeda to share some of her knowledge with me and would be pleased to see me when I visited the village. I was ecstatic; this was progress. The headman and the wise woman had accepted me. Hopefully, such acknowledgement would extend throughout the village and that in time we might become friends.

I followed Breeda and as she carried Luc to her own hut, others from the village came to see what was going on; she gossiped away with them showing off my son. I was a little nonplussed, as I wasn't sure what was expected of me, if anything. The women poked and prodded at Luc who, surprisingly, took it in good part. His black hair, blue/green eyes and olive complexion seemed to be of the greatest interest and, as I looked around, I realised that everyone's hair was in varying shades, from what can only be described as a muddy straw colour to dark brown, their eyes grey or brown and their skin quite pale. Luc's would surely have looked quite foreign to them.

I held back and let them fuss over my son; it was another way of connecting with these people. Eventually, though, Luc had had enough and started to wail, stretching his lungs to capacity and making the women chuckle. I hurried over and Breeda handed him to me. I guessed he might be hungry and felt awkward that I would need to ask for a little privacy. Senna stepped in again guiding me into Breeda's hut, settling me on some rugs and keeping the others away.

By the time Luc was full and sleepy again, I decided it might be a good time to leave. Now that we had been approved, as it were, we could arrange to come back any time to talk about healing methods. Senna agreed that this would be appropriate and, once I had settled Luc back into his pouch, we explained that it was time for us to set off home. Breeda thanked us for coming and we arranged to meet again in two days. Petronius rejoined our little group and soon the four of us were on our way. I felt like singing; I was so happy with the results of our morning's venture and couldn't wait to visit again. Remembering to collect some of the fleshy leaves and the yellow flower on our way, we made it back to the fort by mid-afternoon.

I was a little fatigued, so after placing the plants in water and making sure Luc was comfortable, I left Senna in charge and went to take a short nap. The other woman came to me as I slept, fluttering into my mind like a ghost, her sadness a tangible thing. I could still see the images that caused her sorrow, but was unable to interpret them; I would have to wait until she spoke before I would understand. For now, it was enough that we were one again.

.......oooooOOOooooo.......

I was dreaming that we were in Rome, wandering through the Forum, the ruins captivating my senses. Max was holding my hand and we were talking about when to get married. Neither of us wanted or needed to wait. We'd been together for eighteenth months and known each other for well over a decade. There was nothing we didn't know about each other and no reason for a prolonged engagement. I heard his voice soft and mellow like honey, flowing around me as we made our plans and I felt a smile tug at my lips. Suddenly, strangely, it felt as though I was enfolded in his embrace. Was that his heartbeat? Then the horror crashed back into my mind: the flames, the smashed fuselage, the emergency services and, hard as I tried to push them away, they refused to go. I felt my other world envelop me and found its sweetly seductive call irresistible. Max's voice faded and I let go.

****

Max knew the moment Hannah slipped through; he watched her disappear. He was sitting next to her on the bed, her back tucked into his chest, their hands wrapped over one another, his chin resting lightly on her head. He had been talking about Rome, reminding her of when they were planning on getting married. He was sure she had begun to respond; he felt her push against his chest as if snuggling closer and sensed rather than saw her start to smile. Then she stiffened; a low moan tore from her throat and her body seemed to fold in on itself. Quickly turning her in his arms, he watched as her whole countenance changed, as though her soul had just left her body — and he knew. Holding Hannah to him, he could not prevent the tears from coursing down his face. He couldn't lose her, not now. He refused to let her go, whatever it took, he would bring her back to him.

.......oooooOOOooooo.......

Chapter Nine

Yet again I was fighting someone; why did they persist in shoving me around?

"Let me sleep," I muttered crossly, turning over. "I'm not bothering anyone." The someone turned me back.

"Hannah, my love, it's Luc, he needs feeding and, as much as I would like to help, he doesn't want me." The voice, belonging to a man, sounded amused. Who on earth was Luc and why did I need to feed him? There was something about the voice though; I felt I should recognise it but just couldn't quite put my finger on it.

"Who's Luc?" Silence. Now what? Was I supposed to know who this Luc was? Not really caring, I snuggled back under the sheet and batted the hand away. "Leave me alone. Please."

"Hannah!" The voice was no longer amused. "Hannah, Luc is your son." I shot upright, my eyes flying open. I didn't have a son. What on earth was this man talking about?

A face looked down on me, so familiar yet not quite who I was expecting. Where was I? Who was this Luc? Well...okay yes, apparently he was my son but I was pretty sure I didn't have children. Was I dreaming? I looked down at myself. I was wearing a long tunic, my skin was darker than it should be and I could see rich chestnut curls trailing over my shoulder. I stared up at the man in shock.

"Oh no, what have I done?" My voice was barely a whisper. "I didn't mean to fall." The man sat next to me on the bed, his expression anxious.

"Hannah?" I gazed at him, shaking my head as if that would change the picture.

"It was just too easy, it was safer and there was no pain."

The man took my hand and began rubbing his thumb against my palm. I watched for a moment allowing my brain to catch up and then faced him again.

"Maxentius, I'm sorry, I'm so sorry."

"Why are you sorry, my Hannah?"

"I shouldn't have come, I should have stayed and dealt with it, but I was too afraid."

"I think you might need to give me a bit more." Puzzled now. I drew a shuddering breath and steadied myself.

"There was a plane crash, there was fire and wreckage, he was in it, there were no survivors. I think I collapsed when I saw it on the news and it was easier to stay where I was than face the world. A world without Max, a world where I would have to explain what happened over and over and over again. There was a moment when I thought he was still alive, that he was talking to me, but it was impossible; so what was the point? I remembered that this world felt safe, there was no pain, no grief, I could be part of something here, even though I'm only really in your Hannah's head." I knew I was speaking too quickly and my last sentence was nothing short of preposterous, but he would understand.

He gazed down at me, his expression still a mixture of bewilderment and concern, and I realised that much of what I'd said would be incomprehensible to him.

"It'll be okay Hannah, we will work it out." He hesitated. "Do you think you could feed Luc while you talk to me? He's crying for you." Still rather mystified over the whole having a son thing; although I vaguely remembered knowing that she — the other Hannah — was pregnant, I nodded. Maxentius leaned in and kissed me gently, squeezing my hand. Suddenly, I was aware of a forlorn wail. My chest tightened and it was all I could do not to run towards the sound. Maxentius rested his hand on my shoulder.

"I will bring him to you, my love, just wait here in the quiet." I relaxed against the pillows, my mind whirling. She and I were together again and it felt so natural, even though I accepted that this time it was my own cowardice that had allowed me to slip through. I just hoped that if I held any kind of knowledge that might help them, I would get the chance to use it.

Maxentius came back in with a wriggling bundle. He laid it carefully in my arms and, without thinking, I shifted my tunic so that the child could feed. Instinct, as ever, had taken over and I was already adjusting to my other world. I stared down in wonderment at this small baby, my — well, her — son, taking in his dark hair and blue eyes that were showing tints of green. I looked back up at Maxentius and began to cry. Desperately, I tried to stop the tears, but found I couldn't. This beautiful child had cracked the ice around my heart and it was like melt waters after a big freeze.

I sobbed for my lost love and my lost life. I sobbed because it had taken me so long to realise I loved him, so many years wasted. I sobbed that I would never know the joy of holding a child like this, and I sobbed because I knew that my time in this world was probably finite; that one day I would have to leave and lose this family all over again. Incredibly, the child didn't falter in his intent; he carried on feeding as if his mother having a crisis was quite normal. Maxentius moved to sit behind me, drawing both of us onto his knee and cuddling me against him, let me cry it out.

Slowly, very slowly, the tears abated. Unfazed by my distress, Luc had taken his fill and Maxentius laid the child next to me on the bed so that we could watch him. I couldn't stop touching him, he was perfect; I counted his fingers and toes and then counted them all over again. I ran my fingers over his little body feeling his soft skin and I was unable to prevent myself from stroking his hair. I was in awe of him. I remembered Claudia having the same effect on me when she was a baby, but it seemed so long ago. I didn't want to break this tableau. The force of my emotions had left me wrung out and I was loath to let either Maxentius or Luc out of my sight.

Maxentius hadn't released me from his embrace; he continued to hold me close, wrapping his hands over mine in a gesture that reminded me, painfully, of Max. As my breathing steadied and I stopped hiccuping, he asked me to explain what I meant by a plane crash and how everything else had fallen apart. It took some time, although that didn't seem to worry Maxentius, and I worried, vaguely, whether he was supposed to be elsewhere, that he still had duties to complete. First I tried to describe what a plane was. I then went on to tell him about the accident, that no-one had survived and that I had retreated inside myself rather than face a world without Max.

"You, well Hannah, my Hannah, talked about fiery boxes. Would this be the crash you talk about? How is it in a box?" I smiled rather ruefully, realising he was talking about television. How on earth did I explain that one? In as simple terms as possible, I tried to clarify the television to a man who didn't even know what electricity was. Oh boy! To be fair, he heard me out, but I could see he wasn't convinced. I patted his hand.

"Just believe me and trust that it is so," I said. "It is the only way, otherwise it'll do your head in" My phraseology made him chuckle. It was such a lovely sound and suddenly I relaxed, leaning against him, resting my head into the crook of his neck.

"What time is it?" I asked wearily, not really caring.

"Around the tenth hour, I think."

"Should you be at work?"

"Marcus can finish up. I can tell him what happened when he joins us for dinner."

"Oh," I said, straightening up. "Am I supposed to be cooking a meal?" Panicking a little, as I am a rubbish cook — in both my worlds — my saving grace being that in my modern life there are packet mixes. Maxentius guffawed at this — how rude — and explained about the staff.

"Oh phew, I was worried for minute there." I leaned back against him, luxuriating in the comfort his body and gentle hug were providing. I didn't want to move.

Luc shifted on the bed, kicking his feet about and trying to roll around. He was chuckling and burbling in the most amusing manner and I wanted to get a photograph, just as I remembered that there were no cameras in this world — oh, that was such a shame! I glanced around the room noticing the portraits of the other three children and my heart skipped a beat.

"Oh, they've grown." Maxentius followed my gaze and grinned.

"Haven't they?" he said proudly. "They are a credit to you, well her, well actually both of you." He stumbled a bit there and I turned in his arms to caress his check with my hand.

"It's okay, Maxentius, I know what you mean, and the credit belongs to you too. I — she, we — haven't done this alone." He rested his cheek on my head for a few minutes and then said that we should probably get ready for the meal. Marcus would be there and Mabina would be disappointed if we didn't eat.

I nodded and reluctantly moved out of his arms, feeling the cool air from the window cut between us. Luc was still chattering away to himself and, as I picked him up, he cuddled against my neck, his little hands fisting into my hair. My heart warmed and I realised that I loved this little scrap as much as Hannah did. As before, when our minds had melded, so had our hearts. I remained motionless, enjoying the moment, unwilling to put him down again, but recalling that there was a girl who watched him — Senna — and that she would be waiting for me to take him to her.

Maxentius watched me, love radiating from his eyes and before I left the room I smiled and reached up on tiptoe to kiss him.

"Thank you," I said softly

"What for, my love?"

"For being you." I carried the now rather sleepy child along to his room, where Senna took over his charge. I thanked her and went back to the bedroom, needing to freshen up. All that crying had left me feeling rather uncomfortable and I knew a change of clothes would go some way to restoring my inner balance. Letting instinct guide me, I managed to find some clothes and once ready, Maxentius took my hand and we made our way to the triclinium where Marcus was already waiting.

Marcus was looking out of the window; the evening was drawing in, the days not so long now. Annant had lit the lamps and the room looked inviting. I tried to familiarise myself with a quick glance and then realised that I didn't need to; I already knew it. Dishes of food lay on the low table between the sofas and we sat unspeaking until Annant had poured the wine and had quietly left the room. Marcus had to know; she had already told him that I was close and it was his right.

I let the men take over the conversation while we ate. I was still rather weary from all that slipping through time and crying — I know, absolutely no staying power! As the dishes were taken away, I glanced at Maxentius; he smiled encouragingly and I took a deep breath.

"Marcus, there's something...well, rather I need to...it's like this..." I stopped before my incoherence got the better of me and tried again. "You know what I was telling you the other day? Well, she's back. It happened this afternoon and I don't think it's because of some kind of calamity, it's because she's grieving." I heard the words as they tumbled out of my mouth. Seriously — they sounded perfectly ridiculous and I was very thankful that walls didn't have ears. Unsure whether I was making any sense at all, I stopped abruptly, watching Marcus' face, trying to gauge his reaction.

He sat for a moment, ruminating over my words and then asked whether I knew why. I told him, much as I'd told Maxentius, that it was because the man she — I — was in love with, the man who was now her — my, here we go again — husband had been killed in an accident. I left out the part about the aeroplane. It was too hard to explain again and, to be honest, irrelevant to Marcus' understanding of what was happening. Like Maxentius, he accepted my words, trusting me as he had always trusted me and, after making sure I hadn't had a repeat of my funny turn, turned the conversation to other matters. I liked that he didn't labour the point, just listened, believed and moved on. There was nothing any of us could do anyway; we just had to see how life unfolded.

Later that evening, as we were getting ready for bed, I thought about my convoluted life. In this world Maxentius was my husband yet this term sat awkwardly with me — I had a husband in my other life. Then I remembered: I didn't, he was gone! Maxentius was my only husband and, although he loved me beyond time, I knew that I missed Max and was unable or unwilling to let him go. I sat down on the edge of the bed, distracted by changes that I had dreamed would end my pain, but had only made it worse.

Preoccupied, I fiddled with my tunic, folding and unfolding the material, crushing it in my fingers, not wanting to undress, suddenly realising that I was shy. In this world, I was the same person who had slept with this man every night and had been woken by his kiss every morning, yet I'd forgotten what it was like for us to be together, to be intimate, even though all but a small part of me had known him for close to fifteen years.

Maxentius came round to where I was sitting and crouching in front of me, untwisted my trembling fingers from my tunic to hold them in his hands.

"What is it, my Hannah?" His voice, gentle and soothing, wrapped itself around me ensnaring my senses and I sighed, unsure how to phrase my hesitation. "Come on, my love, whatever is bothering you is better shared, I doubt I will be surprised." I lifted my head and we locked eyes. He held my gaze for what seemed like a lifetime as I tried to form the words, which would help him understand.

"Its hard for me to say this, for I have known both of you for many years." Momentarily distracted by another thought, I added. "You and he are related, did you know that? You can trace his family line right back to you and me — well, Hannah. I think that my Max is a descendant of Luc's, yet the clasp will be passed down through Claudia." Forcing myself to get back to the point. "Anyway, you I loved almost from the moment we met, yet with Max, although he was my best friend, it took me a long time to recognise my feelings for him. So here I am, a woman in love with two men in two different worlds. You and I are bound by this love down the centuries and I believed it would continue with Max. Now Max is gone but I still love him as much as I, through your Hannah, love you and I didn't have him for long enough." I stopped, unsure whether I was making even an iota of sense. Maxentius smiled and squeezed my hands.

"Usually, when I come through time, I am aware that there is a kind of invisible force that holds me to my other world, that somehow Max can draw me home when whatever I have to do here is done. In the same way, when I feel the call of this life, this same thread pulls me back here. When Max was killed, I lost my anchor, there was nothing holding me in that world, the bond was broken and I wanted to be here, I wanted to be part of your lives. I thought it would ease my grief, but even though I know you, I can't remember and I think I've made it worse." My words sounded even more irrational than when I had first tried to explain myself to him so many years ago.

Maxentius was quite still as I trailed off and my heart clenched. What on earth was the matter with me? I should not have assumed. He loved Hannah, not me. How dare I try to share their lives? Once again, I was racked by pain, only this time it was in my heart, the enormity of my error making me quake. I reached out wanting to touch him, but dropped my hand back onto my lap.

"I'm sorry, I'm so sorry, I don't know what I was thinking, this was a grave mistake. Maybe I can work out how to go back and leave you to your lives, I should never have let myself fall; to intrude in such a way was folly." My voice, husky with grief, had no strength and before my sadness engulfed me I tried to untangle myself from his grasp, to stand, to back away. "I will sleep elsewhere, then you do not have to worry about me being two people. When I am gone, your Hannah will find you." Maxentius refused to let go of my other hand, his expression open and untroubled.

"Hannah, my beautiful Hannah, we have been here many times, you are two people in one body more than you are not and I have never found it to be folly. When I fell in love with you, you were two people. You were two people for the first six years we knew each other and as these two people, sharing the knowledge you held, saved our lives twice. I know that there are times when you are not part of our lives, but to me you are just my Hannah, whether one or two. My love for you never changes, it will always be thus."

I stared at him and he smiled — a lazy, toe-curling, heart-stopping smile and I felt my heart flip-flop, the pain receding just a little.

"I think I know a way that may help you remember." He leant towards me, brushing my lips with his. I bent my head, the shyness returning and I felt hectic colour wash up my cheeks. With his free hand he stroked my jawline, one finger resting under my chin and I felt a ripple run down my spine. Tilting my head he kissed me again, feather-light, while the hand that held mine interlaced our fingers.

It was like a first kiss, a learning kiss; we had never really had one like this. The first time he had kissed me was when Sergius had died and it had been hard, quick and totally unexpected. This was tender and languorous, as though we had forever to discover each other; and except for our hands and our lips, no other part of us touched. I leaned away to look up, searching his face seeing his eyes twinkling down on me, glowing with green fire.

He moved to sit next to me on the edge of the bed still holding my hand. I gazed down at my small slender fingers enveloped in his huge, yet beautifully tapered ones, then back up to his face. He kissed me again, no less gently than before, cupping the back of my head, his caress pulling memories into my mind. Resting my free hand against his chest, I felt his heartbeat, breathed in his familiar scent and finally let go sinking into his embrace. It went deeper and deeper until I was oblivious to anything else save this man, my Roman, my husband. The veil fell away and I remembered.

Chapter Ten

The next few days were a bit of a blur, for although I let my instincts guide me, it was little while before I became accustomed to everything. Soon enough, however, I felt comfortable and relaxed in my new environment. It was strangely familiar too, as this fort was close to where we lived in my other world. In fact, the museum I had been working at was almost on top of its remains. I knew the weather and the landscape, even where the other forts were, so apart from the fact that there were no modern amenities, no cars, no electricity, none of the modern accoutrements and rather more in the way of woods and forests, it was exactly the same. I became part of my ancestor's life as though I'd never left after the eruption of Vesuvius and I embraced it.

Two days after my return, I went out to the village again with Senna and Petronius, although this time I left Luc at home, one less distraction. Marcus, who didn't have any other pressing duties, had offered to watch him, commenting that looking after his namesake was part of being an uncle. Good luck with that, I thought, knowing that he'd be very glad by the time I relieved him of babysitting duties. Once I had made sure he knew what to do at feeding time, I left them to it, amusement playing around my mouth. Maxentius was aware, obviously — Marcus being his deputy — and had promised to be there for back up should the need arise, but had found the whole thing very funny.

It was a cool day, despite the bright sunshine and the autumnal colours were beautiful. The trees were laden with richly coloured berries, as were the hedgerows and a plethora of flowers still blanketed the fields. Once we were at the village and had gone through the welcoming formalities, Breeda began to teach me which herbs, berries and leaves could be used for healing and how they were best applied. Some needed to be ground finely and mixed with wine or water, some to be applied topically. Many had multiple properties, even suitable for hot drinks or to add flavour to food. Then there were those that should be avoided at all costs.

Time flew by and it seemed that we had only just arrived, when it was time to return to the fort. I thanked Breeda and said we would meet again soon. On the way home, I collected some of the black berries growing in the hedges, which Breeda had told me were sweet and made good eating. I added some more of the fleshy leaves and the yellow flowering plant. Satisfied that I had enough, we carried on home. On the way we had to move out of the way of a group of soldiers marching back to the fort. They were being led by Gratius Albus who sneered at us as they passed, seemingly unperturbed that they had forced two women and one of their own soldiers off the track. I questioned Petronius who shrugged his shoulders; he had no idea why this man was so aggressive. Surely he wasn't holding a grudge still over the position of legate!

We made it back without further confrontation and I decided not to mention it to Maxentius; he had enough on his plate. Taking the leaves to the hospital, I handed them over to Atius who was already drying some, which he intended to mix with oil to make a balm. Once we had treated them, all the affected soldiers had recovered quickly and completely with no apparent after-effects, so we knew these leaves were definitely the answer. Atius informed me that he thought the fleshy plant was from the rumex family of plants and had several applications; not only could it be used as a herbal remedy, but also could be added, in small amounts, to foods such as stews or soups. He believed he would be able to preserve some if he added vinegar to the ground leaves. He was quite excited about our discovery and we chatted about it for some time.

Eventually, though, I needed to go home. Luc would no doubt be crying for me, well for food at least and, Marcus would have likely long since regretted his offer. The house was quiet as I approached; fingers crossed that all was well. I went into Luc's room to see Marcus fast asleep in the chair; Luc snuggled in his arms also in the land of nod. They looked so sweet together that I wanted to show Maxentius, who just happened to be in his office within the house.

He accompanied me back along the walkway to our son's room, chuckling quietly at the scene and commenting that Luc must have run Marcus ragged, as he'd never known him to nap in the middle of the afternoon.

"Luc's far too young to tire a grown man out, surely?"

"Remember how tired you get and you're used to it." He grinned. Oh dear, I thought, Marcus will never suggest that he look after his nephew again. Maxentius went back to work and I carried the basket full of plump and delicious-looking berries along to the kitchens where Mabina was concocting something which smelled divine. I handed her the basket and asked her, in my sweetest manner, whether they might be added to whatever would be served after the main meal, unless of course she had already had something planned — knowing that she had but also knowing that she would incorporate these berries into it if it killed her!

Thanking her profusely, I left her to it and went along to our bedroom to change. I was very dusty from all the walking and sitting on the ground at the village, and thought I should at least try to look presentable for the evening meal. As I finished, I heard a familiar cry and sped along to Luc's room, to find Marcus rocking my son and singing an army song — honestly they looked so adorable together and again I wished I had a camera — come on Hannah, let it go! I watched them for a moment until Marcus turned and saw me; grinning self-consciously he handed over my son.

"How did you do?" I asked. "I noticed the pair of you needed to rest your eyes for a few minutes; must have been a tough day."

"We were fine, thank you, I'll wager that he was as good as a baby of his age can be." Which didn't leave a lot to the imagination. "I enjoyed today, I really did." I stared at him unsure whether he was joking, but apparently not, for he grinned and patted me on the shoulder saying, "I'm serious, my nephew is a delight." I looked at them both suspiciously and muttered.

"Who are you and what have you done with my real son? A delight is not the word I would have used, unless of course he's asleep." Marcus smiled and said he'd be back shortly, he just wanted to change. I watched as he left and spotted a splatter of something questionable down the back of his tunic.

"Marcus," I said, trying not to laugh, "did you by any chance turn your back on Luc while you were feeding him?"

"Maybe, I can't recall; why?"

"You may like to put your tunic in the laundry, it seems he may have used you for target practice. So much for being a delight!" Marcus twisted around trying to see what I was talking about but couldn't. I waved him away and he stalked off to his quarters, still turning himself into weird shapes in an attempt to see the damage. I giggled and then frowned in mock severity at Luc who merely gurgled and pulled my hair. "You are a minx, my child," I said, smiling, as I settled him against me to feed and my son looked positively angelic — a bad sign — as he took his fill.

Later, after I'd laid Luc in his cot, I joined the two men in the triclinium and told them about my day at the village. Although I had no intention of mentioning the incident on the path, I asked whether there'd been any more hassles with Gratius Albus, then had to explain 'hassle' as neither of them had heard the term. Once that was clarified, they shook their heads, although Marcus commented that one or two of the soldiers who had come with us from Rome had complained about his attitude.

"He will bear watching, I think," Maxentius noted. "He is aggrieved about my being in command and his ire seems to be increasing rather than abating." Marcus agreed and I filed away this comment, determined to keep my eyes open where this man was concerned. My two Romans continued to discuss the situation for a time and then Maxentius mentioned that he had received orders to travel to one of the other forts for meetings with other garrison commanders. Something about a missive from Rome, it got quite technical and most of it went over my head. Maxentius said he'd probably be away for several nights and couldn't give me any more detail except that he'd be leaving in two days. Marcus would not accompany him, remaining in charge here at Magnis, a decision, which made me feel much less uneasy.

The meal was as tasty as ever and the black berries were delicious, sweet and succulent, with some kind of creamy sauce drizzled over them — heavenly. The two men enjoyed them as well, so much so that I vowed to find more the next time I went to the village. It was quite late by the time we said our goodnights. I was dropping asleep in the chair, my head lolling against Maxentius' shoulder, much to his amusement. Marcus went along to his rooms and my husband tried to get me to move, but I was just too tired.

"Just leave me here, my love, I'll sleep on the couch." He chuckled and, lifting me into his arms, carried me to our bedroom. By then, I was so fast asleep that I wasn't aware that he had put me to bed, had drawn the covers over me and had gently pulled me against his chest; I was far away in dreams.

.......oooooOOOooooo.......

Day four since the plane crash and, although Hannah had finally got up, she still didn't acknowledge anyone. Somehow she showered and dressed and ate, albeit not enough then went outside to sit on the bench in the garden and simply stared into space; going through her days without really living them. There was no way she could go to work; Max couldn't be sure she even remembered that she had a job. For him it was enough for now that she was functioning, hopefully the rest would follow.

Both sets of parents, along with other family members, had visited for the first couple of days, but Max had asked that they leave it for a little while, worried that the constant stream of visitors would overwhelm his wife, making her think they were there to support her through her grief and not to persuade her that Max hadn't been killed. It was rather unnerving being near her; it was as though he was invisible. Even when he was right in front of her, she didn't seem to see him. Mind you, she didn't seem to see anyone else either, which was of some comfort.

Her dreams gave him some indication of what was going on in her head, as she often muttered about her other life. He had worked out that it revolved around a fort, a village, a small child and traditional medicines, but so far not much had made any sense.

Dr Stephenson had come to check on Hannah every day on his way to or from work. He had provided Max with an abundance of information on her condition as well as the treatments available, some of which seemed rather extreme. Still believing that they could talk her out of it, given time and patience, Max was unwilling to resort to drug therapy yet, but it was encouraging to know that certain treatments had a very high success rate — just in case.

Today, he was going to the museum. He had spoken to Nate, explaining what he wanted and his friend had agreed to meet him at the archives offices. Cate had offered to sit with her daughter while he was out, for despite the fact that Hannah was up and about, Max didn't want to leave her alone. Once Hannah was settled in the garden with a coffee, Max left her in her mother's capable hands and drove the short distance to the museum, meeting up with Nate in the reception area.

After a few minutes when they greeted each other and exchanged news, Nate led Max through to Hannah's office. It was very tidy; papers stacked neatly, all labelled and dated. A notepad by the computer and a box on the desk, which had a sheet of paper stuck to the top. It was Hannah's note asking that this artefact be left, as it had not been catalogued. Max knew this to be the one she had been telling him about. Nate was curious and after pulling on gloves, they removed the sheet and carefully opened the box, noting that the item was encased in a cloth bag. Unwrapping it, Max laid it on the cushion, just as Hannah had done less than a week ago and they both stared at it.

"Its quite stunning." Nate said, turning it over in his hands. "Whoever carved this was very talented. He studied the brief record made by the archaeologist who had uncovered it. "This is dated to first century AD. I can't believe it's survived." Max looked at his friend and had a sudden urge to confide in him, but knew that it was unlikely that Nate would believe him.

"Hannah was struck by its incongruity and had an idea that it was made elsewhere, brought here by either a soldier or maybe one of the auxiliaries. She said that it looked like a pomegranate and since they are not grown here, surmised that maybe it reminded the owner of home." Max wasn't sure that his explanation was credible and Nate glanced at him questions in his eyes.

"Hannah seems to have an unusual knack for coming across apparently innocuous artefacts that end up being highly significant, doesn't she? Some even seem to affect her physically," referring to those odd incidents when they'd been on Masada and in Pompeii. Max bit his lip; was it worth the risk? To share this burden with a friend and be able to talk about what was really going on would be such a relief. If Nate didn't believe him, he would lose a friend and possibly the help he needed to bring Hannah out of her stupor. On the other hand...his thoughts trailed out as he stared at Nate, then made a decision.

"Nate, do you trust me? Do you trust Hannah?" Nate looked at him for a long moment and nodded his head.

"Yes, I do. Why?"

"For reasons I have yet to fathom, I'm about to tell you something that will seem completely outlandish and so far beyond the plausible that you might think I'm going mad. Hannah wanted to tell you two years ago, but didn't dare. However, it's reached a point that I have to take the risk. If I can't get her to believe that I'm still alive, I might lose her." Nate's expression had gone from curious to baffled, but he didn't interrupt. Max continued. "Before I tell you, though, I want your word that whatever you think, however mad you suppose me to be, you will still ask the chief archivist to let me take this artefact to my wife. You will understand why as I explain."

Nate sat down on the spare chair, reflecting on Max's words for several minutes, then said —

"I trust you, Max. I have known you for many years and have never known either you or Hannah to do anything that calls into question my trust in you both. Now you have piqued my interest, especially as there have been times when matters surrounding your wife do not appear to be quite what they should be." Max released a breath he didn't realise he'd been holding and smiled at his friend.

"Thank you Nate, and I'm warning you now that this will require you to suspend your belief in everything you think you know. It took me some time to accept that what Hannah experiences is true and not in her imagination, so I know it will take some swallowing." Nate was looking even more intrigued so, hoping that he wasn't making a dreadful mistake, Max explained everything to his friend, carefully talking him through what had happened at Masada and Pompeii and now here in the north of England. He concluded by saying that because he was the only one, until now, who knew of Hannah's other life, it might prove to be the only way for him to persuade her that he was still alive. It needed to be something only he would know.

When he had finished, he sat back in the chair, a great weight rolling off his mind. Even if Nate chose not to believe, he'd talked about it with someone. Now he knew how Hannah felt when she first told him. While he waited for Nate's reaction, Max picked up the wooden pomegranate, admiring the intricate carving, sensing the love that had gone into its creation. Would this work? Would this bring her out of her trance? He remembered Hannah talking about an inscription, but it wasn't on the desk. Had she taken it home with her?

He turned on the computer and watched the screen come to life. Hoping that her password was saved, he tried to log in and — wonder of wonders! — it let him. Smiling wryly as Hannah's favourite tabs opened up, he checked through her browser history and clicked on her last search on the day that he had come home. The page opened, showing a photo of a partial inscription, with the translator's best guess as to how it might have read. Max glanced down at the notebook next to the screen, noting that Hannah had jotted it down, along with her own theory, in cryptic comments.

Even if she hadn't done so, Max knew what the inscription meant — that her ancestor, along with her husband, Maxentius, had definitely been living here at Magnis sometime in the late first century AD. Making a note to check Hannah's backpack when he got home, Max had a quick look through her notebook but nothing else struck him as being important. So, he closed down the computer and tidied up the desk, leaving it just as she had. Turning back to his friend who hadn't said a word, Max sat quietly, hoping he hadn't misjudged him. It was a good ten more minutes before Nate finally spoke.

"I'm not sure I am able to believe what you are telling me, but neither can I credit anyone making this up. It is so far outside the realms of possibility that I fear my brain might explode. It also explains much about Hannah and her strange turns, especially if you're telling me these usually meant a part of her had disappeared through time. Listen to me, I can't believe I just said that." Max grinned at his friend.

"Now you know what I'm dealing with, mate. Okay, so the problem is that she thinks I'm dead and she's slipped into her ancient world with no reason to come back here. I need to find a way to draw her home." He paused. "It's as though she's a ghost of herself, a wraith moving through the days, unaware of the world around her, merely existing rather than living."

As Max spoke, the memory that had been haunting him finally surfaced and he remembered what she'd said.

"One day when we were in Pompeii, Hannah said something about me being the only thing that kept her sane and anchored to this world and, that if it wasn't for me, it would be very easy for her soul to separate from her body and never come back, leaving her lost out of time. Nate, please, you have to help me." Nate took a deep breath and sat forward resting his elbows on his knees and his chin on his hands.

"Ok Max, I'm on board; what do we need to do?"

Chapter Eleven

Later that day, Max returned home, with the box under his arm. Nate had managed to persuade the manager of the archives to allow Max to take the pomegranate home, under the strict proviso that he would return it to the office by Friday. That gave him four days. It would have to be enough. Nate also said that he had some video footage of the Gladiators' School and the House of the Hebrew as well as some from Masada, taken during the excavations that Hannah had been involved with. He thought they might be of help and said that he'd email the files as soon as he was able.

Max entered his kitchen to find Cate preparing something that smelt heavenly. Greeting her with a quick hug and thanking her for her kindness, he asked how Hannah had been.

"Much the same. She's upstairs at the moment, but spent most of the day on that bench. I worry that she'll get a chill sitting for so long without moving but as the days are not that cold hopefully she'll be okay. I managed to persuade her into eating some lunch, just a bowl of soup, but that's more than she ate the last time I was here. How did you get on?" Max smiled gratefully.

"I had quite a productive day. I think I have something that might help and a friend is going to send over some video of our time both in Pompeii and Israel. Not sure whether it'll do any good, but anything's worth a try. Are you going to stay for dinner or is David expecting you home?"

"I think I'll leave you alone. The more time it's just you two, the better chance you have of her hearing you. Just simmer this for another ten minutes, by which time the rice will be done. I think I've made enough for a couple of meals; that should get you through the next day or so."

Smiling his appreciation, Max chatted with Cate for a few more minutes as she gathered her things together and picked up her car keys.

"I'll call you tomorrow, Max. Remember to take care of yourself too." She patted his cheek and he grinned a little guiltily; she knew him well.

"I promise. Drive safely and thanks again."

"Anytime, Max." She smiled and waved as she strolled down the path and got into the little car. Turning it carefully in the lane, she drove away, still waving. Max chuckled; his mother-in-law and his wife were similar in so many ways — bright, funny, intelligent, completely irrepressible and didn't suffer fools gladly. He realised, rather wistfully, that his wife was missing a few of these qualities at the moment and he wished he could bring the light back to her heart.

Retrieving the box from the kitchen bench top, he carried it into the study at the back of the house and placed it on one of the shelves in the cupboard. No-one would know it was there; it was the safest place he could think of. He didn't want to try showing Hannah tonight; rather, he'd wait until the next day. Making sure the stove was turned off, he went upstairs where he found his wife asleep on their bed. Even though she needed to eat, he was unwilling to disturb her and, picking up his book, sat in the large comfortable chair next to the window and enjoyed the peace.

It was another hour before Hannah finally woke, by which time Max had eaten his dinner, setting a bowl aside for her. She floated down the stairs and, coming over to the table sat down and began her meal. She spooned the food into her mouth, eating mechanically — chewing and swallowing but without seeming to taste it at all. Max talked to her all the time, telling her about his day and that he'd been to the museum and seen the artefact she'd been telling him about along with the inscription.

He deliberately mentioned Hannah and Maxentius being at Magnis and thought he detected the glimmer of a response. Careful not to push it, he left it for now and after Hannah had finished her meal, she went back outside to the bench to watch the sunset. He took her a hot cup of tea. She accepted it, thanking him, but showing no sign that she recognised him. Frustrated, but determined not to force the issue, he left her to the evening and went inside to check his emails.

As good as his word, Nate had sent through the videos. Max watched them all the way through, checking to make sure none of them would upset her or make matters worse. He didn't think they would and he was in quite a few of them but there was nothing he could do about that. He hoped he'd be able to talk her through what they were watching, mentioning little incidents that only they would know about, one of which included the inscription on the entrance wall of the House of the Hebrew in Pompeii — that was definitely one to show her.

It had been this inscription that had reconnected her with her ancient ancestor and he was the only one who knew this. There was also some video of the interior of the house that had been her home and it was here where he had proposed to her. There were things he could talk about, things she had told him about of which no one else was aware. Hope flared as he mulled over the best way to introduce these images to his wife.

****

I was sitting on a bench, a chunky jumper shrugged over my shoulders, watching a sunset. In my hands was a cup of tea, which had cooled and I sipped at it without really tasting the delicate flavour. The landscape in front of me was incredibly beautiful, but seemed veiled as if shrouded in a transparent blanket. I realised that I wasn't really here; maybe it was a dream? I snuggled into the jumper, which had faint traces of a familiar scent clinging to it. I recalled a tall man, one whom I felt I should recognise, but when I searched my memory all I found was pain, such agonising pain that I stopped trying. The scene started to shimmer, dissolving into darkness and I welcomed its sanctuary.

.......oooooOOOooooo.......

The days were much colder now and after a spell of unseasonably summery weather the change had come quite quickly. Leaves were falling from some of the trees and occasionally the mornings had been frosty. Maxentius had been away for over a week and I hoped he would be back soon. Despite the fact that I had a household full of people, along with Marcus and several of the other Romans whom I considered to be friends, I missed my husband. It was a very rare thing for us to be apart; in fact the only other time prior to this had been when he had left Pompeii just before the eruption.

Don't get me wrong, it's not that I can't function without him. I am perfectly capable of managing on my own; I have plenty to keep me occupied and love the tasks that fill my days. I just prefer having my husband close by. I think much has to do with my dual worlds and being able to share the knowledge I carry with the one person who understands it. Marcus was a good stand in, but he still struggled with the concept and, unless absolutely essential, steered clear of any discussion surrounding my future self. Moreover, if the wrong ears overheard us, anything I said might have serious consequences, especially as Gratius Albus and the few soldiers under his influence were seeking any excuse to oust Maxentius — or worse.

This day, I was walking back from the village with Senna and Petronius — Luc cuddled into his carrying pouch — having spent a fascinating day with Breeda learning about the medicinal benefits of certain local plants and herbs, as well as their growing seasons. I hoped to be able to build up my collection of treatments with some of them, so I wanted to know how to cultivate them and what part of the plant you could and couldn't use. As the weather cooled, ailments such as coughs and chest infections were rife; therefore it was good to know what I could find in the local area that would help fight such sickness. Also, there were many soldiers who had never lived in this kind of climate and an outbreak of unusual illnesses was likely, so I wanted to be prepared.

In exchange for her tuition, I shared my knowledge of the balms and tinctures I had accrued over my time as a healer. Certain medicines, or ingredients, were available here only if brought in by traders and, many plants could not be grown in this cool climate. However, I had managed to bring a goodly amount of such things and readily shared them with Breeda. It took a little time as Senna had to translate, or we used a kind of show and tell method. We made good progress though and I was learning so much.

Everything I discovered I shared with Atius, who was just as excited. We experimented with infusions and tisanes to see how long certain plants would last, whether we could drink them in a diluted form, or were more efficacious as a concentrate added to a very small amount of water or wine to make them more palatable. I discovered which plants could be used on burns, what was good for nausea, what helped you sleep and what could be beneficial on wounds or to staunch bleeding. As I was unsure whether I would be able to replace any of the remedies I had brought with me, these days with Breeda were proving invaluable.

Luc was fast asleep and we three adults were gossiping cheerfully about our day as we ambled along. Suddenly I heard the sound of hoofs behind us and made to step off the track, but was prevented by the group of riders who bore down and surrounded us. For a split second I remembered a time in Pompeii when I thought I should be killed by a rearing horse and panic coursed through me. I have absolutely no idea what happened next, there was a flurry of movement as the riders dismounted, then jostled into us, herding us as if we were sheep.

I was being pushed and pulled, rather unnerved now and unable to see where any of my companions were or what was happening to them. I called out to Petronius who shouted something back, but his words where drowned in the chaos. I felt someone pin my arms to my sides and lift me onto one of the horses, another pair of arms gripping me tightly. Struggling to escape, I bent my head and bit down on the hand of whoever was holding me, drawing blood and causing him to yell in pain. Luc woke and started to whimper and fearing for both of us, I somehow freed my arms; wrapping one of them round my son holding him close to my chest, I swung out at the man with the other. I missed, but he retaliated hitting me so hard across my face that I saw stars. My vision distorted and there was a buzzing in my ears. I heard a solid thunk, a grunt of pain and Senna screaming. Then nothing.

My head was throbbing and my face ached. I tried to move, but it was too much of an effort and my limbs seemed hampered. Concerned, I forced my eyes open, but I couldn't see where I was, darkness surrounded me. Where on earth was I? I waited for my eyes to adjust, but even after several minutes, I was none the wiser. I knew I wasn't anywhere familiar; whatever I was lying on was not a bed, it felt prickly. There didn't seem to be any windows and the area smelt of animals. Remembering anything seemed too hard and brought a wave of sickness over me so acutely, I stopped trying. I shut my eyes, willing my insides to settle and the blackness overtook me once more.

I have no idea how long I was unconscious, but the next time I opened my eyes it was daylight. Fingers of light streamed through cracks in the wooden walls. Slowly, I turned my head to look around and realised I must be in a barn or stables. Two horses stood, tethered loosely at one end of the space, facing away from me and I was lying on a bed of straw. Attempting to get up proved futile, for I was bound hand and foot. Now I was really scared, who would do this and why?

Suddenly I remembered my son — oh good grief — how could I have forgotten him? Where was he? I started to struggle against my bonds, which seemed to be made of a kind of twine and although the fronds cut into my wrists as I fought to free myself, they began to slacken. I shuffled myself into a sitting position, the nausea coming back with a vengeance every time I moved my head, but I was determined. After what seemed an age, I was sitting up and leaning against the wall of the building.

There was no sign of Luc. My son would be hungry and likely very upset. He didn't like his routine disrupted and I did not know how long I'd been here. I heard footsteps walking in my direction and, unwilling to let anyone see how close I was to being free, buried my hands into the folds of my tunic. A cloaked figure entered and dropped a hunk of bread at my feet. I asked for some water and without speaking, he pointed to the trough from which the animals drank. Oh delightful.

"Where is my son?" I asked in what I hoped was a firm and steady voice. He grunted and shook his head. Angry now, I shouted at him "What have you done with my son? He needs food, he needs me. Who do you think you are taking him away?" The last sentence was a shriek, as the figure ignored me and strode away.

I continued to yell and scream, but nobody came back. I was very scared now, not just for me, but for Luc, Senna and Petronius, What had happened to them? My imagination ran riot and a terrible fear began to creep over me. I might have to face the reality that they were all dead, the mere thought of which made me whimper in distress. I tried to get a grip of my panic — come on Hannah, I instructed myself, you have to get out of here and find them. Leaning back against the wall, I had another attempt at loosening the bonds. Slowly, very slowly, the twine was breaking, I kept at it, taking a breather every so often to clear my head, concentration making me dizzy all over again.

Finally, I did it and when my wrists came free the relief was indescribable. I grabbed the hunk of bread and nibbled at it, it was stale, but I was hungry enough not to care. Crawling over to the trough I peered in, it didn't smell too bad and I needed fluids, I knew I was probably dehydrated along with everything else. Despite the fact that I realised there could be all sorts of revolting things floating in the water I had to risk it. There was no alternative. Taking a deep breath I drank deeply, the water tasted brackish but not stagnant, hopefully it didn't have too much filth in it. I rinsed my face and neck and tried to wash some of the blood from my wrists.

Now I had to get the rest of the bonds off my ankles. Whoever had tied me up had done a good job and I chewed over why they had felt the need to restrain me? As far as I could tell, I'd been unconscious anyway; it's not easy to escape when knocked out. I yanked at the twine, fiddling with it, but I found it hard to remove. Glancing around the dim room, I spied a few jagged sections of wood in the slats that made up the walls. Maybe I could cut my way free. Shuffling back over to where I had been lying, I pondered my options, working out that my best chance was to try to break one of the shards and use it to slice through the twine.

Grabbing hold of one of the pieces of broken wood, I twisted and pulled and twisted again, trying to be as quiet as possible in the hopes that whoever had left me here had assumed that I was incapable of escape. Finally, a piece snapped off in my hands and I silently cheered my efforts. Finding the sharpest edge, I began to saw through the fronds. It wasn't easy or quick, but it worked and, although my hands were covered with splinters and my ankles were bleeding from where the fronds had sliced into my skin, I was free. I drew an exhausted breath, trembling with the effort and the fear that I would be caught.

I remained seated for a while, listening to make sure that everything was quiet, letting my heart resume it's normal rhythm and my hands stop shaking. Certain that no one was coming, I made to stand up, using the wall for support, feeling the blood beginning to circulate through my body again after lying down for so long. I was still quite stiff and my head was thumping, but I was upright. As carefully as possible, I tiptoed over to the door, which swung open. This seemed odd, although as they thought me restrained maybe they had not felt the need to lock me in as well. I peered out — no sounds just the gentle breathing of the horses. I tried to decide whether I dared steal one.

As I was standing there trying to decide what to do, one of the horses nickered. I looked over and to my complete and utter shock realised that it was Gemmula. Whaaaat??? Was I actually in the fort? Hidden in plain sight? Or had whoever taken me, also stolen my beautiful mare? It all seemed very muddled. I crept over to her and stroked her nose; she nibbled at me with her soft lips and nuzzled my hair.

"Oh Gemmula, what do I do?" I stood for several moments, pondering my next move. Then, worried that I might be seen before I could escape, I glanced around to see where the main entrance was.

I followed a passageway running between the stables, which were mostly empty. Was it the fort? Had I been home all the time? Why was there no noise? Surely if we were at the fort I would hear the sounds of the soldiers going about their duties? Not helping, Hannah, I reasoned; just get out. Hardly daring to breathe, I made my way towards the opening and, pressing my back against the wall, peeked around the wooden pillar trying to get my bearings. It was so bright outside that my eyes needed a moment to adjust. Yes, I was home; there was the principia and next door to it my house.

Confused, I remained hidden behind the doorjamb. What on earth was going on? Why would anyone hold me captive in our own stables? It seemed rather counterintuitive. Doubtless someone would have heard me having the screaming habdabs sooner or later and come to find out what or who was causing such a racket! Risking another look, I checked the compound; no sign of any soldiers — most peculiar. Staying in the shadow of the building, I moved cautiously along the wall until I reached the corner, then stopped and waited. Still nothing and nobody. I chanced a peep around the end of the wall. The route across to my house was clear, but I would have to be quick as it was quite a long stretch of open space.

Taking a deep breath, I hitched my clothes up and ran as fast as I could across the quadrangle and shot around the corner of the principia, slamming hard into something solid as I did so, knocking the breath out of me. I slithered to the floor and, panicking again, tried to scramble back onto my feet; terrified that I had been caught by the very people I was trying to escape from. Then a familiar voice spoke —

"Hannah?" I could have cried; it was Julius.

"Julius? Is that you?" I felt his hands lift me, helping me to my feet.

"Where have you been? The whole camp is searching for you?" As he held my arms steadying me, he took in my dishevelled appearance and noticed the blood on my wrists, which was running freely again. "I need to get you to Atius; you are bleeding and your face is all bruised." His voice reflected his shock.

I waived his comments aside —

"How long have you been looking, Julius? How long have I been missing?"

"Nigh on two days." I stared at him in consternation.

"What about Maxentius, does he know? Please tell me he doesn't know. My son, where's Luc and Petronius and Senna?" I was babbling in my alarm, stupefied by the events of the last few hours. Julius shushed me gently, telling me they were safe; Senna had Luc and Maxentius wasn't back yet. Marcus, however, was frantic, debating whether or not to send out a messenger to let my husband know what was going on, but who was out searching for me at the moment.

"They'll be back before long, it's nearly nightfall, they cannot search after dark, Marcus will return soon. In the meantime, you must let me get you to the hospital; Atius needs to check your wounds." I glanced down at my wrists, I'd forgotten about them and suddenly realised that they were very sore. My knees buckled and I felt myself start to slump. Julius caught me and virtually carried me over to the hospital. Atius was walking along the long ward and, as we entered, Julius called out his name, the medicus hastening to help.

They guided me to one of the beds in a smaller room where there was no-one else, giving me some privacy. I was zoning in and out and, although the two men were talking and asking me questions, their words were distorted and I struggled to tell them what had happened. I'm sure it was just garbled nonsense. I felt someone, Atius I presume, washing my wrists and ankles, cleaning the blood and applying something that was soothing and cool. Determined to hang onto consciousness, I attempted to get up only to be pushed back against the pillow. A blanket was pulled over me, its warmth making me relax as the stress of the last few hours took its toll and I remembered nothing else.

Chapter Twelve

The room was dim and cool, the bed I was lying on was comfortable and I felt better — less disorientated. Images flooded into my mind as I recalled what had happened: men crowding us, a horse, my being bound. I started to panic all over again and tried to sit up, but was prevented from doing so by a gentle hand. Someone was sitting next to the bed out of my line of vision. Turning slightly, I saw Marcus watching me, his expression one of concern.

"Oh Marcus, it's you." Immediately my fear subsided and I felt safe, finally my brother was here. "Please, let me get up, I have things I should be doing, a child to look after, I can't lie here any longer." Marcus moved his chair so that he was facing me and clasped my hand in his.

"Luc is fine, Hannah, Senna has been feeding and watching over him. You should rest now. Tomorrow you may get up."

"What happened to me, do you know?" He shook his head.

"All I know is what Julius told us; he found you in the compound. Well, actually you ran into him. Where did you come from?"

"The stables." Marcus stared at me in disbelief. "It's true, I woke up in the stables but I have no recollection of how I got there."

I proceeded to tell him all I could remember, which really wasn't that much. Marcus had also had Petronius' version of events, however and together they made a clearer picture. Apparently, when the riders had corralled us, they shoved Senna and Petronius away from me, while one of the men lifted me onto his horse. That much I knew. Then they snatched Luc from me, handed him to Senna, mounted their horses and rode away. It was bizarre.

"Did you hear any of them speaking, or see how they were dressed?" Marcus asked.

"It was so quick, all I remember is biting the hand of the man who lifted me, then I tried to punch him, I missed, he didn't." Ruefully, running my fingers over my sore face.

"You do have a nice bruise on your cheek. Honestly, Hannah, Maxentius will have my hide for this." I grinned across at him.

"No chance. How on earth could you have known that was going to happen? I have been going to the village for weeks now, it's no secret and we have to be able to move freely around the area. Isn't that why you're here? To give the locals and us freedom of movement. Maybe they were disgruntled tribespeople from further afield. We should ask at the village and tell them what happened, Bearach may know."

Marcus agreed with me and said he would ask Petronius to go and speak to the headman the next day.

"You haven't sent a runner to Maxentius have you?" I whispered. "He doesn't need to know, he has enough to worry about."

"No, I didn't, but he will have to be told. Hannah, you were missing for nearly two days, they targeted you, which means they want Maxentius to know what happened. It's the fact that they held you in the stables that worries me, it can only have been people from inside the fort, how else would they have got you inside?" We discussed this for quite a while and were both of the opinion that Gratius along with some of his cronies were the likely culprits, but had no proof.

"One of them will have a deep bite on his hand though." I muttered. "I know I drew blood, so you could check their hands." Marcus chuckled.

"Only you would think to do that, Hannah. You do not go quietly do you?"

"What do you expect? I'm not just going to stand around like some useless wimp and let anyone take me against my will. I was more concerned that Senna and Petronius had been badly hurt or worse, there was a lot of screaming and I heard a thud."

"They gave Petronius a bit of a thumping, but only enough to stop him from coming to your aid. I don't think they wanted to cause any serious injury. This is why it is so peculiar." Marcus looked totally perplexed and I could understand why, the whole incident was baffling.

"Maybe it'll seem clearer tomorrow. Are you sure you won't let me go home?" I gazed at Marcus beseechingly.

"I'm sure, Hannah. I'll come over in the morning but Atius will have the final say as to whether you are fit to leave."

"I wasn't hurt badly, just scuffed around my wrists and ankles. I'm fine really." He smiled down at me, shaking his head at my persistence.

"Just rest, Hannah. Trust me, Luc is in good hands and we have a guard on watch over both him and you."

"Oh," I said, surprised. "Really? How kind." Suddenly I realised just how tired I was, I yawned and felt my eyes drooping. "Thank you Ma..." and I was asleep.

The next time I opened my eyes, it was daylight, sun was streaming through the windows whose shutters had been thrown back to let the air circulate. Realising that I was alone, I decided to take matters into my own hands and get up. I swung my legs down from the bed, noticing the state of my ankles — they were covered in angry welts from the twine and sore to my touch. I glanced at my wrists, which were much the same. Absently, I rubbed them, wincing as my fingers brushed the raw skin. I shook my head in exasperation. Honestly, Hannah, I admonished myself, you do get into some scrapes.

I was making my way out of the door, when Atius came in, turned me around and pointed me back to the bed.

"I might have known. You cannot leave Hannah, not until I've checked those wounds, you should know better." I grinned at him sheepishly and sat back on the bed. He sat in the chair Marcus had used the night before — well I assumed it was the night before — and examined my wrists and ankles thoroughly. He rubbed some more balm into the abrasions and then bandaged them. "I can't afford you to get sick as well, Hannah; you never know when I might need your help." He winked then quickly checked my pulse and temperature. "I think you're good to go, but you must wait for Marcus, he'll be here shortly."

As he said this, an auxiliary came in with a platter and I realised how hungry I was. Other than that stale hunk of bread, I couldn't remember when I had last eaten. Thus, acquiescing to Atius' demand and thanking him, I sat back against the pillows and enjoyed the food. I mulled over the events of the past few days, still confused about what was really going on and it brought Maxentius' absence into sharp focus. It was hard enough him being away when everything was going swimmingly, now with all this, it was ten times worse. Then there was Luc, my son, without his mother for what must now be three days; the poor little soul will think I've abandoned him. I felt useless tears start to form and was hastily scrubbing at my face with the sheet, as Marcus strolled through the door.

With one glance he had summed me up and sitting down, gave me a quick hug.

"Hey, Hannah, it's going to be okay. Come on let's get you home." I rested my head against his shoulder just for a second, wishing he was Maxentius, then pulled myself together.

"I'm ready." I said, in a voice that wasn't quite steady. Then with an effort. "Have you any more news?" he shook his head.

"No, not yet, but Petronius is on his way to the village now with Annant. Let us hope they are successful with their enquiries."

We walked over to the residence, still discussing the strange incident. Senna came to meet us, hugging me and saying how relieved she was that I was safe. I responded in kind, apologising for leaving her with Luc for so long and asked how my son was faring.

"He's fine, Hannah, maybe a little grouchy, but he's been eating and sleeping and there has not been very much crying. It was not as though you deliberately left him." I squeezed her hand, thanking her for everything she had done for my son and me. Not many young women would have been so solicitous of another's child. Marcus came along with us to Luc's room, where my son was crawling all over the floor, chattering away to himself in baby talk.

As we went in, Luc turned towards us his little face lighting up when he saw me. He reached his arms out in the universal sign for children wanting a cuddle. I collected my son in my arms, holding him close, breathing in his baby smell and kissing him all over. He suffered my attentions by fisting his hands into my hair and pulling at it, chortling all the while. He hadn't forgotten me; the realisation of which made me go all wobbly again and I sat down abruptly. Marcus looked at me, eyebrows raised, but I shook my head.

"I'm all right Marcus, just relieved. I thought he might have forgotten me." Marcus smiled, as did Senna.

" I do not think you are so easy to forget, Hannah." Senna said.

"I know, but he's only young and it's been three days." The two of them chuckled and Marcus took his leave.

"I'll be back once Petronius has returned. Come and find me if you need anything." I thanked him for everything and he waved it aside. "Not only are you my commander's wife, you are also my sister and you know I'd do anything for either of you." I blushed and grinned.

"See you later then." He left us to it.

I spent the day with my son. I had a need to reconnect with him, to re-establish the bond I was sure had been stretched to its limits if not actually broken by my absence. Also, I was hesitant to venture beyond the safety of the house, nervous of being caught up again in whatever was going on. By the evening, I was very tired and accepted that I was still feeling rather wrung out. I fed Luc and settled him into his cradle, before indulging in a bath and changing clothes. Once I felt presentable, I went along to the triclinium, where Marcus was waiting as, to my surprise, were Petronius and Julius.

"Okay, what's going on?" I asked warily.

"I thought you might like to hear what these two found out today and it's easier to hear it straight from them rather than second hand."

"Oh, definitely." I sat down, expectantly, the three men doing the same, Petronius telling us what he had discovered at the village. Strangely enough, the villagers had claimed they knew nothing of any planned attack. Despite the fact that it was only a little over ten years since the rebellion organised by Venetius of the Brigantes, the people in the local area had grown accustomed to the presence of the Romans and had acknowledged that they felt more secure. The constant patrols and regular meetings had gone a long way to protecting not only their livelihoods, but also their trade routes. As things stood, they had no desire to see any change to the status quo.

It was a puzzle, and none of us could see the point of the attack, nor why I was held in our own stables. We discussed it throughout the meal until eventually I had to say what was bothering me —

"We all believe this to be the work of soldiers within the fort and if we all accept that this is the case, then we must also accept that the likely ringleader is Gratius." I looked around and the three men nodded. "Question is, who else is involved? Who do we trust? At this moment, the only people I am sure of are we four, Atius and Maxentius and probably those who are with my husband at the moment. I doubt whether any of the soldiers who accompanied us from Rome would get caught up in any kind of mutiny, but we can't be certain."

"I think it might be better if we simply carry on as though nothing happened and be more observant," said Marcus. "You two," nodding at Julius and Petronius, "listen to the other men when you are going about your duties. I presume that if they intended serious harm, you, Petronius would not have come away from that skirmish with only a thump to the chest and Hannah would not have escaped as easily. I feel sure this is all to do with Maxentius being legatus, there is nothing else that would create such a divide...." he paused, then added "...and I fear this was merely a warning, a hint of what they could do, should they so choose."

"I fail to see why they are disgruntled," commented Julius, "Maxentius has never been anything but fair. He is a good man, treating all under his command with respect. I am appalled at this dissension in his ranks." Petronius nodded his agreement, both men had been in Maxentius' garrison from the time of our arrival in Pompeii and both had acted as my guardian and escort regularly. Petronius had helped me escape the town on the eve of the catastrophic eruption of Vesuvius. I had trusted and would continue to trust my life to all three men sitting here.

We went round and round the topic, but could not shed any more light on it. Vigilance appeared to be the only answer for now. Marcus told me that a guard would be stationed at the house at all times until Maxentius' return. I thanked them all for their concern and bid them goodnight, knowing that they would secure the house. I wished that my husband were with me; he had been gone for too long.

Chapter Thirteen

I had a very restless night. I couldn't stop thinking about what had happened and, when I finally did fall asleep my dreams were filled with garbled images of hooded men and galloping horses. I kept waking with the need to check on Luc to make sure he was safe. Eventually, I gave in and got up. It was still dark, I had no idea what time it was and really wished that I had a watch, dismissing the notion with a faint chuckle. Really Hannah!

I checked along the corridors and through all the rooms of the big house, assuming that once I knew all was quiet and secure, my mind would settle. Nothing helped. Any other time, I would have saddled Gemmula and gone riding, even that pursuit was not worth the risk at the moment, plus it was dark. Frustrated, I picked up one of the lamps and went along to my medicine rooms, thinking to distract myself by checking my supplies.

Usually I found working with ointments and tinctures soothed me, but not tonight. Finally, I went along to the kitchens. They were empty; all the staff were in bed, so I knew it was still very early in the morning. I stood in front of the massive fireplace over which Mabina could roast whole pigs if she chose. The flames were burning low in the grate and I placed a large log onto the ashes, watching as the fire coiled around it, sparks shooting up the stone chimney. I poured myself a goblet of calda and, dragging a large chair over to the fire, huddled into it tucking my feet up under my legs, resigned to being awake for the rest of the night.

I had been sitting for maybe an hour, my thoughts faraway, contemplating my dual life and what I might have been doing had Max still been alive. I was staring at the embers in the huge grate, the fanciful part of my mind trying to picture my destiny in their flickering glow and unconsciously running my fingers over my bandaged wrists, when the door creaked open and Marcus poked his head around.

"Oh, it's you, Hannah. I saw the light and wondered what could be amiss at this hour."

"It's just me. I can't sleep; this seems the most comfortable place to be. So sorry," ruefully, "I didn't intend to disturb your rest." Marcus pulled another chair over to the fire and poured his own drink, topping up mine in the process. We had been sitting in companionable silence for quite some time, when Marcus spoke.

"What do you consider to be an acceptable age difference between a man and a woman?" I gaped at him. That came out of the blue!

"Err...mmm...for why?" Marcus looked rather embarrassed and I could see that he was trying to decide whether to tell me what was really going on. "Marcus?" Curiously.

"Well, I was just thinking. Am I too old to consider marriage?" Any other time I would have burst out laughing; it was such an odd question and Marcus had never shown any real interest in marriage. He knew the rules concerning soldiers and their wives and I had presumed he had decided not to marry, as any union would not be recognised officially until his retirement from the army. His question floored me — he was serious.

"Marcus, you are never too old to consider marriage, not if you truly love someone." As I was saying this, a series of scenes floated through my head and abruptly I realised for whom he had feelings. I am usually very good at noticing such things; how could I have been so blind? "Senna?" I asked gently. He looked across at me in shock.

"How on earth did you work that out?"

"It just popped into my head. I suddenly remembered the way you two look at each other when you are talking. Your expressions, your body language. Oh Marcus, I know this is an intimate question; but do you love her?" He hesitated, this was so very personal.

"I don't know whether I know what love is. I know that I can't stop thinking about her, that my heart beats faster when she is near and that I miss her when she is not around. When she and Petronius told us what had happened the other day, I felt as though I had been punched and I had to struggle not to drag her into my arms and kiss her fear away. The thought of her being harmed in any way would destroy me."

As he said the last few words, he dropped his head staring down at his arms, which rested on his knees, his hands clasped loosely, uncertainty radiating off him. He was in unknown territory here. I reached across and brushed his hand.

"Do you know whether she feels the same way?" He looked at me, shaking his head, not so much as a negative, more in confusion.

"I cannot tell. Sometimes when she looks at me, or when we talk, I think she cares for me, but more likely she just sees me as a protector, just another soldier and, probably too old for her anyway. I dare not ask her."

"I think you might find she is not indifferent to you, my brother. Leave it with me, I will find out," raising my hand as he started to protest. "Give me some credit, Marcus, I will be subtle." He didn't look convinced and to be fair, subtlety is not one of my more obvious traits. I have been known, however, to use it on occasion with great success — which is why it's not obvious!

He smiled rather diffidently and we let the matter rest, for now. While we had been talking, the light in the room had changed; dawn had broken and soon the staff would bustle in ready for their morning duties. I checked to make sure the fire was safe and said I was going to try to snatch an hour's sleep before the day was upon us. Marcus took the goblets and rinsed them out, placing them on the table. We went quietly along the hallways and parted, he to his quarters and I to mine.

I managed to get some rest, not nearly enough, but thought I might be able to sneak in a nap during the day if it proved necessary. When Luc's demanding cries woke me, I felt as though my head had barely touched the pillow. Groggily, I dragged myself out of bed, stumbling through to his room, still half asleep. He was lying in his cradle angrily pumping the air with his fists. It was actually quite amusing to watch him. I'm sure he thought he was being very fierce, but he just looked cute. Scooping him up and crooning softly, I fed him, his grumpy cries becoming delighted snuffles as he satisfied his appetite.

Once he was full, I bathed and dressed him, by which time Senna had appeared. Taking Luc so that I could go and dress, Senna said that she'd be out in the yard. The two of them had taken to watching the soldiers every morning, something else that hadn't really registered with me until now. I knew that Marcus, as second in command, always inspected the troops, so

I decided that this morning I would go along and observe Senna without her realising. You see...very subtle!

After a thorough and very refreshing bath, using fragrant oils that went a long way to clearing my head, I found some clean clothes and hastened to join my son and his guardian in the quadrangle. The soldiers marched out, the highly polished metal of their armour blinding in the early morning sunlight. For the most part these soldiers did not wear armour in the course of their regular duties, but they did for inspection and it was a formidable sight. Hundreds of men standing in perfect lines, shoulders back and heads held high, proud of their position. I watched as Marcus strode out to begin his daily inspection. Cutting an imposing figure and nearly as tall as Maxentius with that same regal bearing, he walked the lines chatting with his soldiers, commenting occasionally, a smile here and a nod there. It took quite some time, as this was not a drill that should be rushed.

Unexpectedly, it reminded me of my other life. My brother-in-law was in the airforce and I remembered watching his graduation parade. That was impressive enough; this was on a whole other level and, despite the fact that I had seen it many times, it never got old. I felt the familiar wrench in my heart as, unbidden, memories flooded through me. With a valiant effort I pushed them away — not now, I couldn't handle them now. Now, I needed to concentrate on this life.

I forced my attention back to the parade ground and shifted my stance slightly in order to watch Senna, without appearing to. She was pointing out different soldiers to Luc telling him all about the inspection, as though he understood her completely. But although it seemed that her attention was on my son, she was staring at Marcus, her dark eyes following his every move, with an expression that could only be described as smouldering. I smiled to myself; Marcus had nothing to worry about, Senna was as besotted as he. I would just need to work out a way of getting them together, without them realising it. It cheered my heart. I would like Marcus to find the same happiness I enjoyed; he deserved it.

Wanting to get on with my day, I told Senna I would see her later, and went back home to grab a quick meal, which I inhaled with little regard for what was on the platter. Then I made my way over to the hospital. Atius had said he wanted to check my scratches, so I presented myself dutifully while he examined, applied salve, then re-bandaged my wrists and ankles, telling me he thought I'd be able to remove them by the end of the day.

"I just don't want you to get dust and dirt in the cuts, Hannah and you know how easily that happens. If you have a long-sleeved tunic, that would give the bandaged area a bit more protection, especially if you intend to go out to the village." I thanked him and went to look for Petronius who, at this time of day, could usually be found in the stables.

I found him filling the feeding frames with hay and topping up the water troughs and I asked whether he would be free to accompany me to the village. He wasn't sure that Marcus would be happy for me to go rambling through the countryside after what had happened, but I said we could clear it with him before we left.

"Maybe Julius could come also?" I suggested. "An extra soldier can't be a bad thing." Petronius thought this idea had merit, so we went to look for Julius before we set out. He was happy to fall in with our plans and the three of us went over to the principia to ask Marcus whether he would allow us to travel to the village.

Marcus merely advised us to take extra care and be aware of what was going on around us; and told me, very tongue in cheek, not to get kidnapped again. I smiled demurely as he said this and promised I'd do my best. Then, just as the other two left the room, I crossed over to the table where Marcus was standing and very quietly told him that he had nothing to worry about. He stared at me, momentarily confused, until I dropped a very slow wink and grinned. He blushed, actually blushed and thanked me in a voice that didn't sound quite like his. I squeezed his hand and left him to his day.

Senna had said she would remain at the fort with Luc and, I knew it was safer than taking them with us after recent events. I found a tunic that Atius could not object to, its sleeves long enough to fall right over my hands, tucking the cuffs under the edge of the bandages to hold them in place; it was probably a more suitable outfit anyway for these colder days. By the time the three of us set out, it was into the fourth hour and, even though the sun was shining, the day was still rather chilly. I surmised that winter was closing in quickly and was quite looking forward to seeing what it would be like, so far north. The ground was hard with frost, but we all wore boots and I had my heavy winter cloak slung around my shoulders, caught at the neck by my beautiful clasp. We chatted as we walked, but I noticed that my two guardians kept a vigilant eye on our surroundings.

We arrived at the village without incident and Bearach and Breeda welcomed me. They asked me what had happened and took turns to look at my damaged wrists. Breeda carefully unwrapped the bandages, nodding in approval at the balm that Atius had smoothed into the cuts, before re-binding them and tucking the cuffs of my sleeves back under the cloth. Bearach said that he had no idea who had done this. None of the locals wished to antagonise the garrison. Life had been very settled in the past few months and they did not want a return to the constant tribal upheaval that marred their usually relatively peaceful existence. Neither was kidnapping an unarmed woman who was carrying her baby their preferred method of getting attention.

I agreed with him and without giving too much away, said it was possible that unrest within the fort may be behind the incident. Bearach stared at me for a long time as though weighing up whether to share something of importance. I sat patiently, knowing he would tell me in his own time; and after a little while, he took my hand, turning it over and pressing my palm.

"Your husband is a good man, but there is one within the walls of the fort who wishes him harm." I felt a trickle of ice run down my spine. I fought to remain expressionless and merely nodded. Bearach continued, speaking slowly, making sure I understood the gravity of his words. "Be careful of the tall, angry soldier; he is twisted by a hatred that clouds his senses. Heed my words." I shuddered, fear roiling through me. I was right: this was all to do with Gratius, but we had no evidence of wrongdoing, nothing to tie him to what happened to me. Expect the man whose hand I bit — I thought — he would have a nasty scar.

"Thank you, Bearach," I said solemnly, "I will heed your warning." He inclined his head and I bowed mine. He went on his way and, pushing the warning aside for a little while, I spent a happy couple of hours learning more from Breeda. Petronius and Julius were dragged into silly games with the children until, eventually tired by all the running about, Julius called a halt and began to teach them how to make simple toys by twisting pieces of young, green sapling into shape. He was very good at it and patient too; the children were fascinated and by the time we were ready to leave they were engrossed.

Extracting a promise that he would come and help them again, Julius was allowed to come with us, although for a moment or two I thought they were going to keep him. Grinning in delight, he agreed and said he would come with me the next time I travelled to their village. The three of us set off home. We were about halfway there and too far away from anything like a stand of trees in which we could secrete ourselves, when we heard the thundering of hooves.

Stepping away from the track and fearful of a repeat of the recent incident, I cowered against Petronius, who pushed me behind him and drew his sword. Julius did the same and by the time the group approached, I was quite scared; after all, there were only three of us. Suddenly a shout went up from one of the riders. It didn't sound threatening; it sounded friendly. Who were they?

"Petronius! Greetings. It has been many days." Petronius yelled back, then turned to me.

"It is your husband and his guard, Hannah. They have returned." I gaped. We had received no warning of his impending arrival. My heart began a rapid tattoo in my chest; I had missed him so much. Where was he? I couldn't see him; to me it was just a gaggle of soldiers, then one separated himself from the others. A tall man dismounted and strode towards us. I just stood, frozen to the spot. His dark hair, caught back by a narrow leather strip, peeked out from under his helmet. His eyes, green as a forest — I could see them twinkling from where I waited — and his smile, that toe-curling, heart-stopping smile. My legs went a little wobbly and I grinned foolishly.

He stopped just in front of me. I gazed up at him, drinking in his broad shoulders and muscular physique. I couldn't speak. I opened my mouth, but nothing came out. I felt like an idiot. Not so my husband, who took one more step and gathered me into his arms and in complete disregard for military etiquette — not to mention all his soldiers — kissed me soundly. A cheer went up from his men, all of whom I knew and liked. Flushed with embarrassment, I tried to push him away, at once mortified by this overt display of affection, yet inordinately pleased by it. Maxentius was having none of it and held me close.

"My Hannah, oh how I've missed you," he whispered, kissing me again.

"The feeling is mutual, Sir." I smiled up at him. Resisting the desire to fling off his helmet and run my hands through his hair, I compensated by smoothing my hand along his cheek. For a moment the rest of the world disappeared and it was just the two of us. I couldn't quite believe he was here and that I was in his embrace. I rested my head on his chest, breathing him in, then common sense reasserted itself and I made to move out of his arms.

"No. You're riding in with me, my girl." I shook my head.

"That is not proper, Max. You should ride in as their commander, not as my husband."

"I am always their commander, my love, but I have missed being your husband and I am not on official business; I am returning home, to my family and my garrison. Come on, it'll be much quicker than walking. Capitulating, albeit a little reluctantly, I allowed him to lift me up onto his horse. He settled behind me, his arms around me and, holding the reins loosely, we set off.

Petronius and Julius followed after us, one or two of their comrades dismounting to accompany them. I recognised that this was a relaxed arrival, no ceremony, so I stopped fretting and, leaning back against my husband, enjoyed the ride.

Chapter Fourteen

I slid off the horse just before we entered the fort, ignoring Maxentius' protests. With everything else that had happened while he'd been away, I thought it prudent to let the soldiers ride in as a body without my presence. I waited until Petronius and Julius arrived and walked in with them. I knew that there would be army protocols to follow and presumably Marcus would need to present a verbal report to Maxentius regarding the daily affairs of the garrison. My position as Maxentius' wife was secondary to these procedures and I would need to wait for our own reunion.

My first port of call was to the hospital, to apprise Atius of my latest visit to the village and what Breeda had taught me. It had become our habit to make note of what I had learned along with any information on plants or herbs that may prove useful. We were creating quite a large pile of tablets, each one neatly labelled and all stacked carefully in order. Some tablets could be threaded together, which was useful should a particular treatment or mixture require more than a simple description. Where possible, I had divided my own collection of remedies in half and had painstakingly copied the ingredients and marks from my personal set of jars and tablets onto a set for the hospital. It didn't do any harm to have duplicated medicines. The pair of us were very excited about how much information we were gathering and, I had persuaded Atius that he should accompany me to the village. I knew that he and Breeda would get along famously.

Once that was completed, I went home to see how Luc and Senna had filled their day. They were in Luc's bedroom sitting on the rug that covered most of the floor. Senna was singing and making shapes with her fingers; Luc was trying to copy her and his earnest expression was very funny. I joined them and we continued to play for a while longer, until it was time for Luc's feed.

He was down to two feeds a day now, having taken to more solid food with gusto — although his habit of throwing it at all and sundry hadn't quite been broken. Senna left to enjoy her free time while I settled myself into one of the chairs and let Luc feed to his heart's content. These moments were so precious; soon he would no longer rely on me for sustenance and, although I knew it was simply a part of growing up, I would miss it.

After Luc's hunger had been catered to, he nestled against me and fell asleep. I knew he would rest for longer if I placed him in his cot, but I was comfortable and enjoyed the closeness. I rested my head on the back of the chair and felt myself relax; it would be very easy to slip into a doze. Bearach's words came back to me in the quiet and I ruminated over them. As soon as possible, I needed to share the headman's warning with Maxentius and Marcus as well as with Petronius and Julius, who seemed to have resumed their role as my guardians; something they had initially undertaken in Pompeii. I was just sad that the threat was from within the fort.

I heard footsteps along the passageway and smiled to myself, knowing who it was before he came into the room. Maxentius opened the door quietly, his face lighting up when he saw me with our son. My heart did its familiar flip-flop and my breathing quickened. He was so tall and handsome and even though it was only a couple of hours since we'd greeted each other, his long absence meant we still had quite a bit of catching up to do. He came over and knelt by the chair, taking my free hand and drawing it against his chest. I gazed at him, drowning in the dark-green depths of his eyes. We didn't need to speak; words were never necessary. He leaned towards me, caressing my lips with his and desire coiled around my stomach.

"Maybe Luc could rest in his cradle," my husband murmured, "I would like to say hello properly."

"I thought you did that quite beautifully in front of all your soldiers." I smiled.

"Ah, that was my official greeting; I think now it is time to be somewhat less so." I giggled at his expression, which was nothing short of flirtatious. Disengaging my hand I placed Luc gently into his bed, covering him with the blanket and making sure he was tucked in. I rocked him for a moment in case the movement had disturbed him, but he stayed fast asleep.

Maxentius reclaimed my hand, pulling me to him, but as we touched he let go, running both of his hands through my hair and then, cupping the back of my head, bent to kiss me. His lips were firm and cool, his hands gentle, as one tangled itself in my hair cradling my head while the other began to trail along my body. My arms went around him as I responded to his kiss, which deepened as we became enraptured by each other. Time slowed and I forgot everything else except how much I had missed this man — my lover, my husband, my Roman.

After what seemed like a lifetime, Maxentius lifted his head —

"Oh, my Hannah, I really do not like being apart from you, but our reunions do tend to be most satisfactory." I grinned up at him, my heart in my eyes.

"Hmmm," I said casually, twirling my fingers across his chest, "I suppose that wasn't bad, but I..." Whatever I was going to say was cut off as his lips captured mine sending heat scorching along my veins and making my legs buckle. With no intention of letting me fall, he held me tight in his embrace, continuing to plunder my mouth, causing delicious sensations to ripple up and down my spine. Long moments later, he broke away and stared down at me, a wicked light in his eyes.

"Now, what were you saying?" I was breathless and my legs still refused to hold me. I knew my face to be flushed and my hair would now be completely dishevelled.

"As you said, most satisfactory." My voice was husky as I tried to regain control of my senses. "Well, good Sir, you certainly know how to say hello." Maxentius chuckled and said —

"Better, my beautiful wife," before kissing me again, this time butterfly light. "Now, although I would like nothing better than to pursue this to its obvious conclusion, I think it is nearly time for the evening meal. I understand Marcus has things he wishes to discuss in private.

"Oh, would you prefer that I did not join you?" I asked, maybe a little more flippantly than I should have done, knowing exactly what Marcus wanted to talk about and thinking their discussions may be easier without my presence. Maxentius looked at me questioningly.

"Now why on earth would you suggest that, my Hannah? Do you have some inkling as to the matters that Marcus wishes to discuss?" I blushed and dropped my gaze. Maxentius lifted my chin and looked into my eyes. "What is it?" he asked. I hesitated a moment then —

"There was an...err...incident and I think I should let Marcus tell you; it is better coming from him. But if you wish, I will join you. I think you will find Petronius and Julius will also attend." Maxentius looked rather perplexed and not a little anxious. I lifted my hand to cup his cheek, starting to tell him not to worry, but the action sent my sleeves rolling up my arm and he saw my bandages. Those long sleeves had hidden the bindings most effectively. Taking hold of my wrist and running his fingers over the cloth, he stared long and hard at me, suddenly noticing the fading bruise on my cheek. He brushed the hair off my face to get a better look, his gaze darkening. I bit my lip, suddenly unsure of how to explain what had happened. I knew he would be upset and frustrated that he hadn't been there to prevent it, although quite how he could have done was a mystery to me — I just knew how his mind worked. "Just wait until the meal," I whispered hesitantly, "then it will be clear."

He frowned, then nodded and made as if to leave the room, but I could tell he wasn't happy. I clutched at his hand and held it until he turned back to me, his features tight, unyielding.

"Maxentius, please don't turn away from me like this, it wasn't my fault." He had only just come home; he had just been kissing me, now this sudden change of mood! I couldn't bear it if he was going to get upset with me for something totally out of my control. My husband stared at me, his eyes hooded, his jaw clenched, reading my expression, which I knew must have been one of dismay, but he simply turned on his heel and left.

I sank back into the chair in consternation, feeling as though someone had thrown a bucket of cold water over me. What had brought on this sudden change in attitude? I felt tears forming but blinked them back determinedly. My first instinct was to go after him and demand an explanation — actually more likely to hit him. Then my anger started to burn and I decided he could stew on it. I waited until I thought he would have finished getting freshened up and changed before I ventured into our bedroom.

I fussed about for longer than was necessary, but in the end chose to dress in my deep emerald green undershift and lime-green tunic. The last time I had worn this was at his mother's villa and I hoped he would remember how much he had liked it then. The material was gossamer fine, the colours dissolving into one another. I combed my hair through, pinning it loosely off my face, rather than twisting it into its usual plait; again something Maxentius preferred.

It felt a bit strange, making such an effort after Maxentius' odd behaviour. I really should just have worn my scruffiest tunic, but I felt the need to dress up, as though I was arming myself. Before I left the bedroom, I picked up my clasp, rolling it around in my fingers, staring into its ruby depths, wishing it could tell me what was going on.

Eventually, I could delay no longer. I walked into the triclinium, my head held high, but I refused to look at Maxentius. If he wanted to be petulant, so be it, but my ire continued to build and I had no desire to play nice. The other three men were already there and had also made an effort, all wearing togas over their tunics. Maxentius was deep in conversation with Julius and Marcus was chatting with Petronius, but they turned to greet me as I entered the room. As Marcus hugged me, I whispered that Maxentius was all uppity and that we needed to tell him about the attack sooner rather than later. Grinning, he nodded and released me. I went over to the smallest of the sofas and sat down, reclining, as was the custom. I usually sat with my husband on one of the larger ones but not tonight — he'd blown that!

I kept the conversation light until the meal had been served and then let Marcus take over. He cleverly turned the discussion to what had been happening while Maxentius had been away. I still refused to make eye contact with my husband. I was now fuming and more than a little upset with him. Never had he walked away from me and I was not going to let it go. Petronius took over when it came to the attack on our little group. He explained as much as he was able, then I wound the tale up, telling how I'd been knocked unconscious and then discovering that I'd been taken somewhere and bound to prevent my escape; and that I'd been able to break the bonds only to find I was held captive in our own stables. I concluded with what Bearach had said to me that morning.

My words were stilted, my voice cold and harsh and after I had spoken, an odd silence fell over our little group. Then I stood and in icy tones, told them that they could continue their discussion without me, as it appeared my presence was superfluous to requirements. Petronius and Julius looked bewildered, sensing undercurrents; Marcus smiled sympathetically. I had studiously avoided my husband's gaze throughout the evening, but as I turned to leave the room, I looked straight at him.

Maxentius' expression seemed chagrined and he appeared as though he might come to my side, but I glared at him in utter fury daring him to move, my eyes spitting green fire; then bidding them all a crisp goodnight, left the room with as much grace as I could muster. I almost ran along to Luc's bedroom to check on him. He was still sleeping, so I carried on along the corridor, through the atrium and out of the main door, finding a wooden bench near the principia and sitting there for a moment trying to calm my wrath and distress.

Bubbling under my anger, was the realisation that Maxentius' actions had left me feeling bereft, as though something had shifted in our relationship; only for the life of me I couldn't work out why. It was as though my anchor had broken its mooring. Thinking of anchors made me recall the other me and her life. I knew she was in my head still and I couldn't understand why she thought her Max to be dead. As far as I could tell, he was very much alive and trying to make her believe the same. My head was whirling with too many thoughts and I very much wanted to scream.

Deciding that this might not be the most sensible option and without stopping to consider my actions, I stalked out of the fort, through the main gate, nodding to the guard on watch. It seemed a bit odd that the gate was open, until I remembered that the last patrol was probably still out, so I had a little time. It was a very cold night and the air smelt a little sour, something I registered subconsciously as being a warning sign, but immediately forgot. I had not thought to pick up my cloak, but I didn't intend to stay out for very long — just long enough to clear my head. The sky was cloudy and there were no stars to light my way; neither had the moon yet risen, but I could just make out the road — it was enough.

I stomped along with no real thought about where I was going. Having worked myself up into a raging temper, I wanted to burn it off in case I blew my top in front of everyone. As I marched, my mind churned over all the whys and wherefores and I was so caught up in being righteously angry that I had no idea how long I'd been out or how far I'd gone. When I finally paused to catch my breath, I turned around and realised that the fort was no longer in sight. I hadn't strayed from the road, though, so I knew it was just a matter of retracing my steps.

As I thought this, I felt the light touch of something on my arms. I looked up into the sky seeing that it had started to snow. I held my hand out, catching a flake; it was so delicate, like a cobweb.

"Oh dammit," I muttered to myself crossly, "now it's snowing. That's just great!" I knew that I needed to head back to the fort, so I about-faced and started for home. I had been walking only a few minutes when the wind picked up and what had started as a gentle fall suddenly turned into a blizzard, the snow covering the ground, quickly obliterating my route. My consternation growing, I scuffed through the whiteness trying to see the huge flat stones that made up the road, but it was coming down so thickly that it became too hard. My sandals were soon soaked through and my feet felt like ice.

Frustrated with myself for being so incautious, I pushed on, hoping to see the light from the torches dotted around the fort, knowing that they would guide me back. The snow was falling so fast that the dizzying dance of the flakes mesmerised me. Maybe I should sit down and rest a while; wait until it stopped. This seemed like an eminently sensible plan, so I found a very useful bush and curled up against it, wrapping my arms around my body.

I wanted to shut my eyes, but a voice in my head told me not to, telling me to get up and move. I ignored it for a while, but it was most insistent. Finally, I got up, noticing that the snow was changing the landscape to one of unfamiliar flatness. The dips and mounds, usually so recognisable were being blanketed over rapidly and there was no sound, the deep snow muffling everything.

I realised that nobody would even know that I was here; the four men were no doubt still engaged in discussions over the events of the last few days and probably presumed that I had gone to bed. No-one would even know I was missing until it was too late — oh, except maybe the guard at the gate, he might remember my leaving. Oh well, I mused, that'll save Maxentius having to be angry with me anymore. I trudged on, in a bid to keep moving than in any hope of getting back to the fort. I was lost, hopelessly lost and more than a little frightened, the cold making me very sleepy. Oh Hannah, I thought, you are an idiot!

Determined to stay awake and upright, I thought about my children and how I missed the older three. This kept me going for a while, but it was getting harder. The snow was over ankle deep now and I was colder than I ever thought possible. Now Maxentius would have every right to be upset with me. I found I didn't care. I was still mad with him; two could play at his game.

Without warning, I walked bang slap into something very hard. I put my hands out trying to work out what it was. It wasn't a tree, it was bigger than that and it wasn't round. I felt along, my fingers tracing the shape of the object. I realised it was some kind of fence. A spark of hope flickered. Was there any chance that this was the palisade for the fort? I realised that I must be close to the gate or I would have fallen into the ditch. The thought of being warm and safe spurred me on and I hugged the wooden structure until suddenly it opened up and I fell through a gap.

As I was thanking all the gods for guiding me home, I wondered why there were bright lights dancing about in front of me. That was weird, I thought hazily, maybe they were fairies or fire sprites. No matter, I couldn't go any further, I was totally exhausted; perhaps the fire sprites would watch over me until the morning. I lay down on the blanket of snow, which was surprisingly comfortable and shut my eyes.

Chapter Fifteen

Millennia away and day five since the crash, Max was connecting up his laptop so that he could play directly through the television the videos that Nate had emailed him. He had told Hannah what he was doing but she hadn't responded. Her expression when he spoke hurt his heart. He knew she could hear him, but he also knew that she thought she was imagining it. Once everything was set up, he simply turned the television on and let the videos run. He had already watched them through and knew there were scenes within them that Hannah should recognise. Sebastian had videoed the whole of the interior of the House of the Hebrew including the inscription and Nate had done much the same at the Gladiators' School.

Picture and sound were very clear. Max sat back and waited to see whether Hannah would react. In one scene she was laughing at something Nate had said, her head falling back and her hair catching the sun. Max's breath hitched — she had to come back to him. He sensed rather than saw his wife come into the room. She walked over to the television and sat on the floor in front of it, her face alive with delight. It was the most animated she had been since he'd come home. Max watched as she leaned forward taking in the images. Suddenly the inscription appeared and she moved even closer, her fingers stretching out to trace it, murmuring the phrase under her breath.

The scene changed; they had moved into the oecus, or main room of the house. Sebastian was recording the frescoes, but voices wafted through. Nate was discussing something with the other person in their group, a girl; Max remembered her name was Liz. They were arguing about the pots in the back garden and why they would be there.

"They were empty. There was no point filling them again, the ash would bury them." Hannah's words fluttered over the room. Max grinned; she was responding to something, finally, but he had no desire to distract her, so he remained in the chair as still as a stone. Hannah smiled as she watched the screen, adding her own perspective to the days as the scenes unfolded.

While they were still watching the video taken in the House of the Hebrew, Max decided to talk about the day he proposed to his wife. He waited until the recording was that of the back garden and he began to speak. He talked about where the chicken coop and the vegetable patch were, the spot where a table was placed so that Hannah and her two colleagues could try to save Tobias. He described the upper floor where Aliza lived and how the garrison headquarters was next door, along a short walkway. He mentioned how he had kissed Hannah in the middle of the garden, after she had said yes to his proposal.

His voice died away and he waited to see whether any of his words had reached her. She touched the screen and whispered his name, as though willing him to walk through it to her, and a solitary tear ran down her cheek. He couldn't help himself; Max went over to her and curled up behind her on the floor, pulling her into his embrace. She sighed and rested against him. He started talking again, talking about things only the two of them could know — things about Pompeii, her other life, her other world and the people in it.

He talked about Maxentius and Marcus, about the children and her work at the Gladiators' School. He knew she was listening. She interjected here and there, adding things to the story he was weaving around them. Her hands wrapped over his and she traced the back of his hands with her fingers. A tiny spark of hope began to sputter into life. He knew it would be a long haul and it was unlikely she would come back to him this night, but it was a start.

The video ended. Unwilling to push her too far and waste the progress he'd made, Max simply gathered her in his arms and carried her upstairs. She undressed and snuggled under the sheets and was asleep in minutes. He watched her as she settled, then went back downstairs to turn off everything. He'd have another go tomorrow. Once the house was secure, he joined his wife in bed. He had decided that whether she believed him dead or not, her nights were less disturbed when he was next to her; and as he drew her close, she relaxed against him and they both slept.

****

The television was playing a video of the dig at Pompeii. I could see the inscription that Maxentius carved for me — well, her. I wanted to touch it, run my fingers over the words. Scooching up closer to the television, I listened to the argument Nate was having with Liz about the amphorae in the garden. Even though I knew they couldn't hear me, I couldn't help but tell them — I knew why the pots were there. While I was sitting, I could hear Max's voice talking over the top of the video. That was strange; why was I hearing him? He was talking about the chicken coop and the garrison. I wanted to cry, his voice was so lovely. I felt a tear run down my face and suddenly I could feel him. His arms were around me and I was holding his hands.

How was that even possible? Absently, I stroked my fingers over his hands listening to him as he talked about Maxentius and Marcus. Only Max could know these things. How was I hearing them? Was my mind running on overdrive? The screen went blank. I felt myself being lifted and carried upstairs. My senses were tumbling. What was going on? Was I going mad? I knew that grief could send people over the edge; was that what was happening to me? I was in bed and two-thirds asleep, when suddenly I felt Max lie down behind me, pulling me to his chest. It seemed so real. If this was a fantasy of my own making, then I was definitely losing my marbles. "Or maybe," a very small voice whispered at the back of my mind, "Max isn't dead." Afraid of opening my eyes and looking to check, I simply enjoyed the feeling of my husband's arms wrapped around me and I slept.

.......oooooOOOooooo.......

I was dreaming about my other life; Max was talking to me about Pompeii and I was snuggled in his arms. It was so lovely. Without warning, I was wrenched back, hands were lifting me and somebody was holding their fingers against my throat; I knew that was one way to check for a heart beat. I remembered all the snow and being very cold and contemplated whether I might have died. Oh well, if I'm dead, I can't be mad with my husband; I didn't think dead people had feelings. Hmmm...I could haunt him though! That would teach him to get angry with me for no reason. Yes, but if I was dead, I wouldn't be able to feel the fingers. I could feel a giggle rising in my throat; my thoughts were completely insensible.

A voice was talking to me and I felt that I should recognise it, but it wouldn't come to me. I had the impression that I was in someone's arms, but I didn't know whose and that something warm like a cloak or a blanket had been wrapped around me. I couldn't concentrate and it was too hard to respond, so I didn't. The giggle rose again and this time I could not stop it from bubbling up. I bit my lip thinking that it sounded as though I was a bit hysterical. The voice spoke to me again; I think they were asking me questions, but I had no idea what they were saying, so I ignored them — very mature Hannah!

I realised that I was probably hallucinating because whoever was holding me seemed enormous, probably a giant, and I thought it wise to check, so I asked him. I felt a chuckle rumble through his chest and he assured me that he wasn't. Well, it was a fair question, I thought.

"I saw fire sprites, so you might have been a giant." Another chuckle. I felt as though I was floating, my head simply would not connect to what was happening around me. A thought came to me.

"Do you know M-Maxentius?" I whispered through lips that were stiff with cold.

"A little," the voice answered, "why do you ask?"

"P-please don't tell him," my teeth were chattering now. "I was v-very angry and I think I chose the wrong d-dress to take a walk in and I d-don't want him to be even m-m-more upset with me." I could barely speak now and was too tired to think straight. Even to me my words sounded slurred. "I think y-y-you should put me d-down, not sure you sh-sh-should be carrying me."

Rather than heed me, the person merely held me closer, the warmth from his body starting to penetrate through whatever they had wrapped me in. He said —

"I don't expect he will be."

"W-will be what?" The fog in my brain had thickened and I was fighting to concentrate.

"Upset with you."

"Oh, b-but he is. Too h-hard, too m-many other things to worry about, easier if I r-r-return to Rome." My voice caught as exhaustion played havoc with my emotions and I started to cry. The man stilled for a moment and then carried on walking.

Suddenly, I realised what I was saying and clamped my mouth shut. What on earth was I thinking? Sharing a private matter with someone I didn't know; really Hannah! In a last ditch effort to marshal my thoughts, I took a deep breath and muttered —

"S-sorry, not your p-problem, I should n-not be speaking of such things, but if th-this is a dream, you won't be able to h-h-hear me. Oh dear, I'll sh-shut up now." My stammered words were totally incoherent and I felt another sob rise in my chest.

"Hush, my love, there is no need to cry, rest easy all will be well." Woozily, my brain registered that he called me his 'love', but I couldn't process it.

"You are v-very kind, thank you for c-c-carrying me." Again I felt laughter and the voice, now full of amusement, said it was his pleasure. Whoever this man was, he was holding me close and, without thinking I tucked my head under his chin trying to banish the chill. I was so tired that my thoughts became even more jumbled and I couldn't hold onto what little awareness I did have, so I gave up and let the darkness swallow me.

It was still night when I eventually came round and opened my eyes. The only light was from an oil lamp burning in the far corner of the room. Where was I? The last few hours of my recollection flooded into my head. Honestly, Hannah, how do you manage it? You are not fit to be let loose. I was very comfortable and didn't seem to be suffering from any ill-effects from being in the snow. Cautiously I lifted my head to check my surroundings and realised I was in our bedroom.

My movement caught the attention of someone sitting near me and a familiar voice, deep yet very gentle, spoke making my heart thump.

"You are awake?" I refused to speak, remembering that I was steaming angry with him. "Hannah, my love?" I still did not answer. He took my hand and held it in his, rubbing his thumb over my palm; my breath caught and the tears began again. Oh, you are absolute rubbish, Hannah; so much for being mad at him.

"I'm mad with you," I stuttered miserably. "Why am I here? You obviously don't care what happens to me." I knew my accusation was untrue and that I sounded petulant, but I couldn't help it.

"Now why would you think that?"

"You walked away — you saw I had been hurt and you walked away. You had just been kissing me as though you never wanted to stop and then you turned your back on me and walked away. Have you any idea how that made me feel?" The tears were running freely now and I tried, rather unsuccessfully, to stop the sobs that were building in my throat. Maxentius made an inarticulate sound and pulled me to his chest.

"Oh, my love, I am sorry. I had missed you so much and then when I get home, I find that someone had hurt you while I was away. I was so angry that I couldn't trust myself. I wanted to flatten whoever had done it and thought it better to leave rather than let my anger explode in front of you, who least deserved it."

"You could have said. Why didn't you just say? I thought..." I trailed off.

"What did you think, my Hannah, that it would be easier on me if you returned to Rome? My love, I would never want you to think that." At his words, a glow began to blossom in my heart.

"How did you know that's what I...?" I hesitated, remembering a strange conversation with a giant. "Were you my giant?" He chuckled, such a lovely sound and said that indeed he was. "Oh dear," I muttered, "I...errr..." my voice dried up, not knowing really what to say.

"It was a most interesting conversation." His voice smiled in recollection. "I thought your dress beautiful, but you were right, maybe not the best choice for a stroll in the snow."

"I did think it a trifle odd that someone I didn't know thought it appropriate to call me his love." Giving up and snuggling into his arms, which tightened around me — yes I know I was supposed to be angry with him, but I found being cuddled was preferable. Maxentius kissed the top of my head, then said —

"I couldn't understand why you were so reluctant to tell me how you had been hurt. Then later when all four of you explained what had happened, my only thought was that I had not been here to protect you, that I had let you down."

"Let me down? You could not have prevented it, even if you had been here. That's why I didn't want to tell you; I knew you'd think it was somehow your fault. It happened while I was outside of the fort and I had Petronius with me; even that didn't stop them." I muttered against his chest. "But even after we told you, you made no effort to comfort me. I know that you are the garrison commander, I know that we were sitting with three of your soldiers, but that didn't slow you down when you got off your horse and kissed me in front of all your men. I was kidnapped, Maxentius! I was held for nearly two days and who knows what might have happened if I hadn't escaped!" His arms tightened round me.

"You didn't really give me much of a chance, my love, stalking away in a flaming temper," he said mildly. Conveniently ignoring the fact that he was not completely wrong, I countered —

"Hush, I haven't finished yet." He smiled patiently and let me continue. "Worse, it was done by soldiers from within the fort. I didn't even want to tell you, but Marcus said we had to, because whoever was doing this was targeting you and although you have a right to be upset, a little consideration for me would have been nice."

I twisted in his arms so that I could look at him.

"So there! Stick that on your needles and knit it!" I realised that my last sentence would make no sense to him; it was not in use yet, wouldn't be for centuries but I didn't care. Trying to regain control of my emotions, I continued quietly. "We have always been able to talk, Max, that is part of what makes us so strong; you should have just told me. Whatever the cause of your anger, even if it is something I have done, you need to tell me so that we can talk it through. Remember when you were so upset with me in Pompeii?" I searched his face and he nodded, recalling that particular afternoon. "Once we had talked about it and we each understood the other's worry, it was easier to bear. Your behaviour without explanation left me feeling not only furious, but also hurt; it felt as though I had been cast adrift for no reason that I could think of. You are my husband I have loved you since first I saw you wounded and bleeding. I will always love you, however pig-headed you may occasionally choose to be and because of that you have the power to destroy me — you might remember that."

I gazed at him as I spoke and his eyes never left mine. I put my hand on his chest, feeling his heartbeat and the rise and fall of his chest as he breathed; I could smell his scent, which was far more intoxicating than any exotic ointment or perfume. These were the things that made me feel secure and safe.

I think I must be programmed not to be angry with Maxentius for long because as I stared up at him my breath caught and unable to help myself, I ran my fingers along his jaw, my fury fading. Something about this thought tickled at my memory, but I couldn't hold onto it. Then it was gone as Maxentius leaned down, brushing my lips with his — lightly, gently, like the touch of a dragonfly wing. I shuddered, feeling my heartbeat increase, but tried to ignore it, suspecting that this may not be the most opportune of moments.

"Forgive me, Hannah," he said, "it was never my intent to cause you anguish. Sometimes we men do not think straight when those we love have been in danger. We think with our gut, not our hearts. When you were out in the snow, I realised that it was me who had caused you to go and if anything had happened to y..." I placed my finger on his lips.

"It wasn't you who made me go, Max." He raised an eyebrow. "Well not specifically. I just wanted to clear my head. I was so furious with you and hurt and very confused and I just didn't think. I'm..." whatever else I'd been going to say was lost as my husband's mouth descended on mine with a fervour that took my breath away. I leaned into him, the tumult of emotions that had been rolling around in my head and my heart, coalescing into an all-consuming passion. "Max..." I murmured his name and he lifted his head for a moment, looking down at me, his green eyes darkening.

"Yes, my Hannah."

"I think I may need you to show me how much you love me." He smiled then, his slow, heart-warming smile and did just that.

Chapter Sixteen

Very much later and as we should have done hours before, we started talking about everything that had gone on since Maxentius had left for his meetings. We needed to clear the air, so, as you might imagine our conversation lasted quite some time. Maxentius told me what else he and the other three had discussed the previous night after I had left them to it and I reiterated all I knew, including what the local villagers had said. We knew we needed to be extra careful until the dissent had been subdued and it seemed as though our family was the main target.

Presumably this was aimed at 'persuading' Maxentius to hand over the command of the garrison. He would never do such a thing, so the risks to his person might be more than either of us wished to contemplate. However, if they threatened Luc or me, it might be a different matter and this may have been why they captured me. Bit pointless though, since Maxentius had been away at the time. There did not seem to be much logic or thought behind their behaviour — we would just have to wait it out. I told him about biting the hand of whoever had hit me, which meant they had something concrete to check out, should the need arise.

Mindful of what had happened to me, Maxentius carefully peeled my bandages away, examining my wrists and ankles. The damaged skin was healing rapidly but still looked rather red and sore. Finding some of the balm I had been using, he gently rubbed some over the abrasions and then replaced the bandages; after which he looked at me for a long time, his hands cupping my face and again asking my forgiveness for his crass behaviour. I shook my head and, hoping I didn't sound too trite, said —

"We have both done foolish things today, Max. Instead of calling you back and asking you to explain, I overreacted. Neither of us is blameless. Our love is a precious gift; we should not take it for granted." I took one of his hands and, kissing his palm, placed it on my heart.

Despite our discussions about the incident, I think Maxentius hoped it was all a storm in a teacup, but I knew Marcus, Petronius and Julius were not of the same opinion. As the dawn broke, tired, yet much happier than I expected to be given recent events, we slept.

I was awoken by someone kissing my nose; it was delightful and for a moment I was unsure which world I was in. I opened my eyes, recognising Maxentius' deep forest green ones staring into mine. Smiling, I put my arms around his neck and entwined my fingers into his hair, pulling his head closer to mine.

"Is it time to get up?" I whispered, touching my forehead to his.

"Probably," murmured my husband, his fingers beginning to bewitch my senses, "although I'm sure nobody would mind if we were late for once."

"That's the answer I was hoping for," I replied, and let my body do the talking for the next little while.

It was mid-morning by the time we finally got up, although neither of us appeared in the slightest abashed about having an impromptu lie-in. Once bathed, I dressed in warm clothes, for even though we had fires lit all over the house, it was rather cold. I went to find Luc and minister to his needs while Maxentius went across to the principia to attend to his duties and catch up on anything he had missed while away. The snow lay thickly on the ground and, as I looked out over the compound, I realised how lucky I had been to find my way home. You are absolutely crackers, Hannah, I remonstrated with myself; learn to think before you act.

Senna was with my son and we chatted about our plans for the day. There was no way I could visit the village in this weather, and Senna had some things she wished to attend to. It was rather nice just Luc and me and we spent a happy few hours together. In the early afternoon, while my son was napping under the careful watch of Annant, I crunched across the snow to the hospital to see whether Atius needed me for anything. He asked how I was feeling and I assured him I was fine.

He told me that several of the soldiers had been looking for me, as the guard on the gate had noticed that I had not returned before the snowstorm started. Embarrassed for being the cause of such anxiety, I thanked him for his concern, explaining that I had not realised such bad weather had been imminent. He did demand that he be able to check me over but was satisfied that I was none the worse for the experience. Thankfully, despite being extremely cold and tired by the time I found my way back to the fort, being wrapped in blankets and taken quickly to my bed had ensured I had avoided taking a chill. Silently blessing all concerned, I followed Atius along the main ward.

He had a few patients under his care, none of whom was in any danger, but he was struggling to work out the best treatment for them because they weren't responding as he had hoped. I went with him to check on them and most seemed to be troubled by a chest infection. I told him that I knew of a remedy that might help and, leaving him to his rounds, dashed home to mix up some of the vile-tasting concoction I had taken when I had been so sick in Pompeii. It usually worked quite quickly and, although I knew a chest infection had to run its course, the draft should alleviate their symptoms somewhat. Carrying the flagon back carefully, I handed it over to Atius with instructions for how much to dispense to each sufferer.

Satisfied that I had done my bit, I was about to go, when the medicus suggested that I let him examine my wrists and ankles. Reluctantly, I acquiesced, as I would have preferred to attend to them myself. However, Atius had done the initial treatment, so it was only fair. He pronounced himself pleased and, after smoothing in some more balm, said I no longer required the bandages. Thanking him, I left him to it, saying I'd come back over the next day to see how his patients were doing.

Luc was just waking as I went in and rather than feed him in his bedroom, I decided to take him along to the triclinium. I would be able to lie out on one of the couches and maybe the both of us could chance a nap. The day before had been one of extremes and Maxentius and I had talked until dawn. Neither was there anything else calling for my attention. I tucked Luc against my breast and let him feed, then once he had taken his fill, reclined against the edge of the couch. My body stretched out along the cushion and I wedged Luc between my shoulder and back of the couch, so he couldn't fall. I crooned a lullaby to him, stroking his cheek and rubbing my hand gently up and down his back until he dropped off. Yawning prodigiously, it wasn't long before I joined him.

We were still there when Maxentius finished his duties for the day and came to find us. As he lifted our son out of my embrace cuddling him close, I roused, trying to remember where I was. I gazed up at my husband who was watching me, while Luc tugged at his hair and tried to chew his tunic. I smiled at the pair of them; Luc was the spitting image of Maxentius, something my husband was not yet aware of; probably all to do with a complete lack of any mirror-like item. Once again I wished for a camera. How I would love to capture this picture and keep it forever. People in the twenty-first century do not realise how lucky they are to have the technology that can preserve such an image.

"How was your day?" I asked in low tones, gazing at my husband ridiculously pleased to see him.

"Busy, but everything is complete for now and I have time to relax. Shall we take a walk?"

"Are you sure you trust me?" I grinned, wickedly.

"Hmmm...as I will be with you, I think it will be fine," he chuckled. "It's very cold though, so we will need to wrap up well. Maybe we should leave Luc here, I do not want him to get chilled." I nodded. Senna should be back now and I believed that she would watch over Luc. Maxentius carried our son along to his room. Senna was indeed there and gladly agreed to take care of Luc while we were out.

We changed into clothes designed to keep out the cold and I dragged my heaviest cloak from the cupboard. Securing it with my clasp and then pushing my feet into the sturdy leather boots that were so useful in this weather, I was ready. Maxentius dressed similarly, choosing to wear under his tunic, the light woollen trousers or braccae favoured by the men at this time of year especially when outdoors. We set out. Despite it being very cold, it was a beautiful day. The days were very short now and the sun was beginning to dip towards the horizon, but there was time enough before dusk for a proper walk. Some of the soldiers had cleared the snow from the road, so we wouldn't lose our way; and in any case in daylight the fort was easily seen from every direction.

Maxentius held my hand and we set out at a brisk pace. We had been walking for about half an hour and were just about to turn around when I felt the strangest sensation and tugged at my husband's hand.

"What's wrong, Hannah?"

"Nothing's wrong it's just..."

"Just what?"

"Hard to explain. It's as though I've been here before, that I've spent time here, not just a few moments, but days, weeks, maybe even years."

"Well, we know that's not possible..." As the words left his mouth Maxentius hesitated. Of course it was possible, it just wasn't this me, it was the other me.

"Please, could we just wait for a moment and let it flow around me? Maybe I can work it out." He nodded and we stood together looking out over the winter landscape. I would not have believed that there could be so many shades of white if I hadn't seen them myself; the undulating ground was highlighted in hints of blue, pink, purple and cream. The sky was a very pale blue, but beginning to turn yellow at the horizon and although there were no clouds near us, they were building in the distance, heralding more snow. The usually dark and forbidding forest rose up behind us, blanketed in snow diminishing its menace and all was still. It was so quiet, even the birds had stopped singing, probably huddled in their nests. Yet despite the starkness, it was breathtaking. Unbidden, a phrase popped into my head — it was like Christmas-card land.

"Oh Max, it is so beautiful, so harsh, wild and untamed, yet it feels like home. I don't know whether I ever want to leave this place. I feel more connected to this land than anywhere we have lived. How can that be?"

"Maybe because in your — her, other world, this is where you — she spent much of your — her — life." It seemed as reasonable an explanation as any, and I nodded.

While we were talking, pictures began to unfold in my head. One was of a house, which had two levels and was made of stone with a pitched roof. It had many windows around it, and a beautiful garden encased within a low wall, and the view from the house was the same one we were looking over now. Then it faded, to be replaced by another image. This time it was a much larger building in a style unfamiliar to me, with huge square windows, which seemed to have glass in them — goodness, how did they make it so thin?

She — the other me — was sitting at a table that had the strangest looking box on it; a bit like the flashing boxes she had been attached to at Masada, only very slender, no wider than my fingers. It had words on it, but I couldn't make them out. In front of her was a cushion with a wooden object nestled on it. She was gazing at it in amazement and I recognised my pomegranate. What? No way! How on earth did she have it? I must have made an odd noise, because Maxentius gathered me to him. Memories started to filter through and I felt everything tilt; the image dissolved and for a moment everything went fuzzy. Then my vision cleared and I was relieved to note that I was still standing in the snow.

Taking a deep breath, I waited for the world to right itself, clinging onto my husband as the one solid entity near me. Holding me close, he stroked his large hand gently over my back letting me steady myself, then asked what had happened.

"I found it, I found the pomegranate, the one you carved for me on Masada. It was in an archive box. I was so shocked to find it and didn't know how it came to be here. Then I did a search on the Internet to see whether there was any trace of you, and there was. It was an inscription on stone; soldiers under your command had made something and they wanted to record it, although I have no idea what it was. The reason I feel as though I've been here before is that I have, only not yet. I'll be here in two thousand years, so I think I'm recognising what I know to be here, even though it won't be for centuries.

I spoke too quickly and realised how incomprehensible I sounded, but that's par for the course in my life. Maxentius accepted it without question; such was his understanding of my other world.

"I need to ask you what on the earth an Internet is, but first I want to know how did your pomegranate get there, to her I mean?"

"I have no idea," I grinned at him. "Pretty impressive that it survives so long, don't you think? Someone so far in the future finds something that you carved while we were on Masada and it has travelled from there to Pompeii, survived an eruption, then ended up in the northern wilderness of Britannia." Then I attempted to explain the Internet — I thought that trying to explain television was bad enough — this was a whole other level of confusion. In the end, I told him to just accept that it was a technology that would not exist for hundreds of years and he didn't need to worry about it. That worked.

The afternoon was waning, the temperature dropping and I shivered as we were talking about what I had seen. Maxentius rubbed my shoulders trying to warm me and then suggested we make our way back. He set a brisk pace, the movement getting the heat back into our bodies quickly and soon we were home. Just before we entered the gate, I turned and looked out over the landscape finding comfort in the knowledge that this was something else that bound us.

Chapter Seventeen

Maxentius wanted to check something in his office, saying he'd be home for the evening meal. He swung in through the doors of the principia and I carried on into the residence to find Luc and Senna. They were in the main room; Marcus had joined them and he was playing with Luc. The two of them were sitting on the floor and Marcus was trying to teach my son some kind of clapping game, which looked very complicated. Luc was trying to copy Marcus; his little face scrunched up in concentration and Senna's face was a picture as she watched them.

I lingered quietly in the doorway — they weren't aware of my presence — taking all this in and, again, I had no doubt of Senna's feelings. I knew, however, that Marcus still considered himself too old for her. I pondered over whether I needed to play matchmaker, or stay well out of it. I would ask Maxentius later when we were alone, he would have more of an idea. He was several years older than I was, but I never even thought about it and I assumed Senna would feel the same. As far as I could tell, love had no age barrier.

I tiptoed away, then retraced my steps, coughing as I approached the doorway, giving them every chance to hide anything they did not wish me to see. Marcus carried on playing with Luc. He had moved on from the clapping game to singing a children's ditty, making Luc chortle by pulling the most ridiculous faces while he sang. Luc was laughing so much that tears were streaming down his face and he was hiccuping.

I walked into the room, grinning at the scene. They all turned as I entered and all smiled back. For a split second, it appeared as though they were the family unit and my heart did a strange flutter. An image rose in my mind of Marcus and Senna with children who weren't mine and, all of a sudden I relaxed. I knew that somehow these two would come together and that they would be very happy.

We chatted for a few moments and then I gathered Luc into my arms carrying him away for his feed, saying I'd be back shortly. I hoped the other two would enjoy a few moments of private time and use it to their advantage. Later, after I had sorted out my son and settled him into his cradle, I changed, and then rejoined Marcus and Senna. They were sitting on the largest of the three couches, not quite next to each other, but closer than acquaintances would have been. They jumped apart as I approached, but pretending that I hadn't noticed anything, told them about our walk. Mundane conversation is a great way to distract people and soon we were talking about nothing of any substance, but it was comfortable and easy.

Maxentius joined us and Senna got up to leave us to our meal. I very nearly asked her to stay and eat with us, but decided it was maybe just a bit too soon for that. I thanked her for looking after Luc and asked whether she thought we might be able to get to the village the next day? She considered this for a moment and agreed that it would be possible, as long as it didn't snow again. Then she went on her way.

We had a lovely evening, just the three of us and by tacit agreement kept the conversation on lighter topics. Later, after we had enjoyed more than one goblet of spicy calda, Marcus said his goodnights and went to his rooms. Maxentius and I remained in the triclinium, relaxing in front of the fire, which was still burning merrily. I leaned against my husband, resting my head on his shoulder and he slung his arm around me drawing me to him. The flickering flames were having a soporific effect on me.

"I feel that it is rather late. Do you think we should go to bed?" I murmured. Maxentius smiled and said as far as he was concerned that was the second-best invitation he'd had all day.

"What was the first?" I asked sleepily. He whispered in my ear and I blushed, making him chuckle.

"Sorry, my love, that was too easy. Come on." He pulled me up from the couch and kept his arm around me as we sauntered along to our room. I tried to get undressed, but found my fingers wouldn't do what I wanted them to. So I gave up and slithered onto the bed. Maxentius carefully removed my clothes and somehow got me into my night shift, then tucked the bedcovers over me. He got in beside me, gathering me to his chest and within minutes we were both lost in dreams.

It ended up being several days before Senna and I were able to go back to the village. The snow fell continually over the next forty-eight hours and it would have made travelling difficult and dangerous. There was no way that Maxentius would agree to me leaving the fort in such conditions and for once I was happy not to argue. I assisted Atius at the hospital. The soldiers suffering from the chest infection were almost well enough to be discharged, but one or two others had injuries from sword training. An extra hand was always helpful.

Maxentius and his most trusted soldiers maintained their vigilance, but the cold weather seemed to have dampened any enthusiasm for rebellion and the garrison remained untroubled. Marcus had discussed the situation with some of those soldiers who had accompanied us from Rome. Telling them of their concerns, he had asked them to report any suspicious behaviour. All of them knew us well and had been involved in the search when I had been kidnapped. They professed themselves more than happy to be part of the covert surveillance, which also, unbeknownst to me, included them keeping a special eye on Luc and me, just in case.

It was maybe a week later before, finally, the weather had improved enough for Maxentius to give Senna and me permission to travel to the village. Petronius and Julius would be coming along, as would Atius. His hospital was empty at the moment, a good thing — and he really wanted to meet Breeda. Maxentius had offered to look after his son, as we both felt that it was too cold for him to come with us. I wasn't sure how well this would go, but Maxentius assured me that he would be fine.

The walk took a little longer than usual, as the snow still lay quite thickly on the ground, but it didn't bother us as the chatter back and forth kept us going. Almost as soon as we arrived at the village, Julius and Petronius were dragged away by the children, who were very excited to see them again, clamouring to be taught how to make more toys. I introduced Atius to Bearach and Breeda, and once the headman had greeted and accepted the medicus formally, Breeda invited us into her home where we spent most of the day learning more about traditional remedies.

I had taken some of my salve and, with the help of Senna, explained in halting Brythonic how I made it and what it was used for. Breeda was very interested and most pleased when I told her to keep the jar. We became so absorbed in what we were doing that Petronius had to come and warn us of how late it was getting. I asked Breeda whether she would like to visit the fort and see the hospital. If she was interested, the next time we visited the village, maybe she could return with us and spend the night, making the journey less arduous. Senna talked to her aunt, explaining what I was asking and Breeda nodded excitedly. It was agreed and the five of us set off home.

The weather was closing in again, the wind was gusting quite strongly and the clouds were scudding across the darkening sky. We made it back to the fort before the snow started to fall, but only just. Atius hurried to the hospital and, after thanking Petronius and Julius, Senna and I made our way across the rapidly whitening quadrangle to the residence. I shook the snow from my cloak, hanging it on a hook that someone had fashioned out of a piece of metal and driven into the wall near the main entrance. It would dry there and wouldn't drip onto the lovely rugs on the floor of our bedroom. Senna went to her room, saying that she would watch Luc after I'd fed him.

I looked to see whether Maxentius and Luc were in the house, but there was no sign of them, so I contemplated trying to get over to the principia. Glancing through the shutters, I decided that even though it was mere steps from the house, the snow was coming down so heavily that it was foolish to think of it, so I collected the basket of mending and settled in the main room, knowing that they would come to me eventually. It was maybe another hour before they appeared and I had just finished my task. Luc was fast asleep against my husband's shoulder and, as happened every time I saw them together, my heart swelled. Maxentius was so tall and burly and our son was still very small, yet the gentleness with which my husband cradled Luc was something very few would ever witness.

He grinned as he came in and carefully handed Luc to me. The child stayed asleep and, speaking in low tones, so as not to disturb him, I asked when he had had his last feed.

"Around the eighth hour," Maxentius replied in the same quiet tones. "He ate a whole bowl of what looked like mashed vegetables, after which he helped me work on some reports, supervised some of the soldiers while they trained, then he fell asleep." I giggled at the image his words created. Luc started to wake, then thought better of it, snuggling back against my shoulder, snuffling at his fists. Maxentius smiled and kissed the top of my head saying he was going to freshen up.

I carried Luc along to his bedroom, placing him in his cradle. Then I asked Senna if she would come and get me when he woke, as he hadn't had his last feed. Senna nodded and went back to her weaving, totally preoccupied with the complicated pattern she was evolving with the beautiful threads. I watched her for a few minutes, before going along to the triclinium.

As well as Marcus, Julius and Petronius joined us for the meal, something that was becoming a very pleasant habit. There were things they wished to discuss regarding those soldiers who had been concerning them. In deference to me, they waited until we had eaten and I listened for a while, then Senna came for me and I went to feed Luc. Once he was settled for the night, Senna withdrew to her own rooms and I rejoined the men. They were so caught up in their discussion that they didn't notice my return, so I sat on the edge of their group, sipping warmed, spicy calda and listening to them.

They still had no concrete proof of any dissent among the soldiers, although some of those from Pompeii had mentioned that one or two of those who had been stationed here for some years seemed unhappy about the burgeoning relationship with the local tribes. Apparently, they considered these people to be savages and should be treated as such. They weren't to be trusted and any sign that the garrison were relaxing their position would likely end in us being overrun at the very least and at worst massacred. I felt a cold chill run down my spine at this. Massacre was not a word I liked to hear. Three of us had been far too close to one several years previously and none of us wanted a repeat performance.

Unable to help myself — well you know I can't keep quiet — I asked whether those suggesting that there might be an uprising from the native population had any evidence of rebellious intent. Petronius said that as far as he could tell, it was nothing as much to do with the tribespeople, more that those particular soldiers wanted to be feared, preferring to rule by coercion and intimidation rather than cultivating an amicable relationship with the locals, forged through ongoing mediation, empathy and mutual respect.

"There is a brutality amongst these men," he said, "they do not think their role is to strive towards a long-lasting stability, they wish to crush them." I looked at the faces of the other three sitting around the table, who were nodding in agreement. I was aghast.

"Surely not?" I asked, "Why would they prefer destruction to peace?"

"Because they have been trained to exterminate anyone who stands in the way of the Roman Army. For them, collaboration means impotence," Marcus replied. "Unfortunately many still believe that this is the only way to subjugate nations. Although I accept that Rome wants to expand its empire and that we are holding a frontier which Agricola fought long and hard to secure, the only way we will hold on to it is with continual negotiation and the building up of trust between us and the locals. I suppose that for us here in this room, our time as part of the peacekeeping force in Pompeii proved that there are other methods."

"You can catch more flies with honey than with vinegar," I murmured, this phrase popping into my head unexpectedly. The others looked at me askance. I grimaced, remembering where I was. "I mean, if you are pleasant to people and listen to their concerns and try to deal with them compassionately and respectfully, you will get a better response than if you are cruel." They all nodded and the discussion continued for a while longer. The answer was the same as before; just be aware. Now that some of the antagonists were known, maybe it would be easier to limit their engagement with the locals. I still didn't know who it was I had bitten, and mentioned it now almost as an afterthought.

Julius suddenly snapped his fingers.

" I don't know why I didn't think of it before. There is a soldier called Calidius Balbus who was struggling with his right hand a little while ago. He said he had cut his hand on his dagger. This is such a common thing when it is cold; your hand slips while trying to grip the hilt and accidents happen. I never gave it a second thought. He always seems such a serious soldier, the last person I would think of to get involved with Gratius. Maybe it was him." I thought about it, then said —

"I'm not sure you will be able to tell now; it is many days since I bit him. Although a bite does not leave the same marks as a cut, we have no reason to check his hands. Unless Atius decided to call something like a hygiene inspection; you know, check cleanliness of hands, feet, hair and so on. I know that he does them periodically to make sure all the soldiers are adhering to the health regimen he set them."

Maxentius thought that this might be a good idea and said he would talk to Atius the next day. The four of them carried on talking for a little longer, but I was too tired to concentrate, so just sat back and let their conversation waft over me. I felt safe and protected. These Romans were the most important men in my life and I was so glad they were all here, far from everything that was familiar.

.......oooooOOOooooo.......

Chapter Eighteen

Nearly two thousand years away, although not quite so far in distance, it was day six since the plane crash and Hannah had slept reasonably well. For once, there had been none of the anguished cries and feverish mutterings of the previous nights and no getting up to roam the house. Max decided to let the day unfold, as he had every other day since the accident; let Hannah follow her usual daily routine, then during the evening he would try the next video. He knew that at least one of them was from Masada and he thought he might play that one today.

While Hannah was sitting in her favourite spot on the bench by the front door, Max took the opportunity to contact the aviation authorities, explaining what he needed. He was hoping that they might provide a list of the people on the doomed flight giving him written proof that he had not been on the plane. He accepted that his request was unorthodox, but once he had mentioned that he was supposed to have been on the flight and that his wife had gone into a kind of grief-stricken stupor because she believed him to be dead, he started to get somewhere. The conversation went on for a long time and in the end Max was advised that because of the confidential nature of such documents, the matter would be referred to the manager. A response would be forthcoming within twenty-four hours. That was all Max could do.

After lunch, he persuaded Hannah to go for a walk. He found it strange that she would go with him, for there was no communication between them and no acknowledgement of his existence. Dr Stephenson had said that this was not unusual in such cases and just to keep the conversation going. They walked as far as the museum and then turned for home. They were about five minutes away from the cottage when Hannah stopped and stood with her head on one side as though she were listening to someone. Max glanced around. There was no-one there yet Hannah smiled as though she could hear quite clearly. The hairs went up on the back of his neck and a chill ran down his spine as she murmured something about the pomegranate and the inscription.

Watching her made his stomach clench. She was interacting with someone he couldn't see, yet he knew that in her mind they would be right in front of her, clear as day. He waited quietly, holding her hand, rubbing his thumb over hers, until it seemed as though the discussion had ended, then calmly turned and continued along the path.

Arriving home, he let go of her hand and Hannah went to sit on the huge sofa. He made a hot drink and took it through to her. She accepted it, without words or even seeming to see him. Max sighed and went back into the kitchen to prepare dinner. Cate had left some food and he simply reheated it, laying the table for Hannah and himself, lighting candles as they always did and turning on some classical music.

After dinner, they sat with a glass of wine. Max kept up a flow of chatter, nothing heavy, just things about their families and what they'd been up to. Then he suggested to Hannah that she relax in front of the fire and he'd bring her a cup of tea. She drifted away and it was all Max could do not to shake life back into her. He concentrated on tidying up in the kitchen and then went to join his wife. Turning on the computer, he found the video from Masada and pressed play.

It was from the day they had found the silver pin. Someone, Max thought it was probably Sebastian or maybe Andrew, had videoed almost the whole of the plateau including those working on the excavations. Hannah's face lit up as she watched the other archaeologists bantering with whoever was behind the lens. Geoff pretended to heave a huge Corinthian capital at them, Nate threw an empty finds tray and Hannah blew a kiss and winked while he, Max, jokingly pulled her away. It was all happiness and enthusiasm, the views out across to the Dead Sea, the mosaics. Then later Max was telling the video screen that they'd found a beautiful little pin.

Hannah froze and, concerned that this might not be having the effect he'd hoped for, Max repeated his actions of the night before and sat next to her on the sofa, drawing her into his embrace. Speaking in low tones, he said that they had taken the pin to Geoff who had cleaned it and decided that it was from a cloak. Then, knowing that only Hannah and he knew the origin of the pin, repeated the story that she had told him; that she had used it to hold her mantle closed, that Tobias had pulled it off, and that Maxentius had gifted her a gorgeous clasp to replace it on the birth of their daughter Claudia.

Aware of the risks he was taking by talking about her other world, especially how the pin had been broken, he had to do it — only he would know. Without thinking, he reached for the ruby clasp, which Hannah had placed on the little side table, and pressed it into her hand. His wife gazed down at the beautiful brooch, which sparkled in the firelight, the burnished gold surround glistening.

"This is what binds us, Hannah," Max whispered. "Maxentius gave it to you two thousand years ago and it came back to you, a gift from your grandmother." A quiver ran down her back and she relaxed against him. Max held his breath and willed her to hear his voice, to accept that it was him talking, not her mind playing tricks. Unable to help it, he kissed the back of her neck, then again, as he done the night before, carried her up to bed.

****

I remembered taking a lovely walk through the lanes as far as the museum. Then on the way home, I suddenly realised that I had stopped and was leaning against a wall, talking to Maxentius about the pomegranate and how I had found it in a box. Odd; was I in two worlds at once? That had only happened once before, when we were in Rome, and there my ancient ancestor had also been with us. More disconcerting was that I felt as though Max was with me holding my hand and, although I knew that this couldn't be right, I didn't want it to stop. His hand was so warm and he was rubbing my thumb with his.

Next thing I was watching the television. I don't recall getting home or eating. To be fair, this was not unusual at the moment; the pain in my head seemed to obliterate so much and, owing to the pain I think, I lost whole portions of my day; a bit like a record jumping when it's scratched. The screen was filled with images of Masada. We were all there laughing together and enjoying our days. Suddenly Max was holding me talking about the pin and how we found it and that Maxentius gave me the ruby clasp when Claudia was born. I was holding the clasp and it was glowing in the firelight.

My mind refused to accept that any of this was even remotely possible, but my body ignored it and I felt myself relaxing into his arms. I was almost sure that I felt the touch of his kiss. As I did the night before, I simply welcomed his embrace without questioning it. As also happened the night before, I had the sensation that I was carried up to bed and that Max drew me to him, my back to his chest. Funnily enough my headache, which had been almost blinding earlier in the day, now was barely noticeable. Slumber called and, for the first time in days, without the fear of nightmares.

.......ooooo OOO ooooo.......

The weeks flew by and I spent as many days as possible at the village, weather permitting; accompanied by Atius as often as his duties allowed. We were learning more than we ever expected to and were also able to share much of our own knowledge with the villagers. Breeda did come to the fort and exclaimed in disbelief at the facilities we had in the hospital. To her eyes it was so bright and clean and far removed from anything she had seen. Atius showed her the medical manuscripts and even though she was unable to read the Latin, she could interpret the drawings of many of the plants and minerals.

We had also begun to gather information on plants that were poisonous, either by touch or ingestion. Senna knew many of these as well, growing up in an area where you had to be aware of what you could nibble on and what might kill you. I wanted to know what these plants smelt like and looked like, whether other plants could mask their taste or smell and whether there was an easily obtained antidote.

Atius thought I was rather overzealous about these things, but I had realised that poison would be an easy way to hurt someone. Even if the poisoner didn't intend to kill, a victim could be very sick for many days, leaving them vulnerable. Taking Atius into my confidence, I had explained why we needed to be aware and that there were those within the fort whose behaviour may be detrimental to both soldiers and civilians. I'm sure he believed it was all a result of my overactive imagination, but I would far rather that than miss the warning signs.

I had begun to build up my stock of medicine, ointments balms, potions and salves, concerned that there might be an attack on those loyal to Maxentius from those who supported Gratius, which could end in serious injuries or worse. I had spent long hours talking with Breeda and Bearach and knew that Maxentius had the backing of all the local villagers, and that Gratius would struggle to persuade any of them to join him in a raid on the fort. I knew also that, although some of the garrisons further along the frontier still faced rebellion from a resentful populace, here at Magnis there was a cordiality between the Romans and those they had subjugated. That despite the occasional minor fracas, for the most part, their relationship was stable. Maxentius and his predecessor had worked hard to maintain this goodwill, accepting that neglecting to understand any issues the locals had could lead to bitterness and a resurgence of strife.

Not only was Gratius an angry soldier, but he was also of the belief that the only method of keeping the locals pacified was to rule by brutality and fear. There was nothing we could do at the moment; he hadn't made a move or threatened anything or anyone overtly. Nevertheless, the word had gone out to those soldiers Maxentius had brought with him from Rome. We knew that to a man they were loyal to their commander and could be trusted to be on guard for conflict within the ranks.

Still, there was a sense of disquiet around the fort. What had been a haven and place of security, now felt less so; in fact I felt safer out at the village with Bearach and his tribe. A sort of stalemate was in place, waiting for someone to make the first move. I knew it wouldn't be Maxentius; he would let Gratius show his hand. I just wanted it to be over; however bad it was going to be, the waiting was far worse.

Adding to the mental discomfort were the physical restrictions dealt out by the unpredictable winter weather. As the season wore on, we suffered days of almost constant blizzards, leaving our usual routes blanketed under feet of snow. Once it stopped, the sun would shine, its meagre heat melting the snow quite quickly. This seemed to be a blessing until we realised that it left the tracks and pathways muddy and virtually impassable. Then without warning, the temperature would drop and everything would freeze over, creating an icy and very slippery lake where the mud had been. Despite the fact that the snowy landscape was stunningly beautiful to look at, it made deciding whether to risk going out to the village impossible, and I was confined, to the house for what felt like weeks. I spent hours with Luc and Senna, but even though Luc was now toddling and old enough for me to begin teaching him the basics, he still needed his afternoon sleep and Senna had her own routine. This meant I had periods during the day when, because of the weather, I was virtually a prisoner in my own home. Even after doing all my own chores, I still ended up whiling away my free time sitting in the triclinium just watching the fire. It left me with too many hours to think and, bearing in mind that I had two people in my head, this was not necessarily a good thing.

Eventually, more to relieve my boredom than anything else, I asked Maxentius whether he would teach me how to wield a sword, or even just a pugio, the small dagger that soldiers used as a secondary or back-up weapon. He seemed reluctant, which was possibly something to do with my complete lack of coordination, but did not dismiss my request out of hand. I simply felt that it would be wise to have some way of protecting myself if I were ever out on my own, or if something happened to one of my escorts. Let's face it, this was not without precedent!

During this time, I had recurring dreams about my other life. I saw myself, or rather her, watching television or sitting on a bench looking out over a hauntingly familiar view, even taking walks. I saw Max holding her — me — my dual selves struggling with these images. How could this be? Wasn't he dead? It was so confusing and I couldn't work out which me was in the dreams. Was I back in my other world, or simply summoning up a life I no longer had? I knew I was still bound to the world of ancient Britannia, but I kept feeling a strange pull back to my modern life. It was as though something was trying to persuade me to return, but I couldn't fathom it. I believed my connection broken, my anchor gone, leaving me no reason to do so. I had the vaguest recollection of my ancestor telling me that Max was still with me, but I wasn't sure whether that was as a memory or as a reality. The more I tried to grasp it, the more convoluted it became and it exacerbated the pain in my head, so I gave up.

Chapter Nineteen

Maxentius gave in and did start to teach me the finer points of how to handle a sword. Deciding that the gladius or short sword, was more practical than the pugio to train with, he had one of his men fashion me a wooden one, as these are heavier than the actual weapon. It was deemed that if you were able to fight with the cumbersome wooden swords, you would be twice as effective with the real thing. He taught me to strike and counter-strike, to thrust and deflect, how to anticipate my opponent's move by the swing of his arm or the stance of his body. Whenever I could, he had me train against the same wooden poles that the other soldiers used.

Then, as I became more familiar with the weight of the weapon and how to manipulate it, he asked Petronius, Julius and Marcus to have practice duels with me. Each man fought differently, which gave me a better idea as to what I might face should an actual scuffle ever occur. Maxentius never got involved with these sessions, as he tended to hold back; and even though the other three were careful, there was less emotional entanglement.

Strangely enough, the training methods reminded me of those employed by the gladiators I had known in Pompeii, as they seemed, to me anyway, to be almost identical. Images of the days I had spent at the Gladiators' School kept popping into my head as I was practising and I tried to copy some of the techniques I recalled them using. These moments were bittersweet however, as although I found it helpful, it was a constant reminder that most of them had likely died in the eruption of Vesuvius. I overcame this by thinking that they might be pleased I was trying to emulate their styles.

The more I trained, the more I loved it. The feeling that I was able to swing a weapon with some competence was exhilarating and it gave me a measure of confidence that I had the ability to protect myself — little knowing that I would be very glad of what I had learned in the not too distant future.

Eventually, the weather started to improve and we were able to venture out of the fort into the countryside again. The days were mild and there was a change in the colour of the sky. The cold harsh blue of winter gentled into a softer hue and those trees that had shed their leaves began to sprout forth new growth in shades of some of the brightest greens I had ever seen. The ground was carpeted with flowers in whites and yellows; I had no idea what they were but they were very pretty.

As the snow slowly disappeared from the woodlands between the fort and the village, its place was taken by the most exquisite delicate bell-shaped blue flowers, which blanketed the ground under the trees. Unable to resist their beauty, I collected great handfuls, placing them in little pots around our home and, when I'd filled all the spaces there, the hospital. I had never seen such a colour in nature and could not get enough of them; they seemed to reflect the glorious blue of the sky. Birds began to flit about in a very businesslike fashion, their song filling the air with promise. This precursor to spring was absolutely captivating.

The change in the weather meant I was able to go horse riding again. To my joy, Maxentius and I managed to escape every now and again for long rides, me on Gemmula, of course. Maxentius' mount was a magnificent black stallion named Ajax and my husband was the only person he would tolerate on his back. Those little breaks were marvellous, a way to clear the mind and also get to see much more of the countryside around us than we would have ever done on foot. We got to know all the different ways to and from the fort, some quick and some more convoluted, but no less interesting.

Getting a measure of the land around us was also another way of protecting ourselves. Although the fort had watchtowers and those on guard could see a long way from such high vantage points, there were blind spots and areas hidden from view by copses of trees or low hillocks. The patrols covered a wide area, but there was always the chance that we could be caught unawares, these points of concealment being advantageous for anyone with nefarious intent. Maxentius and Marcus, however, were wise to such possibilities and ensured that those soldiers whom they trusted also learned where danger might lurk.

Luc was growing quickly; now just over one year old. He had finally taken to solid food and only occasionally required sustenance from me, which I'm sure, was more for comfort than anything else. I had been teaching him to talk; well trying, he didn't seem very interested. I couldn't even get him to say 'Mama' or 'Papa' — so different from Claudia who had been managing easy words by the same age. However, Luc could already toddle about, something Claudia had taken much longer to master. He often came with us when we visited the village and I was pretty sure that by the time he did talk he would be bilingual, as all the villagers spoke to him in Brythonic.

Atius and I had resumed our trips to the village as soon as the weather permitted travel and had become very comfortable in the company of Bearach's tribe. We had met some members of the neighbouring tribes too and, so far, all had been nothing other than cordial. I didn't expect any of them to fall all over us in friendship, but I was very happy with the courteous relationship we shared. I think because we were so obviously under the protection of Bearach, they trusted us.

Both Atius and I were also becoming much more fluent in the local language, practising on each other when we were working in the hospital. We had a long way to go and could reduce the villagers to gales of laughter with some of our attempts, but I think they respected the fact that we tried. In return, we helped them with the common Latin that most of the soldiers spoke, which meant that communication became a little easier and confusion or misunderstandings less likely.

The time that Petronius and Julius spent with the children of the village while Atius and I were with Breeda, and our attempts to learn their language and understand their culture, along with the weekly meetings that Maxentius or Marcus held to address any upsets or problems, helped to preserve and maintain our rapport — something that soon would be tested sorely.

Spring took hold and the last of the winter was banished under cloudless blue skies and bright sunshine. Occasionally we had a cold night and the odd morning where frost lay on the ground, but this was rare. The countryside acquired a whole new aspect and I delighted in the plants and herbs that sprang up in the oddest of places. Breeda taught me the properties of those that were useful and how to recognise those to avoid, either because they were of no use or were poisonous.

I continued practising with my wooden gladius and once he felt that I had mastered it, Maxentius presented me with a beautiful iron pugio made by the metalworkers at the fort. It was smaller than the gladius and nestled in a sturdy leather sheath, as Maxentius felt that this was easier for me to conceal beneath my tunic rather than the unwieldy short sword. The handle had intricate swirls carved into it and an 'H' had been fashioned into the top of the blade where it met the tang. It was a splendid piece and I carried it with me whenever I ventured beyond the palisade.

By my reckoning, it was a little more than two months later when discontent began to raise its ugly head again. During the winter months there had been no problems, as though the cold weather cooled the fanaticism of those who wanted to challenge Maxentius' command. One or two of the soldiers had mentioned to Maxentius that they had heard rumours of dissent, and vigilance was tightened. Marcus organised for several more details of soldiers, taken from those who had accompanied us from Rome, to patrol the fort and surrounds. Overtly this was in case of unexpected attack from outlying clans, which was always a possibility, especially from those beyond the boundaries of the local tribes; in reality it was to observe any suspicious activity, which might challenge the safety of those within the fort.

The tension was almost palpable and I escaped to the village as often as possible, although now two soldiers, usually Petronius and Julius, but occasionally others whom I knew from Pompeii always accompanied me. Several weeks passed without anything untoward happening, however and we dared to hope that our fears had been groundless. Then one day, when I was returning to the fort with my usual escorts, the three of us chatting about our long day at the village, a huge and belligerent crowd of men swarmed past us shouting in a strange tongue and uncaring that they were shoving us off the path. Rather surprised, we stopped for a minute and tried to work out what was going on.

They were dressed similarly to the local tribespeople, their clothes quite different from those worn by the soldiers, coarse material and rough footwear, their cloaks covering their heads, which seemed rather odd, as it was not a cold day. They ignored us completely, but their behaviour was peculiar in the extreme and unease tickled at the edge of my consciousness. Something was not right about this, but I couldn't put my finger on it.

"I don't think we should tarry," I muttered to my two companions. "Something is very wrong here." They nodded, and even though I wasn't entirely sure what we could do, disquiet spurred me on. We were nearly home, less than half a mile away and we were almost running by the time we reached the fort. We dashed through the gate into a scene of complete pandemonium. My jaw dropped. The mob that had raced past us was attacking everyone they could see. A warning must have been issued, albeit rather tardily, as soldiers wielding weapons were spilling out of barracks and from workshops, using tried and true military tactics in attempting to subdue their assailants, which appeared to be working. I could hear what sounded like orders being shouted by those leading the throng, but the language was unfamiliar, like a mixture of local dialect and Latin, but not quite. I knew enough of Brythonic to know that they were yelling words that made no sense.

Petronius and Julius had each drawn their sword and had entered the fray, but my only thought was for Maxentius and Luc and, by extension, Marcus and Senna. Despite the fact that I knew my husband and my brother were perfectly capable of handling themselves in a scrap didn't mean I wasn't worried for their safety. I grabbed my dagger from its sheath, which was strapped to my ankle — a very convenient place to conceal a weapon — and ran towards the residence. Our staff was milling about in terror and, as best I could, I calmed them down, telling them to either hide in the storerooms or try to leave the fort through the side gate closest to the house and hide in the forest until it was safe to return. Promising that someone would come and find them when everything was under control, I eventually managed to get them to listen, but it took precious minutes to deal with. I thanked all the gods that we had Annant, who took over and whose composure in the face of their panic did the trick.

I ran through to Luc's bedroom; neither he nor Senna was there. Worried, I hesitated for a moment chewing my lip, trying to decide where Senna would go, probably to the principia to find Marcus or my husband. She would feel safe with them; problem being that if this was what I had started to think it was, the principia would be the last place that offered any safety. Carefully, I made my way through our home checking all the rooms; despite the hubbub going on outside, here all was eerily silent, no-one remained at all. Half of me was thankful, but the other half was fretting over the whereabouts of my son and his guardian. Satisfied that they definitely were not here, I crept cautiously around to the principia, hugging the walls between the two buildings and keeping low so that I couldn't be seen if someone glanced out of one of the windows.

The sounds of fighting were very loud, voices of the soldiers barking orders blending with the raucous yelling of their attackers; it was difficult to distinguish one from the other. It reminded me of the first time I had any awareness of my ancient world while watching the rout of the Romans by the Zealots at Masada. My stomach roiled when I recalled the devastating aftermath of that particular incident. Swallowing on the nausea that threatened, I gripped the dagger and pushed on. Finally, after what seemed like hours, but could not have been more than five minutes, I arrived at the back of the principia.

Pushing open the door, I moved quietly along the passageways to Maxentius' offices, checking every room I passed. Still nobody. Fear was prickling along my spine now; the building was almost a silent as my house. Surely there would be soldiers in here trying to organise a counter-attack, or maybe they had already done so and were putting it into action. I reached the main office; the huge table had been overturned with everything that had been on it strewn across the room — tablets, papyrus, styli, goblets and a flagon of water. All the chairs had been smashed and, to my horror, there appeared to be blood on the floor and walls and still no sign of my son or Senna.

Trying to control my alarm, I followed the corridor along to the main entrance and peeped around the door. The scene in the quadrangle was shambolic, but the garrison's soldiers were gaining the upper hand. Bodies lay across the ground, some of which looked beyond help. Atius would need me, and I was torn between rushing over to help him and continuing the search for Luc. As I deliberated, one of the brigands, a tall, hooded man whose demeanour seemed vaguely familiar, suddenly bellowed an order and his horde of bandits retreated with a rapidity that suggested detailed knowledge of the fort and its surrounds. I frowned as I watched them flee, my niggling supposition solidifying.

Breathing a very ragged sigh of relief, I tucked my dagger back into its sheath and ran across the compound to the hospital, calling for Atius, hoping that he hadn't been hurt. He came along, his tunic covered in blood, but I realised almost immediately that it wasn't his.

"Atius, we will be very busy for many hours, I think. There are many badly injured men outside." He nodded abstractedly and moved towards me, grasping my hands in his.

"Hannah, you need to come with me."

"In a minute. First we need to organise some of the soldiers to carry those who are wounded in here and we should gather everything we will need to treat them." I wasn't concentrating on Atius. I kept glancing outside at the number of men lying on the ground and trying to work out how on earth we could help them all. "We should check each one and treat those with the worst injuries first; some may only have minor wounds and can wait a little." Atius pulled at my hands.

"Hannah, please, you must come with me." Something in his voice arrested me and I stared into his face. He looked very sombre and my heart began to beat far too rapidly.

"Atius, what is it? What aren't you telling me? Luc?" He shook his head and led me through the main ward to one of the rooms at the back of the hospital in a quieter part of the building. There lying on a bed as white as the sheets covering him was Maxentius.

Chapter Twenty

I let out a horrified moan and almost fell into the room, suddenly realising that Marcus was leaning against the wall and, as I glanced at him, saw that he was bleeding also. Unable to think straight, I shot across the room to my husband. He was unconscious and I could see that he had a nasty gash on the side of his head. Atius had staunched the bleeding, shaved and cleaned the damaged area, although he hadn't bandaged it yet. I knew that head wounds could bleed copiously, but it was Maxentius' pallor and shallow breathing that frightened me. Was there something else going on here? Something I couldn't see? For the moment, knowing that everything possible had already been done for my husband, I turned to Marcus and asked him what had happened. He spoke with difficulty; his wounds must be more severe than he was letting on.

"They came in without warning, there must have been at least ten of them and I have no idea how they got past the guards at the entrance to the principia — unless..." Marcus didn't finish that thought. "There was only Maxentius and me in the room; before we could draw our weapons, they were on top of us. One of them swung what looked like an axe at Maxentius and I thought I was going to be run through with at least one sword." I shuddered at the image that rose up in my mind, but I was determined not to let it rattle me; I needed my wits about me. I had healed these two before and I was damned if I was going to lose them now. Turning to the medicus, I said —

"Atius, please ask one of the soldiers to fetch another cot into this room. Marcus can stay here with my husband, it will be easier if they are together." Atius nodded and disappeared.

I grasped Marcus' hand. "It will be all right, Marcus, you shall not die, I do not permit it." I grinned encouragingly at him, drawing a small smile in return. "That's better. Now just a quick question. Did you see Senna at all when the attack was in progress?" Marcus shook his head, then he realised why I was asking him and, if possible, his face blanched even more.

"Senna?" he whispered. "What has happened?"

"I don't know where she is. I assumed that when she heard the attack, she came to find you and Maxentius, but I haven't been able to find them. Don't worry, Marcus, they're probably hiding in the stables or the storerooms." I remembered that I'd told our staff to hide and would need to get someone to tell them it was safe to come out. So much to do.

As I was thinking this, two soldiers came in with a cot, which they placed against the wall opposite to where my husband's bed stood, allowing enough space between the beds for a chair and a small table. I tucked fresh sheets around the comfortable woollen mattress and left the room while Atius helped Marcus to undress and get into bed. I hurried over to the residence and filled a large basket with as many of my ointments, balms, potions and cloths as I could carry. No sign of our staff, I needed to get on to that, or they'd be outside all night.

By the time I returned, Marcus was lying down and I could see several lacerations across his chest and abdomen. Praying that these wounds were not as bad as the ones I'd had to deal with on Masada, I began to examine him. Meticulously, I checked every gash, nick and scratch. I was very relieved to see that they weren't too deep, which begged the question as to the point of the attack. Why would you leave your opponent alive? Something I mused on out loud while I was cleaning the injuries. Marcus agreed.

"There were enough of them to kill both of us, but they didn't. I do not understand it." I could see that the effort of talking was tiring him, so I shushed him and finished my work in silence. Pushing my trusty salve into each wound and then placing a cloth soaked in the same mixture over those that concerned me, I finished up by bandaging everything into place. I glanced at his face as I rinsed my hands noting that his jaw was clenched and his eyes had a pinched look.

"Would you like a little poppy juice, Marcus?" I asked gently. He nodded gratefully, and I poured a few drops into a goblet of water, smiling as he grimaced at the taste.

"Did it taste this awful when last you persuaded me to take it?" he asked through gritted teeth. I grinned and said it must have done but that he'd been too sick to care. Using a damp cloth, I wiped his forehead, pushing his hair back from his face and then held his hand and talked to him for a few minutes while

I watched the opiate take effect. Just before sleep took him, he gripped my hand tightly.

"Please find Senna." And he was out of it. I made sure his breathing was steady and checked his pulse, but all was as it should be.

I moved to my husband. Although Atius had already cleaned the head wound, I wanted to make sure there was nothing lodged deep within that might cause infection. It wasn't that I didn't trust Atius to be thorough, but I had to check for myself. I had seen more times than I cared to count, the result of not being careful enough and there was no way Maxentius was going to be placed at risk. Wrapping a thin piece of cloth around a dowel, I probed the gash, but could see that it was clean. As with Marcus, the damage was not as bad as it could have been, but the area of the injury worried me. Head wounds were notoriously unpredictable and I would have to keep a close eye on Maxentius in case of any swelling.

My hands were trembling as I searched through the basket for my jar of arnica. Mixing a few drops with oil, I massaged it around the wound, taking care not to let it drip into the gash itself. Then I pressed salve into the cut, covering the whole thing with a piece of cloth, and bandaged his head. Mixing four more drops of the arnica into a goblet of water, I lifted Maxentius' head very gently, managing to get most of it into his mouth. I had learned that arnica taken internally was very good for head injuries and as I didn't have access to modern-day scanning equipment and a surgical team, I had to hope this would work.

The room was cool, quiet and dim, which should ensure a peaceful sleep. I checked the rest of Maxentius' body thoroughly to make sure that there were no other injuries but it was only the head wound. Only — it was quite enough thank you very much.

It was hard to drag myself away but I could not in all conscience leave Atius to deal with all the other wounded men. I kissed Maxentius' cheek, whispered that I loved him and left, shutting the door behind me. The main ward of the hospital was full to bursting. There were men everywhere, sitting, leaning or lying. It was chaotic and we had to gain control of the situation. Standing on a conveniently located stool, I put my fingers between my teeth and blew. The piercing whistle had an immediate effect; everyone shut up and looked at me.

"Right you lot, settle down. You will all be treated, but please stop making so much noise. Some of your comrades are seriously injured and we must look after them first. If you can walk, please go to the next ward," I pointed through the door to the adjacent room, "and wait there — quietly. Those who can manage only with help, stay where you are. Anyone who is here just to support a friend and has no injuries at all, please leave. The quadrangle is a mess; it needs to be sorted out. Any bodies need to be dealt with appropriately, so please carry them to the long room at the end of the hospital and lay them on the benches." I took a breath. "Any questions?"

Silence, finally!

"Right then. Please would one of you go and check my staff; they were hiding in the storerooms of our house or had fled to the forest. They need to know that it is safe to return home. Find Annant first, he'll know where they've all gone." One of the soldiers volunteered for that task and, as I thanked him, he shot off. "I also need someone, or maybe several someones, to look for Senna and my son Luc. They are missing." The soldiers gaped at me, as though trying to decide whether I was joking. I shook my head. "No, I do not jest. I have no idea where they are. They weren't in our residence or in the principia. Please check the fort thoroughly and let me know what you do or do not find." My breathing caught as I wound up and I had to force back the tears that threatened, refusing to let these men see me cry.

Just as I was getting down from the chair, Petronius and Julius came into the room. I was so relieved to see that they were unharmed that my legs went wobbly and I had to sit on the stool I had just come down from. They came over asking what was wrong. I told them about Maxentius and Marcus and also about Senna and Luc. Petronius told me that he estimated there to have been about fifty or sixty in the band that sped past us on the track. I couldn't understand how such a large group had managed to get into the fort unnoticed. Something Petronius agreed with when I mentioned it and something he intended to get to the bottom of. Had one of the guards on watch been part of it?

Making a decision I said —

"Petronius, you will have to take charge, I know that's what Maxentius would want; and Julius, you will be his second." I realised that I had no right to promote anyone, but Petronius had taken this responsibility before to great effect and, besides the fact that it was the logical option I wasn't prepared to let someone else assume the mantle of commander. Who knew where that might lead? Julius collected the group of soldiers who had volunteered for the search and they all headed out to look for Senna and Luc, while Petronius went to the principia to begin his new, albeit temporary, role. I left them to it, knowing that everything would be back in order very quickly.

Turning my attention to Atius, we set about categorising the soldiers' injuries into levels of severity. The auxiliaries were a great help, all of us working together as a team and, although it took several hours, we examined and treated all who needed it. None of them was very badly hurt, although a few would need watching. Infection was always a possibility despite our best efforts. To those soldiers who were causing us concern, we dispensed a small draft of poppy juice, ensuring that they got a decent sleep. Once we had dealt with the living, we went to where the dead had been placed.

I assumed that they would be cremated and a small headstone inscribed with pertinent details, but we would worry about that later. We cleaned their bodies and laid them out with dignity and respect, wrapping each one in a shroud, on which I laid a sprig of rosemary. Finally, we were done and could rest and eat. I went back home to check on our staff. They were all back at their respective duties and pressed me for information on what had happened. I told them all I could, which wasn't actually very much, but informed them that both Maxentius and Marcus had been injured and that Senna and Luc were missing.

None of them knew anything and they were all very upset. Annant recalled that he had heard a commotion in the house just before the attack, but when he had gone to find its cause, there was no-one to be seen. A cold finger traced itself down my spine and I faced the fact that my son and his guardian may have been removed forcibly from the fort. It didn't bear thinking about; we would have no idea where to search. Pushing that awful thought aside for the moment, I asked whether I might possibly have some food to take over to the hospital for Atius and myself, as well as something for my two Romans. Then there were all the other wounded men; they would need sustenance also and I wasn't sure what was happening in the main kitchens. If there was anything like soup that would be most welcome and would do for all of us as it would be hearty and filling. Mabina said she was happy to oblige, and patted my arm.

"It'll be all right Hannah, you'll see." I smiled and gave her a quick hug, before going to my bedroom to change. I dumped my blood-spattered clothes into the basket of dirty laundry, indulged in a brief but thorough wash and found a long-sleeved undershift and light woollen tunic to wear. I decided to take my heavy cloak with me, as I knew I would be in for a long night and it was better than a blanket if I had the chance to grab some sleep. I topped up my basket of medicines and made my way back along to the kitchen to see whether the soup was ready. It wasn't, but Mabina told me that someone would bring it over to the hospital for me and that there would be enough for everyone who wanted some. Thanking her again, I headed back to see how Atius was managing.

The medicus looked as tired as I felt and I shooed him off to go and have a rest, telling him there'd be some food coming soon. We would both be needed round the clock for a few days until the worst of the injuries were on the mend. As I was leaving the medicus' office, Petronius came in to let me know that he had done all he could for this night and would be free to sit with Maxentius and Marcus if we needed the extra help. I nearly hugged him.

"Oh, Petronius, if only you knew how much your offer warms my heart," I said, grasping his hand and shaking it up and down. He grinned and added that it was no problem; he would just let his comrades know where he was in case he was required in the next few hours. As he disappeared to do just that, I checked along the ward to make sure all those injured were comfortable, telling them that food would be along shortly. Then I returned to the back room to see how my husband and brother were.

Both he and Marcus slept still, so I merely observed them, trying to determine whether there had been any changes. Maxentius' breathing was rather shallow and his skin was very clammy; so without disturbing him, I gently touched his wrist, relieved to note that his pulse was regular and strong. I repeated my actions with Marcus, whose vital signs were also steady. I thanked all the gods that these two were robust, healthy men, who ate a good diet and exercised daily. I wasn't overly concerned about Marcus; his wounds were relatively superficial and they had cleaned up well. Maxentius was another matter. Even though he seemed stable, I knew that those who suffered serious head injuries could deteriorate without warning, even when seemingly on the mend.

I needed to check whether Maxentius had been conscious at all since he was attacked; I needed to know where my son and Senna were; and I probably needed to eat something. My head whirled with what I felt I should be doing, realising that I was unable to address any of them satisfactorily, my thoughts tangling up on themselves. Giving up any attempt for now, I sat on the chair and prepared myself for a long night.

Chapter Twenty One

A short while later, Petronius knocked quietly on the door and poked his head round.

"Annant has brought you some food, Hannah; would you like me to sit here while you go and eat it?" I shook my head.

"Thank you, Petronius, I will eat it here. I want to try to get these two to eat a little as well, if at all possible. I might need your help though, if you do not mind." He smiled his agreement, coming right into the room with a large bowl of something, which was steaming and smelt delicious.

I devoured a large portion of it, realising that I hadn't eaten properly since my first meal of the day, which was well over twelve hours ago. Then I woke Marcus, who said that if we could help him sit up, he would be able to feed himself. Petronius went to find a smaller bowl and we poured some of the soup into it. My brother was still rather groggy and I knew he was trying to put a brave face on things, but could not prevent a wince as he tried to get comfortable. He tucked into the meal gamely, but even though he managed quite a bit, the effort soon became too much and he couldn't finish it.

Removing the bowl, I gently laid Marcus back down and checked his wounds quickly. There was no sign or smell of infection, so I presumed that it was just the wounds themselves, which were causing discomfort. Not that this was anything to be pleased about, but it was one less worry. Encouraging him to take another draft of the poppy juice, I watched until I could tell that the mixture was into his system. Just as Marcus was about to drop off, he murmured Senna's name. I took his hand and squeezed it.

"They are looking, Marcus; rest easy, they will find them." He tried to smile, but the draft was working its spell and he was asleep almost before I'd finished speaking. I moved my chair over to Maxentius' bed and rested my hand lightly on his forehead. It didn't feel overly hot, but I wanted to check the wound again before I tried to wake him. With infinite care, I unwrapped the bandages and lifted the cloth covering the gash. To my everlasting relief, there was no sign of infection here either. I didn't want to mess with the wound again, so I simply placed a new piece of cloth over it and re-bandaged his head.

I tried to wake my husband, but he was deeply unconscious and, as I didn't want to cause him any more pain, I let him sleep. Hopefully, he would come round naturally and we would have a chance to determine whether there was any underlying damage. I knew that he would have a terrible headache when he woke, so I wanted to see whether we had any remedy on hand to treat it. The arnica would help reduce the shock and trauma of the injury, but I wasn't sure how effective it would be for the pain itself.

Asking Petronius to stay with the two men, I went along to Atius' office where the medicus was enjoying his own meal. He waved me in when I approached and asked me how my two charges were. Once I'd updated him on their condition, I asked him about headaches. I had heard of a plant that was supposed to be highly effective in curing head pain, but I had no idea whether we had any of it here. I recalled that it was grown far from Rome, but that it had been mentioned in the medical manuscripts that Atius had.

Atius nodded excitedly when I mentioned this and, trying to swallow his mouthful quickly, nearly choked in his enthusiasm to tell me what he knew. Apparently the plant was called febrifugia, or fever reducer, and a daily dose of two to three leaves should be sufficient to cure the worst of headaches.

"Please, please tell me we have some in the stores? I begged him. "Whenever Maxentius wakes, he's going to need something for the pain and we don't need that type of ache to mask others that might be related to his injury." Atius smiled triumphantly.

"I have a large pot of the dried leaves, which I brought from Rome. I searched long and hard for a trader from the region where it is grown and he agreed to carry some back for me. The fresh leaves are better, but this way we have a supply that will last." I grinned at his excitement; it was the first time I'd felt like doing so since we'd seen that band of men hurtle past us, however many hours ago that was. That reminded me of Luc, however, and my grin faded. Pushing my anxiety aside, I patted Atius' arm and asked him to have some of this remedy ready so that it could be administered immediately Maxentius woke up.

I walked slowly along the main ward, glad to see that most of the injured soldiers here were enjoying their meal. When I reached the small room at the rear of the building, Petronius said that neither man had roused and I thanked him for his time, suggesting that he might like to go and get some rest himself. He would need all his wits about him the next day, to try to get to the bottom of the attack.

"Have Julius and the others found Luc and Senna yet?" I asked hopefully. Petronius shook his head.

"They are definitely not in the fort; it has been searched thoroughly. Senna either fled with Luc and they are hiding, or we may have to consider the possibility that they were taken." He spoke gently, knowing that I would have already worked this out. Even so, it was not easy to have someone else voice my fears. There was nothing I could do at the moment; it was dark and I had a hospital full of patients who required my attention, not to mention my two Romans. I just couldn't help thinking about my small son and his young guardian in the hands of those ruffians, and it was hard not to give in to my panic.

"I-I..." taking a deep breath, I tried to find the words I needed. Petronius pressed his hand on my arm in a gesture of comfort.

"Do not worry, Hannah, we will find them. Now please, you need to rest. I will watch these two, and Atius knows where you are if he needs you." I doubted that I would be able to sleep, but I knew it was sensible to try. I pushed the chair against the wall and curled up in it, leaning my head against the wooden slats and, pulling my cloak up over my shoulders, shut my eyes.

After a very long night, during which both Atius and I had checked all our patients several times, I finally fell so deeply asleep that when I woke up I was completely disorientated. Daylight was filtering through a shuttered window, but the room was unfamiliar. Where on earth was I? Then the events of the previous day flooded back and I shot out of the chair. Big mistake — I was so stiff from sleeping in such an awkward position that my legs gave way underneath me. My muscles screamed from being all twisted up and it was all I could do not to yell out. Checking to make sure that my actions hadn't disturbed anyone, I stretched my aching body, arching my back and rolling my shoulders. Flexing my hands and hearing my joints pop into place, I started to feel less uncomfortable.

Petronius was no longer in the room, but someone had placed a platter with some bread and fruit on the small table along with a flagon of water. Hoping that this was for me, I fell on it, silently thanking whoever had been thoughtful enough to provide it. In the dim light, I gazed at the two men, who were both still asleep and breathing much more easily than either had done during the night. I had checked them many times, as they had been tossing and turning, and although neither had woken during my ministrations, I was concerned that they might be succumbing to infection. I had been heartened that so far their wounds were clear of poison and I put their restlessness down to shock.

As I was watching them, Marcus woke and smiled sleepily at me. He tried to get up but I shook my head and went over to his bedside.

"Stay there, Marcus," I said quietly, "you need to rest a little longer. Your wounds may need a day or two." I paused for a moment and then asked whether he was hungry. He nodded. "I'll organise something in a minute. His expression asked me what he feared to say. "Nothing yet, but I'm sure they will be found very soon." I infused as much conviction into my voice as I could manage and it seemed to work. Marcus settled back onto his pillow and I went to find him some food. The two main wards were both peaceful; these soldiers still fast asleep. Atius was in his office poring over his manuscripts. He looked up as I approached and motioned me in.

"How are they, Hannah?" I wobbled my hand.

"So, so," I replied. "Maxentius still hasn't come round and both of them had disturbed rest; not enough to tear open their wounds, but enough so that I know they will be feeling very weary. Marcus is awake; I am going to get him some food. Would you like me to bring you something?" Atius thanked me saying he would be most grateful.

I walked out into the sunshine. The morning was cool but already hinting at a warm day ahead, the sky a glorious blue. The quadrangle had been cleared up and anyone just arriving would never know the chaos that had occurred here the previous night. The efficiency of the Roman Army never ceased to amaze me. I traipsed over to the principia, where Petronius was already at his desk. There was no sign of Julius, and Petronius told me that he was still out looking — he would be exhausted. It was now over eighteen hours since the attack on the fort and it was as though Luc and Senna had vanished into thin air. It was all I could do to stop my dread from flattening me. After updating Petronius on Maxentius and Marcus, I left him to his duties and went home.

Making my way to the kitchen to see whether I could scrounge up some food, I saw that all our staff were already there. That would save me having to tell them one by one. I gave them a report on their two bosses and then asked whether I might be able to have enough food for three. I sank into one of the chairs while they bustled about and I could feel the irresistible call of sleep. It was so comfortable here, surrounded by the familiar smells of baking bread and cooked spices, that I closed my eyes for just a minute.

.......oooooOOOooooo.......

I woke to the sound of birds chattering outside the open window. It was another beautiful day and another day without Max, although I dreamed that he was still alive; and that when I felt him near me, it was real and not some hallucination brought on by grief. I was still too afraid to believe, because every time I did the images from the television would swamp me. I was more than a little concerned that I wanted him to be alive so badly that I had conjured him up out of my head and into my life. Maybe I was going mad. Maybe I should be considering some kind of treatment or therapy.

I got up and showered, then dressed in jeans and an emerald green long-sleeved T-shirt. I knew Max liked me in this colour; he said it brought out the green in my eyes. I don't know why this mattered when he wasn't around to see me, but for some reason it did. I wandered downstairs and found that breakfast was already laid out. I remembered that this happened every day — how odd. Was I setting this out before I went to bed? Unable to answer my own question, I simply accepted it, downing a bowl of cereal before taking my mug of hot tea out into the garden and, stretching out on the bench, watched the day unfold.

The sun had begun its journey across the cloudless sky and the air was full of familiar sounds: birds singing, big fat bees buzzing around gathering pollen and I could hear the distant baa-ing of sheep — sounds of the countryside, sounds that wrapped themselves around my senses letting me lose myself in them.

My head hurt this morning, maybe I hadn't slept as well as I thought and I felt rather out of sorts. As I rubbed my forehead in a vain attempt to soothe the pain, I remembered that I'd dreamed about the fort. There'd been an attack and Maxentius was hurt. My heart began to beat rapidly and my agitation increased. This hadn't been a dream; this was happening, now — okay, well not now, nearly two thousand years away, but right here, not far from where I was sitting. I needed to go back and help. Luc! Luc was missing and I heard myself make a distressed sound.

Suddenly, I was aware of movement and someone sat next to me, pulling me into their embrace. I stiffened. Who was this? A quiet voice spoke.

"What is it, Hannah? What's wrong?" It sounded like Max. My head was fuzzy. I knew that this couldn't be right, but he would know what to do. I rubbed my head again; I missed being able to ask for his advice.

"Maxentius has been hurt, Luc has disappeared and there was an attack on the garrison. What do I do?" My voice rose in panic. For goodness sake, Hannah, you're talking to yourself now; seriously, you really do need some help.

Then a reply —

"Do you think you should go back to help them, Hannah?" I nodded, tears forming.

"They need me," I whispered. "I know I can help."

"How?" Such a quiet voice. I wanted to turn and see whether it was really Max, but I daren't, certain that if I did, all I would see was an empty space and that, I could not bear. Pathetic, you are, Hannah, absolutely pathetic!

"I'm not sure, but I feel that I will do more good there than here. Here I am only half alive."

"Will you come back?" The tone of the question sounded as though my answer was really important. I mulled it over for a long time, realising that despite my aching heart, I belonged here and not in Roman Britain. I had to learn to live again.

"Yes, I will come back." My words were scarcely a breath, but I believed that those arms tightened their hold just for a second.

As I was talking, something registered in my brain. Was I actually making a conscious choice to slip between worlds? I had wanted to go back when I thought my life here was over and it seemed as though I was choosing to return to them now. I couldn't remember deciding to come back to this world, but maybe it was that whole thread thing again. Max had been my anchor; it was his love that held me here; he was my connection to this life. Surely if he was dead, there was no link.

The pain in my head increased and I tried rubbing my temples again. I felt a hand take one of mine and I was certain that a thumb began rubbing along my thumb. After a little while, the pain diminished, although did not dissipate entirely. Max used to do this; only he knew that this worked. A useless tear ran down my cheek but, before I could wipe it away, a gentle finger caught it. I shuddered, the confusion in my mind shattering my composure. Darkness circled my vision and just before it took me, I heard a voice say —

"It's okay, Hannah, let go. I love you and I will always be your anchor. I'll be here when you're ready to come home."

And I was gone.

.......ooooo**OOO**ooooo.......

Chapter Twenty Two

I slowly opened my eyes onto a familiar scene. I was in the kitchens and Mabina was shaking my shoulders. I remembered something about an anchor. The word resonated with me, making me feel warm and safe. I knew it meant something, but I couldn't quite recall. Mentally shrugging my shoulders, I stored it away for now.

"Here you are, Hannah, this should keep you going for a while and please tell Atius that we will arrange for the main kitchens to send food over for the other soldiers in an hour or so," Mabina said, pushing a basket full of food into my arms. I smiled wearily and thanked her, apologising for falling asleep in her kitchen. She smiled at me in a motherly way and said it was of no matter. I gathered up the food and said I would let them know if we received any news. I made my way back over to the hospital, trying to push the terror about my missing son and Senna out of my head. I had to carry on and let those who knew the area continue with their search, but it was becoming harder with every passing minute.

Determined not to crumble, I fixed a smile on my face and handed Atius his food. He thanked me and said that he would be doing his rounds again shortly. I said I would accompany him, once I'd given Marcus his meal and eaten a little more myself — I was still rather hungry. The room at the end of the hospital remained cool and dim. Although the shutters could be opened, I decided not to bother just yet; it was better that it not be too bright. Marcus had managed to sit up and I gave him the breads and fruit along with what looked like a mix of cereals and milk. It seemed quite sloppy, but Marcus said it was very tasty. I was happy to let him have it all.

He ate everything I put in front of him, which was a good sign. Once he had finished, I asked him to lay back down while I examined his injuries; cleaning out the old salve and replacing it with fresh, then binding them up. I knew he wanted out, but by the time I had completed my ministrations, his face was white and his jaw clamped.

"Please, Marcus, there's nothing you can do for anyone at this stage. Rest and you will be able to help later if they need you. If you don't do as you're told, I might have to bring maggots into the equation." I winked as I said this and he chuckled weakly, raising his hands in mock surrender.

"Okay, okay, I give in, no maggots, please."

"Do you want some poppy juice?" I asked. He shook his head.

"No, I'd rather manage without if I can." I was happy with his decision; it meant that he was feeling a little less awful. I took his hand and held it between mine for a moment.

"I'm sorry, Marcus, there is no news yet." He gazed at me, the worry clear in his face. "I promise to wake you if you are asleep when they are found." Suddenly, realisation swept over his expression and he tried to sit up.

"Oh, by all the gods, Hannah, it's just dawned on me that you keep saying 'they'. Luc is missing as well?" I pushed him back down on the mattress and nodded unable to speak. "I am sorry, I've been so caught up in my own misery that I hadn't registered that Luc would have been with her. Please forgive my selfishness."

"There is nothing to forgive, Marcus. You love Senna and it is only proper that you worry for her. I will worry for Luc; between us there is enough worry to go around." I paused. "Now, rest, I am sure they will be found soon." He gripped my hand and smiled, settling back on his pillows. By the time I'd moved the chair over to Maxentius, my brother was fast asleep.

I sat for long moments looking at my husband. Then, trying not to disturb him, I lifted each eyelid to see if his pupils would react to the change in light. They did — phew, that was something. I checked his heart rate and his pulse, which were steady and rhythmic. His skin was still clammy, but that was to be expected. I really wanted to check under his bandage again, but needed more light. As the window was quite high in this room, I decided to open the shutter just long enough to do what I needed to; in this way I would not let too much brightness into the room. Standing on the chair, I did just that, the fresh breeze wafting across the space, pushing out the stale air.

Gathering all my things together, I rinsed my fingers in a bowl of clean water and then poured this out, refilling it with fresh water, salt and frankincense. The scent of the spice permeated the room and I felt calmer as I breathed it in. Carefully, I removed the bandage and the piece of cloth soaked in salve. Wiping any residue away with this same piece, I began to rinse the wound. Without thinking I crooned a lullaby, one I used when our children couldn't sleep, which seemed rather counterintuitive as Maxentius was out for the count, but it was soothing me too.

I worked as quickly as possible, but ensured that the wound was completely clean and that there was no sign of infection. I got close enough to take a good sniff and there was no noxious aroma. Applying the salve and arnica again, I put a clean piece of cloth over the gash and bound it in place. I wanted to cry; Maxentius looked so vulnerable, his face pale and gaunt under the white of the bandage and he didn't even know his son was missing. Closing the shutters, I sat back in the chair and held my husband's hand for a little while, watching him. Then I straightened my shoulders and went to help Atius with the other wounded soldiers.

It was hours later before I was able to return to my two Romans. Both still slept, although Petronius, who had popped in to check on things, said that Marcus had been awake for a little while and they had enjoyed a brief chat. It was now well over twenty-four hours since the attack, a very long time for two people, one of whom was a very young child, to be missing. I knew my hands were tied; I would be no use anyway and there were plenty of people involved in the search. Petronius mentioned that they had found some evidence as to who was behind the attack and would I be able to join him over at the principia later. I nodded, confirming that I would be there at the last hour, and went back to my husband.

Sitting on the chair next to the bed, I took hold of his hand again and, smoothing my fingers over it in long, steady strokes, started talking quietly to him. I told him that we needed him to wake up but that Petronius was in charge of the garrison. I refrained from mentioning anything about Luc and Senna, probably not the right thing to say to bring someone out of a coma. I know that hearing is the last thing to go and that people who were deeply unconscious can usually hear conversations. I talked about a letter we had received from his mother filled with everything our children had been doing and that they'd even put their names to it. I mentioned that it would be lovely if they could come and live with us again. I talked and talked, willing him to hear.

Eventually, I had to stop; my throat ached. I leaned back in the chair and closed my eyes, but found I could not let go of Maxentius' hand and continued to hold it, my fingers interlaced with his. I ruminated about the day, thinking that I was quite hungry, as I worked out that I hadn't eaten anything since the first meal; this was becoming a habit. Marcus was still sleeping, but he seemed close to wakefulness, which would give me a chance to check his wounds again. Not doing anything, however, gave me time to think, and that led to dark places, so I dragged myself back into an upright position and glanced at my husband, straight into his deep green eyes.

"Max?" My voice was so quiet it was barely a whisper. I think I stopped breathing actually. I hardly dared believe he had woken.

"You finally say my name." I stared at him, flummoxed.

"Say your name? What do you mean?" Another fear began to circle at the edge of my senses.

"You have been calling Marcus and Sergius by their names for days now. Why not me?" I gaped at him.

"Maxentius, where do you think we are?" Knowing what his answer would be before he said it.

"Masada, of course. Why do you ask?" No, no, no, no, no, this could not be happening. I'd just got him back and he'd lost a huge chunk of his memory. Please let this just be temporary. I replied in as calm a voice as I could muster —

"Oh, my love, there are things I need to tell you, but you have suffered a bad head injury and I'm not sure how much of our conversation you will remember later." He looked at me askance.

"You call me 'my love.' What am I missing here?" He squeezed my hand; his thumb rubbing my palm and my heart ached.

"Are you sure you want to know?" He nodded, then grimaced as pain lanced through his skull. He paled and I grabbed a bowl in case he was going to be sick. He refrained but only just and, telling him I'd be a moment, left the room, hurrying along the ward to find Atius. Asking for the febrifugia, I gabbled something about Maxentius being awake but had problems with his memory and was in severe pain. Atius handed me the pot and explained the dose, saying he'd be along to check shortly. Returning, I mixed the dried leaves into some water and held the goblet so Maxentius could drink it easily.

We sat quietly until I observed the rigid cast of his face relax as the medication started to work. Taking his hand again, I told my husband the very basics, as much as I felt he could handle in order for him to try to process what his memory could not recall: that we had been married for around eleven years; that we had four children, two of whom were my brother's; that we had left Masada and spent time in Pompeii; that we were now on the frontier of northern Britannia; and that his head injury was a result of an attack on the garrison. I left out the bit about Luc; I didn't think he needed any extra worry.

As I finished speaking, I stared at Maxentius, hoping the information wasn't going to have an adverse effect. I was suddenly very shy of this man whom I had known for nearly fifteen years; our whole life together was missing from his mind.

"I should leave; you probably need some time alone. It is a lot to take in. Marcus is here, he will be of help to you when he wakes." I tried to disengage my hand. Maxentius was having none of it, however, and pulled me closer until I was on the edge of the bed. "Be careful, Max, your head..." His free hand went round the back of my neck and, very gently, he drew me down so that his lips brushed mine.

"Seems I was a very wise man and if you are now my wife, surely I am allowed to do this." He smiled a little. My heart thudded and I released a breath I hadn't realised I was holding. I cupped my hand against his cheek, which I was pleased to note, felt quite cool.

"I believe that your memory will probably come back as your head wound heals, but there is the possibility that some things you may never recall. The garrison will trundle along quite well until you are feeling better. There are already soldiers searching out those who attacked us." He started to sit up. "No, Max, you must rest. Your injury is serious and you need to regain your strength before you go gallivanting out after a bunch of rebels."

I could see that even just that movement was painful, despite the febrifugia and he needed to sleep properly. "Petronius is in charge and he looked after the garrison in Pompeii when you had to go to Rome." My words confused him as he tried to search his mind for the memory. "Do not worry, my love, it will come back; please trust me." I was aware that Marcus was stirring in the other bed and I knew I needed to attend to him. Just as I was thinking this, the door opened and Atius came in.

"Hannah, Petronius has asked for your attendance. Do not worry about these two, I will check their injuries and I need to talk to Maxentius." I was loath to leave, but I knew I had to find out what was going on.

"I'll be back as soon as possible," I murmured to my husband, whose lips curved just a little and he dropped a slow wink.

I tidied my things into my basket and pushed it into a corner, I would likely need them later. Thanking Atius and with one last smile at Maxentius, I left quietly. I paused for a moment, leaning against the wall and drawing deep breaths, trying to get my emotions in check. Just don't think, Hannah — I instructed myself — don't even try, just accept and move on.

I walked out of the hospital into the evening sunshine.

Chapter Twenty Three

I walked slowly across to the principia, wishing that I could just go home, go to bed and when I woke up this would all be over and that it was all a very bad dream. Maxentius wouldn't even remember that there were two of us in my head, that the woman from my other world was entwined in our lives and that she was helping me, that she had always helped us. Before I allowed the screaming habdabs to overcome me, I forced my anxiety to the back of my mind. I knew that at some point it would all blurt out, but hopefully by then everything would have returned to normal.

I knocked on the door of the legatus' office and Petronius bid me enter. There were several soldiers standing around the desk, all of whom I recognised. Julius was propping himself up in the corner and looked absolutely exhausted. I smiled at him sympathetically and he grinned wearily in return. The room had been tidied up and all traces of the bloody fight removed; if I hadn't seen it earlier, I would not have believed it had ever happened.

Petronius was explaining that the evidence suggested we had been attacked by a large band of disgruntled tribesmen and some of the soldiers present were all for rushing straight out and taking revenge on the locals. The thought of anyone attacking my friends in the village filled me with dread. I listened while Petronius talked through what they had discovered, yet something still wasn't right. After a little while, when the discussion had moved to what our response was going to be, I asked whether I might speak. Petronius nodded and I, rather hesitantly for me, took the floor.

"While I accept that some may have been local malcontents, I believe that the majority were not." They all looked at me, and one of them demanded to know how on earth I'd come to that conclusion. I clarified: "When they charged past Petronius, Julius and me, their voices were very distinct and their language was not that of the villagers." I held up my hand as another soldier started to question me. "I have been learning this language and I understand it a lot more than I can converse in it. I am able to recognise the cadence and style, even if I cannot grasp the meaning, and the words these men used sounded nonsensical. Also, much was in Latin, almost as though they were mixing the two together. It was no language I have ever heard, and I believe created to fool us into misdirection."

I watched as they mulled this over. Then before they could deny it, continued —

"You men in this room are Maxentius' most trusted soldiers; you have been together for many years. You know that he and Marcus were concerned about the dissent within the fort from a quarter, led by Gratius who believed he should have been placed in charge when Fabricius Habitus retired. I have been on the receiving end of his enmity and I can tell you it was not much fun." Collecting my thoughts, I went on —

"It is my contention that they dressed as tribesmen and attempted to sound as though they were locals in order to destroy the tenuous relationship that has been growing between the garrison and the villagers. You all know that I, along with Atius, Petronius and Julius, have spent many days with them, learning their traditions and being accepted as friends. Maxentius and Marcus have met with them twice a week, every week to help resolve any issue, which may have arisen because of our occupation of their land. All of you here have been patrolling the surrounds to keep everyone safe. If we fall into this trap, we will take revenge on those who least deserve it, while the perpetrators will continue to undermine this garrison. Gratius wants to be the legatus and I think his desire has escalated into a vehement hatred against anyone who stands in his way." I paused again and let this sink in.

"My last point is that if these men had been intent on destruction, more soldiers would have been injured, and I suspect that even though some were killed in this attack, a determined assault would have resulted in many more deaths. Marcus told me that about ten men who could have killed them both easily set upon him and Maxentius, but they did not. I believe that this is because, although Gratius has many in his thrall, most do not wish to murder fellow soldiers. Also very sharp implements like the gladius inflicted these wounds, leaving little dirt in the cuts. This suggests that whoever wielded them cleaned and honed his weapons regularly. This does not sound like a local tribesman, who would likely use an axe or a club or something similar. Moreover, how did they get in here without the guard on watch noticing their approach? We need to know whether any of those soldiers who regularly stand watch are part of this."

I sat down, feeling drained. I hoped I had said enough to convince them; it hurt my heart that they thought Bearach and his men would attack us. I said tiredly —

"I will go to the village and ask them; maybe this would persuade you that they are innocent." I dropped my head into my hands. I was so fatigued that I could barely think straight and still my son hadn't been found. The longer they were missing, the more I feared that the worst must have happened to them. I wanted to cry but found I did not even have the energy for that. The soldiers settled down to what sounded as though it might be a long discussion. I motioned to Petronius that I would leave them to it. He nodded imperceptibly and came over to see me out.

"Please do not let them urge you into something that we will come to regret, Petronius. I know you are an honourable man. Maxentius has woken and, although there are some memory problems, he is still a soldier and your commander. He will be able to provide counsel."

"Trust me, Hannah. I will not act without proper consideration of all the information I have." He patted my shoulder and told me to try to get some rest.

"Chance would be a fine thing, my friend. Atius and I have a hospital full of wounded men, my son and Senna are still missing and my husband has lost some of his memory. I think sleep will elude me for a while yet." A thought pushed itself forward and, although it sounded preposterous in my head, I needed to voice it. "Petronius, if Gratius, or whoever it was who attacked us, took Luc and Senna, do you think that they might try to force Maxentius to do their bidding in exchange for the safe return of his son? Which is rather ironic as he doesn't remember he has one." I tried to smile but failed and a tear rolled down my cheek. I scrubbed it away fiercely. Come on, Hannah, get a grip!

Petronius swore under his breath and confirmed that they had indeed considered this, but had hoped I hadn't.

"I don't think they would hurt a baby, Hannah. If they want Luc for a bargaining chip, there would be no point in harming him."

"I hope you're right. We must keep the issue with Maxentius' memory a secret for now; they do not need any more fuel for their argument." I gripped my friend's hand and left quickly before I burst into tears.

The evening shadows were lengthening, the amber light softening the hard lines of the palisade and watchtowers. I lingered for long moments breathing in the balmy air. Everything was tranquil, in complete contrast to the cacophony in my head. The familiar scents and sounds of my life pervaded the turmoil and I felt calmer.

Unexpectedly, I thought about Max and my other world. My heart told me he was alive, but my brain told me it wasn't possible. I usually followed my heart. Was it time to trust it? I knew, though, that whatever I decided, I had to see this out first — the voice had said he would wait. Maybe I still had my anchor and, even if I didn't, my memories of him would sustain me for a lifetime.

I trudged home, intending to wash and change. I rinsed my hair while I was at it, running sweet oil through it in an attempt to untangle the unruly mop. After combing then tying it back into its usual plait, I dressed in a warm outfit. I would remain at the hospital overnight again. Being alone in this huge house was not a welcoming option at the moment. I went along to the kitchens to give everyone an update. They were pleased that Maxentius had woken and worried about his loss of memory. I assured them that it should only be temporary, dampening down my own fears that he would never recall any of our life together. Finally, I reported that Senna and Luc still had not been located and, before they could commiserate with me over that particular point, I thanked them and fled.

Instead of returning to the hospital straight away, I decided to write to our children and Claudia, Maxentius' mother. They deserved to know what had happened, even if all was well by the time they received it. It took a little time as I didn't want to scare them, but they needed to know the truth. My hand was aching by the time I finished, but I was happy with my effort and sealing it with a blob of wax, detoured by the principia to drop it off with Petronius. The group of soldiers were still talking, so I handed the missive to Petronius and slipped away unnoticed.

As I retraced my steps of earlier in the evening, I tried not to think about anything other than getting Maxentius sorted out. Maybe if I talked to him about our life, something would click and what was missing would drop into place. As I was thinking about this, I remembered the head injury I had sustained in my other life. They had been very worried that I would lose my memory and Max had talked to me all day every day hoping I could hear him, telling me all about our days on Masada.

Out of the blue, I recalled sitting on the floor of a quaint room and listening to someone talk about my life; that voice was Max's too. In fact the more I thought about it, the more I realised he, well, at least the voice, had been doing this for several days. Was he doing it again? Was he talking about my life with him and what he knew of my other life, this life, so I would know, not only what to do, but also that he was actually alive and not just a ghost in my head? Was this what had drawn me to my ancient world? If I could help Maxentius regain his memory would I accept that what was in my heart was true?

Arrgghhh...it was too hard. My head was full of so many things vying for top position. I would just have to deal with them one at a time and see what happened. Right now, the most important problem, at least the one that I had any control over, was my husband's injury — my husband in this world. See, even that sounds ludicrous!

Pushing it all aside, I entered the hospital and found Atius sitting chatting with one of the soldiers. Most looked quite bright and would probably be able to leave within the next day or so. A few were quite listless and two were asleep. These were the two we were most concerned about. They had sustained quite serious wounds and would need monitoring. Atius turned as I walked into the ward and came over to me.

"I think you'll find that Maxentius has fallen back to sleep. I believe, however, that it is a natural sleep, although I did give him a drop of poppy juice in his drink; a settled rest will be better than all the tossing he did last night." I agreed with him and asked after Marcus. "He might well be awake. I've cleaned and rebound his wounds, and I think he'll be able to leave tomorrow as long as he promises to remain on light duty for a few days."

"Like that's going to happen." I grinned. Atius smiled back and asked what news from the meeting. I reported all we had discussed and he supported my opinion that the villagers would not want to upset the entente that had been achieved. "All we can do is hope the soldiers don't get drawn into something that will have dire consequences. Petronius has a sensible head on his shoulders and is not one to act first and think later, which is reassuring. I have no doubt he will want to talk to Maxentius as soon as that is possible."

"Maybe later this evening," replied Atius. "If he pops in, I'll send him along." Thanking the medicus, I continued along the ward, stopping and chatting with those who were awake. I looked over the two who were sleeping, noting their dry skin and erratic breathing. Atius joined me and we conferred, briefly, about their respective conditions. All we could do for now was monitor them and keep checking their wounds. It reminded me of the many times in my life when people I knew were hurt. Masada, Pompeii and now Britannia. Even though I loved being a physician and having the knowledge to heal, it was always hard to watch those you cared about suffer.

I said I'd be back in a little while, and went along to the room where my two Romans were. Marcus was indeed awake and I pulled the chair close to his bedside where we could talk without disturbing Maxentius. I told him everything that had been discussed in the meeting at the principia and Marcus said he hoped Petronius would be over sooner rather than later. Then we moved on to my husband's memory loss. I explained that I thought it might be to do with where he had been hurt and that sometimes the swelling from an injury to the skull could cause temporary loss of certain functions: sometimes memory, sometimes speech, sometimes coordination and so on. I was not cognisant enough with the pathways of the brain to know which area could be affected by what damage, but had to have faith that as the swelling reduced and the wound healed, his memory would come back bit by bit.

We had been talking about this for quite some time when Petronius appeared. I left them to it, going back to check on those two soldiers who had been asleep. Repeating the same actions that I had done on all of them, I washed out the wounds and rubbed in salve, binding a piece of material soaked in the same mixture over every cut, even the very smallest ones. One of them — and with a shock I recognised Livius Atellus, the soldier who had blundered into the stinging plant so many months ago — came round as I was finishing up and asked whether his wounds were really bad. I squeezed his shoulder and informed him in no uncertain terms that he should be back on patrol by the end of the week and that nobody died on my watch. He seemed convinced and was persuaded into a little poppy juice just to give him an undisturbed sleep. I told him I would check up on him again soon, but to call either Atius or me if the pain got worse. By the time I had tucked the sheets back over him, he was fast asleep.

I walked down to Atius' office and we spent a little time discussing the other patients. As we were doing so, I was moved to question what had happened to those of the attackers who were wounded. As far as I was aware, the only men we had in the hospital were the soldiers who had repelled them, and the dead. I recalled seeing several of the so-called bandits on the ground. How on earth did the others get them away so quickly and who was looking after them? We looked at each other, then along the ward and then back to each other, the same thought crossing both of our minds. Had we inadvertently brought some of them in here? Had they somehow shrugged off their disguises and all we had seen were their regular tunics? My heart began to hammer in my chest; we could be in real danger.

"I'm going to talk to Petronius," I muttered. "Do not speak of our fears." Atius inclined his head and I moseyed along the ward nodding a greeting to all who glanced my way, trying to act casually. I took note of those who were not quite as familiar as the others and, with a jolt, I realised that one of them was Calidius Balbus, the soldier whom Julius thought was the one I had bitten.

Oh my!

Chapter Twenty Four

I almost fell into the little room beyond the main ward in my haste to share our suspicions. After making sure that the door was closed, I told Marcus and Petronius what Atius and I had just theorised, adding that Julius thought Calidius might be the soldier I had bitten, that he was now lying wounded in the ward and that if he was sympathetic to Gratius' cause he may have been with the attackers.

We had no proof of Calidius' involvement, but both men accepted that given the speed with which the bandits fled the fort, there was no way they could have carried all their wounded with them. Petronius said he would ask those who cleared up the mess whether they remembered picking up any unusual cloaks or footwear. I checked my ankle to make sure my dagger was in place. The two soldiers gaped at me in astonishment.

"What? Do you think I'm going out there without some form of protection?"

"You have us, Hannah," Petronius noted, quite reasonably.

"I know, but if things get out of hand, you don't need to be worrying about me. I'm quite good with this, you know, and I am really, really angry about what they've done." I spoke in fierce undertones, standing there with my hands on my hips, all five feet and a bit of me; my hair coming out of its plait, my clothes splattered with blood and goodness knows what else. I saw that both men's lips were twitching and from the other bed a deep voice said —

"You know there is no point arguing with her, she will get her way in the end." I spun around, my face lighting up in delight.

"Oh, you are awake. Atius said he thought you would likely sleep the night away." Uncaring that Marcus and Petronius were right there, I went to his side and sinking onto the floor next to the bed, kneeled up to kiss his cheek gently. He turned his head slightly and I caught his lips. "How's the pain?" I asked, unwilling to break the contact.

"Quite bad," he murmured, "but a little less so now you're here." I grinned a ridiculously foolish grin.

"I'll go and get you some more medication; it will help. These two probably want a word with you." I left the room and shot down the ward to Atius, asking for some of his febrifugia again. He asked how Maxentius was and I explained he'd only just woken up, but that he remembered I could be stroppy.

"This is a good thing, yes?" I queried expectantly. Atius smiled.

"It is, yes, but it is early days. Please do not pin all your hopes on this one thing, Hannah. We have to consider all the possibilities and problems.

"I know it's such a small thing, but it's better than nothing, don't you agree?" Atius did agree and came with me to see for himself. By the time we returned, all three men were involved in serious discussion, although, to be fair, Maxentius was mostly only listening. I mixed up the herb and returned to my seat by my husband, holding his head while he swallowed the draft.

"This should help," I said in a hushed voice.

"You being here helps, this is just a bonus." I beamed at him and sat back in the chair, letting the discussion go on around me.

The four men came up with a plan. It wasn't all that brilliant but it was okay, was simple enough to work quickly and required minimal organisation. I was instructed to stay in this room with the door closed. Maxentius obviously couldn't be moved and Marcus was not well enough to be involved, so my job was to guard them. I knew that in reality the four of them thought that they were keeping me out of harm's way, but I was quite happy to fall in with their decision. Atius was told to go back to his office and bar the door until told it was safe to come out. Petronius left through the back door of the hospital to go and round up those soldiers he trusted.

As the three of us who remained waited, Maxentius asked me some more questions about our life. Without overburdening him with information, I outlined what had happened on Masada. Uncertain how much he would recall after another night's sleep, I told him we could go through more the next day. His face no longer seemed quite so drawn and I knew that the febrifugia was working. Not even asking whether he wanted any poppy juice, I suggested he try sipping some calda; he agreed, unknowing that it had the opiate mixed in.

While he was relaxed, I rechecked the wound; it was looking as good as wounds of this nature could look and I cleaned and re-bandaged it with as little fuss as possible. By the time I'd finished, I could see that he was fading, so I held his hand and crooned the lullaby again. He smiled slowly and succumbed to dreamland.

I looked over at Marcus and asked when his wounds had been checked last. Apparently it was not that long ago, so I refrained from examining them again. We chatted desultorily about this and that, until the sounds of a commotion shattered the quiet. Voices raised in anger and the clash of weapons could be heard. My stomach clenched and I stared at Marcus, fear ratcheting through my body, followed almost immediately by a burning fury.

I drew my weapon; it was only a small dagger but no-one was going to hurt these two men, if I had to die preventing them — I know, I'm sure I looked very scary. Marcus started to get up from his cot. I shook my head, placing my finger to my lips.

"Do not make a sound," I whispered. "I do not think anyone will venture along to this room. I do not need either of you in any more battles today, thank you very much." I turned to check Maxentius who, to my relief, hadn't been disturbed so far. The racket continued, but seemed to be abating.

Very quietly, I slipped out of the room and tiptoed along to the main ward. Peering carefully round the doorway, I saw that the room was in turmoil. Beds had been overturned and three soldiers lay on the floor groaning. I recognised two as being part of Maxentius' contingent from Pompeii, and the third was Livius. Making my way over, righting their cots as I did so, I carefully, but with as much haste as possible, helped them back into bed, murmuring that I would return forthwith.

No sign of Atius or Petronius or any of the other soldiers who, until half an hour ago, had been lying in bed. How they had managed to get up and either help or run was beyond me. I carried on to the end of the ward and through the door, along the corridor and out into the quadrangle. All was calm, no sounds of a skirmish, no bodies strewn about.

Puzzled, I rushed across to the principia and through to the main office. Petronius was there looking as though he'd just had a stroll through the park, not been involved in hand-to-hand combat along a hospital ward. I approached him, still gripping my dagger.

"What happened?" I asked. "You look remarkably tidy for someone who's just been in a dust-up." He grinned and said that it had gone very easily. They had caught a large number of the perpetrators, but some had run, which confirmed our suspicions. These men were being pursued by half a centuria — about forty soldiers. Of those soldiers remaining within the garrison, some would guard the prisoners; others were checking the fort itself in case any of the stragglers had secreted themselves within the barracks or stables, hoping to avoid detection until nightfall.

"How many ran?"

"I think eight or ten, not as many as I expected. It is unlikely that those giving chase will stop until they have their quarry. The majority must have fled when the initial retreat was called. I just don't know what their next move will be. If they are out in the countryside they will have no shelter, which means they will most likely return at some point. Of course, we have to accept that many of those involved may well have returned to the fort, behaving in a manner expected of loyal soldiers. There is no way we can know for sure; however I doubt they will risk another attack just yet. Then it will be simply a matter of rounding them up."

He paused, then added, his grin widening, "I think it's safe for you to sheath your dagger now, Hannah." I looked down at my hand and grinned back, doing as he had bid.

"What will the punishment be for those who mutinied?"

"Worst case — death. All soldiers charged with mutiny are liable to be executed or we could impose decimation." I stared at him in horror.

"No! Surely not? That is very extreme."

"Hannah, these men have attacked the fort, have injured, some fatally, several of my — well Maxentius' — soldiers, and have potentially kidnapped the legatus' son and his son's guardian; not to mention the fact that they had previously taken you captive and had left you bound in the stables. I have no idea what they intended to do with you; it is a good job you escaped." I sighed, realising that he was right. Just because we were so far from Rome did not mean the same rules didn't apply.

Death by decimation was horrible. All to be punished were organised into groups of ten, one of which was drawn at random. The soldier whose name was drawn was stoned or clubbed to death by the remaining nine. The rest, while still liable for execution, were then made to camp outside the protection of the fort and had to survive on raw barley — rather than their regular, far more varied diet — for a number of days. This sentence was carried out immediately, regardless of rank, reputation or level of involvement of any soldier found guilty of the offence.

The idea that you could be forced to kill a comrade was abhorrent to me and I hoped that Maxentius would be merciful. I could not believe that he would choose to execute these soldiers despite their heinous acts.

"Will they not realise that as soon as they return, you will arrest them?" I asked curiously. "Why would they risk that?"

"If Gratius believes that their ruse has been successful and that those who have just fled are caught before they can rejoin the rest of the mutineers and warn them, he may think it safe to return during the night. He will assume that we suspect the native tribespeople, not our own soldiers, and that he and his co-conspirators can resume their regular duties, to all intents and purposes assisting us in the search for the perpetrators of the initial raid." He paused, then continued in thoughtful tones —

"Although, surely, Gratius would realise that those we have caught would be recognised as our soldiers rather than villagers." He drew a tired breath. "I find Gratius' strategy to be convoluted in the extreme; there is no logic behind his actions. I just want it over with, so we can get back to normal." I went round the desk and rested my hand on the arm.

"I know this must be an awful thing to deal with, Petronius, but you are doing a sterling job. I am so proud of you and I know Maxentius will be too. I think you might feel better — we all might feel better — if we got a decent night's sleep," knowing this to be an improbable luxury. The young soldier nodded abstractedly and I said I'd be over at the hospital if he needed me. By the time I'd reached the door, he was immersed in his work.

I hurried back over to the hospital. It was dark now. Atius had returned, as had a few soldiers, and they were helping to put the ward back in order. Saying that I'd be back to assist momentarily, I went along to the room at the rear and entered quietly. Maxentius was still asleep, for which I was truly thankful. Marcus was sitting up looking rather agitated.

"What's wrong, Marcus?"

"What's happening? No-one's been to tell us and you have been gone ages. I was starting to worry."

"Oh, I'm so sorry, my brother, I went to find Petronius. It seems they have caught some and are chasing others. The majority probably escaped when the initial retreat was called and Petronius believes that they may try to return under cover of darkness, not expecting us to have figured out their plans." Marcus nodded in agreement. I tried to change the subject. "How are you feeling?" I asked. "Are you still in pain?" He shook his head.

"Not too much, I'm sure I'll be up and about tomorrow." I stared at him, my eyebrows raised and he smiled rather sheepishly. " Well, maybe the next day." I chuckled.

"I do admire your persistence, Marcus, but you need to rest. I need you healthy, not causing me more problems because you are too stubborn to listen." Then I told him it was time to inspect his wounds, which to be fair were healing very nicely. Re-bandaging them, I offered him some calda, which he accepted. Marcus nodded off almost instantly. Even accepting that the few drops of poppy juice I had added to the flagon earlier had something to do with it, the speed with which he fell asleep confirmed my suspicion that he wasn't quite ready for active duty just yet.

Checking my husband's vital signs, which were steady and strong, I left the two men sleeping and went to see whether Atius needed my help. The medicus and his assistants had tidied up the ward and all the beds were back in their neat rows. It was very late now and I hoped the rest of the night would be peaceful. Each face of all those present was etched with exhaustion, and I knew I looked like a wreck. Between us, we made sure that the three soldiers who had been tipped out of their beds were settled and had not sustained any further injuries.

As we were finishing up, several more, who must have left their cots to assist in the chase, came in and were persuaded back to bed, even if it was just for this night. I was relieved to note that their wounds had not been opened up by their enthusiasm to hunt down the mutineers, but they accepted our ministrations gratefully. Another hour went by and all was quiet. The soldiers were asleep; the room in darkness save for two oil lamps. Atius said he would take a nap in his office and I went back to my two Romans. As I had done the previous night, I curled up on the chair, covered myself with my cloak and leaned my head against the wall letting slumber claim me.

Chapter Twenty Five

I jolted awake sometime around dawn. Unsure what had woken me, my eyes roved over the two men who slept peacefully still. I listened, there was no sound, but I was wide-awake now. Quietly, I left the room and walked through the hospital, checking the ward and the side rooms. Nothing untoward — Atius was snoring gently in his chair, his head resting on the desk. I glanced around but all was as it should be.

Ambling over to my home, I went along to the kitchens, knowing someone would already be up and preparing the day's meals. Mabina was bustling around and I could smell fresh bread. I greeted her and asked how she and the other staff were doing. She told me not to worry about them, they were all fine and to look after myself. I gave her the latest on Maxentius and Marcus, but that there was still no news about Luc and Senna. She enfolded me in a huge hug, and for a moment I rested my head on her shoulder and enjoyed the comfort her embrace offered.

Determined not to cry, I disengaged myself gently and thanked her for her kindness. Asking whether I might take some of the hot water from the huge bucket hanging over the fire, I left her to her preparations and went to wash and change. Using the private bath, rather than just the stone sink that Maxentius had built in an alcove in our bedroom, I poured the hot water in, adding some cold to make the temperature more acceptable. Then lathering up a sea sponge with my mixture of oil, lavender and salt, proceeded to scrub myself clean.

The scent of the lavender soothed me and I felt some of my stress washing away with the water. I refilled the bath and washed my hair, removing all the dust and other questionable things from it. By the time I had finished my ablutions, I felt much more able to face the world. I rubbed a little sweet oil over my skin and through my hair; then, wrapped in a drying cloth, went to get dressed.

My home seemed abandoned at the moment. No sounds from next door to our bedroom where a small baby played. No sounds of Maxentius getting up and preparing for his day. I couldn't even hear the staff moving around attending to their duties. I roamed around the room, running my fingers over the surfaces, touching familiar items. I picked up each likeness of the three of our other children and kissed them; half of me wishing they were here; the other half glad that neither one of them was witness to such bloodshed. Dressing in a light blue shift under a darker blue tunic, cinched neatly at the waist, I shoved my feet into a pair of leather sandals and went back to the kitchen.

Mabina had laid a platter for me full of breads, cheese and fruit. It was delicious and I savoured every mouthful. I drank a cup of the hot sweet drink she regularly made. I have no idea what it was but it was like nectar. Wiping the last of the cheese with a piece of bread, I smiled in contentment.

"Thank you, Mabina, you are an angel." She waved aside my comments and hustled me out of the room, muttering something about young women always getting under people's feet. I did not imagine, however, the quick squeeze of my hand or her quiet chuckle as she did so. I grinned at her then left, rushing back over to the hospital, feeling somewhat restored. Petronius and Julius knew where to find me if I was needed. Atius was nowhere to be seen, so I hoped he'd taken advantage of a little peace and gone to get a proper rest and some food.

I checked all the soldiers still in the ward; all but the three who'd been tipped out of their cots the previous night would be able to leave today. These other three bore watching a little longer, one of whom was still very lethargic. I examined them thoroughly but was gratified that there was no sign of infection. Washing, applying salve and redressing the wounds, I told them that food would be brought to them shortly and to shout if they needed me.

I made my way back to the room where Marcus and Maxentius were, to find them both awake and chatting.

"Well, this is a rather lovely surprise. How are you feeling?" I glanced at them both as I spoke, taking in everything they thought they could hide. Marcus still looked wan and moved with difficulty; Maxentius' face had a greyish pallor, his eyes were hooded and his jaw clenched. "You two think you can pull the wool over my eyes?" They looked at me in confusion, and again I remembered, sadly, that Maxentius could not recall anything about my other life and that even though Marcus did, this colloquialism was beyond him. "Sorry, I mean you are trying to hide the fact that you're both still in pain."

Refusing to acknowledge that I was right, Marcus said he was sure he'd be fine, if I would just tell Atius I was happy for him to leave.

"But I'm not, Marcus, not until I'm satisfied you are able to move without wincing in discomfort." He got up from the bed with a flourish and might have convinced me had I not been watching his face very closely. His forehead furrowed and the pulse along his jawline was beating too rapidly. "Sit back down, you lump," I grumbled at him, "you are not going anywhere unless it's to your own quarters." As I spoke, I pondered on whether that might be better for both of them. Familiar and comfortable surroundings, quiet, calm building. Not even any children to disturb them. My heart clenched as I realised this and for the thousandth time worried about the wellbeing of my son.

I bowed my head, fighting back useless tears. I would not cry. Biting my lip, I forced them back, blinking quickly before lifting my head again. Maxentius looked at me questioningly, but I shook my head imperceptibly. I couldn't tell him, not yet, it wasn't fair.

"May I check your wound, my love?" I asked my husband. He agreed and I carefully unwrapped the bandages. With gentle fingers I wiped away the salve and cleaned the wound thoroughly. I was gratified to see that it was starting to heal. There was no sign of necrosis or infection and the edges of the wound were a healthy colour, which was more than I could say for my husband's face which, if anything, went greyer. As I expected, just as I finished reapplying ointment to the inside of the gash and arnica to the skin surrounding it, Maxentius was very sick. I had a bowl handy and held it for him, then without any fuss removed it and washed his face, giving him a goblet of water to rinse his mouth.

Before I bound the wound, I took the time to wipe a wet cloth over his hair, rinsing out the rest of the dried blood which was matted into what remained of his silky black locks. Such a small thing but I knew it would make him feel less grimy. Then I bound his head with clean bandages. Dipping another piece of cloth into a bowl of fresh water and squeezing out the excess, I calmly wiped his face, neck and arms, talking to him all the while, distracting him from what I was doing. Before he had time to feel uncomfortable, it was over and the sheets were tucked back around him.

I carried all the dirty bandages and bowls to the domestic area at the side of the hospital where everything was washed and made ready for the next time it was required. It was a large, airy room with huge racks for drying sheets and blankets. A large fireplace had a bucket of hot water bubbling over the crackling flames and I scooped some out to wash my bowls and some more for my cloths, which I'd dumped in another bucket. Leaving everything to soak. I did a quick check along the main ward before returning to my two Romans. I was struggling to remember how long it was since the fort was attacked; my days had merged into one long one. I thought it was probably three, but I wasn't certain.

Exhaustion and fear were my constant companions and I felt as though their combined weight was crushing me slowly. Shaking my head to try to clear the fuzziness caused by lack of sleep, I told myself to get a grip, and opened the door to the back room. In my absence, someone had brought each of them a platter of food and Marcus was tucking in with a healthy appetite. Maxentius, however, did not look in the slightest bit interested in his.

"Do you want to try something?" I asked in undertones. He looked at me, agony clear in his eyes. "Would you rather I get you something for the pain?"

"Yes, please." he muttered through gritted teeth. I ran my hand along his arm and went to find Atius. The medicus was chatting with one of the soldiers and readily told me where to find his jar of febrifugia. Locating it, I hurried back to my husband and administered the required dose, making a note to repeat it within three hours. We needed to control the pain or he wouldn't get a proper rest.

Once he'd taken the remedy, I encouraged him to take a sip of the opiate-infused calda. I sat next to him, holding his hand and quietly singing another lullaby. His eyes started to glaze over and within minutes he was out for the count. Marcus had finished his meal by this time, so I removed his platter, and on the way back swung into the ward to ask Atius whether he thought Marcus might be able to move to his own quarters. Atius was not against my suggestion, but asked that we leave it until the end of the day just to be on the safe side. I nodded and returned to tell Marcus of his decision.

"I need to go and see how else I might help, Marcus," I said. "Is there anything you want?"

"Only news about Senna and Luc," he murmured. I smiled sadly and assured him he would be the first to know. Then leaving him to rest went out of the hospital into the bright morning sunlight.

Going across to the residence, I checked through Marcus' rooms making sure everything was clean and tidy should he be able to come home that night. Then I moved to our bedroom where I scrubbed everything within an inch of its life and changed all the bedding, hoping that Atius might let me nurse my husband here rather than over at the hospital.

Once I could do no more there, I walked over to the principia where I found Petronius already hard at work. He looked up as I knocked on the office door and invited me in. I sat for a few minutes and updated him on the condition of his two bosses. Then he told me that the reason the watch hadn't sounded an alarm was because the group had arrived at the gate in an orderly fashion, stating that they were a deputation from an outlying village, come to meet with Maxentius.

A small contingent had been escorted to the principia, the remainder waiting in the quadrangle. Up until this point they had behaved politely and there had been no perception of threat or danger. Petronius said that they must have had some kind of signal, upon which everything went pear-shaped — my words not his! I was astounded at the lengths Gratius had gone to carry out his attack, it was at once shrewd yet completely half-baked. Why he would imagine that a garrison of over five hundred soldiers and auxiliaries would simply sit back and allow a gang of rather crudely organised men to attack and then assume control of the fort was beyond me. I shook my head at the insanity of it all and brought my mind back to the question I'd wanted to ask.

"Do you wish me to go to the village today?" I asked him. He shook his head.

"No, it is not necessary, Hannah; Julius has gone with Annant. They want to apprise Bearach of what has happened and find out whether they have heard anything of Senna and Luc. I have also asked Julius to mention that we fear a small number of soldiers are the perpetrators and not to believe anything they are told unless it comes from Julius, you or me." I smiled at him, relieved at this piece of information. It meant that the villagers would know that we didn't hold them responsible in any way.

Thanking him and saying that I'd be over at the hospital, I took my leave. Even though I was desperate for information, any information, I also accepted that Petronius had to consider the danger to any soldier leaving the protection of the fort. While Gratius and his band of merry warriors were abroad, another ambush was still a possibility and Petronius would not risk the security of the fort for two people, regardless of who they were. After last night's round up of renegades, he was somewhat less concerned, instructing a moderately large contingent of soldiers to travel with Julius and Annant and to patrol the area at the same time.

Much later, I was sitting with Maxentius and Marcus. The former was still asleep, but Marcus and I were chatting about this and that. He was telling me that once Senna had been found, he was going to ask her whether she would be interested in marriage to a crusty old soldier.

"You are neither crusty nor old, Marcus," I admonished him gently, "Senna would be lucky to have you, and I do not think for one second that she would turn you down. Although how would this play out with army regulations?"

"I am coming to the end of my agreed term. I know many soldiers marry, especially on the frontiers, but I also know that, regardless, Senna may not be recognised as a Roman citizen. I am thinking, however, that I may prefer to remain in Britannia anyway. I rather like it here; it has a favourable climate and although there are risks living on the frontier, there are risks everywhere. Nor do I wish to take Senna away from her family." While he was talking, a smile played across his features and his eyes seemed to glow with an inner light.

"Oh dear, Marcus," I said, "I fear you are completely and irrevocably in love." He grinned a little self-consciously and said that as long as she felt the same, he didn't care. I was very happy for him, a happiness only tempered by the fact that we still had no idea where Senna was.

The day moved on and I spent most of it with my husband and brother. I did assist Atius with those few soldiers, who still needed attention, including Livius, but the medicus had the situation under control and it was reassuring to know that the worst had passed. Atius came to check on both my Romans and stated that as long as Maxentius would agree to be carried over to our house, both men could be removed there at the end of the day. Evening was falling and both Maxentius and Marcus had just stirred when we heard a flurry of footsteps along the corridor.

Anxiety gnawed at me and I quietly slid my dagger out, hiding it within the folds of my tunic. The door opened and Julius stuck his head round, his face a study in excitement. I relaxed and, replacing the blade in its sheath, motioned to him to come in. In hushed tones, I asked what was wrong.

"Nothing's wrong, Hannah, everything is right." He was fairly bursting. I asked him to speak as quietly as he could and, although I could see it was a strain, he managed. "They've been found, Hannah! They've been found!" I stared at him, my jaw dropping. I couldn't take it in.

"You mean, L..." I stammered, my voice trailing away, unwilling to say what I thought he meant in case I had misunderstood him. He nodded.

"Yes, they are with Breeda. Senna heard the furore and hid in one of the storerooms, then when she thought it was clear, ran out by the side gate and through the forest to the village. She wasn't coming back until you or I or Petronius told her it was safe to do so." My head was whirling.

"Please tell me they are both unhurt," I whispered. "Please tell me our son is unhurt." I sensed my husband's shocked gaze as I spoke, but I didn't dare look at him. My control was slipping and I needed Julius to say the words I was desperate to hear.

"They are both fine. All the women were spoiling Luc; they are out of danger there. Have no fear, Hannah." I tried to thank him, but my mouth refused to form the words. I knew I was crying but could not stop the tears. My vision blurred, there was a roaring in my ears and I felt the world start to spin as all the strain of the last few days finally overwhelmed me. I tried to stand, but my legs gave way and the last thing I heard was my husband's voice.

"Hannah, Hannah, Hannah!"

.......oooooOOOooooo.......

Chapter Twenty Six

I was running along a dark tunnel. Voices were calling to me, but they echoed off the walls and I couldn't tell where they were coming from.

"I'm coming, I'm coming," I kept saying, but they just kept calling. Disembodied faces from both my worlds appeared, like wraiths, but dissolved before I could reach them. The tunnel was so long that the pinprick of light in the distance didn't seem to be getting any bigger. I was too tired and it was too far. I sank onto the ground and put my hands over my ears. "Please leave me alone, please. I can't find you, I can't find you." I was sobbing brokenly, my words lost in the depths of the tunnel.

"Hannah, Hannah, my love, it's okay, I'm here. I've got you." The voice — male — rippled around me like a summer breeze — familiar and very dear. I was afraid to open my eyes. In one world my husband was injured and didn't remember much about me; in the other I thought him to be dead. Great options there, Hannah.

I seemed to be sitting on something very comfortable and I realised that whoever was speaking was also holding me; I could feel the strength in this arms. This wasn't much help either — both of my husbands were tall, strong, athletically built men. Oh my, I groaned inwardly, listen to yourself, Hannah, 'both my husbands' indeed! You're a loon! The voice was speaking again.

"It's okay to open your eyes, Sunshine." I froze. Only one person in the whole world called me 'Sunshine.' I was wary now. Was I imagining this? Was I dreaming or was he really, truly alive and calling me home? I heard myself moan.

"No, no," I stuttered. "If I do and you're not real, I'll..." my voice dried up. I couldn't say it.

"I'm real, Hannah. Please wake up. I need you to wake up." As fearful as I was, I knew I had to. Even if there was no-one there, I had to open my eyes. If he wasn't alive, I had to face it and somehow get my life back together. I recalled a conversation about my coming home and him telling me he would always be my anchor. I remembered thinking that I had to trust my heart.

The voice continued, calm and soothing. His voice always soothed me.

"I know you think I died in that plane crash, but I didn't. I got an earlier flight. I was coming up the path as you saw the report on the news. I found you on the floor of the kitchen." His words I recalled hearing them before but I had lost faith in my senses. Why should it be any different now?

He was still speaking and I tried to concentrate.

"It has been a week since that day and I know you retreated to your ancient world. I know you can't bring yourself to accept that I'm here, but I have something that may help you believe." The voice paused and a cool round object was placed into my hands.

My fingers ran over its surface. At first I thought it was a cricket ball. Confused I tried to work out why on earth a cricket ball would help. It was carved, one half was smooth, one half covered in tiny bumps and immediately I knew what it was. My breath caught and I spoke, my own voice barely a murmur —

"It's my pomegranate." Now I had no choice. The only person who knew what this meant to me was Max. How had he got hold of it? As if anticipating my thoughts, he spoke again.

"I asked Nate to speak to the museum. The curator agreed that I could borrow it in order to help you. I have to take it back tomorrow." He paused. "I also have the copy of the inscription, the one about Maxentius."

It was the moment of truth. I had to risk it. My heart in my mouth, I opened my eyes.

Straight into a pair of green ones, dark as a forest and so deep I felt I might drown in their emerald depths.

"Hannah, my only love." I just stared, drinking in his face. Lifting my free hand I touched his cheek. It felt firm. I didn't think this was a ghost. At least if it was, it was a really, really good one.

"Are you real?" The face moved ever so slightly and the lips kissed my palm. I shuddered.

"Trust your heart, Hannah." My own thoughts came back in his words. I leaned further back to get a better look. He seemed solid; I couldn't see through him. He slipped his hand over mine and, curling them together, held both to his chest. I could feel his heartbeat through his shirt. I was pretty sure ghosts didn't have hearts. Still concerned that I had wanted him to be alive so badly that I'd actually managed to manifest his image, I didn't move. Speech was beyond me. I waited.

"Hannah, sweetheart, may I kiss you?" Tenderly asked. I nodded, biting my lips to stop them from trembling. Please let this be real. I felt his lips brush mine. The barest hint of a kiss. A pleasurable quiver ran along my spine. Even now I held back. My heart was thudding and I felt a little faint. I heard the rustle of paper.

"Just one more thing, love. I think this might convince you." A sheet was thrust over the top of the pomegranate still resting in my other hand. I didn't want to break eye contact, fearful that if I looked back he would be gone, vanishing into memory.

"Don't let go," I whispered, searching his face. He squeezed my hand.

"Promise."

I glanced down at the sheet in my hand. The room was shadowy. The only light came from a lamp on the table at the end of the sofa, and I struggled to focus on the words. It was very official looking, stamped all over with 'confidential' and other strange markings. It took me a few moments to realise that it was a printout of a passenger list for a flight. I looked at the flight number; it was the one Max should have been on. The words seemed muddled and my breathing went funny. I drew several deep breaths and slowly, as my vision cleared, was able to see the list. Seventeen names, I read every single one — twice — and not one of them was Max's. I gripped the pomegranate and raised my head. Back to those beautiful eyes that still watched me.

"You're not on the list."

"No, I'm not on the list." He lifted the sheet out of my hand and placed it on the table in front of us. Then he removed the pomegranate and laid it gently in its box, which sat next to the paper. Taking both of my hands in his and said, "Now do you trust your heart?" I nodded, still incapable of speech. The tears that I had been holding back, in this world at least, since the day of the crash, began to cascade down my cheeks, sobs catching at the back of my throat. I didn't want to cry, but I didn't think I had anything left to stem the flood. Max murmured, "It's okay, Hannah, let it go." He pulled me to him, enveloping me in his embrace, running his hands through my hair and down my back. The dam broke.

I have no clue how long I cried, but I suspect it was rather a long time; I cried until there was nothing left. Max just held me, continuing to stroke his hands along my back, consoling me. Eventually, I managed to control myself and drew a tremulous breath. I needed to tell him, to explain why I had left. Raising my head from his chest, I gazed up at his face, studying his expression, which was so full of love that I nearly started to cry all over again. He looked down at me, kissed my nose and tucked an errant strand of hair back behind my ears, his fingers teasing along my jaw. He smiled then, his slow, toe-curling, heart-stopping smile.

"Oh Max, you have no idea. I thought you had been killed. The pain, my head..." I stopped, my voice husky from so many tears. He kissed the top of my head, but didn't interrupt. "I didn't want to live anymore, not without you. I know that sounds cowardly, but it was easier to go back, to hide in my other world. Every time I thought I might be wrong, that it was your voice I heard, that it was your kiss I felt, that somehow you might have survived, I saw the images of the crash. The wreckage strewn all over the grass, the flames, the debris, I couldn't believe anyone could have escaped. Okay, now I know you weren't even on that flight, but you see why I couldn't trust my heart? My head told me that it was impossible, there was no way you could be alive." I paused, trying to gather myself.

"It's okay, Hannah, I understand. The doctor explained what had happened, that the shock and grief was too much for you to cope with and your mind had shut down." He grinned at me. "Although we both know it wasn't quite shut, just two thousand years away. I watched you go. I knew the precise moment when your other life called you and I was so afraid that I wouldn't be able to bring you home, that whatever I tried to do, you would not trust that I was still alive. I remembered you telling me, when we were in Pompeii, that I was your anchor and that without me your soul could easily separate itself from your body and remain lost out of time. I wasn't sure I could bear it."

He hugged me close as he said this and I wrapped my arms around him, delighting in the feel of his body. I had thought never to do this again. I snuggled my head under his chin and he lifted his legs up onto the sofa so we were more comfortable. The peace of the room washed over us and for several moments we were quiet. I waited; I knew he had more to say. After a little while —

"It was different this time, though; it was as though you were living in two worlds at once. You existed here at the same time as you were back with your ancient family. You went about your day, albeit as though in a trance, but you weren't unconscious or asleep. I talked to you, your family talked to you, but none of us could reach you, not even your chatty niece."

I chuckled at this; Lara is a garrulous nine-year-old who can talk the hind leg off a donkey!

"You were breathing, eating and sleeping, but only enough to keep you alive; your mind, your consciousness was elsewhere. Then when I played the videos of Masada and Pompeii, I began to think there was a chance. You seemed aware of me, could hear me when I talked about what we did at each place, things only you and I would know about. You even spoke, pretty much for the first time since I found you on the floor, and I had hope. Then yesterday you said there'd been an attack, that Maxentius was hurt and Luc was missing and that you had to help them. For a moment I thought that was it, that I was going to lose you forever, but you said you'd come back to me. It was then that I thought maybe you'd started to believe."

I watched him as he spoke; his face was so grave and I hated being its cause. I tried to clarify.

"Even though I imagined that I heard your voice and felt your touch, I was sure that it was my mind playing tricks; that I missed you so acutely that I had somehow magicked you into existence. I remember thinking that you sat behind me on the floor while we watched a video of our time in Pompeii and I touched your hands. One night I thought you lay next to me in bed, my back against your chest. Every time this happened, I was terrified that if I turned my head to check whether you were there, I'd see nothing but an empty space, so I didn't. I accepted that I was probably going completely mad, but even a make-believe you was better than no you at all." Pausing, I rubbed my eyes, which were sore. I wasn't sure I was making much sense, but I had to tell him the rest.

"I think I must be able to control when I go back." Max looked at me in astonishment. "I know it sounds weird, but I made a conscious choice to let go, to fall through time; I wasn't drawn there against my will. It seems to be connected to moments when my emotions are heightened. Then when you asked whether I'd come home, I realised that my life was here, whether or not you had lived, I knew I belonged here, in our home, in this life. I knew, however, that not only did I need to return to them, that whatever I had to do wasn't finished, but also that it was me who was making that decision, not the circumstance, like with the massacre or the eruption." I heard my words and they sounded about as clear as mud, so I paused for a few seconds trying to collect my thoughts before continuing —

"My time with my ancient family is only fleeting, a precious memory that I will always have in my heart; and I think that this time it is they who have rescued me, not the other way round. I believe that finding the pomegranate, then discovering that they had lived so close, almost next to where we are now sitting, was destined to be — probably written in those millions of stars we admired above Masada — and because part of me was able to go back to them, to be involved in their lives again and have a purpose, it allowed the other part of me, the part that stayed here, to begin to adjust to a life alone. Without that I think that I would have simply stopped living."

I glanced at Max to see whether he understood what I was trying to say.

"When you told me you'd always be my anchor, I knew I could let go, that I could return to my ancient world because somehow the thread still bound us, you and me, even though I thought that all I had was an echo in my heart; your love for me, regardless of whether it was only a memory, would be strong enough to entice me home when my time with them is done." I stopped speaking, concerned that in an effort to explain, my well-known lack of coherence was getting the better of me. Also, exhaustion was clouding my head and I was fighting to stay awake. I sighed, and whispered, "I'm sorry, I know I'm not making much sense, but...do you see?"

"Oh, Hannah, strangely enough yes, I do see, but I guess, from what you've just said, you have unfinished business with your other life. Am I right?" I nodded.

"I think so. They've just found Luc, but there are still one or two rather significant issues to be dealt with and I believe I'm part of it. As with all of these 'visits', I have to see it through. But now I know that you're here, not a figment of my very vivid imagination, it will be so much easier for me to come home. If it is true that I have learnt to control it, I should be able to merge with the other Hannah without fuss. You say it is only a week since the crash?" He nodded. "My life there was coming up to a year, so I don't expect to be away from you for long." I cupped his face in my hands and stared at him for a long moment. "I can feel its pull, but I don't want to go quite yet. I need to feel you, to draw strength from you..." I paused and said rather diffidently, "...will you be able to let me go?" He stared back, his eyes penetrating mine as though he could read my soul.

"I don't think I have a choice, but if you promise to come back to me, I can let you go."

"I promise. Now do you think you might kiss me?" His eyes widened at my question and, smiling his slow smile, bent his lips to mine.

Chapter Twenty Seven

A long time later, we finally surfaced for air. Safe in Max's arms, I could have stayed there forever, I never wanted to move. I supposed we didn't really have to, but it was late and I felt wrung out. Incredibly my head wasn't aching, a first, especially considering all the emotional upheaval; accepting that my husband truly was alive was momentous, then there was all that crying, not to mention everything else whirling around in my head from my other life. Max could see that I was flagging, but neither of us wanted to let go of the other. So we ended up securing the house, tidying the kitchen and going to bed holding hands the whole time. Ridiculous, I know.

I could feel the call of my other world and I realised that it was likely I would be back there soon, probably as I slept, but I was less concerned now. My world here was as it should be; Max was alive and he would wait for me. I could not stop smiling; it was as though I had been given a whole new life. As we walked slowly up to bed, arms around each other, not an easy feat up our narrow stairs I can tell you, I said —

"I don't want people to know yet."

"To know what?" Max asked curiously.

"That I'm okay, or sort of back, or whatever it is I am when I'm no longer not here. What?" He stared at me smothering a laugh at my garbled reply.

"Oh, Hannah, please don't ever change." Hugging me close, I could feel his chest rumble as he tried to control his amusement.

"Well, you know what I mean." Plaintively.

"So, you would prefer that we don't tell anyone that you have come out of your state of shock? Catatonia is what Dr Stephenson called it." I nodded. "They'll want to know you're okay, Hannah, they've been very worried."

"I realise that, but I don't want to deal with people for a little while. I want to savour this time with you without having to be polite and answer questions about thinking you were dead and all that." We were in the bedroom now. "I need time to come to terms with what's happened — well actually, what's still happening — and I think if everyone comes over I'll want to run and hide and you know how that might end." I smiled a little ruefully. Max grinned and kissed my nose as he mused over my words for long moments.

"I think I should at least tell the doctor and our parents. Dr Stephenson's been here most days since you collapsed and both sets of parents have been frantic. If I explain that you need time to readjust, that we need some space, I reckon they'll understand. They'd be so hurt if I didn't tell them and let them go on thinking you had not recovered." I gazed up at his face and seeing the distress that my — what had he called it? catatonia — had caused etched in the lines around his eyes, I realised that I wasn't being fair to any of them, so I acquiesced.

"Fair enough, but no visitors until we're ready. Deal?" I put my hand out. Max shook it, grinning.

"Deal! Now, young lady, I think we could both use a good night's sleep." I squeezed his hand and brought it to my heart. Not wanting to cause him any more anguish, but knowing I had to say it —

"Max, I can already feel a gentle tug on the thread that links me to my ancient world and I think that I may return to them before we wake. I must allow myself to go, for I believe that my part is not yet over, but it will be soon and I will come home to you. I love you more than you know, please remember that." My words sounded old-fashioned, but they suited my mood. I held his eyes, willing him to understand.

"I love you too, Sunshine, now shut up." With those words, he cupped one hand around my neck, entwining his fingers into my hair and curved the other around my back, cradling me against him. Then, breathing my name, he kissed me. Gently at first, but as it deepened, became more passionate, time slowed and we forgot everything else except each other for quite some time, and when Max lifted his head, finally, I was breathless with desire.

"Don't stop," I whispered.

"Hannah, my darling, much as I would like nothing more than to spend the rest of the night making love to you, I do not think it would be fair," he said in a voice that wasn't quite steady. "That was so you won't forget me." I drew his head back down to mine.

"I will never forget you, now please kiss me again." He readily obliged.

Sometime during the night I awoke and raised myself up on one elbow to make sure he was still there. In the pale glow of the moonlight through the window I could see his face, relaxed in sleep. My heart thudded as I finally accepted that it wasn't a dream; it wasn't fantasy; it was real. He was here next to me, not dead in a fiery crash. Unable to help myself, I traced the line of his jaw with my finger and brushed his lips with mine. He stirred and, although did not wake fully, gathered me to him, turning me so that my back rested against his chest. He nuzzled my hair and kissed my neck, sending a frisson down my spine. I wrapped one hand over his and rested the other on his thigh, curling my fingers around his leg. Safe in his embrace, I let slumber take me once again.

.......oooooOOOooooo.......

The next time I opened my eyes it was daylight, and I knew immediately that I had moved between worlds. The room was different, although it took a moment for me to place it. Confused, I turned my head to see my husband watching me, my other husband that is — oh dear, I know that sounds rather absurd, but I'm sure you're used to it by now. I was lying on a cot in the same room where he and Marcus had been ensconced. My head felt groggy and I struggled to sit up, but was forestalled by a large hand.

"Rest, Hannah, you must rest." I shook my head trying to clear it. Julius' words flooded back to me. My son had been found.

"No, I need to see Luc."

"He is safe, do not fret, my love. We will go and bring him home soon." I tried to sit up again, but found I didn't actually have the strength; my limbs felt heavy and refused to do my bidding.

"What happened? How am I here? Wait...did you just call me 'my love'?"

"You fainted when Julius told you of Luc and Senna, then we couldn't wake you. Atius said it was because you have been so worried and have not slept properly since the attack on the fort." Sounded feasible. "Hannah, why did you not tell me that Luc was missing." I looked up at him, noticing that his face was still pale and he was obviously in pain. I bit my lip, feeling stupid tears building. I was sick of crying, but wasn't sure I would be able to stop myself.

"You had enough to deal with," I said, my voice sounding cracked and weary. "Your poor head and not really knowing who I was, or even that we had children, how could I add to it by telling you that the son you could not recall was missing, possibly kidnapped or worse? That would have been cruel..." then, "...what are you doing there? You should be lying down, not sitting in that chair waiting for me to wake up."

"Do not worry about me, my Hannah, I am fine." His hand took hold of mine and he began rubbing his thumb over my palm. My composure, such as it was, began to crumble.

"You always do this; you have done this since the time I collapsed on Masada after Sergius died. You have no idea how soothing it is." He smiled down at me, his deep green eyes full of some emotion I could not fathom. Then his endearments came back to me. "Just a second, you have called me 'my Hannah' and 'my love' in the last two minutes. Have you remembered anything more?" Fervently hoping this to be the case, I needed something, anything, to hang on to.

"I remembered that I love you with every fibre of my being, that you bewitched me from the moment I first laid eyes on you and that without you my life is not worth living." I stopped breathing and gazed into his face and, for the third time in what was probably less than twelve hours, I burst into tears. Oh, for goodness sake, Hannah, I thought, you are a veritable waterspout!

Maxentius lifted me onto his knee, ignoring my sobbed protests about his head, and held me close, my head on his shoulder and his arms wrapped around me. He murmured sweet nothings as I cried, his voice calming me in a way nothing else could. His hands gently stroking my back in a gesture that was endearingly familiar. Eventually I regained some form of control and, worried that my husband should not even be out of bed, never mind be holding me like this, tried to get off his knee. He refused to let me go, however and simply held me tighter, so I gave up and snuggled back into his arms.

A long time later, when finally I felt able to speak, I asked him what else had happened after I'd fainted. It seemed that Marcus had been allowed to return to his quarters, although he had wanted to stay and help look after me. Atius had persuaded him that a husband and a doctor were perfectly able to manage. Atius had suggested that I be taken to another room so that both Maxentius and I could rest without disturbing the other; but Maxentius had declined saying he preferred me to be close to him. I could not stop the silly grin that spread over my face when he told me this. My husband was returning to me, bit by bit.

Gratius and his supporters had not yet been located, but extra guards — trusted soldiers — had been posted around the fort in case they tried to sneak back in. One thing was certain, following several very thorough searches; Gratius was definitely not in the fort. Petronius had carried out an inspection, working out how many soldiers were absent and who they were. That was small consolation, as he realised that there could be others within the fort, smart enough not to draw attention to themselves until Gratius required their services again. Not one to sit back and wait, however, Petronius had instructed those soldiers not on watch nor incarcerated for mutiny to prepare for another attack. Maxentius, Marcus, Petronius and Julius had decided that it would be inevitable; they just didn't know when or in what form it would occur.

I asked my husband how long it was since his wound had been checked. He chuckled, softly.

"You can't stop yourself, can you, my Hannah?" I lifted my head to frown at him. "You should trust Atius, he is a good medicus, he only checked it about an hour before you woke."

"I know," I muttered. "It's just that you're my husband and I need to b..." He cut me off rather delightfully by the simple method of kissing me soundly. I made a half-hearted attempt to stop him — he was still very unwell — but found it far more pleasurable to be kissed, so gave in to the bliss of the moment. When he finally lifted his head several minutes later, I was trembling.

"If I forgot everything else, I don't think I could ever forget the touch of your lips," he murmured.

"I think that's one of the nicest things you've ever said to me, my love..." I said quietly, waiting for my heart to resume a steady rhythm, "...but shouldn't you be lying down, resting?"

"Probably, but I find I do not wish to let you go." I giggled at his expression as he said this.

"You look as though you think me a hot meal, not your wife."

"Much the same thing." He chuckled. I blew a raspberry at him and made to get up. He still tried to prevent me, but I managed this time.

"Maxentius, you have to rest. Your head was badly gashed and exhaustion can slow your recovery, as well you know." I tried to sound stern but failed dismally, as Maxentius just smiled his slow smile, making my insides melt. "Please, I feel much better now and you should be back in bed." He gave in and I helped him out of the chair and into his own bed, pulling the cool sheets over him and making sure the blanket was within his reach, if he needed it.

As I was doing this, Atius appeared and demanded that he examine me just to settle his mind that my fainting fit was as a result of stress and nothing more sinister. I submitted reluctantly, but he seemed satisfied with what he saw. Then he gave Maxentius a quick check over before persuading him to take a mixture of febrifugia and poppy juice to dull the pain that we all knew he was suffering from, then told us to rest.

It was mid-morning now and I realised that I was rather hungry. I could not recall how long it had been since I'd eaten in either of my worlds. I mentioned this to Atius who said he would bring me a platter shortly, ignoring my suggestion that I could go and get it myself.

"Give yourself today, Hannah. You cannot go and bring Luc home; they tell me it is too risky to do so. He is safe with Senna. Marcus is keeping an eye on things with Petronius and Julius. They have everything under control. What good are you to anyone in this state?" I bowed my head feeling more than a little chastised, but looked up just in time to see that Atius was trying not to laugh.

"He knows you too well, Hannah, you'd better do as he says." Maxentius' words were a little slurred as the pain remedy took effect, but he was grinning wickedly.

"You two are conspiring against me." I grumbled, doing as I was told. The bed did feel very comfortable, however, and I thanked Atius for his care. Before the medicus had left the room, I was asleep.

The next time I awoke, the light was different and I worked out that it must be late afternoon. I turned and saw that Maxentius was still fast asleep, but that his face appeared more relaxed. It would take a long while for such a wound to heal, but I hoped that his healthy constitution would be in his favour. I would need to ask Atius how the injury was looking. There was a platter on the table between the two beds and I knew I should eat, but couldn't be bothered.

I lay for a few moments, mulling over the last couple of days; learning that Max was alive in my other world and that my husband in this world had remembered how much he loved me. I could feel a smile spread over my face as these thoughts gladdened my heart, and nearly laughed out loud at the idea of me trying to explain the utter incongruity of them to anyone other than the two men in question.

I sobered quickly enough as the threat of a further attack niggled at me. Several of those who had mutinied were locked up, punishment yet to be determined. Would the remainder try to break them out, or leave them to their fate? What form would the next attack take? How long would we have to wait? Would they attack quickly while we were still trying to regroup or employ a longer-term strategy? Many of the men at the fort were all battle-hardened soldiers, used to long campaigns and bloody warfare. Despite all these concerns, however, there was nothing I could do; I just hated feeling impotent.

Trying to distract myself, I forced my mind back to more practical things, such as going back to our house, having a bath, washing my hair and changing into a clean outfit, having a proper meal in the triclinium and not having to worry about a bunch of resentful soldiers bent on destroying a fragile peace. There it was again and ruefully, I accepted that it was futile trying not to think about the probability of another attack; it loomed large in everyone's mind and would not go away until the mutiny was quashed and all those involved, dealt with.

Suddenly I felt hungry...it'll be all that thinking, I smiled to myself. Sitting up, I helped myself to some of the bread and cheese, washing it down with whatever was in the goblet. It tasted sweet, as though there was honey in it, but I couldn't be sure. It was quite delicious and I drank the whole goblet. Wiping my face and hands on the cloth laying beside the platter, I got out of bed, carefully and tiptoed over to Maxentius.

I rested my hand lightly on his chest, noting that his heart and breathing were steady. His countenance was still very pale but, I surmised, less so than earlier. I really wanted to check under the bandage but there was no way I was going to disturb him. I stared down at him, taking in his craggy features and now unkempt hair. I loved the slightly fierce aura that surrounded him; it was in such contrast to his true nature but meant that others would never assume that he was an easy mark. He was a force to be reckoned with, even injured. I was about to go back to bed when his hand caught mine.

"Maxentius, you're supposed to be asleep." I said in undertones.

"I'd rest better if you were next to me," he muttered.

"I cannot — your head — go back to sleep."

"Come here, woman," he growled and drew me down to the bed, "there is room for two, especially as one of us is very small." I giggled as he snaked his arm around my waist, his pull relentless. I gave in and lay down, careful not to nudge him and he gathered me to his chest, hugging me close, my head fitting neatly under his chin. "See — that's so much better. Now I can sleep."

I wriggled a little to get comfortable, causing a groan from my husband. "Be careful, Hannah, my head may be injured, but that part of me is completely undamaged." I was laughing helplessly now. "Shush, you'll bring Atius in and we'll be in trouble." I tried to take deep breaths to stop the laughter, without much success, I might add, and was still hiccuping with mirth, when Maxentius kissed the back of my neck. That did the trick. My breath caught and a quiver ran down my spine.

"Don't you dare do that to me," I whispered, trying to twist away. "Neither of us is in any fit state for that." I felt his chest rumble.

"Now you know how I feel when you wriggle against me, my love!" He chuckled, holding me still. I nestled back against him.

"I love you, Maxentius."

"I love you too, my Hannah; now, go to sleep." And being very obedient, I did.

Chapter Twenty Eight

My dreams were confused. One moment I was in my modern world with Max, we were sitting on the bench in the front garden, watching the sunrise, or strolling along country lanes; the next I was with my other family in Ancient Britannia, playing with Luc, enjoying dinner with my two Romans, visiting the village. My dual lives melded and the more I tried to separate them, to work out where I was, the more enmeshed they became. Maybe it was because my emotions had been sorely tested these past few days; maybe it was because I had feared for the lives of the two men whom I loved most in the world; maybe I knew that my time in the past was coming to an end.

Whatever the reason, everything was getting very garbled. Then, without warning, the picture changed, fading away to be replaced by images of men fighting, swords clashing and blood running. I began to panic. Was this really a dream? If it was, I needed to wake up but was unable to. Oh no — was this actually happening? Not more wounded; I wasn't sure I could cope.

Suddenly, I became aware of an arm around me, the steady beat of a heart against my back, the touch of lips on my neck and someone murmuring to me, trying to calm me. Still in the throes of sleep and with no idea where I was, I tried to speak, but my words seemed jumbled.

"The wounded, we have to help them. There are so many. Don't let me go, don't let me go. Please, please."

"Hannah. I'm here, it's okay, but you need to stop thrashing." I heard a grunt as my elbow connected with something solid. "Ooof...that was my ribs! Come on, my love, wake up. There aren't any wounded." The tones were low, but firm and I recognised my husband's voice. If he was with me, I was safe. My eyelids felt like lead. If they were closed, I must have been dreaming — oh thank goodness!

I moved, turning onto my back, then rubbed my eyes before opening them slowly. The room was very dark, a small oil lamp burned in the corner. I was lying on a cot looking up at Maxentius, who was gazing back at me in concern. I drew a shuddering breath, taking a moment to adjust to where I was.

"Oh, I'm so sorry. I hope I didn't hurt you. I told you it was a bad idea to sleep like this." He chuckled.

"Everything was fine until you started yelling out and waving your arms about. Honestly, Hannah, you're like an octopus, all arms and legs."

"How on earth do you know about octopuses?" I asked in astonishment, diverted momentarily.

"Saw them when we put into port at Lechaeum in Corinth on the way to Armenia." I gazed at him, a little awed.

"You have seen so much, things I will never see. Wait...you recall this?"

"It was before I was on Masada, Hannah. I remember everything up to Masada, that's when it becomes hazy. Bits are coming back here and there, much is still completely blank." I realised he may never remember anything about my two worlds. I would have no-one to talk to about the fact that I shared knowledge across millennia. I felt unutterably sad about this. Marcus knew, but it wasn't the same. Maxentius had listened, understood, accepted and still loved me knowing I was part of two lives.

"Typical." I tried to sound upbeat, but it came out rather forlorn.

"What's wrong, Hannah?" Gently asked.

"Nothing, never mind, you don't need to think about anything else but getting better." I infused practicality into my voice.

"Hannah, it's the middle of the night and after your antics we're both wide awake; we have time to talk. Tell me what's upset you." I stared at him for a long time, biting my lip, unsure of how much I dared mention. I started to speak, only to flounder, searching for the right words. I tried again —

"There are things about me which you likely do not remember, may never remember, things which would seem outlandish in the extreme and totally irrational. I took a great risk and told you once many years ago. It was long before we were married, but after we had spoken to each other of our feelings and against all the odds, you believed me. These things have helped me save us from certain death at least twice and provided me with an awareness of much that no-one else in this era knows. Eventually I had to tell Marcus, but he struggles with it and would rather avoid any discussion about it unless absolutely necessary. You, on the other hand, you have always been so understanding of who I am and what I experience, but if this is lost to you and then things happen, I…"

I stopped abruptly. I heard the words as they rolled off my tongue and knew that they sounded peculiar. How could I explain this to him in a way that didn't make me seem completely mad? This was way more complicated than the first time. I had so much more to lose now. Before it was just me; now there were four children and our friends. I wasn't sure I could cope if he never remembered or found he could not trust that my story was true.

My head swam with the convoluted nature of my two worlds and for the first time I wished that I had never fallen back through time, that Hannah could have just met and married Maxentius without all the extra complications. Ah, but then they would have all died in the massacre on Masada, the rational voice in my mind admonished me.

Nervous of his reaction, I didn't know where to look, so I stared straight ahead, which happened to be at my husband's chest. I could see the outline of his muscles through the lightweight garment he was wearing, which did not help my concentration one jot. A finger ran along my cheek, settling under my chin and lifting it, allowing Maxentius to search my face in the dim light.

"You fear that who you are will be too much for me and I will no longer want you in my life?" he asked quietly. I looked at him, unable to voice my qualms. To my utter frustration, my eyes had filled with tears, which was impressive, as I didn't think I had any left to cry. I refused to blink, for that would send them spilling down my cheeks and I was not about to give in to such nonsense. "Oh, Hannah. I know that often your conscious mind melds with another's from eons away; that she shares her knowledge of history to help us. I have a vague recollection that we actually met her — or should I say you — in Rome not too long ago. Am I right?"

I gaped at him, temporarily robbed of the power of speech. I was so shocked that of all the things he might have remembered, all those momentous things in his life, he remembered this.

"When...was it...how...had you...?" For the life of me I could not form a coherent sentence and my voice cracked with the effort not to cry.

"This has never been lost. Even when I thought we were still in that sick room on Masada, I remembered that you were different. The rest of it came back when you told me about our lives there; I think it happened when you mentioned sitting under the pomegranate tree and talking. Hannah, even if I hadn't remembered any of it, I would never push you away. What kind of man do you think I am? You would just have had to tell me all over again." He winked. "I also remember something about the moon and a park. Care to elaborate?" I smiled ruefully.

"It was just before I explained about who I was. You told me that you could not stop loving me even if I told you that I'd floated down from the moon and I said..."

"...that once you'd told me, the moon thing would seem like a walk in the park." Maxentius took my words from me. I nodded. "It still holds, Hannah. I accept that there is much I cannot recall, but I am aware that there have been times in our lives when you have felt uncertain, when circumstances seemed to threaten what we have, what we share, but I will never stop loving you, I will never leave you or let you go. You captured my heart the first time I saw you and it is yours forever. You just need to learn to trust your own heart."

My breath caught. His words were so familiar that I had to look twice to make sure it was still Maxentius and I hadn't inadvertently gone back to Max. As I stared at him, an unnamed dread buried so deeply I did not even know I carried it suddenly shattered, it's place filled by a serenity I had never known. Finally, after so many occasions when I had asked myself whether I was worthy of this man — as happened when my unusual upbringing, my work as a healer and my inability to conform to social expectations had brought undeserved and often unwelcome attention to our union and our family — I realised that I did, I did trust my heart. Maxentius had never let anyone else dictate to him, he had never let anyone persuade him that I was not the right woman for him. I was the one with all the speed wobbles.

Whatever we had to face, we were meant to be together, almost as though it were our destiny, which if the clasp and my future self were anything to go by, it probably was. Despite attempts by others to tear us apart, either by words or actions, the opposite had been achieved and, if possible, we had become closer. Even the whole 'woman from the future in my head' thing had not scared him away, and he'd had to get used to that happening several times.

"I'm sorry, Maxentius, I have been all kinds of a fool." He started to speak. "No, please, I need to say this. Everyone I have ever loved has been snatched away — my parents, my uncle, Aharon and Raizel, my friends. I lost them all and I think somewhere in the darkest recesses of my soul, I have always expected that one day something or someone would take you from me, that such happiness could only be fleeting and that I would never be as lucky as to have you forever. Finding you in the most unlikely place; loving you and being able to share your life was a gift so extraordinary, yet so ephemeral that I think a tiny part of me refused to accept that it could last; that maybe I wasn't deserving of such love." My voice dropped to a whisper, Maxentius groaned and made as if to wrap me in his arms. I held him away, shaking my head, determined to say it all. I drew a deep breath and continued —

"Yet, whatever was thrown at us, you never wavered. Even now, hardly recalling anything of our life together, you never questioned that we should be together and never lost faith in us. In spite of the fact that I love you more than life itself, I have always been the one who needed reassurance. Your unshakable confidence in us and unconditional acceptance of who I am, with all my err...eccentricities, is humbling. Please forgive my faint heart." I stopped, biting my lip, hoping that he had understood.

"Oh, my Hannah, your heart is that of a lioness, there is nothing to forgive; and why would you ever think you are not deserving is beyond me, you goose! Our love is indeed a gift, one that will last several lifetimes, even millennia if I am not mistaken and I am more than happy to keep reassuring you." He winked. "We are blessed and that is an end to it. Okay, now that we've bared our souls, do you think I might kiss you? I fear I am forgetting you again." My eyes widened, worried that I had overtired him with all this talk, when I spotted the twitch of his lips. He was distracting me and I was grateful. Deep and meaningfuls do have a tendency to become rather emotionally taxing. I chuckled.

"Hmmm...forgetting me, huh? I'll see about that." Lightly brushing my lips against his. "That do?" Impudently.

"Why you..." bending his head he possessed my mouth with a passion that took my breath away. Squirming, I tried to tell him that he needed to be careful of his injury; his head didn't need blood pounding through it, but my words were swallowed under his kiss. My arms went round his neck and, mindful of his wound, I ran my fingers through his hair. The world around us faded into nothingness and I let everything go.

Moments passed and still we kissed. I felt the embers of desire, which always smouldered between us, threatening to burst into flame and knew I had to break it off. Maxentius was in no fit state to take this any further, never mind that we were in the hospital with no privacy at all. Just as I was thinking this, I heard footsteps along the corridor. Maxentius released me and, in the blink of an eye, turned me over and pulled me to his chest, muttering something about feigning sleep. It was all I could do not to burst out laughing as our hearts were beating rapidly and trying to control our breathing was a complete waste of time. He drew up the sheet and rested his chin on my head. I shut my eyes managing, what I hoped was, a fairly creditable job of appearing to be in dreamland.

I heard Marcus say something and Atius reply. A smothered chuckle, then the door closed. Slowly opening one eye, I risked a peek and saw that the room was quiet once more.

"Not sure we are all that convincing but at least they left us alone." I giggled, twisting so I could see his face. "I do feel quite tired, though. How is your poor head? Do you want a sip of calda? There's poppy juice in it; might help."

"Somewhat painful, but it was worth it for that kiss..." He wiggled his eyebrows then winced as the action stretched his wound. I made to get up, "...and no, I would like to try without the opiate if possible." I settled back on the bed.

"Rest my love, I'll examine your gash later. I think we should try to have some more sleep. Hopefully, later today I can take you home.

"Sounds perfect." He gathered me back against him and within moments his breathing became quiet and rhythmic, the rise and fall of his chest soporific and soon I had joined him in slumber.

Chapter Twenty Nine

The day was reaching its midpoint, when we woke again and I had slept better than I had in many nights, an untroubled dreamless sleep. For what seemed like an age, I had been battling demons which had crossed both my worlds — the loss of Max, my very short-lived kidnapping, the threat to the garrison, my missing son and Senna, then the injuries inflicted on both my husband and Marcus. My refusal to allow myself time to reflect on any one of them for more than a moment or to grieve had manifested itself in my dreams. As I opened my eyes and stretched like a cat, I realised that I felt happy. There was much that still had to be dealt with, but somehow I knew that it would work itself out. I smiled contentedly.

"Now that's a picture to wake up to." A voice murmured from beside me. I turned to see Maxentius watching me in much the same way as he had been doing hours earlier. I raised my hand and caressed his cheek.

"Morning, my love. I hope you slept as well as I did." I lifted myself up and kissed his jaw. "I must examine your head."

"You never give up, do you?" amusement threading through his words.

"No! Now, please don't be pesky and let me check you out." I slid out of bed, noticing the food had been replenished and a flagon of some kind of drink was standing next to it. "Do you feel up to eating?" Maxentius said he did, so I handed him the platter, then padded through the hospital to see if Atius was around. The medicus was in his office. He smiled as I entered and asked how I was feeling.

"Rested, thank you." I smiled back. "I'm sorry, I know I look like a wreck, but after I've checked Maxentius' head, would you come and see whether he is fit enough to go home? I'm sure he would do better in the quiet of our rooms and I can look after him just as easily there as here." Atius pondered this for a few moments and then agreed, as long as he was satisfied that the wound was healing properly.

"I'll leave it unbound until you come. Give me a quarter of one hour and I will be ready." He nodded and I left him to his work. On the way back to the room, I popped into the laundry to freshen up. I had been in the same clothes for what felt like days, although it was probably only about thirty-six hours and had nothing to change into, but a splash of cold water over my face and neck worked wonders.

Back with Maxentius, I told him what Atius had said. He was pleased with this decision and submitted to having his head examined in as gracious a manner as he could muster.

"I know you hate this, but it has to be done. You were never a very good patient." He grunted a less than polite response, which I ignored. Making sure there was no residual salve or ointment in the gash, I cleaned it thoroughly. It was healing more quickly than I expected. We still needed to be aware of increased headaches or vision disturbance, but other than his loss of memory, he was definitely on the mend. Atius appeared on schedule and pronounced himself very pleased with Maxentius' progress, confirming that as long as my husband promised to take things easy for the next few days, and rest most of the time, he could go home.

Maxentius' look of gratitude was almost comical. I applied the salve and arnica and re-bandaged the wound while Atius left us to sort ourselves out, saying he'd be back to assist us over to the residence. It was the first time Maxentius had been out of bed since his injury, other than to perform necessary ablutions and I guessed he would be feeling rather unsteady. Once we were ready, I draped his cloak snugly around his shoulders and we began the slow walk home. Atius came back with Marcus and between them they managed to make it look as though they were just strolling across the quadrangle having a chat, not making sure their commander didn't collapse in a heap. I was very grateful for their sensitivity.

We got my husband into bed and tucked the blankets over him. His face had a greyish caste now, the exertion telling in his clenched jaw. While the two men settled him, and out of Maxentius' line of vision, I added a few drops of poppy juice to the flagon of Mabina's warm sweet drink thoughtfully left by the bed. When I offered him a sip, he swallowed it without question. Within seconds his eyes drooped and he was asleep. I knew we could leave him to rest undisturbed. Thanking the other two, I followed them out of the room, leaving the door slightly ajar in case I was needed.

"What news?" I asked Marcus. He shrugged and spread his hands.

"Nothing solid. As you are aware, there are soldiers who were part of the initial attack who have not tried to return. We must assume that there are others within the fort, as those who are absent are too few to have caused the mayhem that was inflicted. It has been several days now, though, and those outside the palisade must need food if not shelter."

"Is Calidius still in the fort?" I asked curiously.

"I believe so. Why?"

"I think he was part of my kidnapping plot, such as that was, yet I'm not certain how much more involved he is." Marcus raised an eyebrow. "Don't ask me to explain it, it's just a feeling. Maybe if I could talk to him, he might tell me what's going on." The two men looked at each other, then Marcus said —

"I cannot see that this would be a problem, it certainly can't be detrimental; I will have him brought to the principia. If he is still in the fort, maybe he has decided that the mutiny was misguided. Make no mistake, though, Hannah, if he was the one who hit you and left you bound in the stables, he will have to face some form of punishment." I nodded slowly, conceding his point.

"Please let me know if you find him." I paused. "I don't suppose I can go and get Luc?" I gazed at the two of them beseechingly. Marcus grinned.

"Nice try, Hannah. No, it is not safe for you to be out there and I cannot spare the large contingent of soldiers that would be required to accompany you as protection; they are needed here. I promise you we will bring Luc home as soon as it is safe to do so. Do not try to sneak out — Hannah..." he paused, waiting for me to respond. Knowing he was right, but finding my desire to see my son far outweighed any risks involved, my compliance was under sufferance. "...I know this is tearing you apart, but you must trust us. Luc is safe with Senna; hopefully we will see them both very soon. In my desperation to see Luc, I'd forgotten how anxious Marcus was about Senna. I hugged him quickly.

"I'm sorry, Marcus, that was thoughtless of me. I know how worried you are." He returned the hug and then said he had to get back to the office and he'd let me know whether they had located Calidius. Atius headed back to the hospital and I went to speak to our staff.

They were all in the kitchen enjoying a break when I knocked and entered. Everyone stood when they saw me, but I waved them back to their seats.

"Please relax," I said, "it's only me." Mabina came over and enfolded me in a huge hug, nearly squeezing the air out of my lungs. The others smiled and nodded, or came over and squeezed my hand in gestures of comfort. I asked if I might join them for a moment to update them on what had happened. They always looked amused when I did this and I realised that most people in my position would do exactly as they chose in their own home. After all, any staff were generally the property of the homeowner; in fact they were usually classed as slaves, a term I abhorred. We preferred to give them some autonomy however, wanting them to understand that we appreciated their hard work and that we did not take them for granted. I think they thought I was a bit potty, but I believed there was a respect between us; plus I reckoned they'd given up trying to work me out a long time ago.

Annant brought a chair over for me and I updated them on Maxentius' condition, confirming that he was here in the residence and, hopefully, would be back to normal soon. I warned them that his memory had not returned fully, so he may need gentle reminders on certain aspects of the house but that they were not to worry about it. I thanked Annant for going with Julius to the village, to tell them what had happened.

"Marcus told us that you had collapsed when you heard that Luc and Senna had been found," said Lynet shyly, the youngest member of our domestic team and Mabina's granddaughter. "I hope you feel better now." The others chimed in with their own concerns. I smiled and said that I was indeed much better, especially now that the two thought missing had been found safe and well. Mentioning that Maxentius did not have much of an appetite but that I expected that Marcus, Petronius and Julius would be joining me for the evening meal, I left them to the rest of their day, asking whether I might have some hot water brought along to the bathing room.

While I had been sitting in the kitchen, I had decided to indulge in a proper bath. I felt sticky and uncomfortable and really wanted to wash my hair. I did not have to wait long for the water. Tam, our odd job man — the closest I can come to describing his multitude of duties — brought the hot water along in two huge buckets, tipping them into the stone bath for me. Thanking him, I closed the door, stripped off completely, dumping my clothes in the basket to be laundered and, after adding some cold water to the hot, luxuriated in a proper bath. It was bliss. I scrubbed all my cares away along with the dust and whatever other indeterminate things might have ended up on my skin over the past, however long it was since I had last bathed. Once I felt clean, I emptied the water out, then filling the smaller sink, washed my hair. I dug through my dwindling supply of the more exotic oils I had brought with me and massaged some of the Sharon rose oil I had 'acquired' from the storerooms on Masada into my skin and through my hair. Its light floral scent with a hint of honey sweetness was soothing and lifted my spirits.

Wrapped in a drying cloth, I went to our bedroom and dressed very quietly. Maxentius was still deeply asleep and I lingered for a few moments watching him, noting his colour and breathing, his face no longer sporting the greyish pallor that worried me so. Everything seemed as normal as could be expected at this juncture and I thanked all the gods that he was a healthy person. I sat with him for a while but he didn't show any signs of waking, so I left him to his rest and went along to the triclinium. It was still only mid-afternoon and the meal would not be served for ages yet, but the room was comfortable so I reclined on one of the couches and relaxed.

I had been there for maybe half an hour, when Julius stuck his head round the door and said that Calidius was in the office if I wanted to try talking with him. I nodded and followed my friend across to the principia. Calidius had been seated in one of the smaller rooms along the corridor from the main office, guarded by one of Maxentius' most trusted men. I smiled at the soldier and he greeted me, saying he would be just outside the door should I need him. Thanking him, I sat down opposite the young man in the room. Calidius looked terrified. He could not have been much more than twenty and three years, if that, and most likely hadn't seen a battlefield. The small skirmishes here on this outpost of Empire were a picnic compared with what Maxentius and Marcus, and probably Gratius also, had seen.

I sat for a moment just observing him, then quietly asked him to show me his hands. He held them out palms down and I turned each one, studying them closely. The heel of his right palm bore a faint crescent shaped scar and when I looked carefully I was fairly sure I could see teeth marks. Julius was right: Calidius was the soldier who had lifted me onto the horse all those weeks ago.

"Why did you do it, Calidius?" I asked gently, pointing to the scar. "This is where I bit you, isn't it?" He stared at me for a long time, his eyes haunted, and finally he nodded.

"Gratius believed that he should have been appointed legatus. We had been here for nearly four years and Gratius had acted as commander on those occasions when Fabricius Habitus was called away."

"Do you know why he wasn't appointed?" Calidius shook his head. "It was because your previous commander felt him to be too unstable. Also he is only a centurion, not a general, a requirement to be promoted to legatus." I paused. "What did you intend to do with me, you know, when you kidnapped me?" He shrugged his shoulders.

"I do not know. My job was to bring you to the stables without being seen. The rest was up to Gratius." He hesitated. "I never meant to hit you, please believe me. I did not expect you to fight me when I tried to get you on the horse and I panicked. I am so sorry. I had no choice. I owed Gratius a debt." His face was a study in misery and I realised that he had been encouraged into something that under normal circumstances he would never have dreamed of becoming involved with.

"What was the debt, Calidius?" I asked curiously. He explained that he had not been in the army very long and had been posted to Isca Silurum, a fortress in southwest Britannia — in an area settled by the Silures tribe — with a detachment sent to augment Legio II Augusta already based there. One evening while on patrol, his unit was ambushed, with several soldiers killed or badly wounded. Calidius admitted that he had been terrified and rather lost his head in the commotion; he would have been cut down had it not been for Gratius, who had saved his life. Here on the frontier, Gratius had called in the debt, leaving Calidius little choice.

I sympathised with this young soldier so far from home, caught between a rock and a hard place. If he hadn't supported Gratius, his superior would likely have threatened to expose him for cowardice or even desertion. Maybe if he'd had the courage to come and talk to Marcus or Maxentius, he wouldn't have been in such circumstances.

"Did you take part in the attack on the fort?" I asked him. "I know you were injured, for I saw you in the hospital."

"I was fighting against them," he said. "I knew that if my part in your kidnapping was discovered I would be in serious trouble, but I could not stand by and let them try to take over the garrison by force. I have friends here, comrades whom I have lived beside for several years. It is enough that we try to maintain a peace outside of the fort; there should not be dissent from within."

I watched his face as he spoke and believed his words to be the truth. It was sheer coincidence that he had been wounded, one which, thankfully, had led us to question the tactics of the mutineers.

"I am not sure what punishment they may be considering, Calidius, but I will speak for you. Thank you for being brave enough to tell me all this; it could not have been easy." He smiled then, a shy smile that lit up his youthful face.

"Thank you, Hannah Valerius. After what I did, I do not deserve such support."

"Oh, I bit you very hard; I think we might be just about even." I winked at him, drawing a hint of a chuckle. I motioned to the guard and rose to leave. On my way out, I patted Calidius on the shoulder. "Stand tall, Calidius, you are a soldier of Rome, not Gratius. I think all will be well." I had to trust that I wasn't giving him false hope; that in the absence of my husband I could persuade Marcus and Petronius to be lenient.

Chapter Thirty

I paused for a moment in the hallway, collecting my thoughts and then walked along to the main office; and after being admitted, found Marcus and Petronius sitting at the desk discussing some strategy or other. They both grinned as I entered, asking how the interview had gone. I told them everything and then appealed for them not to be too harsh in their judgement.

"I cannot promise anything, Hannah, although it appears that he may have redeemed himself somewhat," Marcus stated thoughtfully. "We will have to discuss it with Maxentius. It wasn't just you that day, you know; Petronius and Senna, not to mention Luc, were placed at risk. Petronius did not come away unscathed," Marcus said, softening his words with a smile. "Now go and check on your husband, we will be over shortly. I am looking forward to a proper family meal." I beamed at the two men and thanked them for their time, then left them to finish their day's work.

I breezed home, feeling quite light-hearted. Slowing my steps as I approached our bedroom, I crept in to find Maxentius still sleeping. I ran my eyes over his features. They were relaxed and his skin looked cool. No heat in his cheeks suggestive of a fever and I could not detect any clamminess. I had a little time before the others would arrive, so I went along to my medicine rooms to make sure everything was in order and that my supplies were as they should be. Some of my ointments were getting low and I ruminated on how I would replenish them.

Although there was plenty of trade along the frontier, I wasn't certain whether any of the merchants would carry what I needed. I jotted a few things down on the tablet I kept on the shelf and made a mental note to ask Marcus. I would love the chance to visit Eburaci for a few days; the shops there had looked so enticing with all manner of things available. Probably all I needed would be found there. I could almost feel my fingers itching at the idea of pottering around shops full of herbs and balms and ointments. Not yet, Hannah, I admonished myself;

get your family back together and your husband sorted out before you go gadding about the countryside.

I sauntered back to the bedroom and, seeing that Maxentius was stirring, waited for him to come round so I could check his head. He seemed a little groggy, but I suspected it was sheer exhaustion rather than anything more insidious. I asked whether he would like to join us for the meal, or have something on a platter in bed. He preferred to remain where he was, which confirmed my suspicion that he was far from well. I stayed with him until he had eaten his fill, which was barely enough to keep a bird alive, never mind a burly soldier, but I forbore from saying so. After persuading him to drink some watered-down wine, with a drop or two of febrifugia and poppy juice added, I held his hand until he fell asleep once more. Just before slumber claimed him, he asked —

"Will you be sleeping here tonight, my Hannah?" I raised his hand to my lips and kissed his palm.

"As long as you promise to rest, yes, I will sleep here tonight." His lips curved in a sweet smile as he sank back into unconsciousness.

By the time I entered the triclinium, the other three were already there. I mused on how easily Petronius and Julius had become part of our inner circle — for want of a better term. We had gone from three to five as though it was the most natural thing in the world and I wasn't complaining. I liked that we had such camaraderie and that there were two more whom I could trust to share our lives with more closely than most. They turned to greet me as I walked in, asking after Maxentius. I gave them an update and then we relaxed and enjoyed our meal. It seemed a long time since we had done this, days and days and I voiced my thoughts as we sat with a goblet of spicy calda.

"Hopefully, we can get back to a much more normal life soon; just patrols and training and sword practice and the odd skirmish, rather than pitched battles in the quadrangle with a band of mutineering soldiers." Marcus chuckled at his own wit. I grinned.

"Nice thought; not sure how soon that's going to be though and I still haven't seen Luc or Senna." I remembered to include Senna at the last minute. I missed her as well, but she wasn't my son and she was with her family at the village. I was starting to think Luc would be an adult before I next got to hold him.

"I know it's hard, Hannah, but please put up with it just a little longer. I cannot envisage Gratius waiting more than a few days to strike again, he is too headstrong and is determined to take the fort. He must know that Maxentius is wounded and it is unlikely that he would risk delaying things until he is well. He'll assume that Maxentius could be 'persuaded' to relinquish control if he is in a weakened state."

"He really does not know my husband at all, does he?" I queried, astounded at Gratius' complete lack of insight. Marcus shook his head.

"No, but this might make him more dangerous." My eyes widened at his tone. He explained, "If he cannot get Maxentius to hand over the garrison, he may prefer that no-one has it."

"How on earth does he think he'll manage that? We have several hundred soldiers here, most of who are not in support of Gratius' muddle-headed plans."

"Desperate men will use any means available, Hannah." I smiled wryly, recalling the last time I had heard this said. In fact I think I'd been the one to say it many years ago and thousands of miles away.

"So I suppose vigilance is still our watchword?" The three glanced at each other, then back at me. "What?" Nothing. "What?" Exasperated.

"We are worried that you'll be the one at risk. Gratius might try to get to you again, to force Maxentius' hand. Luc is safely out of the picture but you're here and Gratius knows you won't leave Maxentius."

"I'd like to see him try. I'll punch his lights out if he comes anywhere near me," I muttered angrily. They guffawed and I glared at them — how rude! To be fair, being on the small side, most people think I'm a pushover, but I'm not.

"Please, Hannah, just keep a low profile and make sure you can always see one of us when you're around the fort." I stared at them.

"You're serious, aren't you?" They nodded in unison. "Okay, okay," I said grudgingly, "I'll be careful. Just don't expect me to stop going about my normal business though. I do not intend to let him ruin my life." They agreed that this would be acceptable, but to let them know if something didn't feel right.

We moved on to lighter topics after that and I mentioned my desire to visit Eburaci, that diverted everyone for the remainder of the evening and soon it was time to say our goodnights. Someone had lit the oil lamp in our bedroom and I could see in the gentle light that my husband continued to sleep peacefully. I changed into a nightshift and got into bed as carefully as possible so as not to disturb him. I touched his cheek, then lay back and fell asleep almost immediately.

The next few days fell into a routine. I would get up early and meet with Annant briefly, to discuss what had to be done in the house during that particular day; this was purely because of having an invalid in the residence, in case certain tasks needed to be adjusted to suit Maxentius' rehabilitation regimen. Then I would take a platter of food along to my husband. His appetite was building nicely and he was starting to look less gaunt.

The wound healed quickly, but Maxentius still had huge lapses in his memory; so every afternoon we talked about his life since we had met. The more we talked, the more he recalled. Oddly, some of the more important things, such as the births of Claudia and Luc, the storming of Masada after the massacre and finding me after the eruption of Vesuvius, were still beyond him. I just had to hope and pray that eventually these too would come back.

He needed to regain his strength also, so each morning after the first meal we walked around the house. Initially, he could manage only halfway and had to rest, but he persevered and after three days he could make it all the way without a break and soon he could do it twice. He was chomping at the bit to do more, but knew that it would take time and he had to be patient. It was a good job that he had this particular characteristic in spades.

Marcus had told him about Gratius and the fear that they would attack again. Maxentius agreed and the pair of them spent many hours discussing all possibilities, sometimes with the added viewpoints of Petronius and Julius. While they did this, I assisted Atius at the hospital. This was a working fort and, although the soldiers took every care, there were always minor injuries or accidents. Then there were those who worked in the stores and workshops. Metalworking, woodworking and

231

stonemasonry, to name but a few of the skills and crafts that were employed at the fort.

Not only soldiers, these men were also engineers and builders, constructing or reinforcing the network of roads, using equipment that could do you a fair amount of damage. Thus, there was a constant catalogue of cuts, lacerations, bruises, sprains and even breaks, which kept us busy all day every day. Rarely a day went by when we had no-one to treat.

All this kept my mind occupied. I was still frantic about Luc. Even though my head told me he was perfectly safe, my heart was torn. I was his mother and I hated being apart from him. It was nearly two weeks since I'd seen him and who knew how much longer I would have to wait! Also, I missed being able to get out into the countryside, or to go and meet with Breeda and the other women in the village.

The days were long and sunny and I felt they were wasted, not being enjoyed to the full the way they should be. It made me a bit grouchy, truth be told — yes, I can guess how shocked you are to hear this — and although I tried to conceal it from Maxentius, he had always been able to read my moods. He did his best to calm me and for the most part succeeded, but there were times when I went around like a bear with a sore paw.

One night after everyone had gone to sleep, I lay awake unable to settle. I was troubled and a sense of foreboding had been growing throughout the day. I accepted that it was probably my general unease surrounding the tension in the fort, but this time I couldn't shake it. The day had been as normal as our days were at the moment. Maxentius was much better and had even managed to walk three times round the house. I was restless and, attuned to me even in slumber, he had pulled me to his chest enfolding me in his arms. He was snoring gently and this sound, along with the steady beat of his heart, was usually enough to soothe me into sleep, but not tonight.

I tried everything, from counting sheep to some weird relaxation technique I had learned in my other life at the one yoga class I had taken. Nothing worked and I lay for what seemed like hours. Eventually, certain that I was going to disturb my husband with my fidgeting, I disentangled myself from his embrace and got up. Pulling a blanket over my shoulders for modesty rather than for warmth, I crept through the house checking every room; needing to be sure that all was secure. I could hear sounds from outside, but didn't pay any attention; there were always guards patrolling the fort at night.

I had reached the kitchens when something tickled at my nose. I stopped and sniffed, thinking with mild amusement that if anyone saw me I'd look like a dog sniffing for treats. Nothing. I went into the kitchens, the fire was banked down, there was nothing amiss. As I turned to leave, I caught the smell again. Glancing back over my shoulder to be sure everything was as it should be, I thought I detected movement outside through the slats in the shutters — not a patrol, this was people creeping stealthily. Heart thumping, I crept over to the window and peered out. Dark shadows were flitting here and there and I could not decide whether they were really anybody there or just the weird shapes thrown by the moonlight and the breeze through the palisade.

Then as I was watching, one of the shadows loomed up next to the shutter, their actions furtive. It was all I could do not to scream. It was definitely a person and they were definitely up to no good. Trying not to panic, I flew along to Marcus' quarters and rapped quietly on his door. I couldn't tell whether he'd heard me, so I tried again, this time a little louder. I was dancing about in agitation by the time the door swung open to reveal a rather dishevelled-looking Marcus, his eyes heavy with sleep.

"I'm so sorry, Marcus, but I think something's wrong." He stared at me, trying to work out what I was saying, still not fully awake. I shook his arm. "Marcus, please, there are people outside, they're sneaking about, and before you ask, no it's not the patrol. They were hugging the building." I was speaking in low tones, but my voice was rising and I bit down on my lip to control my fear.

"What woke you, Hannah?"

"I haven't been to sleep." He looked at me in astonishment. "Oh, I don't know, I just couldn't, something was niggling me. Now I know what it was." As we were talking, I got a whiff of that strange smell again and all at once I realised what it was. I grabbed Marcus' arm. He had smelt it too and we spoke at the same time

"Fire!"

Chapter Thirty One

I froze in horror. Fire is my worst nightmare and I've been far too close to one or two in my lifetime; I did not want to repeat the experience. We had people in our care, though and they had to get out. I wasn't sure whether the residence was on fire, but as the fort was built mainly of wood, it wouldn't take much for the whole lot to go up. The days had been long and sunny, we hadn't had any rain for weeks and everything was tinder dry.

"Marcus, please, you must help Maxentius. You will be able to get him outside and to safety far more quickly than I could. I will go and tell the staff. Is there a way to warn the rest of the fort? A bell, or something?" Marcus nodded his head.

"A horn and if that fails, a lot of yelling. Go, I will help Maxentius and sound the warning. Once you have told everyone, do not try to save anything, just get yourself out. We will meet in the quadrangle, it will be safe there." I nodded and shot along the corridor, banging on the doors of the sleeping quarters, making sure they heard me before I went to the next one. People shuffled out of their rooms, looking confused and alarmed.

"There's a fire! You must get out! If you think you can dress quickly, do so; otherwise grab a cloak and some shoes and run. Go through the side door, it opens straight onto the compound. Meet up in the quadrangle. Annant," — as the one in charge of the staff, I knew I could rely on him to make sure they were all accounted for — "please make sure everyone gets outside. I have no idea where the fire is, but we cannot risk people being trapped in here." He nodded and took charge. I left the staff in his capable hands and ran back to our bedroom. On my way, I heard the horn and breathed a sigh of relief; that would alert everyone else.

Grabbing my bag, I dropped in the pictures of the children, then ran to the medicine rooms and shoved in everything I could think of that might be needed for people with burns. Going back to the bedroom, I dressed quickly and pulled on my cloak, fastening it with my beautiful clasp. That meant it was with me. I noticed Maxentius' sword leaning against the wall. I lifted it, very tempted to take it with me, but it was so heavy. I thought better of it and, replacing it reluctantly, I left my bag on the bed for the moment, swinging out of the room and along the corridor.

Exiting through the main door and keeping a very close eye on my surroundings, I hightailed it over to the principia thinking to retrieve any documents left in the office. I could see an orange glow from the other side of the residence, it looked like one of the workshops and I hoped that some of the soldiers would be able to douse the flames before they reached our home. I hurried through the building to the main office where I found Petronius and Julius. They looked as shocked as I did to see each other.

"How did you get in here so fast?" I cried in astonishment.

"Marcus came and woke us. We've been using the rooms near the chapel as we felt we should stay here in case of a second attack. Easier to find us there than in the barracks." I nodded distractedly.

"I was coming to collect any papers left on the desk. What about the standards? Will they be safe in the chest?" The standards for each unit, along with any coin, were stored in an iron-bound chest under the floor of the chapel. There was also the matter of the garrison's documents. I groaned. This was a nightmare. "The documents, what about them?" Panic was making me sound shrill, but I couldn't help it.

"Do not worry, Hannah, we have moved the documents; they are in a safe place at no risk from fire." I didn't really care where on earth this might be. They seemed sure, that was enough for me.

"Sorry, I know it's not my place to worry, but it saves me from going completely mad." They both chuckled. "I'm going back over to our house to see what else I might be able to salvage if the flames do catch hold."

"Hannah, no — wait," consternation clear in Petronius' tones, "you should go and find Maxentius, he'll be worried." I was already out of the door.

"I'll only be a few minutes, I need to get my bag anyway. It's got my medicines in it." I was halfway down the hall, when Petronius called after me —

"Be sure you don't linger, Hannah, these buildings will go up like torches. Let me come with you."

"It's okay, Petronius, I'll be as quick as a flash." I was out of the door and nearly home when I heard a voice, grating and harsh, but one that seemed vaguely familiar. I slowed, listening, trying to work out where it was coming from.

"Give me the garrison, Maxentius Valerius and I will spare your wife." It was Gratius. My steps faltered and I followed the sound around the building until I came to the end of the principia. I wasn't really sure how Gratius thought he was going to spare me when he didn't actually have me. Peeping around the corner, I could see Maxentius and Marcus facing Gratius, who had his back to me. I could tell that my husband was furious, but also that he was in pain and struggling to stay upright, his face ashen in the moonlight. Marcus wasn't exactly holding him up, but was standing close enough to be a support, if necessary.

I edged along the wall until I was in my husband's line of vision. I couldn't understand why no-one had caught Gratius. How had he entered the fort unseen and where were the other soldiers? Surely they didn't intend to just let him get away with this? Confused at the lack of action, I dragged my thoughts back to the scene unfolding in front of me.

Gratius hadn't moved and I realised that he was unaware of my presence. I did a little jig and caught Maxentius' eye, letting him see that I was not being held somewhere against my will. Fatigued as he was, I thought he might burst out laughing at my antics, but he managed to control himself.

"Come on, you fool, surely you do not wish me to hurt her."

"Your words mean nothing, Gratius, my wife is safe from your schemes. Do you think I would let you touch her? Be warned, my men are close, you will not escape the fort this night." He paused and then said with a hint of indifference as if bored by Gratius' words, "Rather than undermine the garrison, your recent actions have had opposite effect, and the loyalty you assumed could be destroyed by your malicious conspiracy has been strengthened. You have become like the fly that keeps banging on the shutters, Gratius, very, very annoying." Gratius snarled in his throat; it was a noise much like the wild dogs made when they were guarding food, and a shiver ran down my spine.

"Ha, your men!" Contempt dripped from his tongue and he spread his arms in a demonstrative gesture. "Where are they all when you need them. I cannot see any coming to your aid. They do as they please, or have likely fled like the curs they are, for you have no control. So much for this loyalty you seem so proud of. When I am in charge, they will bow to my command, because I shall enforce it." Then, almost as an afterthought, "If I find her, I will take her." I saw Maxentius clench his jaw, the only outward sign that Gratius' words were affecting him. He forced himself to ignore the soldier and, waving his hand in dismissal, turned to walk away.

"I shall enjoy taming her," Gratius jeered. "She will know her place by the time I have finished with her." Watching my husband and Marcus, I knew it was all they could do to ignore Gratius taunts. With Maxentius so unwell, neither man was able to bring down the belligerent soldier, for Gratius had taken care to remain out of reach and Marcus would not leave Maxentius vulnerable. They needed back-up, yet strangely there was still no-one close enough to come to their aid and arrest Gratius; presumably they were pre-occupied trying to save others and any building from the encroaching flames.

The fort gates were barred and I knew that Gratius had no chance of getting away, or for that matter gaining control of the garrison. His bid for power would end tonight, one way or another. I was more concerned with how many more would be hurt, or worse, before the dawn broke. My husband and my brother, impotent for now, managed to rein in their anger and refused to rise to the bait. I, however, could feel a murderous rage building up inside me and knew I had to remove myself before I went for him. It was a good job I didn't have Maxentius' sword, for at that moment, I longed to run it through the perfidious soldier.

The smell of the fire was stronger now and I could hear the crackling of flames. I had to get my things. Tiptoeing back to the narrow pathway between the buildings until I was out of hearing range, I hotfooted it into the residence. Flying through the atrium, along the walkway and into our bedroom, I picked up my bag, slipping the long strap over my head. Spotting my carved pomegranate on the shelf, I grabbed that as well. No way was I leaving that to the flames. I was about to leave when I heard footsteps. Thinking it was probably Petronius coming to check on me, I went to the door with a smile on my face expecting to be admonished for taking too long, when I was confronted by a tall unkempt man with a wild expression on his face. My smile died and I backed away.

"Gratius. What are you doing here?" My voice trembled and I swallowed, determined not to appear afraid of this soldier, this traitor. I remembered how angry I was and straightened my shoulders. He sneered at me and advanced slowly into the bedroom; he seemed to fill it — and it was a big room. Maxentius was tall, but this man was huge. I kept backing up until I hit the wall. My mind whirling and hoping to distract him long enough to allow me chance to dodge past him, I asked quietly—

"Why, Gratius?" I had no need to spell it out. He halted, glaring at me.

"This garrison should be mine, there has to be some reward for all the years I have spent in this godforsaken wilderness. We have conquered the natives; now they should be subjugated, forced to abide by our rules, not pandered to; your husband is too soft. Show them a hint of kindness and the next thing, they will kill us in our beds." He growled the words, stepping towards me. I ran my tongue around my mouth, which was suddenly very dry. He had a strange light in his eyes and the fear I was trying to damp down, flooded back with a vengeance. Tilting his head as if contemplating something, Gratius changed tack.

"I just need something to bargain with," he paused, his tones becoming silky, "come here, my sweet, seems your husband thinks you are safe. Oh dear, how wrong could he be? I believe now would be a good time to make you mine."

"Not a chance, Gratius." I was pleased to note that my voice sounded quite vexed. "Get out before you do something you might regret."

"We're way past regret, Hannah Valerius. If caught I am doomed but, if I can take the garrison and remove those in my way, I might let you live as my whore."

Here we go again with the whole 'whore' jibe, I thought abstractedly. What was it with people? I was pretty sure I didn't look like a whore and I certainly didn't act or dress like one. Why did they insist on calling me one? I'd had enough.

"I have never been and never will be anyone's whore," I spat at him. "How dare you?" He laughed, but there was no humour in it.

"I really don't know how you can stop me. Your so-called husband has no idea you are here and I can't see anyone saving you now. You need a little taming, but I think I can handle you." I bit back a moan of terror and pressed up against the wall. There had to be a way out. I remembered that I still had the pomegranate in my hand and, as I registered this, I also realised that Maxentius' sword was within my grasp. Don't look at it, Hannah; you only get one go at this.

He came closer; I edged along the wall, my fingers feeling for the hilt. He stretched his hand and stroked one finger down my throat and over the ruby clasp murmuring almost dreamily. "This clasp will bring me some welcome coin. I will enjoy the challenge of removing it and this cloak from your neck as I break you." I wrenched away, wrapping my fingers over my talisman. Over my dead body, I thought; then gulped, perceiving that it might well be. Gratius was not to be put off, however, and reached out again. This time he caught my hair, which had fallen loose from its plait. I jerked my head, but he held on tightly and twisted a curl around his fingers.

"Such soft hair," he murmured. Then yanked it, making me squeal with pain. "There is no escape, Hannah." His words brought back very bad memories and I could feel nausea rising, followed very quickly by fury. No way, you piece of dirt, I thought, not this time. I lifted my right hand and, with as much strength as I could muster, hurled the pomegranate at him. He was quite close and it hit him square on the forehead, bouncing into a corner. He grunted, in shock rather than in pain I think, and tightened his grip on my hair. I squared up to him and leant towards his face.

"You think you can tame me? Think again." I hissed and bringing my leg up, kneed him hard in his groin. He doubled up and let go of my hair. I moved then, my fingers finally gripping the hilt of Maxentius' sword. It was longer and heavier than the gladius I was used to and knowing its weight was going to be a strain on my arms, I flexed my shoulder and, readying myself, swung it up.

Taking a deep breath, I forced my mind to empty of everything except the sword. Hoping I would remember my lessons and avoiding Gratius who was lying on the floor writhing in agony, I jumped up onto the bed making for the doorway. I knew that if Gratius could catch me, I'd pay dearly for hurting him, but I had the sword now.

Smoke was surging along the corridor, the courtyard acting as a chimney, drawing the flames towards us. I could hear the pop of the wood, splintering as it grew hot and the air was acrid with fumes from furnishings mixed in with the resin from the wood of the buildings. How many were on fire? I started to cough as the smoke filtered into the room. We didn't have long to get out. I had almost made it to the door when Gratius reached me. He tried to pull me back, but I jabbed the sword at him, the blade slashing through his cloak.

"Don't touch me!" I shrieked, waving the sword rather recklessly at him. He edged around trying to force me back into the bedroom, but I was having none of it. I started to slice the blade in lazy arcs in front of me, keeping Gratius one step away from being able to touch me. I knew I couldn't do it for very long. How on earth did Maxentius ever use this thing? It weighed a tonne.

Gratius was laughing; it was a maniacal sound and it seemed that he might well have been taken by madness. As I backed along the corridor I could see flames licking along the walls and across the ceiling. I kept backing up until I sensed that I was near the atrium. The blaze was relentless and, regardless of whether or not he ended up catching me, we had to get out. Trying to talk some sense into the crazed soldier, I raised one hand, still gripping the sword with the other. I was gasping for air now.

"Gratius, we need to get out, this fire will take us if we don't." He ignored my plea and bore down on me. With one last effort, I swung the sword hard and felt it come into contact with something. Gratius bellowed and I screamed as blood spewed out of a long gash across his chest. I was very nearly sick. The only thing that stopped me was that I didn't have time. I was out of strength and the sword clattered onto the tiled floor. Abandoning any thought of trying to use it again, I tried to get to the door.

"No you don't, whore." Really? I thought woozily, still at it? "If I am to die here, you will die with me." I could see the blood soaking through his clothes and dripping onto the floor as he stretched his arm out and caught my tunic. I squirmed in panic, the material started to tear and frantically I pulled away, hearing my tunic rip, as I broke free of his clutch. I was sobbing in terror now as the flames engulfed the building. The door was just there, but I couldn't reach it. Pieces of the walls were disintegrating into the corridor, the whole roof would likely collapse on us. The smoke was so thick that I became disorientated. I knew I had to get low, that the smoke would rise and there might be a little space of clean air near the floor. As I dropped to the ground, I felt a rush of fresh air as the door opened. A figure burst through and there was a blur of movement. I crawled across the atrium to the entrance — so close. Behind me there was a fight. I could hear grunts and thuds as fists hit flesh. A voice yelled —

"Don't you hurt her, you..." the roar of the fire obliterating whatever else he shouted as it blazed over our heads.

"We have to get out," I tried to shout, but my voice was croaky from all the smoke. There was a horrendous cracking sound and I looked up just as the whole roof above me came crashing down. I hurled myself towards the open doorway, wondering rather detachedly whether I would die in my own world too if I died here. I was trapped, encircled by a wall of orange flame and merciless heat. I glanced above me and saw the black smoke billowing upwards, besprinkled with bright sparks shooting up into the clear night sky. Beyond the smoke, I noticed the stars; they were breathtakingly beautiful.

"I'm sorry Max," I whispered, not sure which one of my remarkable husbands I was apologising to. "I tried."

The rest of the building came down.

Chapter Thirty Two

The fort had been reduced to utter chaos, but was slowly being brought back into some form of order. A large contingent of soldiers was passing buckets of water along a line trying to douse the flames, and at long last seemed to be bringing them under control. The orange glow from the fire had lit the sky for miles around and the villagers, realising that something was amiss, had come to see whether they could offer any assistance, an offer that was gratefully accepted. The whole fort was now a hive of activity. Soldiers are always happiest when they have something to do, something to aim for, and this night's goal was to fix up the fort. The locals worked alongside their erstwhile conquerors, and slowly a more positive atmosphere began to pervade the air.

The fire had destroyed several buildings including the legatus' residence. It was still dark and in the light from the smouldering embers there were two who were frantically trying to find Hannah. Before long, they were joined by two more. Petronius and Julius had expected that she would be with her husband by now and were aghast to discover that she was missing.

"She said she was going to get her bag, that she was only going to be a minute and then she would find you in the quadrangle," Petronius informed Maxentius.

"And you let her go alone?" he expostulated as the four men turned to survey what was left of the residence. It was ruined; only one wall remained standing and it was leaning at an alarming angle. Maxentius shuddered and all four moved as one towards the devastation. The area was still searingly hot and they had to take great care. If that wall came down, anyone under it would be killed, or at the very least seriously wounded. Cautiously, they searched where they could. Every step was fraught with danger and Marcus was very worried about his commander who appeared to be on the verge of collapse.

"Maxentius, let us look, you should not be doing this." Marcus pleaded with him.

"I will not rest until we have found her," Maxentius replied through gritted teeth. His head was pounding and he reckoned he was seeing double, but he would not stop until he held his Hannah, even if she was... he refused to finish that thought and waved away any assistance. Knowing it was fruitless to dissuade him, Marcus continued his own search. They had been looking for quite some time when suddenly Julius called them over.

"I've found something." They held their breaths. "It's Gratius." There was a short silence. "He is dead." Another moment of silence, then Petronius asked in a puzzled tone —

"What was Gratius doing here? This is your home." They looked at each other, the same thought filtering into their minds at the same time.

"He was after Hannah," ground out Julius, "the filthy louse."

"I told him she was safe. Why would he look for her?" Maxentius muttered, the torment clear in his tone. "I should have cut him down." Knowing that this had been impossible did not make his anguish any less bearable.

"Keep looking," shouted Marcus, "she must be here somewhere," although he rather hoped she was not. Anyone under this rubble would likely be burnt to a crisp. The thought of losing the woman who had become a sister to him nearly brought Marcus to his knees. She had saved them so many times, but this time when she needed them, they had failed her.

They continued to search, others joining them. Many knew and cared for Hannah and were horrified that it appeared she had been killed in the flames. It was a long and dangerous job, but they did not give up. The body of Calidius was recovered, lying very close to that of Gratius, confusing those combing the ruins as to what he was doing in the residence. His position in death suggested he may have been fighting with the other man, but they had no way of knowing for sure. One of the soldiers found Maxentius' sword between the inner courtyard and the atrium, half buried under what looked like a wall, but nobody could understand how it had come to be there.

Meticulously, they sifted through the wreckage of the building from the back to the front, and just as the dawn broke they reached what had once been the main doorway. Suddenly from the depths of the debris, Julius was sure he heard a groan. He held up his hand.

"Shush." Instantly, everyone shushed. "Did you hear that?" Silence fell across the site. Nobody moved. You could have heard a pin drop. It came again, and as they stood around the scene of destruction like sentinels guarding the last vestiges of the night, an extremely sooty, dirty and ash-covered creature staggered out from under an incinerated heap of wood that may well have been the door itself. It appeared to be a woman. She opened her eyes, the most beautiful green eyes, glistening like emeralds in her blackened face, which widened in astonishment as they took in all the people standing stock-still across the ruins staring back in shock. Her singed and tattered clothing was covered by the remnants of a cloak — well something that resembled a cloak — caught at the neck by a deep red clasp that glimmered in the pale light of the dawn.

"Am I dead then? Are you all angels?" Then, "Oh, they might not know about angels." Unable to help himself, and later he would say it was because he was so thankful that she was alive, Marcus smothered a bark of laughter. Petronius and Julius heaved huge sighs of relief but Maxentius was transfixed to the spot. He blinked and then blinked again. Was it her? Was it really her? Had she somehow survived? He tried to speak, but nothing would come out. Hannah tried to move, but her tunic was caught on a piece of charred wood.

She stumbled and fell to her knees, which galvanised Maxentius into action. Without thought or care, he shot across the splintered wood — which continued to burn in places — carefully unhooking the material of her tunic from the wood and gathering her into his arms. She seemed dazed and confused until he started scattering kisses all over her face. Then she giggled, a sound that rippled out over the quiet, lifting the spirits of those who had been searching, when all they had expected to find was death and sorrow.

"Maxentius, stop, there are people watching. Does this mean I'm not dead?" Plaintively.

"You are most definitely alive, although finding you covered in soot and ash is becoming a habit. Are you sure you're not a fire sprite?" As he said this, Maxentius froze, unsure what had prompted his words, the phrase reverberating through his mind — a picture of Hannah in a huge cistern and another at the end of a street blanketed in ash. Images tumbled into his consciousness, reviving his memories. He could hear Hannah talking to him, asking what was wrong. He nearly laughed out loud — she was asking *him* what was wrong. She was the one who'd been buried under a tonne of burning building. Only his Hannah would worry about others at a time like this.

I heard people calling my name. There was no more fire, but I couldn't work out whether I was dead and it was angels, or alive and actual people were trying to find me. My mouth was parched, so I couldn't shout back. I tried to move and realised that whatever was on top of me had little weight to it. I pushed myself up and managed to stand, feeling something slither down my back. I looked around and saw lots of people standing absolutely still, all staring at me. I felt a bit ridiculous actually. My vision was indistinct and I thought it might be a good idea to check where I was, so asked whether they were angels; then remembered that they probably wouldn't know about angels in this era. Good one, Hannah!

Nobody answered me, which seemed a bit weird. Then I heard Marcus bite down on a laugh; it was such a nice sound. Maybe I wasn't dead. I tried to move but something was caught around my clothing and I fell. It was all a bit too hard, if I'm honest. Then suddenly Maxentius was there, unhooking my tunic and lifting me into his arms. Oh, and what lovely arms. Then he was kissing me...hmmm...so, probably alive then. The soot from my clothes and hair was splattering all over him and I tried to stop him. What was he thinking kissing me in front of all these people? He wouldn't stop and it was quite funny. I couldn't prevent a giggle. I was alive and Maxentius was kissing me — what a relief!

He asked me whether I was a fire sprite. I was looking at him as he said this and everything stilled. He was quiet for so long that I began to worry, as he seemed to have disappeared within himself. Oh dear, this couldn't be good.

"Maxentius, please, what's wrong? Please tell me. Don't go having a relapse on me now. I think I might need you." My husband held me close and whispered in my ear —

"Oh, my little fire sprite, you have worked a miracle today." I gazed at him, biting my lip, thinking he might have actually lost the plot. "I remember." I searched his face looking deep into his eyes, a frisson of happiness running through me.

"Really?" I whispered back. "Everything?" He nodded.

"Everything!" I burst into tears, sobbing helplessly in his arms. Marcus came over and helped Maxentius carry me from the smouldering pile of wood. A cheer went up from the crowd and I felt the hot flush of embarrassment; however, since I was pretty sure my face was very grimy, no one would be able to tell. They rushed me over to the hospital, which was surprisingly undamaged; some scorch marks along the wall nearest the residence but otherwise intact.

"I have to bathe, all this soot, please don't put me on one of those lovely white sheets." They all ignored me and then Petronius came along with Atius, who also seemed rather pleased to see me.

"Hannah! You are alive! I am so happy."

"Me too," I grinned shakily, "but I'm quite dirty; I think I might need a bath." He chuckled but said that they would need to wash me very carefully, in case there were burns to my skin. If they rinsed the soot and filth off too quickly, it could cause further damage. So far Maxentius had refused to relinquish his hold, but the others persuaded him to lie me down.

"Don't leave me," I muttered, trying to reach his hand. He moved to sit alongside me and held my very dirty hand in his, rubbing my palm with his thumb.

"I'm not going anywhere, my Hannah. Let them look after you." I felt more tears spilling over, following the others that had left smeary tracks down my cheeks. I couldn't seem to stop them. "Don't cry, my love, you are safe now. Gratius can't hurt you anymore."

"Is that an Aharon can't hurt you, or a dead can't hurt you?" I asked, my voice rather hoarse. Maxentius grinned, remembering that when Aharon had told us Tobias couldn't hurt me anymore, we'd assumed he meant he was dead, when in fact he'd just been banished.

"He's dead. We have found his body and that of Calidius, although what he was doing in that inferno is beyond me."

"Oh, I might know, I'll tell you when my head stops whirling," I said. "I feel rather odd, maybe I need to sleep." I squeezed Maxentius' hand. "I love you." I murmured, as everything began to spin crazily and then went black.

I have no recollection of the next little while. Later Maxentius told me that they had spent many hours cleaning away all the soot. The scorching heat had melted my tunic and some of it had stuck to me, the removal of which required great care so as not to peel away my skin along with the material. Breeda had joined Atius and they had worked together using their extensive knowledge of remedies to treat the burns that I had not realised I suffered from — although quite how I thought I could come out of that conflagration unscathed, I do not know.

The burns covered quite a lot of my body, but they were mostly superficial, which was some consolation. The fire had flashed over so fast that I had escaped the worst of it, and even though I remembered being surrounded by flames, by the time they actually reached me, they had no more fuel and had burnt out almost immediately. My lungs ached, which was apparently from breathing in too much smoke, but staying close to the ground had prevented any serious damage and Atius didn't think there would be any long-term effects.

Breeda recommended honey mixed with milk to create a balm, which they coated me in, then covered me in damp cloths, leaving it for several hours before carefully sponging it off and repeating the process. It felt rather peculiar on my skin but was very soothing and cool. Much of my hair had been singed and was falling out, so the decision was made to cut its length.

I slept more than I was awake, but on those few occasions when I did open my eyes Maxentius was always there. I worried vaguely that he should be resting as well, but I couldn't wake up enough to tell him. My sleep was filled with the most convoluted dreams, some of which, inevitably, were full of terror. I'm almost certain that I returned to my other world briefly, but every time I came round I was in the hospital in the fort at Magnis, so maybe I only imagined it.

.......oooooOOOooooo.......

His wife tossing and flailing, muttering about fire startled Max awake. He tried to wake her, worried that she was seeing the crash again. She was too hot and her hair was all over the pillow, damp tendrils clinging to her face. He managed to draw her to him, talking to her, trying to reach inside her head.

Eventually she calmed down, but the muttering continued. He couldn't make it out, but it sounded like she was talking about the fort.

Confused over what was happening and unable to do anything except hold her, Max distracted himself by looking over Hannah's shoulder and through the window. Dawn was breaking, illuminating the room with fingers of soft light. A gentle breeze, scented with the honeysuckle that grew in riotous abandon over the porch, wafted over them as he lay, propped up against the pillow, his wife in his arms. It was going to be another beautiful day, a day he would be able to enjoy with Hannah properly for the first time in a week. He remembered that he needed to return the pomegranate today and hoped that his wife would go with him to the museum.

As these thoughts were rolling around, Hannah stopped muttering and opened her eyes. She stared at him for a long time, then lifted her hands and cupped his head, bringing his mouth down to hers. She kissed him with an almost desperate passion, and feeling a familiar desire curling through him, Max tightened his embrace. Then her hands fell away and as suddenly as she had awoken, she had disappeared back to wherever she had just come from.

Stunned, Max stared at Hannah. It was as though he had dreamed it. He pinched himself — no, he was definitely awake — what on earth? There was nothing he could do; he would just have to wait.

.......oooooOOOooooo.......

Chapter Thirty Three

One morning I woke and realised that I must be getting better. My body wasn't thrumming in pain or itching from the burns and I felt as though I could move without expecting my skin to rip open. I was on my side, the only way I had been able to rest, as the burns made it uncomfortable for me to lie on my back. I was also hungry. I knew that I had probably eaten at some point over the last however long, but I had no memory of doing so.

I stretched carefully and then rolled slowly onto my back, settling myself against the pillow. My head felt a bit weird, sort of weightless, and I raised my hand to touch it, realising that nearly all my hair was gone; it was barely to my shoulders. I must have made a sound, for suddenly a hand grasped one of mine and a thumb began to rub my palm.

"Do not fret, my love, they had to cut it. It was all singed." I turned my head to see Maxentius, his face lined with fatigue, sitting in the chair next to the bed.

"How long have I been here?" I murmured.

"A week?" No way! This was ridiculous. I had things to do: a son to be reunited with, a home to fix up, all that smoke — everything would need a really good scrub.

"I have to get up, there are things I should be getting on with. We need to get Luc and sort out the house." Maxentius chuckled.

"Honestly, Hannah, you always refuse to heed your own advice, don't you. Luc is fine and we actually don't have a house to sort out, so you can stay right there until Atius and Breeda say you are fit to get up." I stared at him in shock.

"B-b-but...wait, no house at all? What? Surely not all of it burnt down?"

"No buts. You might have been killed in that fire. The whole house fell down around you; there was only one wall left standing and that one only just. You are exceptionally lucky to have received relatively light burns, and those looking after you would prefer to be satisfied that you are healing properly." I tried to glare at him and may have harrumphed. I didn't feel lucky; my skin had been itching like hell. My expression didn't make any difference; in fact it just made him chuckle all the more.

"Patience has never been one of your virtues, has it, my love?" Pulling a face, I gave in, diverting his attention by asking what had been happening. Knowing exactly what I was up to, Maxentius grinned and gave me a brief rundown of what they had been doing since the night of the fire.

They had cleared the ruins of our house and started to rebuild it. Several of the workshops and two of the barracks had also been damaged beyond repair and they had begun reconstructing those buildings also. They had found several other bodies in the wreckage and even though it appeared that they had all been part of Gratius' mutineers, not soldiers loyal to Maxentius, it was still very sad. Their remains, such as they were, had been dealt with the same respect owed to all dead soldiers and they had been cremated — I know, ironic really — the day after the fire.

Those soldiers who had been swayed by Gratius' argument and had not died in the fire had come forward, appalled at the lengths to which a man they thought suitable to command them had gone to take the fort. None of those who survived had been party to the fire; Gratius and a few of his closest conspirators had set the flames. None had wanted any soldier dead at their hands and had freely admitted to whatever their part in the insurrection had been. Most were just fed up at being so far from home or from their regular army base, and had hoped that if Gratius took command they might get transferred back.

Maxentius and Marcus had deliberated long and hard over what punishment to inflict. Decimation was a real consideration, bearing in mind how fatal the fire had been. They decided on clemency, however, as the ringleader and his accomplices were dead and the remainder appeared truly repentant. They had been banished from the fort and would have to camp beyond its protective palisade — which had somehow escaped the flames — for a week with only barley for rations. It was very unpleasant but was the least harsh retribution for their actions.

These same soldiers would also have to live with the fact that they had risked the safety of all within the fort, not to mention their blatant disloyalty. Many of the garrison had served under Maxentius for years and would not likely forgive and forget as easily as their commander. They would have a long road ahead before their lives could be considered back to normal.

"You said that you found Calidius in the residence as well?" I asked when Maxentius had completed his update. He nodded.

"He was lying next to Gratius. The roof had collapsed on the top of them both and Calidius was crushed under a heavy beam. Neither of them had a chance."

"He came to save me," I said quietly. Maxentius raised his eyebrows in question and waited for me to elaborate. "I was crawling along the floor, trying to get to the door, when it opened and Calidius came through like a whirlwind. I have no idea how he knew we were there. I heard them fighting and Calidius yelling something about not hurting me. Then the roof collapsed, but before I could escape, the walls caved in on us." I shuddered, long tremors running through me as the horror of that night reared its ugly head. Maxentius stroked my arm gently, taking care not to put any pressure on the bandages covering the sensitive skin.

"Why were you there, my Hannah?"

"I went to get my bag. I had filled it with as many remedies and balms as I could get into it and the pictures of the children. Then I spotted my pomegranate and couldn't leave that." I paused remembering, "Oh, no, no, no! I'm sorry Max, I threw it at Gratius, it hit him on the head and bounced away. It must have been destroyed by the fire." I was devastated. Maxentius had carved it for me on Masada and I had carried it everywhere. "My bag, the pictures, my pomegranate, oh and your sword. I used your sword, but I dropped it, it was so heavy. How do you carry that thing?" My words were all over the place, but as coherence has never been my strong point I wasn't overly concerned. My husband was used to me.

"We have your bag. It must have been lying underneath you, for it is undamaged except for part of the carrying strap. I have not seen the pomegranate, but someone found my sword under the remains of the roof. Don't upset yourself. I can carve you another."

"It's not the same. It was carved with wood from the palace and it was special."

"I know, my love, but if it's gone it's gone, we cannot change this."

I muttered, rather despondently, that I supposed he was right, but it didn't make it any easier. The loss of my pomegranate gnawed at me, when out of the blue I remembered the walk Maxentius and I had taken. I gripped his hand, more tightly than I had intended and my husband looked at me in alarm.

"What's wrong, Hannah?"

"Nothing, nothing's wrong, but do you remember our walk? He looked at me askance. We had taken many, many walks. Frowning, he rested his free hand on my forehead and pressed his fingers to the pulse at my wrist. I batted at him, smiling. "Very funny; stop pretending you know what you're doing." I chuckled. "No, the walk just after I'd been out in the snow?" I gazed at him and then said, "Oh, maybe you don't remember all those little things quite yet." I bit my lip.

"I remember everything, my love, I'm just trying to recall which particular walk you're talking about.

"The one where I said that I'd — or rather she'd — found it, found the pomegranate." He stared at me and I willed his mind to catch up. He smiled and lifted my fingers to his lips, kissing them softly.

"I do recall that walk. You said you — she — had found the pomegranate and an inscription." I nodded excitedly.

"I know it seems strange, but even though I haven't got it now, it isn't lost, she'll — I'll — find it in about nineteen hundred and thirty years." I relaxed, completely ignoring how incongruous that last conversation would have sounded to anyone else. I was suddenly very much in need of a hug. "Oh, Maxentius, I know I'm being pathetic, but I really want you to hold me. Will they let you? I don't think I'll break."

He looked uncertain. Atius and Breeda were concerned that too much physical contact would be painful or would rub my scars making me sore. I was past caring. "Please, I need this, I can draw strength from your touch and while holding hands is rather lovely, I find it isn't enough."

My husband gave in, as I expected he would. Very carefully, he got onto the bed his legs outstretched and, moving the pillow so that it supported his back, leaned his upper body against the wall. He lifted me gently onto his lap, bringing the blanket up over the both of us. I curled up against him breathing in his scent, the comfort I desired immediate.

"Just hold me." Over the blanket, his arms went around me and cradling me, he nestled my head onto his shoulder. "How's your poor head?" I asked.

"Much better. We are a bit of a pair at the moment, aren't we? Much as we both miss Luc, I am very pleased he is being looked after by Senna. Neither of us are in a fit state to care for a rambunctious baby at the moment." I leaned away from Maxentius so that I could see his face. He smiled down at me and, unable to stop myself, I kissed his jawline, the stubble scratching my cheek. I giggled, as for some reason this scruffy look always made me laugh; he was usually clean-shaven and the bristles gave him a slightly piratical appearance. He looked affronted and, stifling my laughter, I kissed him again.

"Can't help it, you have that whole dishevelled look off to a fine art." I giggled again and he, very gingerly, moved me so that I was facing him.

"Is that so?" He muttered and cupping the back of my head drew my face close to his. Just when I thought he was going to kiss me, he rubbed his jaw all over mine, my face being about the only part of me where there were no burns. He was merciless, tickling me with the stubble until I was laughing helplessly, trying to push him away. He was much stronger, but I knew he couldn't grip me tightly. I was hiccuping with mirth when he finally relaxed his hold and I fell against his chest.

"So, on top of everything else, now I have stubble rash — charming." Laughing had made me feel better, though, and my thoughts were less dark. Maxentius tilted my chin and then did kiss me, very tenderly. I responded, my body tingling and this time it wasn't the burns itching. The kiss deepened and for long moments everything else faded into insignificance; I was safe and my husband's arms were around me. The passion that never failed to ignite was there, but tucked away, circling the edges of our consciousness, and I revelled in simply being cherished.

Soon after, Atius and Breeda appeared to redress my burns. Rarely leaving my side since the fire, Maxentius took this opportunity to go and check on his garrison. Marcus was perfectly capable of overseeing everything — in fact it was his job — but Maxentius liked to be kept abreast of the daily activities and deal with any missives that had been received.

It was becoming much less uncomfortable to have the bandages removed and the balm washed away. My skin still looked rather red and raw to me, but my two medici seemed very pleased with my progress. I watched them work for a little while then asked —

"When can I get up?" They looked at each other, then back at me.

"I'm not sure you're ready just yet, Hannah, it's only been a week." I bit my lip with frustration.

"I'm so fed up with lying here, I need to see the sky and smell the fresh air and I really, really need to see Luc. Have you any idea how this feels? I haven't seen him for over a month. He will think Senna is his mother. He won't remember either Maxentius or me. The fear of attack on the fort is over, neither he nor Senna are in any danger and I really want my son back." My voice was rising in my consternation and the yearning to be reunited with my son.

Yes, we had three other children and I missed them dreadfully, but I could not have seen them even if I'd wanted to; they were out of reach. My baby, my little boy, was less than an hour's walk away and I was beginning to think I'd never see him again. I blinked hard to stop the useless tears that were forming, cursing myself for being so feeble.

"I'm sorry, I know I'm a bad patient, but this is doing my head in. I'm not used to staying in bed and I'm bored."

Atius and Breeda listened to my litany of woes and, instead of being sympathetic, the pair of them burst out laughing. I gaped at them — how rude! Then Atius spoke in serious tones —

"Hannah, you have only woken properly today. Up until now you have been barely conscious, so I fail to see how you have had the time to become bored. Your burns are healing nicely, but too much movement will stretch the skin making you even more sore. The honey and milk balm is working wonders, but you need to give it time. If Maxentius agrees to carry you, I may..." I started to sit up, but he raised his hand "...I only said may, let you go outside for a little while after the eighth hour when the day is a little cooler. You will not walk about, you will sit quietly and there will be no excitement." I beamed at the medicus.

"I promise. Oh, thank you so much and I'll try and behave." Breeda chuckled.

"Healers are always the worst patients," she said, "and have no fear, Luc will not forget you. You are his mother; you have a bond with him that is unbreakable. Trust me." She laid her hand on my cheek, brushing away the one treacherous tear that trickled over. "Now, we have a little food here." She lifted a bowl of something that smelled delicious and made my stomach growl, to the amusement of the two of them. "Let me help you, then I think maybe a little more sleep before you go outside." Giving up, I let Breeda feed me, feeling like a recalcitrant child. The food was very welcome, though, and I managed to eat it all.

By the time I had finished and had drunk from the goblet she handed to me, I had to admit to feeling rather weary. The simple effort of eating had worn me out. Pitiful, I know. When I mentioned this, they grinned at me and I raised my hands in mock surrender.

"Okay, okay, you win, I'm ready to rest. No need to look so happy about it." Telling me they'd be back to check on me later, they went off to attend to whoever else was in the hospital. I realised with a jolt that it was unlikely that I was the only one hurt in the fire. I'd been lying here feeling sorry for myself, when there could be others with far worse injuries. I would ask Maxentius when he came back. I had just started to mull over how much longer I might be restricted to bed, when my thoughts began to tumble around and I couldn't hold anything in focus. Before I knew it, oblivion came along and claimed me once more.

Chapter Thirty Four

Despite my best attempts, it turned out that it would be several more days before I was allowed to get up. Later that same day, I started to feel quite unwell, nauseous and shivery. Atius discovered that one or two of my burns had become infected, resulting in a low fever and I was advised in no uncertain terms to stay put.

Truth be told, I felt so awful that I was happy to comply. Atius and Breeda put their heads together again and dosed me with a combination of white willow, elderberry and garlic steeped in water. It smelt quite similar to calda actually, and since I was scarcely conscious I didn't notice what it tasted like. All I can remember is that it seemed to be very soothing and certainly helped me to sleep. After three days, they were satisfied that the infection was out of my system, but they made me stay in bed another two, just to be sure.

You would be right in assuming that by this time I'd had enough. No fresh air — well proper outside fresh air anyway — no exercise, no family, nothing to do except lie and be cared for. To some this would seem blissful, but not to me. I hate being unable to look after myself and once they had cured me of the fever, I felt like I was going stir crazy.

Nearly two weeks after the fire, I was finally allowed to leave the hospital, but only for a short time. I was under strict instructions not to involve myself in any kind of activity other than to sit quietly and watch the world go by. Not quite what I wanted, but it would have to do.

Maxentius carried me out, ignoring my protestations that I was perfectly capable of walking, sat me down on one of the benches that hugged the walls of the hospital and wrapped a blanket over my legs. It was a beautiful day, the sun was high and the sky, dotted around with a smattering of white fluffy clouds, was the most incredible blue. I realised that we had been here about a year. The seasons would be changing again soon. The light was less intense than it had been; summer was nearly over. I sighed, a sigh of pure happiness, breathing in the clean air, enjoying the familiar bustle of the fort going on all around me.

"This is lovely, Maxentius, thank you for carrying me out." He grinned.

"A pleasure, my love, it's good to see you looking so much better."

"How soon do you think it will be before they let us go and fetch Luc?" My constant catch-cry.

"Maybe next week. Atius has pronounced himself very pleased with my head and says I may resume full-time duties in two days." He had been doing only short stints while I had been in the hospital, partly because he had wanted to stay with me and partly because Atius had told him to take it easy. Interestingly, my husband had bowed to the medicus' expertise and done as he was told. Hmm...I may have to ask Atius how he managed that.

I leaned against Maxentius and he slung an arm over the back of the bench, resting his hand lightly on my shoulder. Everywhere I looked there were people working. The outside walls and roof of our house were complete, but apparently they had not yet finished the internal rooms. Seemingly, they had reorganised one of the barracks and all our staff and Marcus were sleeping there at the moment.

"Where have you been sleeping?" I asked Maxentius curiously.

"Next to you at the hospital. Atius set a cot up alongside your bed so that I could stay close." You would think I might have noticed this, but he had sat beside me every night until I went to sleep and was either in the same position or gone when I awoke. I smiled at him. All the love I felt bubbled over and I squeezed his hand tightly. "Well, you know you cannot be trusted to do as you're told," he chuckled, "someone had to make sure you followed orders." I couldn't stop smiling, my face almost split with the beam I bestowed on him.

"I love you, Max."

"I love you too, my Hannah."

We sat for a long time, just the two of us, watching all the comings and goings across the quadrangle. While we were there, many of the soldiers came over to spend a few moments with us; chatting about this and that, expressing their delight at my recovery, pointing out the new buildings and what they would be used for, and even explaining that they'd set up a better way of alerting the fort to an emergency such as a fire or an attack.

A large circle of solid metal had been forged in one of the undamaged workshops. It was huge, its shape very slightly domed. Apparently, when it was hit with a wooden club, it boomed and could be heard all over the fort and quite a distance beyond, much louder than the horn. It was to be placed at the main door of the principia and only to be used if danger was imminent. It was a splendid piece, highly polished and shone like silver.

Marcus joined us for a little while, telling us he was taking a break because he was knee-deep in reports, which made me laugh. I knew how much he hated reports. He had visited me every day since the fire and his presence, as always, warmed me. He'd also been out to the village, taking over the regular meetings with the locals while Maxentius had been indisposed, and told me that Luc was doing well. I was glad to hear this, but it wasn't quite the same as seeing for myself. Pushing away my longing, I concentrated on our conversation.

"How is Senna?" I asked, grinning wickedly. Maxentius looked rather confused and I realised that Marcus hadn't told him. I chortled with laughter; oh this was too good.

"Senna is fine; she is looking forward to returning to the fort with Luc when you are ready."

"She could return now. I am happy to have her back as long as she brings my son."

"I think it is better that she remain at the village until you are a little better, Hannah," my husband interjected. "We will both go over and bring them home with us in a few days."

"I'm just not sure Marcus can wait that long," I said innocently. Maxentius looked at the two of us, trying to work out the undercurrents. Marcus tried to look annoyed, but I grinned at him and winked and he could not prevent a huge smile in response.

"Okay, you two, what on earth is going on? What am I missing?" Maxentius sounded aggrieved. I capitulated and, leaning towards my husband, whispered in his ear. He looked at me in astonishment, then back at Marcus. "Is this true?" I nodded. Marcus feigned a scowl.

"I'm assuming she has informed you that I have feelings for Senna. Hannah, men don't discuss this sort of thing."

"Why ever not?" I asked, surprised. "Such an important life-changing event. It will affect both of you in different ways. Plus, we want to share in your joy." My two Romans shook their heads, surrendering to the inevitable. "When Senna is part of our family, you'll find that conversations occasionally take on a much more, errr, personal tone. I can almost guarantee that there will come a time when Marcus needs advice on something related to being married and the only other person who may be able to help him will be you," I said, looking at my husband.

"I cannot see why," he replied looking puzzled.

"Because, you're the only other soldier here who is married. You are like the guru of military husbands," which might have gone down a whole lot better had they the slightest idea what a guru was. By the time I'd explained that, my point was well and truly forgotten. Never mind, I knew that they would remember this conversation in the not too distant future. We moved on to other things and soon Marcus had to return to his duties. He gave me a gentle hug and said he was very glad I was looking better. I smiled and, thanking him, kissed his cheek.

Petronius and Julius also came over to chat but by the time they returned to whatever jobs they had come from, I was very tired.

"Please, I think I need to go back to bed," I murmured feeling rather peculiar. Maxentius glanced at my face and scooped me up into his arms.

"I have kept you out for too long," he said rather anxiously.

"No, I'll be fine, I'm just not used to it." I yawned prodigiously; my head was all swimmy and seemed too heavy for me to hold it upright. By the time we were back in the room that Atius had assigned to me, I was fast asleep. I was right, however; it was simple overexertion, nothing more insidious, and over the next few days my strength began to return. I was even allowed to walk outside, rather than be carried and soon was able to get right around the fort with a little help. From this point on I improved quickly. It would take some time for my skin to recover and there would always be some scarring but, the rapid response of Atius and Breeda with the honey balm had reduced the possibility of it being much worse; something I was eternally grateful for.

Finally, after several more days of being monitored, Atius said he was prepared to let me visit the village and collect Luc, as long as I promised to go on horseback as walking that far would be just too much and that we would take it steadily, not race out at full gallop. Maxentius would accompany me along with a small contingent of soldiers, just in case. I wasn't quite clear on the 'just in case' part, but as long as I was allowed to go, I didn't care what the restrictions were.

We planned to go the next day. Breeda knew we would be going, as she had been at the hospital to check me over when Atius had agreed that I could travel and she said she would inform Bearach. She had given me some ointment that she wanted me to massage into my skin twice a day for the next few weeks, as she believed it would reduce any scarring even further. It smelt rather nice and I guessed it had lavender and myrrh in it and may have been blended from instructions in Atius' medical manuscripts. Whatever was in it was fine by me, as long as it helped. Although mostly healed, my skin was still quite itchy and Atius said it would be for quite some time yet while the new skin strengthened. Ugh!

I didn't sleep very well that night; I was so excited. I kept tossing and turning until in the end Atius threatened to revoke his permission. That settled me and I tried my best to go to sleep. Eventually, in the early hours, I managed a few short hours of undisturbed rest. By the time Maxentius came to collect me, having made sure everything else was in hand, I was sitting on the edge of the bed, almost bouncing in my eagerness to be on my way.

Marcus, Petronius, Julius and three other soldiers would be coming along with Maxentius and me. They were already mounted and waiting in the quadrangle. Gemmula was saddled and standing quietly. I paused for a moment to stroke her nose and chat to her. She nuzzled my neck and blew down my ear, which I took to be a sign that she was happy to see me. I mounted carefully; making sure that the skin on my legs didn't feel stretched. They seemed okay and someone had thoughtfully placed a thick blanket over my saddle for extra padding.

We trotted off and it was absolutely wonderful to be outside, really and truly outside, no longer confined to the fort. As far as I could see the undulating landscape was covered in a purple flowering plant, growing very low to the ground. I made a mental note to ask Breeda what it was; maybe it could be of some use. To our left the great forest rose up, its dark grandeur offering cool shelter along hidden pathways. The sun shone and for once everything was calm.

An abundance of birds flitted about, their throats throbbing with song, silvery notes blending together and filling the balmy air with joyful harmony. Even though we were coming to the end of the summer and the seasons would soon click over, there was a feeling of promise, of new beginnings. Or maybe it was just me; my world was safe and happy; my husband was healed; I was recovered almost fully and we were going to get our son. Life was very good.

As instructed, we didn't rush, enjoying the ride and chatting amongst ourselves. I knew the other three soldiers who were accompanying us, so the half an hour or so it took us to get there was most enjoyable. By the time we arrived, I thought I might be sick with nerves. It was so long since I'd seen our son and, despite Breeda's words, was still terrified that he had forgotten me, us — must remember that this affected Maxentius too.

We reined in our horses as we approached and my husband helped me dismount. One of the soldiers stayed with the animals and the rest of us walked slowly into the village. I was gripping Maxentius' hand so tightly that I thought he might complain, but he seemed able to put up with it. As we came towards Bearach's hut, a whole crowd of people flooded out of their homes. I took a step back, rather uncertain of our welcome. Maxentius pulled me to him, whispering that all was as they expected. Bearach strode towards us, a huge smile on his face. He nodded to Maxentius and Marcus who, along with those who had accompanied us, fisted one hand, thumping it across their chest. Bearach and all the other men from the village who had come out to meet us repeated this gesture.

Apparently this was the way they always greeted each other, after which formality, everyone relaxed. Maxentius and I were invited to enter Bearach's hut and, as we were walking towards it, I noticed a flurry of movement and turned just in time to see

Senna fly along the path and fling herself into Marcus' arms. The villagers were smiling in delight and I grinned at my husband who burst out laughing. Marcus was bright red with embarrassment, but this didn't stop him from kissing Senna very soundly.

"Told you," I murmured to Maxentius who was still chuckling. We spent a little time with Bearach and the village elders, being plied with food and beverages. They all knew what had happened at the fort and many of them had been assisting in the reconstruction effort. I accepted that this was customary, but I was very anxious to see Luc and found it difficult to sit still. I was so fidgety that at one point Maxentius pressed my leg with his in a vain attempt to calm me. I got a hold of myself. After all, it was only a few more minutes after so many weeks without him; I could handle it.

Eventually the discussion concluded, most of it went over my head but I think it went along the lines of thank you very much for trusting that we would not attack you; our friendship is very important and so on. More chest thumping and bowing and nodding. I was becoming quite uncomfortable, my limbs not used to sitting in such a position anymore and so many people in the hut made it very stuffy. Before I had to excuse myself, however, Bearach escorted us back into the fresh air and sunshine. I felt a bit odd; not enough sleep, over excitement and too long in the airless hut had made me rather dizzy.

Determined to remain upright, I reached out for Maxentius, needing his support. I heard myself make a strange gulp. He turned and I felt myself swaying as he grasped my arm.

"Sorry," I muttered, and promptly fainted. I was only out of it for a minute or so and came to lying on a mat outside Breeda's hut. Mortified, I tried to get up, but Breeda shook her head and encouraged me to drink a draft of something sweet.

"No, please, I'm fine I just felt rather stifled in the hut." She helped me to sit up and as she did so, I saw the most beautiful sight. Maxentius was walking towards me carrying our son. Luc seemed taller than he was when I had last seen him, which was entirely possible; bearing in mind it was nearly two months. He was gabbling away to Maxentius who looked as proud as punch.

There didn't seem to be any issue with Luc recognising his father and as they approached, Maxentius said something and pointed to me. Luc followed the finger and his little face lit up with a huge smile and he almost catapulted himself out of my husband's arms in a bid to get to me. He remembered me — oh the relief! With Breeda's assistance, I stood up and waited, my legs still rather unsteady. I could feel ridiculous tears forming and scrubbed them away furiously.

As they reached me, Luc stretched his arms out and I caught him in my embrace, covering his little face with kisses, murmuring his name over and over. I could scarcely believe I was holding him and wasn't sure I would ever let him go again. The tears I had tried so hard to control were spilling down my cheeks.

Never one to be affected by my crying, Luc chuckled and grabbed what was left of my hair, trying to stuff it into his mouth. I noticed that he had several more teeth and that he certainly hadn't suffered during the time we had been apart.

He was losing his baby chubbiness and I felt somewhat wistful that I had missed this stage of his growth; changes happen so quickly at this age. Still, he was alive, safe and, if his weight was anything to go by, had taken well to solid food. Fed up with being snuggled and kissed, Luc hankered to get down and I lowered him gently onto his feet. He wobbled towards Breeda who handed him a piece of bread to chew on. Maxentius pulled me to him and kissed my forehead.

"I told you there was nothing to worry about," he said, "Luc is your son, it would take much more than a few weeks apart for him to forget you." I smiled damply, enjoying the scene in front of me. Petronius and Julius had been dragged into games with the older children and the younger ones were sitting in a circle playing with little carved toys. Luc bumbled about amongst them, uncaring that he was disrupting their fun; neither did the children seem particularly bothered and included him in whatever they were doing until he pottered off on his next mission.

I leaned against Maxentius for a moment or two and then we walked slowly over to join Marcus and Senna, who were looking very pleased with themselves.

"So?" I asked, grinning at them both. Marcus blushed, which was becoming a habit, and Senna smiled at us coyly.

"I have asked Senna whether I may approach her family to request their permission for me to marry her." He hesitated, "I did ask her first whether she'd like to, though, I thought it better to check." I gurgled with laughter; he was way out of his depth.

"I'm assuming your answer was 'yes,' Senna?" I smiled at her. She nodded shyly. "I am very happy for you both," giving her a quick hug, kissing her lightly on the cheek, then adding, "welcome to the family, I hope you're sure about this because life is never boring around us." Marcus tried to look affronted and failed dismally; he was way too ecstatic. "Congratulations Marcus, if you two are half as blessed as Maxentius and I have been, you will have a long and happy union." I hugged him, whispering in his ear, "I told you so." He grinned, hugging me back.

"Go on then, get it over with, you'll not be happy until you've asked." I waved them away and they walked towards Bearach's hut hand in hand.

It was a bittersweet moment for, as had happened so many times in my life, things were changing. Our relationship with Marcus, while always very strong, would undergo a subtle shift. His priority now was Senna and this was as it should be, but the familiar intimacy we had shared for nearly fifteen years would never be quite the same. I rested my head on my husband's chest, his arms came round me and, attuned to my every emotion, he tilted my chin so that he could look into my face.

"Life never stands still for very long, does it, my Hannah?" I shook my head, not quite trusting myself to speak. "At least he will stay close. I have been thinking that I would like to remain here in this place once I have completed my term as legatus. I will be eligible to retire, or maybe serve a short term as commander in one of the nearby forts. How do you feel about that?" I stared up at him. I knew that Marcus would stay, he would not take Senna away from her family and his term in the army would also be coming to an end in a few years. I was comfortable here in the wilds of the north country and had no desire to leave.

Once — a long time ago — I hoped we could return to Masada, but I no longer had the urge to live in such a desolate place. I felt at home here; maybe it was because the other part of me, the modern me, the woman in my head, lived here millennia into the future. I liked that we were close to each other in place, even if not in time. She was still in my head, but I felt that she was returning to her own life. The thread was loosening again, but maybe if we stayed here it would not be broken entirely. An affinity would remain and I believed that if we needed each other, she would come. While all this was running through my mind, I was still gazing at Maxentius, who was waiting for my answer.

"I would like that very much," I whispered. He bent his head and, ignoring the fact that virtually a whole village never mind six of his soldiers surrounded us, kissed me for quite some time. I was breathless by the time he released me and I grinned up at him, my eyes shining and my heart pounding. Oh, I did like that feeling.

"It's settled then." We smiled at each other, happiness radiating from our faces. We had a home and a place to stay, to live, to love and to grow old together.

Chapter Thirty Five

Marcus and Senna rejoined us some time later, their jubilant expressions needing no explanation. Bearach and the village elders had approved their marriage and Senna's family had pronounced themselves agreeable to their daughter marrying a Roman soldier; another step towards greater understanding between the conquerors and those they had conquered. We stayed at the village until the sun began it slow descent towards the horizon. The three other soldiers who had accompanied us had been encouraged to leave the horses — which had been tied to a tree and provided with water and hay — to join in the activities of the village. None of them had been before and it was gratifying to see that they fitted in very quickly and seemed to have enjoyed their day.

We trotted home. Luc was tucked into Maxentius' arms, as he felt that I should not risk the chafing that the carry pouch might inflict on my skin. I was happy to oblige as I was quite tired after all day in the fresh air and doubted that I had the strength to hold my wriggling child all the way home. The gentle motion of the horse settled Luc, though, and he slept the whole of our return journey. We arrived back at the fort just before the tenth hour and Petronius said he would stable Gemmula for me. I traipsed over to the hospital to check in with Atius. We still had no home to go to, but at least we had a private room. I was really looking forward to the day we could move back into the residence. I would put up with having no furniture for the pleasure of being back in our own place again.

Maxentius followed me in and waited until Atius had examined my skin. The medicus was a little concerned at how weary I seemed, but was in agreement that it was probably owing to the long and rather excitement-filled day in the sunshine. He rubbed some of the balm into those burns that had become itchy during the last few hours, but declared that he was satisfied that I hadn't done any lasting damage.

My husband handed Luc over and my son snuggled against me, much to my delight. He would be hungry and I had no idea what Senna had been giving him to eat. I was no longer able to feed him as the last of my breast milk had dried up during our two-month separation. Even though I knew this to be a natural progression, I experienced a fleeting sadness that it had been essentially forced on us both. Just as I thought this, Senna herself came into the room with a bowl of something. I have no clue how she'd had it made up so quickly, but maybe Atius had taken longer than I realised. She handed me the feeding spoon and held the bowl while I fed my child for the first time in what felt like an age. He gobbled it up, emptying the bowl after which Maxentius took over and burped his son; again concerned about the weight of the child rubbing my delicate skin.

Once that was accomplished satisfactorily, Luc was back in my arms. I stroked his little face and ran my fingers through his downy mop, which was beginning to thicken and lengthen; his hair would be much like his father's, something I was inordinately pleased about. Before long our son was fast asleep and Maxentius lifted him from me, laying him in the small cradle that had been fashioned for us in one of the workshops. Atius brought us some food and we fell on it, inhaling the hot soup and fresh bread. A goblet of calda rounded off the meal very nicely and I knew I was ready for my own bed, even though it was still early.

Maxentius had to go and check on the daily reports and anything else that may require his attention. Telling me he would be back shortly, he kissed me and by the time he was at the door, my eyelids were drooping.

The days were shortening, the light had changed and the morning air was chill before the residence was finished. For the last few weeks prior to its completion, Maxentius, Luc and I had removed to one of the barracks. I could not live in the hospital, especially once I no longer required constant treatment. Neither was it the most suitable place for a small child. Luc was now toddling around quite easily and had learned to say Mama and Papa as well as a few other words; all of which he liked to practise all the time and usually at full volume.

Today was going to be special for two reasons. The residence had been completed and the soldiers wanted to have an official unveiling, as it were. Then once that ceremony was over, Marcus and Senna were to be wed.

For once, I took a little more care with my preparations, as I felt both occasions demanded something a little out of the ordinary. Despite the cooler weather, I decided on my dark gold silk undershift with its translucent over-tunic in palest gold. I managed to twist my short hair into a kind of bun, affixing my ruby clasp into its centre. A lightweight shawl made of fine red wool, and gold sandals completed the outfit. Maxentius would wear full armour as befitted his station and would look magnificent.

The whole garrison stood to attention as we came out of the barracks, their polished armour gleaming in the autumn sunlight. The local tribespeople, many of whom had participated in the rebuilding, stood alongside. The residence looked remarkable. Those who had worked on it had done an extraordinary job. It had been rebuilt on the same footprint of the previous house, but almost the entire lower portion was constructed in stone — a small concession to the risk of fire, I think.

The interior was painted in a light wash making everywhere seem very spacious and there were beautiful pieces of furniture scattered throughout the rooms. I could see Maxentius' hand in some of it and thanked him quietly as we were escorted through the house. Even though most of my balms, ointments and other stock had been destroyed in the fire, the soldiers had remembered about my medicines and had built me one huge room with sinks, benches and shelves all made from local stone; stacking neatly anything that had survived.

All those involved were proud of their achievement and rightly so. The aftermath of the fire had actually created a much more cohesive garrison and, after working so closely with the locals, a deeper understanding had grown between them and the soldiers.

As we came out of the very grand main door, carved with all manner of intricate patterns, I noticed something to our left and turned to inspect it. On the highest level of stonework there was one very long slab on which had been carved an inscription. As I ran my eyes over it, my two worlds collided. It was the same inscription that I had found in the museum on the day I saw the report of the plane crash. The transcriber hadn't got it quite correct, however. It was a little longer — presumably the remaining fragments were lost — and it actually read —

'To the divine power of the Emperor and under the command of Legatus L. Maxentius Valerius soldiers from COH II PR LEG XX VV and LEG II A at Magnis with contributions from the tribe of Bearach made this.'

I shivered a little and my head buzzed as I stared at the beautiful lettering, knowing that I would find this again far into the future. Maxentius glanced down at me and I shook my head imperceptibly, smiling gently. I would tell him later. Today was for this world.

The local tribespeople were very pleased to be included in the inscription; it strengthened further the ties that were flourishing between the soldiers and the locals. They had been unfailingly helpful in the rebuilding of the fort and many had begun to assist in the workshops, soldiers and villagers teaching each other traditional techniques and crafts, sharing their prodigious expertise.

Then it was time for the marriage of Marcus and Senna. The fort fell silent as Senna, surrounded by her family, walked towards Marcus looking radiantly beautiful in a simple tunic, her hair wreathed in white flowers. She carried a bunch of the purple flowers that I had noticed the day we collected Luc. Breeda had explained that the flower had many uses; this time it represented good fortune. Marcus, standing tall and handsome in full armour, could not keep the grin from his face. The official Roman ceremony was short and the locals had asked that they be allowed to perform their traditional rituals also, after which the celebrations began.

The festivities went on for most of the day, and for many stretched long into the night, generally involving lots of drinking and singing. Marcus and Senna slipped away at some point, after thanking everyone for their blessings. When the residence had been rebuilt, those working on it had been instructed to add a door between Marcus' quarters and the rest of the house, which provided him and now Senna, and by extension, us, a little more privacy. They even had the option of eating in their own triclinium, but could still join the rest of us in the main room if they preferred.

By the end of the day we were exhausted, but it had been lovely; such celebrations are rare in times of conquest, especially after so much tension and turmoil. It was also marvellous to be back in our own home. As we were walking along to our bedroom, having settled Luc in his cradle, Maxentius returned to his unspoken question from earlier in the day. I explained about the inscription, that I had searched for some kind of proof that we — well, he and Hannah — had been here after I'd seen the pomegranate, discovering fragments of the inscription on the wall of our home listed in an archive. I refrained from calling it a database, knowing the kind of confusion that would cause.

My husband stared at me for several minutes after I'd finished explaining this to him.

"I'm sorry, I know it's weird when I talk as though it's the other me, the Hannah from the future, but it's the easiest way for me to explain. You should be used to it by now." I winked. I felt my other world calling me, it was nearly time to leave — just a little longer I pleaded silently, unknowing what it was that held me here. But there was something, something I couldn't quite put my finger on, and I was not quite ready to relinquish this life.

Maxentius smiled his slow smile and my heart thudded in my chest. He came round to where I was undressing and helped me divest myself of my finery. He unclipped the beautiful clasp from my hair, laying my talisman carefully on the cupboard with one hand while running his hands through my short yet riotous locks with the other. Then he proceeded to remove all of my clothes, piece by piece. As the material floated to the floor, he drew me close and, lowering his head, brushed his lips to mine, so tenderly, but just as I started to lose myself, he pulled away. Confused, I blinked at him.

"What's wrong?" I whispered.

"I don't want to hurt you, your skin..." he paused, uncertainty clouding his expression, his breathing ragged.

"I'm fine, my love, a kiss can't hurt me."

"If you think I'm going to be able to stop at a kiss, you are sorely mistaken. We have a little catching up to do." My breath hitched as I gazed into his eyes, fathomless and burning with green fire.

"Then don't stop," I murmured, "my skin is healed, it just looks rather..." I paused, knowing that my scars weren't particularly attractive, "...errm...unpleasant." Maxentius looked down at me, surprised by my words.

"Oh, my Hannah, please do not ever think that any part of you is unpleasant. They are just scars, they may be of you but they do not define you and to me every single piece of you is beautiful." He kissed my nose and I sighed, lifting my face so that my lips met his.

He plundered my mouth, his kiss hot and fierce, and I sank into his embrace; desire for this man I had known for fifteen years coursing through me like the flames that had consumed the fort. Desire coiled round my stomach as I responded in kind, delighting in hearing Maxentius groan as my fingers played across his back and up around his neck.

"Can't...you need to...never understand..." I felt laughter rumble through my husband's chest as I tried to remove his tunic. I had never worked out how to do it easily. Surely it couldn't be that complicated? I leaned away, letting him shrug out of his clothes, moving back into his arms as we resumed that heart-stopping kiss. Gently, his hands caressed my skin, his fingers tracing the delicate edges of the scars, following each touch with a kiss and sending ripples of pleasure down my spine. Maxentius laid me on the bed, joining me there and we let the night wrap its velvety darkness around us, as we took our time to rediscover that which was so precious and that we had very nearly lost.

Several days later, I was standing at the entrance to the hospital chatting with Atius about one or two of the patients we had under our care. It was quite a chilly day and a little overcast. There had been some heavy showers over the last week and I was mindful that Luc, who was pottering about at our feet, might decide that the many puddles scattered across the compound would be great fun to splash through. He was burbling away to himself, his words an amusing mix of the recognisable and the unintelligible, distracting me from our discussion.

As we were talking, we heard the sound of horses, and at least one wagon, possibly more, appeared at the gate; and, thinking it was probably a supply train arriving, turned to watch its entry. I spotted Maxentius and Marcus appearing from the principia, which was a trifle odd, as they didn't normally deal with provisions.

The train, rather shorter than normal, rumbled into the fort and we could hear the shouts of the soldiers who had accompanied it as they called for the grooms to take the horses. I noticed that there were several people in the first wagon and tried to work out who they were. If Maxentius and Marcus were there to greet them, they were probably visiting dignitaries. Rather unusual so far north, and my husband hadn't mentioned that he was expecting anyone. Intrigued, I sat on one of the benches as everyone climbed down and then did a double take as Maxentius looked to be hugging one of them. I looked at Atius, my jaw dropping, then back to the group. Marcus did the same and by now I was speechless.

Sensing my presence, Maxentius turned and even from this distance — it was quite a way from where we were sitting to the entrance road — our eyes locked. Pointedly folding my arms, I raised an eyebrow and he strode towards me, a huge smile on his face.

"Hannah, come quickly, there are some people you should meet." Standing, I asked Atius whether he minded keeping an eye on Luc for a few minutes and hurried over. Maxentius grasped my hand and dropped a quick kiss on my cheek. "I think you will enjoy this." His grin widened, his face full of mischief, but I was at a loss for why.

"What's so important about these visitors?" I asked.

"You'll see," was all he said. As we approached the group who were talking animatedly with Marcus and something about them made me stop dead in my tracks. For a split second I think I lost my ability to function in any meaningful way. I opened my mouth, but nothing would come out. The woman was tall, nearly as tall as Maxentius and, even after what must have been a very long journey; she was the epitome of elegant sophistication. Standing alongside her were three younger people; a boy — well more a young man really — and two very beautiful girls. The girls could have been sisters; their curly, dark chestnut hair so similar to mine twisted into a neat bun at the nape of their neck, both wearing what was probably very expensive travelling attire. The young man was taller than I am and wore a tunic, but his features were not of this land. My heart was hammering in my chest; my head still couldn't quite believe what my eyes were seeing. One of the girls spoke —

"Mama? Are you all right?" I tried again, still nothing, I croaked something and then the one who had spoken hurled herself at me. "Mama, Mama, we have missed you, oh we have missed you." I held her to me breathing her in, burying my face in the richness of her hair.

"Claudia, oh my darling daughter, I have missed you too, more than you will ever know." I pushed her away from me so that I could look at her properly. Her dear little face, changed from when we had said goodbye over a year ago, but still my baby girl. Liora came over, a little shyly. I was having none of it and drew her into my embrace.

"Liora, you are so grown-up, quite the young lady now. Oh, my precious girls." I was fighting back tears now, but was absolutely determined that they would not fall. Looking over their heads, I could see Efraim shifting awkwardly from foot to foot. He was of an age when being hugged by your mother was not the done thing and it took all my powers of restraint not to pull him into my arms as well.

Relinquishing my hold on my daughters, I walked over to him and bowed my head. "It is good to see you, Efraim," I said, glad that my voice seemed quite steady. "I understand you have excelled in your studies. I am so proud of you." He smiled self-consciously and thanked me. I winked at him and suddenly he was in my arms, hugging me as though he never wanted to let go.

"I love you too, Mama." I bit my lip, relishing this contact. I was still in shock that they were here. I had written to them when Maxentius was wounded but hadn't had a reply, so didn't know whether they'd even received my letter.

"How is this possible?" I stammered, finally letting my son go and turning to my husband's mother, Claudia the elder. She smiled at me, coming forward to hug me, saying that when they had received my letter about Maxentius, the children had begged to come. They were frightened that the worst might happen and that not only might they lose their father but also I would be left on my own. Bless their hearts; they were too young to be worried about such things. Long story short: Claudia had agreed, Maxentius was, after all, her only son.

The preparations had taken longer than they had anticipated, as initially they had intended to be here a month ago. It was fortuitous that they were delayed, however, as had they arrived any sooner we might have struggled to find somewhere to put them. Thankfully, the rebuilding was complete and there was plenty of guest accommodation in the residence.

I was so excited and eager to show my family around. First, though, I went and relieved Atius of my son who was yelling for me. The medicus didn't look in the least perturbed by Luc's antics; quite used to them by now, and when I invited him to join us for the evening meal, said he would be delighted.

We retired to the residence and spent a happy hour or so showing them around, where they would sleep, introducing them to our staff and so on. Then later after some refreshments, we toured the fort. My children had never been inside one. When we lived in Pompeii, the garrison had been outside of the city walls and was not a place for small children. This was a new experience for them and they were enthralled by the hive of activity that represented a regular day here at Magnis.

They chose to rest for a little while as the day wore on, weary from so much travelling. Maxentius and I retired to the triclinium, cuddling up together on the long sofa.

"Did you know they were coming?" I asked him curiously. "It looked as though you had expected their arrival." He smiled.

"I had received a letter recently from my mother full of questions about my injury and that they had decided to come. The date on the letter meant that they would likely be arriving soon and I had one of the soldiers watching for a wagon train. He ran in this morning to say he had spotted one and it appeared to be shorter than the usual supply trains. I was pretty sure it was them."

"Why didn't you tell me?"

"Because you would have become far too excited and I didn't want you to make yourself ill over it; you know what you're like." I smiled ruefully; he was right. I squeezed his hand.

"It was the best surprise. Thank you, my love." He smiled back and hugged me. I snuggled back against his chest and we talked about what we could do and where we could go. "Do you think they'll stay, or is this just a visit?" I asked, dreading the answer.

"I would like to think that they will decide to stay, but we'll have to see, my Hannah. Let's just see where the days take us."

That evening was one of the most enjoyable we'd had in a long time. The house was full of people laughing and chattering. Marcus introduced Senna to her extended family and they all fell in love with her, as we knew they would. Petronius, Julius and Atius joined us for the evening meal, which was uproarious. Later when everyone had gone to bed, Maxentius and I went outside and stood for a moment savouring the quiet of the night. The sky was clear and full to bursting with stars, the moon beginning its time-honoured journey across the heavens.

Suddenly I knew that this was it; this was what I'd been waiting for; it was time to say goodbye. My heart belonged to another and I had to return to him. Half of my soul would forever remain with my ancient family, but it was time to let them go. I turned to Maxentius holding his hands in mine.

"I want to say thank you, Maxentius." He looked at me, perplexed.

"What for, my Hannah?"

"For saving me." He started to speak and I put my fingers to his lips in much the same way as I, she, had done when I, she, told him she loved him — oh boy, this never got any easier — so many years ago. "No, please, let me say this." I drew a deep breath. "When I thought Max had been killed, you accepted that my spirit had fused with that of your Hannah as I re-entered your life. You welcomed me back into your heart and helped me to heal, away from my own world, which I could not face. At first, I assumed it was because I needed to warn you or save you from some terrible calamity, but I believe that this time our roles were reversed. The catastrophe was in my world; it was you who would be saving me." I hesitated, needing to collect my thoughts.

"Being part of your lives gave me the chance to come to terms with my loss. For a while, I did not think I could ever return; that without Max I had no reason to be in that world, the thread that bound me was disintegrating. Then, small things happened which gave me pause to rethink, and eventually I began to follow my heart. She, your Hannah, believed that Max was not dead, but I was so wrapped up in fear and grief that my head would not allow me to trust what my, what our, heart already knew. He does live, yet even if he had died, I know that I still belong in that world. For even dead, my memories of him are enough to keep me warm for a lifetime."

I stopped, swallowing on the tears that threatened to choke me. Maxentius groaned and drew me close. I snuggled against him for a moment, but was determined to finish what I needed to say.

"I don't think we will ever be apart, not truly. My soul is eternally bound to Hannah and to you, and since you are here and likely to stay, I am close in place, if millennia away in time. She — I, still have little recollection of anything before I met you. My life began on a lonely desert citadel when suddenly I had three Roman soldiers in my care and no clue who I was or how to treat you. It began with you. It began with Max in the same place when I decided to trace the origins of an ancient ruby clasp. When Hannah fell in love with you, I was already part of her. That part has always belonged to you and, even though I know that there must have been a time before I loved you, I am unable to recall it. Now I have to let you go so that you two are just you; no weird outside spirits hanging around." I tried to smile, but it was more than I was capable of.

"I love you, I love our family and I thank you from the bottom of my heart for loving me enough to save me." I couldn't go on; tears were pouring down my face. Maxentius held me tightly, murmuring words of love. I tried one last time.

"Tonight is ours. I believe that before the dawn breaks I will have slipped away. And except for several questionable words and phrases," he chuckled, "you probably won't even notice. I have been lucky enough to have experienced things with you that only three people in either of our worlds would ever have believed possible. My life has been irrevocably changed and enriched beyond measure because you have been part of it."

I sighed and the gentle sound seemed to echo down the centuries. "Trust your heart — both you and Max have spoken these words to me and finally I do. I do trust my heart and you will always be in it. I will miss you and Marcus and your, our, children more than you know, but I will be only a heartbeat away, and if ever I am needed I will feel it there where you and she rest." I could not continue; my heart felt as though it might shatter. Maxentius spoke, his voice enveloping me —

"My Hannah, as I said not so very long ago, you have always been two and to me that is how I know you. I am forever grateful that because a band of Zealots decided to ambush a garrison, a beautiful young physician was granted permission to heal three badly wounded Roman soldiers on that isolated citadel. I am sure our paths will cross again and I thank you for being brave enough to share your knowledge with me," he grinned, "and whether one or two, you will always be my love, my wife, my precious fire sprite." Our conversation, as ever, was absurd, yet with us this was normal; his Hannah and I were forever, inextricably entwined.

Then my Roman looked down at me. I was still crying — you are rubbish, Hannah, absolute rubbish! He cupped his hand around the back of my head, tilting my face so that he could look into my eyes, and with that hauntingly familiar gesture, breathing my name, he kissed me. I moulded myself to him curve for curve and for a little while longer revelled in his touch. He lifted me, carrying me into the house and through to the bedroom. Taking his time he wove his spell and made heady, passionate yet exquisitely tender love to me before we fell asleep, as we always did, wrapped in each other's arms.

As the dawn broke, I awoke and surveyed my husband, my husband in this world — I know, ludicrous — one last time in the ethereal light that suffused the room, imprinting his craggy features, relaxed in repose, into my memory as if I could ever forget him! The pull was very strong now and all around me the room started to disappear. My vision grew hazy and much as I wanted to be with Max, this was harder than I had ever believed it would be. I leaned close to Maxentius and, cradling his cheek in my hand, whispered,

"I love you." My ancient world shimmered and, like an autumn mist in the morning sunshine, faded into history.

.......oooooOOOooooo.......

Max knew the moment Hannah returned to him. They were sitting on the bench outside the house with a cup of coffee, enjoying the view, although he could tell that Hannah wasn't really there. Max had realised that, as she told him she would, his wife had slipped back to her other world sometime during the night. This time, however, he wasn't so concerned; she had promised him she would come back and Hannah never broke her promises. His arm was slung along the back of the bench and his wife had snuggled into his shoulder, as though she knew he was there. He just had to wait.

Suddenly Hannah started crying and, disengaging the mug from her trembling fingers, Max drew his wife into his arms, gently running his hands down her back in a soothing motion, talking to her and willing her to return. She stilled. With one hand continuing to stroke his wife's back, he touched her cheek with the other, lightly brushing her lips with his. Hannah opened her eyes, those beautiful green eyes, full of tears that he wanted to kiss away. As she gazed at him, the confusion that clouded her face slowly vanished, to be replaced by an expression of immeasurable love. His breathing hitched. She was home.

****

I felt someone holding me, murmuring my name and running his hands along my back. Unsure of what was happening, I didn't respond, simply relaxed into the sensation. Then I felt a hand rest against my cheek and lips, cool and firm, brushed mine, feather light. Startled, although why I don't know, my eyes flew open and locked with those of my husband, green as a forest. For a split second, two faces swam across my vision and, as I gazed, one dissolved into memory and one remained. The whole of my body was suffused by an emotion so powerful that it would have felled me had I been standing and I breathed his name.

"Max."

I had come home.

"Hey there, Sunshine." Max was looking at me anxiously, searching my face and I realised that I was crying. Had I been crying across worlds, across millennia? Unable to say any more, I gazed back, mesmerised by his eyes, drinking him in, waiting for my head and my heart to adjust to the shift. Even though I knew this was coming and that part of me had desired it above all things, my other life still echoed flickering like the dying embers of a fire. As my world came back into focus, my sorrow at our parting was assuaged by the knowledge that I believed I could reconnect with my ancient family at will and accepted that there may come a time when they needed me again. For now, knowing that they were safe, living in a region that was relatively peaceful and being close to me in place was enough.

I had to choose. I had to decide where I wanted to be and that was and had always been, with Max. I could not go on living two half lives; it wasn't fair on any of us. Yes, okay, I know I didn't really have any say in the matter the first couple of times, but this had been different. Yet, despite everything that I had experienced, the good and the bad, over the last fifteen years in one life and two years in the other, I would not have changed it, or who I was, for anything.

Max was still stroking my back and the ache in my heart began to lessen. I drew a deep breath and rubbed my eyes. No more crying, Hannah, you'll need an ark soon. Turning in my husband's arms, I noticed that we were sitting on the bench in the garden; it was probably mid-morning and it was a glorious day, the breathtaking landscape laid out before us. I rested my forehead against Max's chest, breathing in his familiar scent, a mixture of sandalwood soap and his favourite aftershave, which played havoc with my senses but was also very comforting. After a few moments, he lifted my chin and looked down into my eyes.

"You okay, Hannah? Want to talk about it?" I smiled rather tremulously and shook my head.

"Not just yet; soon, but not yet." I drew an uneven breath. "What day is it?"

"Friday." I leaned back and gaped at him.

"Really? You mean it was only yesterday that I said I would probably go back?" He nodded, seeming puzzled by my comment. Well, you know my time lapses are totally weird, I thought and continued almost absently, "I have been back there for over two months."

"Did you get to see it through, whatever 'it' was?" he asked.

"I did and I will tell you, but for now I would like it just to be us, no ancient family, no missing child, no scary mutiny, no fire." Max looked shocked at my last word, but I shook my head. "Later, love. Didn't you say we had to return the pomegranate today?"

"We do. Would you like to hold it again first?"

"I really would," I whispered.

"Wait here," he replied, and disappeared into the kitchen. He was back almost immediately with the box. Placing it between us on the bench, he gently removed the wooden carving protected inside layers of soft material and handed it to me. I peeled back the cloths and lifted the artefact clear.

My heart fluttered as I rolled the intricately carved ball around in my hands, admiring the detail and the texture; it was so tactile, my fingers would never tire of touching it. I knew that we had to return it to the museum and only Max would ever understand what this meant to me, but I would always know that it was mine. It was as though I had come full circle.

"Do you think we might take a photo?" I asked. Max didn't see why not and we snapped several from every angle. "I really don't want to hand it back. I know we have to, but I'm sad that I can't keep it. I feel as though something of Maxentius rests within it." I shook my head. "I'm sorry, I probably shouldn't be talking about him to you, but my other life still hovers and he carved it for me — well, her. I know how it came to be lost and I would hate for it to be lost again; archived and forgotten, shut away in a dark vault." I paused and then straightened my shoulders. "Listen to me, all fanciful. Never mind, come one let's get ready and take it back before I spirit it away."

"Just a moment, Hannah, I think I need to..." he never finished his sentence, his lips capturing mine and his arms enfolding me. My arms went round him and I surrendered to his kiss, thrilling to the potent pleasure of his touch. As ever when I transitioned, I had to remember that it hadn't been me physically to whom Maxentius had made love to, scant hours ago; it was to his Hannah. I was only an extra sense, an added voice. But her emotions were mine and I needed to separate them.

Max's kiss deepened, becoming hot and fierce, and the slow burn coiling through me, burst into flame as my passion rose to meet his. His love surrounded me, creating what seemed like a cocoon of euphoria so intense that it was almost tangible. After what seemed like hours, by which time I swear I was floating, Max lifted his head, breaking the kiss and, cupping my face in his hands, said very quietly —

"Welcome home, Hannah." He smiled then; his toe-curling, stomach-flipping smile and my heart soared.

A little later and somewhat reluctantly, we gathered everything up and after ensuring that the box with my pomegranate was secure in the boot of the car, drove over to the museum. To my surprise, Nate was there and he expressed his delight in my recovery. We went along to the office that I had been working in; it was strange that it had been only a week since I had last been here. I had lived what felt like a lifetime in my other world. I sat at my desk and fingered my files, not really knowing what to do. Nate sat down in the spare chair and took hold of one of my hands. I stared at him in bewilderment.

"What's wrong, Nate?" I asked perplexed. Nate looked at me, up at Max who was standing behind me, then back at me.

"Max told me."

"Told you what?" I asked, still completely baffled.

"He told me about who you are and where you go." Trepidation flickered. This couldn't be good. I bit my lip and turned to my husband, feeling a little betrayed. Max squeezed my shoulder.

"I had to, Hannah. I needed the pomegranate and I have to say it was a huge weight off my shoulders being able to tell someone else, especially as I couldn't reach you. Nate, well I think it messed with his head more than a little bit, but he took it on board." Nate chuckled.

"I've always known there was something different about you, Hannah; never thought it was quite this different but I'm glad Max trusted me enough to explain. Everything makes so much more sense now." I watched his face as he said this, his expression was clear, his words the truth. Relief surged through me and I grinned.

'Okay, so now you know and for your further edification, I have spent over a year in Ancient Britannia at Magnis with my ancient family." He gaped. "Too much?" I giggled then; I couldn't help it, he looked completely nonplussed.

"See, now you know what I'm dealing with," Max sighed, over dramatically. We turned our attention to the box, which Max had placed on the desk. I touched it, knowing I had to let it go, but the thought of losing it again hurt my heart.

"You'd better take it away," I whispered. Nate opened the box, peering in to check the contents. He didn't remove it, however;

rather he withdrew a sheet of paper from a file sitting next to him, pushing it across the desk towards me saying —

"You might like to read that." I picked up the sheet and glanced over it. It took a moment for me to work out what it was about, but as I read it more closely I recognised certain words. Maxentius, Armenia, Parthia, Masada, general, Pompeii, legatus, Magnis. The passage was badly fragmented and it was in Latin, but there was a translation at the bottom. It was Maxentius' diplomata, or document, given to soldiers on their retirement detailing the whole of their army career.

What was unusual about this diplomata — and something that had slipped my mind — was that under normal circumstances they were issued to non-Roman soldiers who were granted citizenship on their retirement. Maxentius was a Roman citizen; he had been born a Roman citizen. I had thought about trying to see whether there was any record of his, last year when we were in Rome, but never got around to it. This must have been one of the rare diplomata issued to honourably discharged, or retiring generals.

The original would have been carved in bronze across two tablets, hinged together. The outer side of one tablet would be inscribed with detail of the soldier's career, which would then be repeated across the insides. The second tablet would hold the names of the seven witnesses. Joined together then folded and sealed, it was thought that the bearer of a diplomata would take it to the archivist in the administrative headquarters of the province in which he intended to retire. The archivist would break the seals and check that the information therein matched the outer inscription, proving the holder was who he claimed to be.

Maxentius should not have required such a document, but maybe it was because he had decided to remain on the frontier of Empire at his retirement or that the transitional nature of legionary forces deployed during the pacification of northern Britannia necessitated it. Whatever the reason, we had some of it. I was riveted and, even though much was missing, I could fill in the gaps, except for his latter years. My fingers traced the words and I started to talk about what wasn't there. Nate and Max listened intently as I told them of Maxentius' military service, those years that I knew of at least. None of us would be able to share this information, but I could tell that the two men were fascinated.

As I wound up, I continued to stare at the paper in my hands, unable to face either man — too many emotions tumbling through me. The details of my other world were very close and we were sitting almost on top of where they had lived nearly two thousand years ago. I knew that if I concentrated hard enough, I would see them. Maybe it had been a mistake to come here, today of all days.

"How did you find this?" I muttered, after several moments of dead silence.

"After Max told me what had happened and everything about your life, both your lives, I started to do a search to see whether there was any mention at all of this Maxentius Valerius. I found the inscription that you had already discovered through the database and, using the information in that, started to change the parameters. Once you have units and vexillations and places, information can be gleaned if you know where to look." Frustratingly, I could feel tears forming again. I blinked them back by sheer force of will.

"Was there anything else?" I asked, almost inaudibly, not sure whether I wanted to hear. If Nate had found any record of Maxentius' death or of Hannah, I think it would have been more than I could bear. Nate shook his head.

"No, nothing yet, I'll keep looking, but in the meantime I've spoken to the curator of the museum and have managed to persuade him to let you have the pomegranate on permanent loan." I gasped. "It must be stored securely, to be seen by you and Max only, not on view to anyone who was in your home and, if the museum wants it back for any reason at all, you would have to agree to its immediate return. I have a form here for you to sign, should you agree to abide by these conditions." I was shocked; this was unprecedented and I was speechless. All I could manage was a nod and somehow signed the form; despite the fact that I was trembling so much that I could barely hold the pen. Nate smiled. "Max told me how much this artefact means to you and I came up with a very convoluted tale as to why you should be allowed to have it." Without thinking, I hugged Nate tightly, thanking him over and over, my eyes shining as the desolate feeling that had settled over my heart at the thought of losing this precious carving, evaporated.

"Thank you so much, my friend, you have no idea." He chuckled.

"Oh, I think I might. Now go on, off with the pair of you, I have work to finish and you two need to spend some time together, without one of you disappearing into antiquity." He shooed us out back into the sunlight and waved to us as we drove away, the box on my knee.

Once we were back home, Max called our parents and the doctor, telling them that overnight I had come out of my trance or stupor, or whatever they had chosen to call it. He managed to stop them all from popping over, saying I was still coming to terms with everything and would like to have a very quiet weekend. He appeased them by agreeing that they could visit the following week. Then he poured us each a glass of wine and we returned to the bench in the garden.

Max had brought out a long footstool, so we could lift our feet up. Then he pulled me to him, my back to his chest, wrapping his arms around me and interlacing our free hands. It was late afternoon, and although the sun was still quite high, the light was changing, becoming almost translucent at the horizon, the promise of a cool night. It was taking me some time to remember that it was still spring here, not the autumn I had left. The air was like champagne and I breathed it in, letting its fragrant scent envelop me.

"Do you feel able to tell me now?" Max questioned me gently. I pondered this. Could I? I wanted to share everything with him. He deserved nothing less, but I always worried that it would hurt him and, that because I was talking about another man, who had captured some of my heart, Max would find it too painful.

"Are you sure, love? I worry that it's too hard for you."

"Maybe, but I need to hear it all; it affects who you are and why you react to things the way you do. I would rather know than let my own imagination fill in the blanks." So I told him everything, all about the local tribespeople, the fort, the mutiny, even the fire. Max struggled when I told him this last bit. Even though my body wasn't scarred, my soul had suffered and he hated that he hadn't been there to help me through it.

"But you were, Max, in a sense. By then I knew you were alive and that you were waiting for me. The only thing that bothered me when I was trying to escape the flames was whether I died here too if I died in my ancient world; that if I did, I wouldn't be able to tell you why and that I was sorry." He tightened his arms around me and I rested my head against his shoulder.

"My life is here with you, Max, but I hope you are able to understand that they will always be part of me. I do not want to sever the connection and if they need me, I will gladly return to help them. I know it's a lot to ask, especially after what you've been through this past week, but it's who I am. Will you be able to...do you think...is it more...?" My voice trailed away; I wasn't sure I wanted to finish the question. To expect Max to live with the knowledge that I might slip between worlds at the drop of a hat might just be pushing his devotion a bit too far. He turned me in his arms and, smiling down at me, kissed the tip of my nose.

"I'm always here for you, Sunshine; just remember to come home." Then he kissed me until everything around us faded away and we might have been the only two people in the world.

Epilogue

During the next few weeks our lives settled back into a blessed routine. I was offered a permanent position at the museum, an offer I accepted gratefully. To be so close to my ancient family in that place was a gift I did not expect. It also meant that occasionally I was able to divine what was happening in their lives. As when I first felt my worlds meld, it was in my dreams that I would reconnect and it wasn't very long after I had come back to Max that I realised I was sharing my mind with the other Hannah quite regularly.

I managed to convey that I had the pomegranate and that it was safe in my care; she was over the moon and I know she told Maxentius. Throughout the following year, our souls entwined several times, usually when one of us had something of great import to share; Luc finally being able to string a sentence together; the birth of a daughter to Marcus and Senna; Efraim saying that when he was old enough he would like to join the army and was starting to learn the basics of being a soldier under the watchful eye of his father and uncle; and Claudia and Liora asking that their mother train them to be physicians and beginning to assist in the hospital, learning from Hannah, Atius and Breeda. It was a comfortable connection. We both seemed to enjoy it and although I don't know about my ancestor, knowing that they were all safe and well kept me sane.

Max changed jobs as well, joining a small firm of engineers in Newcastle, most of whom spent some part of every week working from home. Computers, the Internet and excellent videoconferencing meant that there was no real need for them to be in the office every day. It suited us both. I still found it hard when Max wasn't near me. He truly was my anchor and my tendency to...err...drift away was lessened by his presence.

My headaches had decreased substantially and I had started taking feverfew, the modern term for febrifugia, as a matter of routine. Despite mixed reviews on its efficacy for headaches, I found it helpful and preferred this herbal remedy to relying on more powerful painkillers. Dr Stephenson had run several more scans and tests and the results were very encouraging. Nothing insidious showed up; he believed it might have been an accumulation of many things, including residual trauma from the original accident, being so unwell in Pompeii, getting married, moving and changing jobs. Max and I had another more interesting theory, but neither of us was about to share it with a doctor of modern medicine.

About five months after I returned to this life, following a rather prolonged bout of what I had assumed to be a stomach upset, we discovered that I was pregnant. Having children was not something either of us had discussed or even thought about, if I'm honest, and even after the doctor told me that the test was positive, I still wasn't even sure that I wanted children — yes, I know, bit late now! I love my niece and nephew, but I didn't think I was in any way the motherly type.

When we got home that afternoon, I sat on the sofa in front of the fire. It was autumn now and the days had turned very cool. Max brought me a cup of tea and came to sit next to me, drawing me against him. I think we were still both in shock.

"Well, that was unexpected," I said ruefully. "What are we supposed to do now?" I felt Max's chest rumble with laughter. "What? What's so funny?"

"Oh Hannah, we're going to have a baby; there's not a whole lot we can do, except maybe be pleased."

"I didn't know whether I wanted children, whether you wanted children, we've never talked about it." I hesitated, then went on to explain how I'd felt when suddenly my role became that of mother to Luc — well, not really but he knew what I meant. "As I held him, I experienced all the love that Hannah had for this child and I was utterly distraught about the fact that I would never experience the joy of having your child, you know, you being dead 'n' all." I winked at him and his face crinkled in amusement. "But even wishing that I might be pregnant, to have something tangible to remember you by, I still wasn't sure I was cut out to be a mother." Then plaintively, "I can't even conjure up any excitement about being pregnant."

Max kissed the back of my neck and was silent for a moment before saying —

"I think the best gifts in life are those that we receive without warning. Like when I looked into your eyes one morning as you were telling me off and suddenly realised that you loved me;

when you told me that I was your anchor; when you said that you would come home, even when you still thought me dead; and when Nate said you could keep your pomegranate. Unexpected they may be, but no less precious, and this is the same. Neither of us anticipated this, yet here we are and as such I believe it was meant to be. Maybe our lives and this path that we were taking was pre-ordained, for if any single thing along the way had not happened, we might not be here. So I for one intend to embrace it. I have no doubt that you will be a great mother. You know that through the other Hannah you have already brought up four children rather successfully." He paused then continued, "We share a love that transcends time and now there will be a child, a part of you and me, a manifestation of that love. Also, we're usually quite sensible people; I'm pretty sure we'll muddle along quite satisfactorily."

His words were quite poetic but they fitted our mood and as he talked I felt a contentment suffuse my body, as though everything was falling in to place and we were exactly where we were supposed to be. Putting my cup on the table, I turned in his arms, lifting my face for his kiss. His response was instant and for long moments we gave ourselves over to the utter bliss of togetherness.

"We'd better enjoy as much of this as we can," he murmured against my mouth, "in a few short months our time will no longer be our own."

"No time like the present," I smiled, "the tea will keep," and, taking his hand, led him up the stairs.

My pregnancy progressed and I assumed everything I experienced was quite normal. The doctors kept quite a close eye on me in case the changes in my body brought about a recurrence of my headaches. Surprisingly enough, they didn't but we did get a huge shock when, after the first ultrasound, they informed us that I was carrying twins. I very nearly fainted. Twins ran in my family but for the life of me I had not anticipated that we would have them. I panicked for a couple of days until Max calmly sat me down and informed me that we had the room, the income and the love for two just as easily as for one. Finally he asked what I thought I was going to do about it — send one back? His question made me giggle, alleviating my consternation. I think I was more flustered at the thought of the actual birth than anything else.

During this time, I found myself drifting back to my ancient world; only in my dreams, mind you — my life was firmly anchored here, with Max. I wanted to share my, our, news with them and maybe subconsciously I was escaping from my own reality just for a little while. The months flew by and my due date loomed. We had fitted out one of the bedrooms as a nursery, in shades of lemon and pale green. We did not know the sex of either baby, so decided that these colours covered all bases. Family and friends had been very generous and our children would want for nothing. I was already worried that they were going to be spoilt.

Finally the day arrived, although it was another ten hours before the first baby deigned to make its presence known. It was a boy, his sister arriving scarcely thirty minutes later. Max was ecstatic and I was exhausted, but managed to hold both babies for a few minutes, in awe that I had somehow created something so perfect. The wave of emotion that washed over me was indescribable, yet I realised that I had experienced this before, when Claudia and Luc were born. Even though it wasn't really me who had given birth to either of them, my heart had been filled with Hannah's all-consuming love.

The next few days blurred into one as I came to terms with being a mother to two tiny babies who always seemed to need feeding and changing at the same time. They kept me in hospital for a week, I think more to monitor my head than any other reason, but at last I was allowed to go home.

Arriving at the house, sitting snugly in that stark, untamed yet beautiful landscape, I breathed an elated sigh. We each carried a baby from the car and I turned to show my son his world. Echoing words my ancestor had spoken a long time ago, I whispered —

"Look at this, my precious child, this is your home. I hope it never changes and that you and your sister are always happy here." Max smiled over at me, our daughter cuddled into his shoulder. They were such tiny mites, so vulnerable, and I was absolutely besotted with them — okay, maybe I wasn't going to make a complete hash of this whole mother thing.

Taking them inside, we lay them in the large wooden cradle, a gift from Max's parents, making sure they were properly wrapped, papoose like. Currently standing in the corner of the lounge, the crib was close enough for us to keep an eye on them, but far enough away that they were unlikely to be disturbed. I rocked the cradle gently and within seconds they were both fast asleep.

I kicked off my shoes and, dumping my bags on the kitchen table, walked back into the lounge and collapsed on the sofa.

"Oh, it is so good to be home." Max chuckled and agreed, switching on the kettle to make a hot drink. Our parents had put their heads together and filled the freezer and fridge with any amount of delicious-looking food, so that neither of us would have to cook for weeks. Max removed a shepherd's pie from the fridge and put it in the oven; then joined me in front of the fire, which he had just lit. We sat for a few minutes enjoying the peace. Being cared for at the hospital had been lovely, but it was never quiet. I missed the silence that we had in our home — no buzzers, no-one yelling for the nurse, no street noise — just the sound of the breeze and the birds.

"Oh, my goodness." I said. Max looked at me, eyebrows raised. "We're parents." I must have looked rather stunned, because it was all Max could do to keep a straight face.

"I'm afraid so, Sunshine. I wonder whether either of them has inherited your special gift." I stared at him.

"I hadn't thought of that. Wouldn't it be lovely if one of them has? It'll probably be our daughter. Regardless she will be given the clasp when she's twenty five."

"Stop! Don't start thinking about it now. We've a lot of years before you need to worry about it. At least you can tell her where it came from. Let's hope she has your perception and can believe what most would never understand." I chuckled, marvelling at how far we'd come.

"I still can't quite believe we're mother and father to twins. You know, we really should try to decide what we are going to call them." We had not been able to come up with any names that we both agreed on. I wanted to call our son Max, but my husband wouldn't hear of it. Too confusing, he said, although he would agree to me using it as a middle name. We had spent hours trying to choose and nothing seemed to fit. By the time we'd had dinner and were sitting with a cup of tea, having fed and changed both children in the interim, I said that for now we should just call them Vallier One and Vallier Two. Max guffawed, drawing me into his embrace and kissing me soundly. My arms went around his neck and I ran my fingers through his hair. Suddenly Max pulled away and cupped my face in his hands.

"Luc and Claudia." I looked at him askance.

"What about them?"

"That's what we should call our children, Luc and Claudia." I gazed at my husband; this man who knew how much my other world meant to me and was secure enough in our love to bring it into this life."

"Are you sure?" I whispered, my breathing going a bit wonky as my heart beat a rapid tattoo in my chest.

"I'm sure — look!" He dragged me over to the cradle where our babies were sleeping, dark lashes sweeping over flushed cheeks, their tiny faces hauntingly familiar in repose. I couldn't speak. He was right, the names fitted. Quietly I drew him away from the children and stood for a moment searching his face.

"Max, this is..." His lips crushed mine with a passion I wasn't expecting. My knees buckled and if he hadn't been holding me, I would have ended up on the floor. I sank into his kiss, feeling the world spin out of control before righting itself around us. After what seemed like an age, although was probably only a few minutes, we came back down to earth. "What was that for? I murmured breathlessly. "Not that I'm complaining."

"I found I couldn't help myself," my husband replied. "I have the most exquisite wife and two beautiful children. What more could a man ask for?"

"A good night's sleep?" I chuckled. More moved than I thought possible, I kissed him tenderly, letting my body tell him what I feared I could never express in words. "I love you, Max. I believe we are the luckiest couple in the world tonight."

"I love you too, Sunshine. Now I think we should go to bed before these two rascals wake and we have to start all over again."

A few weeks later, we were out walking through the countryside. The children were lying together in our ridiculously large double pram, gurgling away to themselves. I had always wanted a traditional pram and even though it was totally impractical, I loved it. It was a chilly day and we were all wrapped up snugly. Over my jeans and jumper, I was wearing a gorgeous deep green cape, the wide sleeves and cowl hood of which were reminiscent of medieval garb, a gift from Max. My clasp twinkled at the neckline, deep red against forest green. Our path took us towards the museum and Max had called Nate to see whether he was around, so that we could show off our babies — I know, not that we were pleased with ourselves or anything!

As we approached, Nate came out of the door followed by a large figure who seemed vaguely familiar. To my delight, I realised that it was Geoff. Neither of us had any idea that he was up this way, but we were overjoyed to see him.

"Geoff, what a marvellous surprise," I said, as I was swallowed into a bear hug.

"Hannah," he grinned "and Max," shaking his hand, "now please introduce me to your offspring." I held back as my husband proudly did as he was bid, lifting one child out at a time, handing Luc to Nate and Claudia to Geoff. Both men were suitably impressed and, as I watched, I noticed how quickly our tiny tots wove their spell around the two gruff yet unfailingly kind archaeologists.

"Two more uncles in the making," I muttered to Max as we waited, virtually forgotten while our children took centre stage. "Even this small they hog the limelight...I blame you." Max spluttered as I winked at him.

"You're the one who chucks wobblies and falls through time...talk about attention stealing." He muttered in my ear, taking this opportunity to plant a quick kiss on my cheek. I giggled and batted him away. Chatting for a little longer, we couldn't linger. It was too cold to stand about for many minutes and the two men had work to do. Discovering that Geoff was staying in the area for a week or so, we invited them both over for dinner the next night, warning them that any meal would likely by interrupted by demanding babies. They didn't seem overly perturbed, and readily agreed!

Carrying on a little further, we came to the place where, had more than just a few bits of masonry and the vallum survived, we would have seen the ancient fort of Magnis. I shivered a little and Max put his arm around me. The view had barely changed since I was last here, nearly two thousand years ago. Sure, there were more houses and the forest had dwindled in comparison with the vast swathe of trees I remembered, but the landscape was much as it had been. I walked forward a few paces but fearful of slipping away, stretched my hand out for Max. He joined me, interlacing his fingers with mine.

"I'm here, Sunshine. What is it?"

"They're here. I can feel them." It was eerily quiet and as we stood there, my ancient world rose up in front of us, as though I had somehow willed it into existence. Gripping Max's hand, I described the fort and where we were standing — near the principia — in relation to the other buildings. As I talked, figures like ghosts appeared in my vision, hazy yet recognisable. The picture sharpened and I could see Hannah, wearing our clasp on her cloak, talking to Atius; Maxentius and Marcus strolling across the quadrangle; Senna was playing with Luc and her own daughter, joined by Claudia and Liora; Efraim appeared leading a horse and I knew it was Gemmula. My throat caught and as I swallowed a sob. Hannah turned and looked straight at me.

Time stopped, my breathing stopped, as she walked towards me calling to Maxentius. He grasped her hand as they approached and, as we had in Rome, we embraced, both of them kissing my cheek. Hannah pointed to the pram and I nodded, showing them our children.

"Twins," I whispered, "a boy and a girl, their names are Luc and Claudia." She gazed at me, then took my hand squeezing it tightly and smiled, such a sweet smile, her heart in her eyes. Maxentius grinned and glanced towards Max. They seemed to be assessing each other — which wasn't possible was it? — when, to my everlasting shock, Maxentius put his hand out and Max, his expression one of stunned disbelief, shook it. Then they both fisted the same hand thumping it to their chest. I blinked, certain that I was actually dreaming now. How on earth could Max see this, never mind interact? He never had before.

Hannah laughed, a sound of pure happiness, which echoed around us like golden bells. She touched my clasp and touched her heart.

"Be happy, Hannah, remember that I am always with you, this is our destiny. We share our beautiful clasp, we share our lives and our loves and we are forever bound across place and time."

Unable to help myself, I hugged her and then released her back to her world. She reached for Maxentius' hand and they walked away, looking back once. The image started to dissolve, like gossamer clouds, vanishing into history leaving, for now, nothing but a memory. My world came back into focus and I started breathing again. I turned to Max who was frozen to the spot.

"Did you...I didn't think...I never expected..." I was totally incoherent, as usual, but I really wanted Max to tell me that he had done what I'd seen him do.

"I...that was...no way...how?" Max was even less coherent than I was, which was a first. He stared at me, his face white. I grasped his hand and he returned my grip, his thumb rubbing down mine, an abstracted gesture, his mind still on the events of a moment ago.

"Please tell me you shook his hand." He nodded, just nodded; words had failed him. I smiled and, drawing my husband close to me, kissed him. His arms wrapped me to his chest as our own magic spun its web around us.

The afternoon began to wane and thoughts of a hot meal and cuddling up in front of a blazing fire tantalised us. As we set off back towards our home, the twins now fast asleep in their pram, I whispered to Max —

"Welcome to my world."

The Pomegranate Tree
Hannah's Heirloom ~ Book One

After receiving an ancient ruby clasp from her long dead grandmother, Hannah Wilson decides to visit Masada, supposedly the place where this gift was given to one of her ancestors. Travelling with her is Max Vallier, her best friend, who was already going to Herod's fortress in the desert, as part of an archaeological excavation team.

Once there, Hannah is disturbed by strange visions. Visions, which seem to revolve around the AD66 attack by Zealot rebels, on the Roman garrison based at the fortress.

As her two worlds begin to entwine, Hannah realises that she is experiencing the events of the past as they unfold, events that so far she has only dreamed about. Pulled into the ancient world, she tends to three Roman soldiers who survived the attack, but who are now captives. Back in the modern world, she finds artefacts that tie her to her ancient counterpart. Meanwhile, her relationship with Max takes an interesting turn, but just as they admit their feelings for each other, a tragic accident tears them apart.

Fate intervenes and Hannah slips into the world of Ancient Masada. There, away from all modern trappings, she must rely on her wits and instincts to deal with the challenges of her alternate life. A life in which she, an unmarried Hebrew woman, is a healer - a trained physician fighting to keep alive the men under her care. This life becomes more complicated as she realises she is falling in love with one of the Roman soldiers, a love that could have deadly consequences.

Unsure whether she will ever be able to return to the modern world, Hannah accepts her destiny, rising to the challenges of living on an isolated fortress and, believing that she has a chance to save those she loves by using the knowledge she has brought with her from two thousand years in the future. The knowledge that, eventually, Jerusalem will fall and, that those escaping the city will make their way to this outpost, followed by an avenging Roman army intent on destruction.

Will Hannah escape? Will she ever see Max again, or is she doomed to die along with hundreds of others as Masada falls - and what does any of this have to do with an ancient ruby clasp?

Echoes of Stone and Fire
Hannah's Heirloom ~ Book Two

Pompeii was once a bustling port nestling under a forbidding mountain. Then in AD79, the mountain erupted, smothering the town under a thick blanket of ash and volcanic debris, leaving it lost for centuries. Now, rediscovered and a world-renowned heritage site, archaeologists from across the globe yearn for an opportunity to uncover the town's past. Some things though, are best left alone - revealing the secrets hidden beneath the stones could prove perilous.

Eighteen months have passed since Hannah and Max left Masada, Herod's isolated fortress in the Judaean desert. The place where, just as they admitted their feelings for each other, they were wrenched apart. Hannah slipped into an ancient world, discovering how her ancestor had received the ruby clasp - her talisman. Somehow she survived the ensuing tragedy and Max's love was strong enough to bring her home. Since then, Hannah has had no awareness of her ancient counterpart and wonders whether the slender thread that united them had been broken, lost beyond time, leaving only a memory.

On a spur of the moment trip to Rome, familiar dreams recur. Unable to recognise where her ancestor is, but realising that she is not on Masada, Hannah struggles to understand the reason behind her visions. Then, a chance meeting with two friends sees Hannah and Max invited to join an excavation team, one whose goal is to determine what lies beneath the ruins of Pompeii. Although excited to be a part of such an investigation, Hannah experiences a growing sense of unease, an unnamed fear circling at the edges of her consciousness.

Her worlds begin to converge and Hannah realises to her horror, that her fear, this reconnection of minds, must be related to Vesuvius and that the woman she is bound to was actually in Pompeii before the eruption. Hoping she can somehow warn her ancestor without being drawn back into her other life, Hannah tries to convey her knowledge through her dreams.

As before however, fate intervenes. After entering a house, which bears a Hebrew inscription, Hannah falls back through time. Although familiar with this fusion of souls, she still has to rely on her instincts to adjust to life in ancient Pompeii. A world where her ancestor is a physician to gladiators engaged in mortal combat, where riotous mobs run amok and where a ghost from the past returns to haunt her. All the while knowing she needs to save her family from the devastation that will befall this town.

Will Hannah escape the cataclysmic eruption? Can she persuade her loved ones to flee before burning debris engulfs the town? Will she ever find her way back to Max the love of her life waiting, not so patiently, millennia away? Or will echoes be all that remain?